escape from
GENOPOLIS

T.E. Berry-Hart

First published in the UK in 2007 by Scholastic Children's Books
A division of Scholastic Ltd
Euston House, 24 Eversholt Street
London, NW1 1DB, UK
Registered office: Westfield Road, Southam, Warwickshire, CV47 0RA
SCHOLASTIC and associated logos are trademarks
and or registered trademarks of Scholastic Inc.

10 digit ISBN 0 439 94310 8
13 digit ISBN 978 0439 94310 9

British Library Cataloguing-in-Publication Data
A CIP catalogue record for this book
is available from the British Library

Typeset by M Rules
Printed in the UK by CPI Bookmarque, Croydon, CR0 4TD
Papers used by Scholastic Children's Books are
made from wood grown in sustainable forests.

1 3 5 7 9 10 8 6 4 2

www.scholastic.co.uk/zone

www.genopolis.co.uk

For Cristina Teixeira, without whose original and inspiring vision of a world without pain, tireless encouragement and ideas, this book would never have been started, let alone finished.

ACKNOWLEDGEMENTS

A huge thank-you to everyone who read and advised on previous drafts of the manuscript and whose belief and support helped me through literary stagnation or many a dark night of the soul; my agent, Clare Conville, my editor, Elv Moody, and all the team at Scholastic; and Cesar Casado, David Mercatali, Jennifer Fieldsend, Alex Berry-Hart, Tiff Berry-Hart, Marian Lines and Pauline McGlade.

And a special thank you to Martin Soames, who started the whole thing off.

NATURAL HISTORY

4,500,000,000
EARTH FORMED

2,000,000,000 YEARS AGO
LIFE APPEARS ON EARTH

4,000 BC TO AD 1750
EARLY CIVILIZATIONS

AD 1750 TO 2040
LATE CIVILIZATIONS

AD 2067
THE APOCALYPSE. . .

PROLOGUE: "PUSH!"

Rain beat down fiercely on the disused railway track. It was the heaviest night-storm that the City of Genopolis had seen that summer, with vicious sheets of spiky rain churning the red earth into swamp. From where the Doctor sheltered, he could hardly make out the distant grey-stone viaduct that spanned the cut between two hills until a flash of lightning momentarily lit up the glistening bulk against the scrambled clouds. A crack of thunder rolled around the sky and a blast of icy air sent another gust of rain slicing into the shelter.

Wrapped in a dripping oilskin, the Doctor checked his timepiece and saw with surprise that almost two night-hours had already passed, with no sign of the guide that he had been promised. Uncertainly he glanced at the lowering sky.

Had the plan gone wrong?

A hand clutched his shoulder. He turned and lashed out, sending a small figure toppling into the mud with a cry.

Instantly the Doctor was on his feet, pulling his scalpel out of its sheath, before he saw in bewilderment that the other was a young Natural girl-child, probably no more than ten or eleven, her black hair plastered dripping against her face. Like most Naturals, she was wolfishly thin and dressed in filthy rags. Her wild eyes swept his face as she flinched from the expected blow. He lowered his arm and stepped back.

"Are you him? Are you the Doctor?" she stammered, although her accent was so strange the Doctor could barely understand her.

"Yes. Yes, I am," he answered. "Where is he? Where is the child?"

But the bedraggled girl had scrambled to her feet and was already scurrying down the slope towards the old railway, beckoning him to follow her. There was no time to hesitate. Pulling his oilskin over his head he ducked out into the full fury of the tempest and stumbled after her. Luckily, on a night like this the boundaries were closed to travellers so no Guardian patrols encountered the two figures, bent almost double under the weight of the storm, as they made their way along the steep track that threaded its way out to the wild Natural Regions that lay outside the City.

From what could be seen of him underneath the dripping hood, the Doctor was a tall, well-dressed man, obviously unused to such exercise. High cheekbones and his fine skin marked him out as a Higher Citizen from a privileged and long-lived background, and a glimpse of his neatly-trimmed beard, velvet scarf and quality medical bag declared his membership of the Inn of Court of Genopolis.

His small guide, on the other hand, shivered violently in the piercing wind, and the thin fingers which clasped the rough length of sacking that served her as a cloak were blue with cold. Rags bound her small feet instead of boots, and her scrawny legs were spattered with mud, though she expertly navigated the huge slimy girders that littered their path from the ancient railway track.

Clouds blotted out the moon for a second and, when the pale light flickered again, the Doctor saw the girl edging her way down a steep cutting that ran down the side of the viaduct. Gingerly he followed her, struggling to keep his balance as the gale ripped viciously at their cloaks and the huge drops of rain pelted them like pebbles. Around them, water coursed down through deep grooves carved into the stonework, feeding a muddy river that surged around the buttresses of the crumbling bridge. Without a moment's hesitation, the girl plunged in, wading chest-high through the stinking piles of rubbish that bobbed and lodged on the dark flood. In disbelief, the Doctor crouched down on the river bank, fumbling for his crumpled medical bag, and brought out a small silver instrument, no longer than a finger. Steadying himself with one gloved hand, he leaned forward and dipped the tube into the racing stream. He held it there for a moment, then withdrew it and checked the reading. It registered well below the safe limit. It might be all very well for Naturals, he thought, but Citizens should not take such risks, even for a journey as important as his.

Despite his misgivings, the Doctor lowered himself almost to his waist in the current, holding his bag above his head with one hand as if to safeguard something extremely precious. To their left loomed the decaying skeleton of a huge train, toppled from the viaduct many years before, protruding like a wrecked ship's hull through the surging waters. Finally the buttresses of the great pillars that supported the bridge rose before them and the Doctor saw a dark alleyway formed by the narrow space between the huge wall of the pillar to the left, and the jagged rock of the cutting to the right. The girl scrabbled her way out of the water like a drowned rat and disappeared into the darkness of the tunnel.

A dank, oily smell wafted up from the shadows. Wrinkling his nose, the Doctor followed her inside. At intervals in the rock face were other, smaller, roughly bricked arches, blocked with crudely nailed planks or thick doors wedged with rusted heaps of machinery. From underneath the last door shone a tiny chink of yellow light. The girl raised her fist and beat a lively tattoo on the wood, three knocks, pause, one knock, pause, three knocks. The light was almost immediately extinguished, and in the resulting darkness the door swung open unseen. When the next shaft of moonlight came streaming through the wrecked clouds the alley stood as lone and desolate as before.

Inside, the hastily extinguished candle was relit.

"It's a wild night to be out," said the Doctor, throwing off his oilskin and drying his face with a rag.

"I found him, Uncle!" cried the girl gleefully, in her absurd accent, throwing her arms around the dark-haired man who had opened the door for them.

The man smiled and tousled her hair affectionately. "Well done, Kira. Go and get dry now. That rain will be the death of you."

Typical Naturals, the Doctor thought contemptuously, not for the first time. But he knew better than to let any of these thoughts show in his face at such a crucial hour. "Angus," he said courteously, extending his hand towards the man whom he barely recognized in the flickering smoky light, "I came as soon as I could."

Angus was probably no more than twenty years old, with eager brown eyes shining from a thin face and a quivering, rather timid smile. Matted locks of hair fell down to his cheeks and faint stubble covered his chin. Ignoring the Doctor's outstretched hand he threw his arms around him, embracing him after the custom of his people. The Doctor politely tried to ignore the fetid smell that attacked his nostrils and, to his relief, the Natural finally broke away, holding him by the shoulders at arm's length, scanning his face closely. "Thank you for coming, Doctor. We were worried when Kira told us the barriers had been closed."

As his eyes grew accustomed to the light, the Doctor took stock of his new surroundings. He stood in the first of a small warren of caves blasted out of the cliff face. Behind Angus he could see a scared huddle of seven similarly-ragged men and women whom he did not recognize. It was rare enough that he saw the same Natural twice with times as they were. As Angus guided him into the second cavern the Doctor saw an old woman tending a boiling pot over a small fire. Beside her, the girl Kira crouched by the warmth, now wrapped in a threadbare blanket and ravenously tearing at a crust of bread.

A gasping moan rose above the murmurs, and the crowd parted to reveal a makeshift bed formed of filthy rags and sacking, and on it a sweating, exhausted figure. As he watched, it contorted suddenly and groaned again. The effect on Angus was electric. Covering his face with his hands, as if he could not bear even to watch, he pleaded, "Please, Doctor. You have to help Gea. You have to. . ."

Kneeling down, the Doctor assessed the patient, a young woman with a smeared face and damp red hair lying exhausted on a pile of rags, her belly swollen. Her breath came in harsh, deep gasps and her dark green eyes glittered with an expression that he could not fathom. Angus stood rooted to the spot, gnawing compulsively at his nails, watching the torn figure of his wife in her agony. At least, the Doctor supposed it was his wife. Again with Naturals, you could not always tell.

Kira crept up to the young woman and crouched down next to her. "It's all right," she muttered soothingly. "The Doctor is here. He will help you."

As if the child's words were a magic token, Angus turned to look at the Doctor, his eyes bright with intensity. "It's so precious. Isn't it?"

The Doctor was puzzled. "That depends on what you mean by precious."

Angus leant closer. "Something bought so dearly. It must be, mustn't it? Something bought with so much pain?"

The Doctor gazed at the Natural, uncomprehending.

Gea suddenly contorted and started to moan again.

"Please, Doctor, help her!" shouted Kira, her eyes welling with tears.

The Doctor opened his sodden bag and reached for his instruments, but it was the old woman who elbowed him rudely aside, sending his kit tinkling on to the stony floor, and crouched over the woman, holding her hand tightly.

"Now come on, girlie! Push!"

ONE

2069 – Foundation of the City of Genopolis.
2087 – First Water Laws passed.
2088 – Second Food Laws passed. . .

Arlo yawned and threw his history book aside in a fit of boredom. He had now read the same dates five times over and still could not remember them by heart. In despair, he stretched his arms above his head and looked around him at the deserted, dusty schoolroom where he was supposed to be studying.

It was too beautiful an evening to be poring over books, he thought mutinously. Late golden sunlight was slanting through the latticed windows. It reflected off the silver models of the solar system, slid past the tattered charts detailing the movement of the planets and spilled on to the globes of the Old World that stood poised and tilted around their central poles. If you wanted to, you could rotate the globes and see lands long dead and long drowned, mountains and whole countries that had disappeared under the waves from the huge tidal floods of 2065.

Groaning in exasperation, Arlo wandered over to the schoolroom window, leaned his arms on the sill and looked out at the great tree that stood outside in the gardens of the Inn of Court. The tree had always held a strange fascination for him. Gnarled and ancient, with a mossy trunk and roots that protruded from the earth to disrupt the neatly-clipped lawn, it was so old that it might have been standing there for hundreds of years, perhaps from even before the Apocalypse, thought Arlo, though nobody that he had asked seemed to know for sure.

All that was certain was that Doctor Ignatius had expressly forbidden him to climb it.

And things that were forbidden were, if you were supposed to be studying for your Citizenship Exams on a sweltering February evening, strangely irresistible.

Almost without thinking, Arlo swung himself through the ground-floor window, tramped gleefully through the geranium patch and over the well-trimmed lawn towards the tree. From his Natural History lessons he thought it might be an oak, or a beech, perhaps. It stood at the bottom of the Inn's lawns in a secluded corner, its leaves gently rustling in the breeze, and the lowest of its boughs hovering invitingly like outstretched arms just a couple of feet above his head. Casting a quick glance around for any disapproving Doctor, he jumped up and caught at the nearest branch. The weight of his own body momentarily surprised him, before he tensed his muscles and managed to swing up first one leg, then the other, and pull the rest of himself up.

From then on it was easy. Gently testing each branch as he went, Arlo climbed up hand over hand, ducking through the bright screens of fluttering leaves with growing excitement. Almost instinctively he could tell whether a handhold would be secure, or if a bough was too brittle to support his weight. Around him the branches swayed and murmured in the soft breeze. He chuckled. Climbing was easy. What on earth had the Doctors all been making such a fuss about?

Yet, as he neared the top of the tree, Arlo hesitated. The greatest of the branches reached out, tantalizingly close, to the ruddy brick wall that surrounded the Inn, separating it from the rest of the City of Genopolis.

Arlo had never been to the City in all his eleven-and-a-half Citizen years, nor had he ever set foot outside the grounds of the Inn. Most of the eighty Doctors who also lived and worked within the Inn's bounds hardly ever ventured outside, except for advisory trips to the Consulate or the Senate. And for a young novice such as Arlo, *going outside* was yet another of the many things that he had been forbidden to do until he had graduated as a proper Citizen. But perhaps, he thought excitedly, if he edged along the bough he could stretch out and perhaps pull himself up on the top of the wall. And then, once on the wall, perhaps he might be able to see. . .

Yet, as he crawled along the branch and reached his

hand out to touch the stone, a lash like an invisible whip suddenly cut across his face. Instinctively he snatched his hand back to cover his eyes and lost his balance. The next moment he found himself plummeting backwards, gasping and clawing at leaves and branches as he fell. He had almost no time to yell for help, as the next second the world turned upside down, a large bough hit him with a wallop in the stomach, knocked the breath out of him, and he was tipped head over heels, to land with a bump on his back in the soft grass.

Winded from his fall, he lay still for a moment, too shocked even to groan.

"Arlo! Arlo!"

Through the roaring in his ears, he heard a voice calling his name. Dizzily he pulled himself up on his elbows and looked up. Through the schoolroom window leaned Doctor Ignatius, eyes wide, gripping the sill with both hands.

"Arlo! Are you all right?"

Arlo tested his hands and feet. Everything still seemed to be in working order, but his face was prickling from the scratches caused by his sudden descent. He was trembling all over and his thoughts were whirling. He struggled for words.

"Something hit me, sir! There was something at the top of the wall. . ."

"But why on earth were you climbing the tree in the first place?" Ignatius scolded. "What were you trying to do?"

Arlo's head started to ache. "I'm sorry, sir, I. . ."

"You're very lucky you didn't break a leg or worse! You're supposed to be studying, not trying to kill yourself!"

Ignatius vaulted through the schoolroom window and came hurriedly towards him. Tall and loose-limbed, with a shock of untidy iron-grey hair that blew in unruly locks above a pair of sharp hazel eyes, Ignatius usually regarded the world around him with an air of gentle mockery. But on this occasion his gaze was unusually firm and direct, and his hands were gentle as he swiftly checked Arlo's head, his pulse and his eyes. Finally, satisfied that nothing was wrong, he folded his arms and fixed his pupil with a stern look.

"You must have touched the electric wire that stops thieves from climbing over and plundering the pantry. You're very lucky indeed! What on earth's got into you these days, Arlo?"

Arlo eyed him uncomfortably. He had a deep respect for his tutor and hated to be caught in trouble by him. "I'm so bored," he burst out. "There's nothing to do here, and I can't go outside, and it's so hot! I just can't learn any more. I can't."

Ignatius sat down next to Arlo on the grass and stretched his long legs out in front of him. "Right then, I think we need to talk. Don't we?"

Arlo waited in sullen silence, nibbling at his fingernails, while Ignatius tipped his head back, half-closed his eyes, and seemed to be pondering what to say next. His tutor's many little eccentricities were well known and often commented on by the other Doctors. Despite the good tailors that often visited, the cuffs and elbows of Ignatius's jacket were always frayed and slightly threadbare, although he never seemed to notice, his clothes apparently having been thrown on at the last moment. Unusually for a Higher Citizen, Ignatius was unafraid to show his full fifty Citizen-years by the web of laughter-lines that issued from around his eyes and curved down around his mouth. Arlo had heard that outside the Inn, the ancient gesture *smiling* was held to be subversive, so most Citizens only indulged in expressions of polite neutrality marked by approval or disapproval. But Ignatius and a few other Doctors of the Inn never had the patience to observe such trifling social customs.

"Listen, Arlo. I know things are difficult for you at the moment. But you need to be more patient. As a novice student of the Inn, tomorrow will be the most important day of your life. You cannot let yourself down – or us."

"I know! I know! Everybody keeps saying that!" moaned Arlo, plucking at the grass. It was so *typical* of Ignatius to give him a lecture at a time like this. Why couldn't any of the Doctors seem to *understand*?

"Well, they're saying it because it's true. You really need to work harder than you're doing, Arlo. Every Citizen-boy and Citizen-girl must pass their graduation examination at age eleven."

This was exactly the conversation that Arlo was dreading, and it took him a huge effort to pluck up the courage to ask his next question.

"And . . . and those who fail?" he started timidly.

But Ignatius glanced away, patted him on the back of the neck and stood up.

"You don't need to worry, Arlo. Just be yourself. That is all you need to remember. That is all we want to see."

Then, with a sudden smile that illuminated his face like the play of light on water, he reached over and ruffled the boy's hair. "Now go and have a bath before supper. You look like you need it."

But as Arlo went off obediently to the wash-rooms, the memory of the invisible lash came back and unconsciously he found himself fingering his cheek and puzzling over it.

What exactly *was* the wire that ran along the top of the wall? The Inn of Court was probably one of the few Institutions that had power supplied directly from the turbines of Genergis, and the Doctors strictly rationed its use, so anything that used power had to be extremely important. As Ignatius had said, the Inn needed something to keep out the many thieves seeking the Inn's valuable food-stores.

But – as he had found – mightn't it be equally effective in keeping people *in*?

Somewhere, down in the murky depths, something was stirring.

It was the smell that always came first, always the

smell, a musty, bitter scent that clogged her lungs and sent her senses reeling. Even though Usha could not see through the suffocating darkness, she knew, with a certainty that was greater than sight, that something terrible was swaying next to her, almost touching her, snuffling, moving so close she could feel the heat from its body, its rank smell choking her—

And then, as always, she took a step backwards, turned and fled down the twisting corridors, through the cells with their barred windows and the labyrinthine maze of doors and windowless rooms. Voices shrieked around her, strangely muffled as if echoing down a long corridor. As she ran, hands shot out from behind the bars and grabbed at her clothes. She shook herself free, but more fingers clutched at her from all sides so that soon she was trapped, powerless, waiting for the shambling thing in the darkness to slowly, slowly emerge into the light and seize her. . .

Usha shot bolt upright in bed, her heart pounding. For a moment she could not remember where she was until her scrabbling fingers clutched the rough blankets. Gradually she recognized her darkened bedroom, the familiar shapes of wardrobe and chair outlined by the tiny slivers of moonlight snaking through the shutters.

She was in her own room, she was safe, she was sound.

But as she sank back in relief, she realized her white nightgown felt clammy and hot. Damp strings of her long fair hair were stuck to her face and the air was stuffy. Throwing aside her coverlet, she stood up on wobbly legs and made her way to the window. She fumbled with the shutters, threw them open and felt the night air on her heated skin. Like cold water it revived her and brought her fully back to wakefulness.

After a dream like that there was only one thing to be done.

Dragging the chair underneath the window gingerly so as not to wake Auntie in the opposite room, she put her foot on the seat and scrambled over the window sill. Auntie had forbidden her to go out into the City at night, but she hadn't actually said anything about the *roof*, Usha reasoned to herself. Nonetheless she moved warily, in case any of the neighbours or the nightwatchmen saw her. She reckoned that it must be around five o'clock in the morning, and everyone in the City would be asleep, or at least confined to their houses for the night-curfew. And Usha was quite sure that of every Gemini in the City, she was the only one awake at such an hour.

Directly beneath her window, a gable protruded over the courtyard to form a natural cornice with the gently-sloping roof. Cautiously, Usha lowered herself down on to the shallow incline, bracing her feet for balance on the guttering until she reached the corner where she could support herself easily. Often she would imagine that she was stranded on an island above the sea of swaying branches in Auntie's garden, able to look directly over to the shadowy City and the jumble of domes, cupolas and towers that made up Central Square. Even at night Usha could pick out the major landmarks: the great Bell Tower of the Guildhall, the spires of the Inn of Court, and the distant beam of the Lighthouse which stood at the port. Over all loomed the enormous Pillars of the Consulate, where all decisions were made by the Governors of Genopolis, and underneath its buttresses the squat headquarters of the Guardian soldiers, who made sure that every good Citizen obeyed them. Usha never went near the Consulate if she could help it. Giant stone statues of great warriors and athletes stood between the Pillars, bleached white and bonelike by the sun, their hollow eyes gazing sightlessly at passers-by.

Since Usha had arrived at Auntie's house, the dream had visited her regularly, and even now, at a nearly-grown-up nearly-twelve Citizen-years old, it still poisoned her sleep and made her wary of going to bed. When she was younger she would often wake from the dream screaming, and Auntie would come rushing in, unable to understand what made Usha make those terrible sounds. When Usha tried to explain, Auntie had curtly said that *a Gemini's purpose was not to dream*, and left it at that. Yet the dreams had not gone away. In time, Usha had learned to control her Outbreak, though it was an automatic reflex when she shot up in bed, as if noise could make the vision of the dreadful figure dissolve away faster into darkness. Usha had asked other Gemini whether they had the same night-visions as her, and they had looked at her, perplexed, and shaken their heads.

So, in time, she had learned to keep it quiet, along with the other visions that sometimes visited her even while she was awake. . .

To calm her thoughts, she ran over the list of tasks that she was required to do on a Tuesday. Firstly, wake up Auntie and take up her early-morning tea and herbs and help her tidy herself. Auntie had been very sick lately, scarcely able to stir herself out of her room, even to bathe. Secondly, tidy the top floor of the house, clean the windows, and then help Auntie sort out her belongings for barter. The last few times she had been to the market, Auntie had sent her out with a pair of gold candlesticks to trade. Candlesticks, in a part of town where no one could even manage to get candles!

Usha had learned, through long experience, not to fall asleep on the roof, unless you wanted to go rolling off and break your back in the courtyard. Once she had actually fallen asleep and started to tilt, but she had jolted awake in time to find herself scrabbling frantically at the guttering, gripping it with her fingers and toes like a fly. In the street you could see misshapen people who had broken their bones in various types of accidents from falling off things or under things, and they would limp and lurch after you, clutching your arm and begging you for food. Auntie had always forbidden her to climb walls or ladders, and Usha had no desire to end up like that.

Instead, she lay back on the roof and looked up at the constellations of stars that wheeled gently above the sleeping City.

"The Pleiades... Casseopeia... Perseus... Gemini..."

Slowly, the sky lightened around her.

As pale morning filtered through his window, Arlo awoke from a dreamless sleep with a heavy, sick feeling of dread in his stomach.

Ever since he could remember, he had woken up to the same view in this small room in the eaves that overlooked the gardens of the Inn of Court. Built around a central courtyard, the Inn was an old building, founded (according to Doctor Ignatius) even before the Apocalypse, and had since then been built in different stages over the years, a strange, higgledy-piggledy combination of ancient styles and stonework, covered in creepers and ivy. In the old days, the Inn might variously have been called a university, a court of law, a monastery or an institute for medical research, but these days it existed only as a centre of scholarly knowledge and learning. This small high turret room was his retreat, a bare room with only a bed, washstand and cupboard, but it was home to Arlo nonetheless. The Doctors frowned on personal possessions, so the room was almost empty of things that actually *belonged* to him, apart from a small cluster of overdue books from the library and the remains of an ancient clockwork train, broken years ago, which Arlo had resolved to mend but had never found the time.

Sleepily, he wandered over to the small basin in the corner to splash his head and neck with cold water. Baring his teeth and sticking his tongue out, he studied the reflection that stared back at him from the old mottled mirror above the basin, a thin, slightly freckled face, topped with short reddish-brown hair and greeny-blue eyes still hazed with sleep. As he usually did when looking at his reflection in the morning, he wished that his nose was straighter, his eyes smaller, his features as regular as other Citizens. He was the youngest in the Inn by a good fifteen years, and sometimes it seemed that everybody around him was taller, stronger and better proportioned, while he was left with large eyes, a slight figure and hands that always seemed larger than they needed to be. But he had no time to worry about his appearance for long. It was too important a morning for that.

The first chimes of the breakfast bell reverberated throughout the Inn, rousing slumbering Doctors and Gemini alike. Outside in the corridor started the usual early-morning noises of doors slamming and footsteps descending the stairs to the mess hall. Arlo's stomach took a sickening plunge. He was out of time.

Quickly he pulled open his closet door and dressed in the sombre garb of a novice student of the Inn, wide black trousers and a long black open-necked shirt. Over all he yanked a long straight gown, slightly pleated and thrown back over the shoulders. Qualified Doctors and Apprentices would wear different coloured sashes depending on rank, but Arlo wore none. As it was a warm February, he jammed his feet into sandals, poked his head cautiously around the door, and slipped softly into the now-empty corridor. A plan was slowly forming in his mind. He would go and find Ignatius, and tell him that he felt ill after his fall from the tree. It might be enough to get him into seclusion in the Sanatorium, which meant at least a week (he hoped) off lessons. Although illness had been officially eliminated with the Abolition of Sickness Law thirteen years ago, the Doctors still took no chances, and every smallest sign or symptom of Infection within the Inn was monitored carefully.

Yes, it wasn't *really* true, he thought, but maybe just this once?

Footsteps behind him made him jump, but it was just the Gemini cook, whistling tunelessly as he tugged the heavy bags of flour down the spiral steps to the kitchens. Like all low-caste Gemini slaves, the cook wore shapeless white trousers and a shirt, bound round with a dusty apron with large pockets. His sausage-like hands gripped the hessian and handled the dragging weight of the sacks with unhurried ease. He bowed to the boy, but Arlo ignored him, as all good Citizens should, though this time he felt a strange twinge of envy. A cook didn't have exams to pass, or Doctors to please. In fact all Gemini, whether they worked in the kitchens, waited tables or delivered supplies, had no ambitions at all. They had little to say and their eyes were uncommonly alike. Arlo tried to avoid spending much time in their company, and treated them with the same amount of disdain and contempt as the Doctors, who had drummed it into him: *the first purpose of every Gemini is to serve a Citizen.*

Yet as he took the first steps through the kitchen garden and on to the sunny courtyard, for a moment all thoughts of examinations, excuses, Doctors and breakfast were driven from his mind. Arlo stopped and gazed in disbelief at the spectacle before him, the history book dangling suddenly forgotten at his side.

For, in the quiet of the Inn's garden, a creature that he had never seen before in his life was staring right back at him.

Usha pulled down with all her strength on the tap of the large burnished samovar, sending a jet of boiling water spouting into the china teapot. She stretched sleepily as the deep, musky scent of tea filled the air. Even though the sun had risen two day-hours since, the kitchen remained dark and gloomy as the sunlight struggled to break through the mass of creepers that covered the windows of the old house. To Usha the greenish light that filtered through the vines felt sometimes as if the whole mansion was slowly submerging underwater, like a rotting ship sinking into the straggling waves of the overgrown garden.

Pull yourself together, she told herself sharply. It was time for Auntie's breakfast nutrition, and no time to linger over such thoughts. Briskly she opened the mouldering cupboards, took out the tea tray and reached for the silver spoons that Auntie was so proud of.

But her searching fingers met only fungus and mildew. With increasing surprise, Usha pulled the drawer out and shook it. It remained entirely empty. She turned it upside down and pounded on the bottom, but only a few crumbs and a dead spider fell out. She stared at the empty drawer, puzzled.

Well, there was nothing to be done about it, but use the old tin ladle that she usually kept to stir Auntie's chicken broth instead. Carefully she measured out two portions of sugar, dropped a herb-poultice, a spoonful of nutrient powder, and a squeeze of lemon-paste into the teapot, lined up the second-best china cup and saucer on top of the ancient lace doily, and decorated the tea tray with a sprig of the basil that Auntie insisted hang over the door to ward off Infection.

As she reached the top of the creaking stairs, Usha knocked quietly on the bedroom door, waited for Auntie's weak greeting and pushed it open. Amid the clutter of ornaments and pictures, Auntie lay propped up on pillows on an ancient four-poster. With her white hair curled like a peony into ringlets and her deep purple bed-wrap clutched around her, she seemed both frail and damp, like a rotting flower in a dark gutter. As she took the cup from Usha the smell of old cotton and lavender rose around her like dust.

She raised a shaking, clawed hand to stroke Usha's cheek.

"You're a good child. The only hope of your poor auntie in her old age. You know that, don't you?"

Usha did know. Unlike most Geminis, Usha had been personally Designed by Auntie herself, which made her feel doubly special. It was one of Usha's favourite stories, how Auntie had wanted a child so much, that she had particularly ordered a little girl to live with her in the big house with the old latticed balconies and the shuttered windows. And best of all, she had selected the colour of Usha's blonde hair, grey eyes, height and the texture of her skin to her own exacting specifications. (Auntie had very high standards.) Whenever Usha thought about it she felt very proud that Auntie had cared so much to Create her with such good taste. Auntie also celebrated Usha's Arrival-day every year, fed her on delicacies, and dressed her in the old silks and satins from her own closets that she had worn herself when she was Usha's age.

Mindful of her good fortune, Usha perched on the side of the bed and supported Auntie as she drank her tea, listening to the old woman's trembling hand beating a staccato rhythm between cup and saucer.

"Auntie," she said timidly, "I tried to lay the tray properly, but the silver teaspoons are missing."

Auntie turned hooded eyes to the girl as she took her last swallow of tea, before scooping up the dregs of the sweetness with a shaking finger, and licking it clean with a wet, sucking sound.

"Is that so, dear? Well, never mind. I'm sure they'll turn up soon."

A sudden thought occurred to Usha. "You haven't . . . you haven't paid the barter-men with them, have you, Auntie?"

The old lady snorted in mirthless laughter. "Of course not. Whatever put that idea into your head? We need to keep *some* standards!"

When Auntie was like this, there was no getting anything out of her. There was nothing that Usha could do but meekly collect the tray and go downstairs to the shadowy kitchen to wash up, Auntie's voice floating behind her.

"We'll have the Master Surgeon over later, dear, so make sure tea and biscuits are ready, there's a good girl."

How nice that Auntie was feeling better today, thought Usha, as she made her way back to the kitchen, balancing the tray precariously in front of her.

But she did not see the yellow glint that suddenly and hungrily lit up Auntie's eyes as she watched the girl downstairs and out of sight.

Arlo stood motionless, hardly believing what he saw. Before him, real and alive under the morning sun, there was an *animal* in the Inn of Court.

From his knowledge of the old encyclopaedias, Arlo could tell that it was either a *dog* or a *cat*, which was more than many people would know these days, now that animals had been Outlawed in the City for some fifty years; but this one was totally unlike any breed he had seen in the ancient books. It was covered in short brown hair, had two semi-cocked ears, a feathery tail and four bow legs, which made it waddle comically when trotting downhill. Watching it move was like seeing one of the pictures from the books come to life, and as it padded along the path, he found himself following it in frightened fascination.

How on earth had anything got through the Gatehouse of the Inn? More importantly, where had it come *from*? Ignatius had told him that creatures were strictly contained outside in the Regions, or else bred for food in the pharms, unless you counted those perfumed and pampered hounds that visiting Senators sometimes displayed alongside them in their carriages as living curiosities. Incredulously, Arlo watched it trot briskly across the central courtyard of the Inn gardens. In what seemed like a second the creature had reached the cobbled path that ran beneath the old wall bounding the Inn and followed it to the library corner with the old diamond-paned windows. Pausing briefly to cock its leg against the drainpipe, it suddenly jerked its head upright and gambolled through the carefully planted daffodils, spraying earth carelessly behind it.

With a curious sensation churning in his stomach as if long fingers were clenching his insides into a knot, Arlo tracked the small figure sniffing along the ivy-covered wall until it disappeared momentarily around the corner leading to the old chapel. From there it had only one possible exit. Glancing over his shoulder to check that no Doctor had yet come out of the mess hall, Arlo scurried across to the shadow of the library window in time to see the creature emerge from the cloisters and prance down the gravelled drive towards the schoolroom.

A crunch of feet on gravel from around the corner made him jump, and the next moment Arlo heard Ignatius's voice, normally pitched in a languorous and easy-going drawl, now raised in disgust.

"But don't you see? We are drawing near to the end of the Experiment! Today we will be able to see the fruits of our labours. Isn't this what we have all been waiting for? You must have patience!"

Arlo's dawning hope at hearing Ignatius was promptly dashed as another voice cut in, cold and curt. "That may be, Ignatius, but the Experiment is long overdue. We will need to see results that please us."

Arlo groaned quietly. Even when he wasn't in trouble, he avoided Doctor Kane by all means possible. Tall, dark and gloomy, with a long, creased face and crooked teeth, he was the total opposite of Ignatius's sunny, unpredictable personality. Something about his manner, as subtle and unidentifiable as a whiff of scent, gave Arlo a cold shiver whenever he passed by. It was a sensation that none of the other Doctors seemed to pick up, even Ignatius, and Arlo had never quite found the words he needed to explain it to them. But all in all, Doctor Kane was the worst possible person to come across a *creature* in the Inn's courtyard. With a pounding heart he withdrew behind a tree, keeping one eye on the gambolling animal but keeping the voices within earshot.

"I cannot promise that we will see results that *please* us," returned Ignatius crisply, "but the Inn is committed to the pursuit of knowledge. And that surely includes knowledge of Naturals."

"Old-fashioned view," sneered Kane. "Hasn't the Experiment taught all you needed to know by now about Naturals?"

The footsteps drew to a halt. Ignatius dropped his voice, so Arlo could not hear his response. Looking back towards the animal he could not restrain a smile despite the emergency of the situation. It was rolling in an ecstasy of abandonment on the grass in the shadow of the chapel, its tail wagging wildly. Arlo punched the wall in frustration. If only Doctor Kane would leave, he could call Ignatius over and show him the creature. Surely Ignatius, of all people, would understand. . .

A door banged across the courtyard as, in the distance, the fat cook left the mess hall and locked up the oathouse. Immediately Arlo heard Ignatius resume a casual conversational tone and the footsteps started to crunch on the gravel again.

"Well, speaking of the Anointment Ceremony for our new Regis, I hear that the Maia have been invited to attend."

"*I* wasn't in favour of the invitation," replied Kane sulkily. "Nobody asked *me* whether *I* approved of their coming."

The Doctors' voices were coming closer as they

turned the corner. The animal lay snoring on the grass, its chest rising and falling. If the Doctors even looked round at the chapel while they were passing, then it would have no chance. Arlo looked round desperately, and then down at the history book in his hand.

Distracting the Doctors from their path was the only plan he could think of, and there was only one way he could think of achieving it. Pulling out one of the loose pages, he crumpled it into a ball and crept to where the ivy hung low enough to the ground to conceal him. Weighing the ball of paper in his hand he took aim and waited, breathing hard, until he saw the Doctors come into sight around the corner, their formal black medical jackets shining like beetles in the morning sun.

Ignatius's usual exuberance seemed to have deserted him as he stalked alongside the thinner, lugubrious Kane, whose squinting gaze and sharp chin were trained on some invisible point in the blue sky above them, as if Ignatius was not really worth his full attention.

"Aren't you ignoring the contribution that the Maia – and the Naturals for that matter – have made to Genopolis?" retorted Ignatius.

Arlo flicked the page gently into the path of the approaching Doctors. Caught on the breeze and slightly unravelling, the paper sailed in a graceful arc, gliding in a spiral over the rose bushes before it dropped to earth and cartwheeled down the grassy lawn, on the opposite side to where the animal lay drowsing.

"This sounds like heresy, Ignatius!" started Kane

scornfully, but, as Arlo had intended, Ignatius's attention had been seized. "Look! *Paper!* From a *book*, of all things! What on earth. . .?"

Biting his nails, Arlo watched covertly as Ignatius steered their course away from the animal to where the offending paper flapped gently on the grass. Ignatius could not see its tail wavings; he did not yet notice its musty smell. Arlo's palms were clammy with sweat.

". . .you persist in your absurd Experiment to prove that we can grant Naturals the same rights as Citizens. . ." pursued Kane, stalking after him.

Ignatius bent to pick the paper up. "Absolutely. After all, before the Apocalypse, Naturals were our ancestors, weren't they?"

A gust of wind tickled the underbelly of the paper, and it bounced tantalizingly out of reach. Ignatius swore. Despite his physique, he was not a young man, and exercise came with difficulty. Arlo watched as they followed the crumpled page rolling slowly back down the grassy bank away from the animal and slowly began to breathe again. In another minute they would be past the chapel. In another minute, they would be around the corner and out of sight. In another. . .

With a grunt, the creature suddenly heaved itself to its feet, rumbling in excitement, raced after the paper and ambushed it, just yards in front of the amazed Doctors. It savaged the ball in a flurry of white shreds and flopped down, its prize between its paws, grinning up at them with a lolling tongue.

The Doctors gazed at the creature in bewilderment.

During the long stony silence that followed, Arlo's insides turned to ice.

"Kane," said Ignatius calmly, once he had recovered himself, starting to back away. "It appears that a *dog* has found its way into our grounds, somehow. Call the garden-boy and tell him to bring his gun."

It was odd that the scissor-man was coming to give Auntie her transfusion even though today was not a Tuesday, puzzled Usha. She liked Transfusion Days and looked forward eagerly to the small hoard of sweets and brightly-coloured bangles that the scissor-man would bring especially for her. And afterwards, Auntie would often feel so much better that sometimes she would come down to the old overgrown garden with Usha and sit in the sunshine for a change.

In the darkened parlour with the windows covered to block out most of the intrusive morning sun, Usha was giving Auntie her morning footbath. The old lady lay back on the couch, one withered foot lying across Usha's lap, and with an efficiency born of long practice, Usha was clipping at her yellowed, curving toenails. The scissors were old and worn, and the toenails rough and horn-like, and a couple of times the nail would splinter despite Usha's best efforts. Sometimes the scissors would slip and Usha would see a small drop of blood come from the tiny wound, which she would hastily wash away. But Auntie would just lie back, oblivious, staring up at the ceiling with faded eyes, muttering to herself.

As she dried and powdered Auntie's feet, Usha wondered idly how many years Auntie had been in decline. She had been thin and fragile ever since Usha had been at the house, and always in need of help when getting dressed or eating. She glanced over, as she always did, at the pictures that lined the parlour shelves. Before Usha's first Arrival-day, Auntie had been looked after by another Gemini-girl, pictured hugging a younger-looking Auntie in the back garden (back in the days when it had been carefully tended). But she had gone away to better herself, said Auntie, and Usha, though privately wondering why anyone would possibly want to leave, said nothing, though none of Auntie's other girls ever came to visit. Next to it hung an earlier picture of Auntie, her face then smooth and unwrinkled, standing with her arm around another Gemini-girl. "That was Galia," said Auntie, smiling reminiscently. "Such a sweet lass. Working over the other side of town, now."

There were other pictures and other girls, but they were too long ago, and Auntie no longer remembered their names. She was getting on and her memory wasn't what it used to be.

The house itself was not exactly a mansion, but it was large and comfortable enough, if a little ill-attended, big enough for Auntie and Usha on the top floor, and the other darkened rooms on the other floors were used for storage. But there were times that Usha would see other people, Citizens and Gemini alike, from her high window, on their way to the chorley-houses or the yearly Games. At these moments she would resent Auntie's frailty, make excitable plans to steal out unobserved, only to have them thwarted by Auntie's petulant and unceasing demands for her hair to be brushed, or perhaps a little chicken soup, a bunch of fresh flowers from the garden. . .

But there was no point in dwelling on such things as these. Usha was very fortunate with her situation, and she knew it. She still remembered the first lessons that had been drummed into her at the pharms.

The first purpose of every Gemini is to serve a Citizen.

Before he had time to think whether it was a good idea or not, Arlo sprang out of his hiding place and ran towards Ignatius. "Sir. Please. Sir!"

Glancing at Kane, Ignatius said warningly, "You'd better get on to your exam, Arlo. There's nothing to concern you here."

Ignatius seemed different when he was around the other Doctors, Arlo thought, as if he was gazing straight through you and talking to someone on the other side, never quite looking at you directly yet knowing with some mystic insight what you were doing even if looking the other way. But on this occasion, Ignatius's glance was surprisingly warning. As Arlo opened his mouth to protest, he swept on. "No backchat, please, Arlo. Immediately."

Arlo shook his head, frantically pointing at the dog that lay a few metres away in a sunny patch of lawn, rolling over as if inviting someone to scratch his belly. "But sir. I was watching him. I've read about . . . *dogs* in the library. He isn't dangerous, I can tell. Look at him, he's harmless. Please, sir."

Kane looked down his long nose at Arlo, lip curled. "Suppose you know all about the diseases these *things* carry inside them, boy? Think that's something we *want* amongst decent Citizens? Any idea where it's even *come* from?"

"Well no, sir, but. . ."

"Doubtless it's escaped from a research laboratory," grunted Kane. "Should get it back there while it's still docile."

"But he *is* docile," pleaded Arlo, rising panic mounting inside him. "He just wants to play. . ."

Kane shook his head. "*Play?* The Inn is not a place for playing! No *creatures* should be running around in here. We should blow its brains out here and now."

Arlo's eyes widened in shock. Seeing this, a smile of malicious pleasure spread around Kane's thin lips. "Of course, we could always make it into a medical specimen of our own. Test its reactions." His long tongue swept out and deliberately licked up a bit of spittle. "Skin it. Or dissect it, maybe." Arlo's face reddened, and Kane's eyes signalled his delight. "Of course, in order to monitor it closely, we'd have to . . . keep it alive . . . during the experiment."

"Kane!" barked Ignatius. "What on earth are you saying?"

The other Doctor shot Ignatius a look of contempt. "Just keeping our backyard clean, Ignatius. Time somebody stood up for principles around here."

Kane stalked away rapidly. Arlo watched his retreating back in rising dismay and turned back to Ignatius, an appeal already forming on his lips. But Ignatius folded his arms with a look of finality.

"You don't want to be late for your exam, Arlo."

Arlo knew from bitter experience that it was impossible to persuade Ignatius to do anything if he did not wish to be drawn. His head spun and his eyes prickled. He started off, dragging his feet, but as he reached the Hall door he glanced over his shoulder furtively. In the distance he saw Doctor Kane making his panting way back across the lawn towards Ignatius and the dog, but instead of the garden-boy his fat companion Doctor Phlegg waddled in hot pursuit behind him. Phlegg carried a long black case over one shoulder, and as soon as he was within range, fell to one knee and started to unpack it hurriedly. All around the courtyard, windows and doors were being flung open and a jumble of Doctors dressed in the same black robes as Arlo peered out and jostled for position to see what the commotion was about.

"Back away," shouted Kane, waving his arms dramatically. "Back away. Phlegg is going to capture the creature for his laboratory experiments."

Ignatius regarded the proceedings with interest. Arlo tugged at his sleeve, pleadingly. "Sir, please, sir. . ."

"Go into the Gatehouse for safety," called Kane, almost dancing on the spot. "Quietly now. Walk, don't run."

The dog's tail thumped on the grass, watching the strange thin man gambolling on the grass. The next second it was off and racing towards Kane, ears pricked, tail up. Kane and Phlegg gave the dog one startled look, then dropped the semi-assembled gun and turned and ran for their lives. Phlegg tripped over but was up again in a flash, charging straight into Kane's fleeing figure and bowling him sideways. With undignified haste, they tumbled into the schoolroom, almost fighting each other as they struggled to close the door on the path of the approaching monster. Their white faces peered out of the small side window, while the dog bounced up and down, its excited barks echoing and volleying around the courtyard as if a whole pack of hounds had suddenly invaded the sedate environs of the Inn of Court.

Ignatius covered the ground to the schoolroom with a speed that Arlo would not have thought possible, unwinding the scarlet Doctor's sash that was wound around his waist. "Here, dog. Here. . .!"

Arlo raced behind him, seeking his chance. "Listen, sir! I can look after him! I can feed him! He'll be all right!"

"Call the guards! Help! Attack! Fire!" yelled Phlegg through the window.

The dog wheeled excitedly to meet them as Arlo and

Ignatius approached. Ignatius slowed to a stop, fished in his pocket and held out part of a biscuit. "Here you are. Breakfast. Playtime over."

He threw the biscuit at the dog, which caught it expertly with a swift sideways lunge. As it held its prey down with one paw and chewed on the end, Ignatius quietly stepped behind the dog and slipped his sash over its head in a scarlet noose, securing it by an elaborate knot. The other end he tied to the iron ring driven into the schoolroom door.

"That's it. Now he can't get away." Ignatius glanced cheerfully at the perspiring faces inside, pressed against the glass. "And, by the same token, neither can they."

Arlo gazed at the dog longingly. "What are you going to do, sir?"

Ignatius winked. "I think I'll keep them in the schoolroom for a while. It'll do them good to stew for a bit. Meanwhile, I suggest you do some last-minute cramming for that exam of yours while Kane is temporarily out of your way."

"But. . ." began Arlo, but Ignatius shook his head. "That's *enough*, Arlo. Go on now. Today is the most important day of your life. Remember that."

The dog grinned happily back at the boy, tongue lolling. Walking away from it was one of the hardest things that Arlo had ever done. As he made his dejected way towards the Old Hall, all the Doctors who had crowded out of the Refectory to watch the proceedings moved aside to let him pass, staring at him curiously. Arlo averted his face and hung his head. Suddenly all the brightness of the day was extinguished into gloom. The sick, burning feeling inside him – as if the old Doctor had let him down, somehow – was so strong that he could not even bear to look back or say goodbye to Ignatius as he left.

On the dot of three day-hours and thirty minutes, the doorbell rang. Its high, tinny note shrilled through the house once, twice, three times. Instantly Usha set Auntie's foot carefully down on its bolster, dried her hands and slid down the long curving banisters to let the scissor-man in. When she was younger she couldn't manage to call him by his proper name of *surgeon* and so, like most Citizens, she had called him the *scissor-man* because of his bag of sharp silver instruments polished to a high glassy shine. Through the stained-glass panel of the front door she could see the outline of his top hat and muffler, distorted into a spider-shape by the fracturing of the many small, coloured panes.

From upstairs Auntie's querulous tones came drifting down. "Let him in, child, for goodness' sake!"

With a mischievous grin, Usha pulled the heavy door open.

"How's my favourite girl?" said the scissor-man, smiling, as he saw the young Gemini standing before him. "Getting Auntie ready for her Operation?"

Usha stood in front of him, cheekily, arms folded. "Where are my sweeties?"

"What sweeties?" The scissor-man jumped as Usha

suddenly pounced on his left hand that he held inside his pocket, and tugged out a small white bag. "Easy, tiger! They'll end up on the floor!"

Usha had no idea what a *tiger* was, but she understood that the scissor-man was meaning to be funny, and laughed politely. Her cheek bulging from a toffee from the scissor-man's pocket, she led the way down the corridor and showed him into the darkened reception room where Auntie reclined fretfully on a divan. The old lady roused herself weakly to clasp the scissor-man's hand.

"Good morning, Master Surgeon. Sit down, and tell me. What news of the outside world?"

"Much change for Genopolis, I hear," said the scissor-man, sitting down quietly at her side. "Word is that a new Governor has been appointed as Regis of the Inn of Court to lead the Regeneration Programme."

"Oh boring, boring, boring!" retorted Auntie, rudely. "I'm too old to worry about politics. When you get to my age, you care nothing about such little things. Usha, darling, tea for the Doctor, please."

As they talked, Usha hurried away to the kitchen. Since her first Arrival-day, Auntie's Operation had been spoken of as a glowing yet unspecified event in the near distance, a source of inspiration and hope to the old lady, a date that was constantly changing according to her health. Poor Auntie, to spend so much time in that darkened room, thought Usha, as she opened the sweet-chest to search out the last of the hard biscuits that nobody ever ate but which would always be presented as a matter of courtesy and likewise politely refused, taken out and returned, again and again, year after year.

As she returned to the reception room, Usha heard that they had dropped their voices almost to a mutter. Her curiosity at the scissor-man's unexpected arrival was re-awakened. Quietly she braced the tray into the crook of her hip and leaned in, pressing her ear to the gap of the door that still lay partially open. She could just about hear Auntie's faint voice.

"She has started to suspect, Doctor. She is asking questions. . ."

Arlo sat alone at a small desk in the middle of the Great Hall, a writing-block and stylus in front of him. Around him the huge walls were hung with old tapestries and paintings salvaged from the Pre-Apocalyptic Period that made up part of the Inn's proud collection, and the light that fell through the Hall's high windows was dusty and pale. On any other day Arlo would have enjoyed looking at the figures and scenes in the ancient paintings; their strange clothes and postures seemed both foreign to him, and yet strangely familiar. But today the smell of the ancient paint caught sickeningly at his nostrils and made his stomach turn. In all the excitement, he had totally forgotten about breakfast, and his mouth was cracked and dry.

He watched as Doctor Kane, lately released from the schoolroom, made his halting way up the Hall, now shrouded in his long medical robe. He heaved himself into the invigilator's chair, eyed Arlo nastily, coughed up something yellow into a handkerchief that he quickly stowed away in his pocket, and tonelessly recited:

"Your Citizenship Examination will last for one day-hour and a half. During the Examination you may not use any reference books, manuscripts or other study aids. Any eating or drinking is forbidden. When you have finished your questions, please hand your writing-block over to me and exit the Examination. The time is now three day-hours and thirty minutes. Now you may turn over and begin."

Arlo obediently turned his slate over and scanned the list of questions. His head hurt and he badly needed to visit the wash-room. As he read, he felt an uncomfortable pinching sensation in his stomach.

1. *Outline the reasons for the creation of the City of Genopolis.*
2. *What are the main differences between Citizens and Naturals?*
3. *Describe the institutions of the City.*

Sighing, Arlo picked up his stylus and began to write.

Question One. The City of Genopolis was created around 2069, but nobody really knows the exact date because there was a big catastrophe called the Apocalypse that had destroyed pretty much everything before it. There were earthquakes and the oceans flooded everywhere and there were lots of diseases that killed lots of the old Natural people who used to live in the world before us. It was all the fault of the Naturals anyway because they were stupid and did a lot of things to poison the earth so it was just as well most of them were killed off. They used to hunt and eat animals because they didn't have anything like the pharms to make food for them. . .

Arlo stopped, suddenly, feeling sick. Meat was often served at the Inn's tables, but only as part of a dressed dish. He had never really considered that meat came from living, breathing *animals* before. Thinking about it made him queasy. Would the ancient people have eaten creatures like. . .?

With an effort, he pushed the thought of the dog from his mind.

There used to be a lot of cities but they were all drowned in the floods, and after the Apocalypse they decided to build one City called Genopolis for special people who are the Citizens. Naturals are banned from the City because they just destroy everything they touch. The man who built Genopolis was called Leuwenkind, and he was a very clever scientist. He is called the Father of Genopolis. He said that Genopolis was all one body, that its Citizens were the head, and the Gemini are its hands and feet. The first purpose of every Gemini is to serve a Citizen. . .

Arlo frowned. He was probably missing something out but there didn't seem to be anything else he could add. Risking a quick glance at the sundial on the wall he noted that he still had another hour to go. Chewing his stylus he tried to collect his scattered thoughts from Ignatius's lessons.

Question Two. Citizen people are very logical and clever and strong. Early Natural people were very weak. They were controlled by eating and drinking, and they were always fighting amongst themselves for more of these things. They were always suffering Infections, or Outbreaks like crying or screaming or laughing and they were very selfish. But Citizen people always work together for everyone's good. This is the main difference between Citizens and Naturals, as well as Citizens are much more beautiful and Natural people are ugly. There are still Natural people hiding in the wilderness, but they are always cowardly and frightened and try to kill everything, even each other. Outside Genopolis there are other wild Naturals in tribes, but they are wicked and sometimes try to attack Genopolis and steal our food. They used to live in Regions outside the City but they were ungrateful and kept trying to rebel, so the Regions were destroyed and the Naturals went to live in the wilderness instead. But that still didn't stop them being trouble, because last week some of them stole the food delivery from the pharms, so we did not have bread for ages. . .

With new confidence Arlo sharpened his stylus, but suddenly a piercing howl sent him leaping to his feet and his writing-slate crashed to the floor.

Again and again it echoed around the Hall, a terrible,

inhuman sound, electrifying every part of him with a wild urge to run.

Behind the door, the scissor-man said something that Usha could not decipher, but a second later she heard the clink of silver as something changed hands. Even though she could not see, Usha knew that Auntie had given the scissor-man her silver spoons in payment for the medical bills.

"I hope that it is true what you promise, Doctor?" asked Auntie.

"It is true," replied the scissor-man. "Death itself has died, and you, Cybella, will be one of the first to triumph over it."

"But young?" asked Auntie eagerly. "Young, as I once was?"

There was a long pause before the scissor-man spoke. "You will not decay, Cybella, nor will you die, but youth, I cannot promise."

"But what good is eternity without health?" grumbled the old lady. "What good is a face without beauty? How can I look forward to the coming years, always weary, always confined to my couch? What good is your proposal?"

"Patience, Mistress Cybella," said the scissor-man soothingly. "Have faith in the new techniques of the Academy. Trust in me."

Usha leaned a little too far, and touched the door with her shoulder. It creaked, and the next moment Auntie cried out, sharply. "Usha?"

She grabbed the tray and backed through the door, trying to appear busy and unconcerned. The old lady was lying back down on the couch, grumbling as the scissor-man bent over her attentively, holding her wrist, checking his timepiece and counting her pulse-beats. Quickly Usha set down the tray on the footstool next to the couch, arranged the cups and china, poured the tea and put two lumps of sugar in her mistress's cup. Finally, she sat down in the chair next to the divan and bared her arm in preparation for a Transfusion, but this time the scissor-man did not bring out the needle and pump. "Not today, Usha. Let's see how you're shaping up instead."

He took out a tape measure and measured from Usha's heel to the top of her head. He asked her to stand on a small box that he took from his bag that calculated her weight. He put a cold stethoscope on her chest, held down her tongue with an aluminium spill and asked her to say *aaah*, took a swab from the inside of her mouth and some clippings from her fingernails, which he put carefully away into a small glass box, humming slightly as he did so, as if pleased with the results.

"You have been looking after her well, my lady."

"She is my future," said the old woman fondly. "She is my dream come true."

Arlo's skin crawled as he stared about the Hall. What on earth had made that *noise*? Although he had never heard anything like it in his life, there was something in the chilling notes of it that struck at him too deeply to bear. In his confusion he turned questioning eyes to Doctor Kane, and saw in shock that his thin lips were pulled back over his teeth in a cruel smile.

"Apparently my learned colleague Ignatius is taking my advice at last with regard to that wretched stray. Back to your Examination, Arlo."

With Kane's words, something exploded inside Arlo's chest. Even afterwards he was barely conscious of what he did; with one hand he picked up the ink bottle and hurled it at the wall, seeing in a blaze of vicious joy the cascade of shattered glass and purple ink spatter all over the walls and floor. As Doctor Kane started towards him, shouting for him to stop, Arlo turned and ran blindly down the corridor, crashing unheeding past anyone in his way.

Breathlessly he flung himself through the doors towards the Laboratories where the noise had come from and stopped short.

Two dripping Gemini servants were trying to hold on to one very wet and howling dog, while an overturned bucket and scrubbing brushes lay scattered around. Looking equally dishevelled was Ignatius, his Doctor's robes spattered with white soapsuds and his hair standing on end. As Arlo appeared, Ignatius straightened up and withdrew a syringe from the dog's shoulder.

"Hullo, Arlo! You've never finished your exam already?"

As if by magic, the howling stopped and the dog started forward as soon as it saw him, tail wagging, but Ignatius held it back. "Now listen, Arlo. I saw your face when they brought out the gun, and I decided that we had room in the Inn for another little Experiment, if only to annoy Kane with all his ridiculous talk of dissecting and shooting. Trial run only, mind. We've cleaned him up a bit, but now, you've got to train him. This one's apparently used to Citizens, but we're not used to him. Keep him off the beds and away from the food, otherwise I won't be held responsible. Understand?"

Unable to speak, Arlo simply nodded. Ignatius handed him the chain. "I've given him a medical and a shot against disease and he seems to be clean. But if anyone shows up that he's Registered to, then you need to give him back, no arguments. And again, any trouble, any scratched furniture or mess in the corridors and he's out. I've gone out on a limb for you on this one, and I hope you'll make it worth my while."

Around him the air was spinning almost too fast to breathe, but Arlo managed a shaky smile. "Yes, sir," he finally managed to say. "You can trust me on that."

Carefully, the scissor-man removed the thermometer from under Usha's tongue, noted down the number, clapped her on the shoulder and turned away. "Good girl. Run along, now."

Suddenly, like a flash of lightning, an image formed in her mind: the dazzle of a bright light in her face, and the sight of his eyes gazing at her, green eyes with brown rims like a muddy lake, and over it all like a silent Outbreak of screaming inside her head, an overwhelming urge to run. . .

"Usha?" the scissor-man was saying. "Usha. . .?"

She blinked herself out of her trance to see Auntie and the scissor-man staring at her in puzzlement. "What is it, my dear girl?" Auntie was bleating. "Standing there gawping in front of visitors. Are you all right?"

Usha could only shake her head. The scissor-man chuckled and poured himself another cup of tea. "Dreamer," he said. "Head in the clouds. What are we going to do with you, eh?"

"You can go to your room now if you want, Usha," said Auntie, abruptly. "You can wash up after our guest has left."

Quickly, Usha turned around and ran up the stairs away from them both, her mind spinning. Bewildered, she sought out the sanctuary of her bedroom, to wait there until the scissor-man had left. Sitting on her bed with her knees under her chin, she pondered the sudden image and what it might mean.

Once she had experienced the same kind of vision when she was crossing the road, a premonition of a splintering crash and a heavy weight on top of her. Confused, she had stood uncertainly on the pavement for a few vital seconds more, and the next moment a runaway pharm-wagon, its axle broken and trailing sparks on the stone, had come skidding around the corner to smash exactly on the spot where she would have been passing. Another time, she had felt a recurring sensation, like a prod in her side, whenever she had talked to the water-man at market. It became so persistent that finally she had asked the errand-boy to take her to the other water-man at the other end of the quarter. The boy had grumbled at the inconvenience but agreed. A few weeks later they found out that the water-man had died from an Infection caused by one of his contaminated barrels, along with a great many of his customers. After this episode, the errand-boy had gazed at Usha with round eyes, and lowering his voice implored Usha never to tell Auntie about the visions, otherwise it would upset her.

So, as with the dreams, Usha had pushed her waking visions away, unacknowledged by other Citizens or Gemini, and indeed almost forgotten by herself. But one thing she had learned. Whether long, short, clear or puzzling, the daydreams were never wrong.

All she could do now was wait and see what this one might mean.

Later that night in the Library as the dog nosed underneath the table, Arlo leafed through the ancient encyclopaedias, searching for a picture that resembled it. Around him rose the giant shelves that housed the Inn's countless books, a huge and labyrinthine maze of rooms, each with their own ancient and now largely forgotten subject – law, medicine, history, mathematics, philosophy. . .

Arlo was in his favourite corner of the library, the few secret shelves that housed the books that did not contain dry and boring lists of facts, diagrams or calculations, but instead contained the ancient stories of what Arlo secretly thought were "real people", people from before the Apocalypse who had thought and felt as he did. Some of the language and names were alien and unfamiliar, but the stories contained inside were as intimate and recognizable as if they had once happened to him. He still remembered the first time that he had picked up one of these books, and the sudden delight that had come over him. For once in his life he had felt himself in the company of what Ignatius called *friends*, and for many years they and the stories they told had been his closest companions. Once he had suffered an Outbreak on reading a particular story, and when Ignatius had asked why, he could only say, "Because I know how he feels." And he did feel, feel as strongly as the man in the story who had found himself, alone and shipwrecked on a desert island, with no one to talk to but the birds and the animals, who spoke a different language to his own.

So engrossed was he in the encyclopaedia that he did not at first see Ignatius and his assistant, the mild-mannered librarian Doctor Kristo, enter with a stack of reference books for filing. He only caught the last scraps of their conversation.

"I'm telling you the truth, Ignatius," Kristo was

saying urgently. "The new Governor Regis has sworn his allegiance to the Regeneration Programme. What on earth are we going to do about the Experiment?"

"We need to protect our research," retorted Ignatius. "The Experiment is the most valuable answer to mankind's future. We can't abandon it now."

Kristo suddenly caught sight of Arlo as he turned. "Oh, hullo, Arlo! What did you think of that book I lent you? *Treasure Island*, I think it was called?"

The next second the dog had pounced on his ankles with a playful bark. Immediately the tower of books went flying and Kristo staggered back against the shelves, his fair face with its placid regular Citizen's features quite distorted with astonishment. "What in Genopolis is that!" he cried. "Ig-Ignatius! There's a . . . *dog* in the library!"

Arlo leapt forward and pulled Rem back. "Down, boy! Down, boy!"

"What did I tell you, Arlo?" thundered Ignatius, but Arlo was already pushing the page of the encyclopaedia excitedly at him. Kristo always had a kind word for him and he had no wish to get into trouble again. "He won't hurt you, Kristo! He's a brindled brown sheepdog," he said eagerly. "There's a picture of him here! He was lost – at least I found him wandering around – and he had a sore pad, and Ignatius let me keep him, and I've called him Rem, and he's going to sleep on my bed at night. . ."

Slowly Kristo recovered himself, looked at the picture

and raised his eyebrows. "You mean to say you found a *dog* . . . wandering around in *here*?"

"He probably escaped from one of the visiting diplomats from Pharmopolis," said Ignatius smoothly. "We put a call out but nobody had Registered him as missing. You know what that lot is like."

Kristo took a step back and stared at the dog, unconvinced. "I still think it's extremely peculiar . . . I would have said that the odds of finding a stray animal in the City were a thousand to one."

"Well, as I said," repeated Ignatius firmly, "he's being looked after by Arlo very comfortably at the moment. And given time, he might even be able to stop him from attacking the ankles of innocent Doctors every once in a while."

And that might have been the end of it, had Arlo not caught the warning glance from beneath Ignatius's bushy eyebrows at Kristo that seemed to be saying that it was best if no more questions were asked.

"WHAT ELSE ARE CHILDREN FOR?"

The baby screwed up its eyes and took its first breath, closely followed by its first scream. Instantly there was a chorus of delight and the crowd of bedraggled Naturals pressed around their new arrival, now bellowing heartily in the throes of its first Outbreak. The old woman sponged its face clean, wrapped it in a sack and placed it Gea's exhausted arms. "Shush!" she cried. "Don't crowd! Let them get some air!"

But Angus kissed Gea, Kira, the baby, the old woman, even the Doctor, in a mood that seemed to combine an Outbreak of both weeping and uncontrollable laughter. All the time, his wife lay watching him, smiling at his antics, trying with kisses and caresses to shield the baby in her arms from the brutality of its new surroundings. Somebody brought out an old violin and scraped enthusiastically on it, although there was no room to dance. Kira carried in a bowl of tea for the gathering, and drizzled in a helping of honey. The thick aroma filled the chamber and the Doctor sniffed distastefully. Hadn't he read somewhere that these people made tea from acorns? As was the custom, they shared it ceremoniously between them, passing it from hand to hand. Fearing Infection, the Doctor politely declined the invitation to drink from the same bowl.

As they celebrated, the Doctor watched them, confusedly. For the first time he felt the uselessness of his Experiment. No amount of study, he felt, could make him properly understand the way that Naturals acted, and no medical book could have given him the intuitive sense with which the old woman had masterminded the birth. With arms folded, he looked on as food was handed round on battered tin plates, an ugly greenish mish-mash of cabbage mixed with potato. As the sweetish smell reached his nostrils, the timepiece on the Doctor's wrist suddenly beeped. It was time for his daily nutrition, and despite himself he accepted the heaped dish that was handed to him. Around him rose the noise of chewing and swallowing as the Naturals scooped up the mess eagerly with their fingers, or with hunks of bread. The Doctor at first tasted his steaming portion dubiously using a spoon taken from his medical bag, but was relieved to find it tasty enough, much like the vegetables grown in the Inn but with a slightly ashy taste. In the corner was a foaming bucket of their home-brewed cider into which everybody dipped cups, bowls and any implements they could find.

"Have you ever seen a baby with as much hair as this, Doctor?" Kira ruffled the reddish-brown tufts on the baby's head, rapturously.

There was a sudden clatter and Angus appeared before him with two more dripping mugs of cider. The Doctor thanked him politely, and put his aside. Angus flopped down in front of him, laughing. "Penny for your thoughts, Doctor."

The Doctor smiled, mystified. "What is a penny?"

"I want to know whatever it is you're thinking," grinned Angus.

"I'm not thinking anything," the Doctor answered pleasantly.

Behind them, Gea raised herself up on her elbow.

"I know what you're thinking."

The Doctor turned to face her, and was unprepared for the look on the young woman's face. It was twisted by a look so extreme that her features were distorted and unrecognizable. Angus too was taken aback. Gea gazed at the Doctor, scowling.

"You despise us. I can tell by the way you're looking at us. At me. At him."

The Doctor shook his head, bewildered. "Despise? I really don't know what you're talking about."

Angus leapt in. "Gea, you're mistaken! He's here to help us!"

The young woman glared at the Doctor. "You think we're doomed, don't you? To a life eternally on the run? We're just fodder to be experimented on, sacrificed for your pleasure, harvested for your immortality. . ."

Angus was already next to Gea, stroking her hair, trying to calm her down, laughing it off. "She's a bit feverish. She always gets like this when she's feverish. You ought to hear what she says to me when she really gets going."

"I understand," said the Doctor calmly. "This night has been hard for her."

"Your time will come, Doctor. It is not far off."

Gea fell back on the bed, the last of her energy suddenly gone, and covered her face with her arm.

In the uncomfortable silence that followed, the Doctor stood up and reached for his bag. It was no use delaying the inevitable. The moment had finally arrived.

"We need to talk, Angus," said the Doctor at length. "But not here. Somewhere private."

Outside, the rain had stopped during the night, and the waters had finally subsided. In the early morning light, the Doctor and Angus made their way to where they could sit astride the old pipes that ran the length of the huge viaduct, their feet dangling over the massive drop. Below them fell the drying riverbed, snaking away into a glitter against the sunrise, and on both sides rose the hills covered with dense scrub and forest. In front of them rolled a plain and the broken spine of the old railway track. It was a desolate but starkly beautiful prospect, and in the distance, silhouetted black against the purple sweep of the morning clouds, lay a city built on a stony outcrop of rock rising vertically from the plain.

They were looking towards Genopolis.

Presently the Doctor spoke. "Have you told Gea, Angus?"

Angus looked away. "No. I... She... There wasn't time."

"There is even less time now," said the Doctor reprovingly. "The next Inspection comes in seven days. Gea was registered as pregnant six months ago. They will come to check on her."

Angus turned to him in sudden decision, his skin flushed with the tint of the golden sunrise. "I'm sorry, Doctor. I can't do it."

The Doctor blinked in confusion. "What do you mean?"

"Our arrangement. I can't do it."

A chill wind whipped around them, and the tears leaking from Angus's eyes dried on his cheeks. He pulled the rough piece of sacking that served as a cloak closer around him, but the Doctor remained oblivious to the cold, staring out impassively at the distant river.

"You don't know what it's like," continued Angus. "Now I've seen him. I've touched him. His eyes, his fingers. . . And Gea. It would kill her. No, I've thought about it. And I can't."

"What other option is there, then?" asked the Doctor, as calmly as he was able. Was the fool really thinking of going back on their agreement?

"We'll hide him. Somewhere. We'll say he died. He died."

"You know it is a crime to bury the dead," warned the Doctor, solemnly.

Angus looked desperate. "Then we'll say he died before he was born. It was over too quickly to inform the authorities. That can't be wrong, surely?"

"It's more difficult than that," said the Doctor swinging his heels. "Registration is becoming more rigid. The City is controlling the births of Naturals in the Regions. You won't keep him a secret for ever. Not from them. Don't you understand?"

"Then we'll move. We'll go east. They've told me that the Controlled Regions end, somewhere, in the swamps. They can't track us there. No Registrations, no curfew. They won't know."

The Doctor shook his head. "You can't make a trek like that in the middle of summer. And definitely not with a small baby."

Angus was mutinous. "We'll manage. I've done worse before now."

"It is a bold plan," said the Doctor diplomatically. At all costs the Natural must be persuaded. He could not have come so far to go back empty-handed. "I just think that this will put everybody at risk."

Angus punched the rail, suddenly savage. "So what's the alternative? Stay here and be trapped? Die in the wilderness? Tell me what I should do! I don't know your people. I can't think with your minds. I don't know what you want! Tell me, Doctor. I don't understand. Tell me. . ."

"Our agreement is the only way," said the Doctor soothingly. "A way that still has a future in it. I cannot promise what kind of future, but it is far safer than what you propose. Your son would have a chance, Angus. And a chance is all that we can hope for, these days."

Angus dropped his head down on to his arms, his fiery determination rapidly draining out of him. The Doctor pressed his advantage. "What better life would your son have, than growing up in the care of a highly-respected Doctor? Think of it, Angus. He would have a future. In a city of culture, he would learn the arts, the sciences, how to read. He would not break his knuckles felling trees or scratch for roots in the Regions."

Angus's face darkened. "And what about us? What future for our people? We need our own blood, Doctor. If our blood *does not run in our veins, it shall not run in theirs. I can't allow it. I won't allow it."*

The Doctor paused to allow the man time to recover himself, but when he finally spoke, his tone was curt.

"You know your danger, Angus. Natural children are being taken at birth and Regenerated in the pharms. You speak of running but you will not get so far as the next Region. You speak of keeping your blood together, but they will drain it from you. Better to keep the last of your sons alive than sacrifice him to feed the bodies of a thousand Citizens. It is your choice, Angus. But you have very little time. They know where you live. They have been watching."

Angus covered his face. The Doctor patted his arm gently, a gesture he often found useful when dealing with Naturals.

"Let him go, Angus. Let him find his own freedom. You cannot use him for your own future."

When the answer came it was so muffled that the Doctor barely heard him.

"But, Doctor, what else are children for?

TWO

"**N**o eggs again," grumbled Doctor Phlegg. "Damned Naturals hijacked the food-convoy from the pharms last week! Time the Consulate sorted those barbarians out once and for all!"

"Oh I don't kn-know," said Kristo quietly as he drained his coffee and left the table, his slight stammer becoming more marked under Phlegg's gaze. "I don't think we can b-blame Naturals for everything that goes wrong around here."

It was almost a month after the dog had arrived. The inhabitants of the Inn were eating breakfast at a long, low trestle table covered with white linen under the shade of the willow trees. Honey from the Court's own hives was heaped in slabs on the delicate porcelain plates, and a few jealous bees buzzed around the damson jam and quince jelly that the cook had made from the fruit that he managed to coax out of the small orchard behind the oat-house. The Inn of Court was unusual in that it tried to cultivate a portion of its own food so that it did not rely so heavily on pharmed-rations, but due to the snobbishness of the Inn's Head, Doctor Benedict, the kitchen gardens and vegetable plots were hidden away around the back of the Inn while the rolling front terraces were bright with beds of beautiful, but inedible, flowers.

Arlo ate steadily away at his bowl of grainy porridge, too used to these sudden deprivations at table to care. Foods like eggs and bacon were scarce at the best of times, and would usually be given to the older Doctors, leaving Arlo and the more junior doctors with plain oatmeal. Although he had never actually seen a real living Natural before and knew little enough about them apart from his Natural History lessons, he had heard enough stories about them to hope that he never did. They were bloodthirsty pirates whose only wish was to destroy the City and every Citizen who lived in it. Doctor Phlegg said that they were jealous of the Citizens' comforts, Doctor Kane that they resented the Citizens' freedom to do whatever they pleased, but it all really depended on what type of Natural they were. Some were part of the rebel movement against the City and others were tribesmen, who lived only to murder, thieve and cause chaos. When Arlo was younger, Doctor Kane had told him lurid stories about the wicked Natural warlord Goren who lived in the swamps beyond the East Regions and drank children's blood. . .

"Well, you'll soon have your wish, Phlegg," intoned

Kane, picking his teeth with exaggerated care using his long fingernail. "Once our new Overloard Regis is appointed, he won't stand for any of this mollycoddling of Naturals."

Ignatius interrupted swiftly, dipping his roll into a glass of bitter black coffee from the last of the Inn's reserves. "Right, Arlo! Ready for your Examination results? Doctor Benedict got the marks from the Academy yesterday. You're to go to his office in one day-hour sharp."

Arlo felt his stomach cramp uncomfortably. "Yes, sir." He wished that the other Doctors were not staring at him quite so closely. Kane sniffed uninterestedly and reached for the last bun.

"I just hope, Ignatius, that our young novice has upheld the reputation of the Inn. It is very important that he does not let himself down . . . or us."

The atmosphere around the table had grown suddenly still. Only Ignatius seemed at ease, ignoring Kane's comments. "And where's that mutt of yours got to, Arlo, that's what I'd like to know?"

"He's tied up round the back," said Arlo, untruthfully.

"Good. Now don't let him go running around and dirtying the lawn again, or we'll all be for it. Remember we're all going to be busy rehearsing for the Anointment Ceremony this afternoon."

Arlo knew. No other event had been so talked about in living memory. All week, the corridors of the Inn had been buzzing with activity like a hive of ants. Old trellises had been dismantled, overgrown rose beds pruned back, and a new load of gravel poured on to the cobbled path that ran from gilded front gate to diamond-paned porch. Ancient hangings in the Hall had been taken down and beaten in the sun, where clouds of dust and mites rose into the air and mingled with the smell of new-mown grass and furniture polish. Steps had been scrubbed and doorknobs shone. The organ in the Hall had been dusted and a carpenter brought in especially to repair the rotted ropes of the foot pedals. The choir had practised at all times and places, their voices echoing down corridors and up the old pipes in an eerie fashion. Even absent-minded Doctor Benedict had put his musty-smelling ceremonial robes in the laundry, and fat Doctor Phlegg had procured a new oversized sash especially for the once-in-a-lifetime occasion that was due to take place, the appointment of a Governor of Genopolis as the first-ever Overlord Regis of the Inn of Court.

Arlo excused himself and pushed his stool back from the table. As he walked back over the central lawns towards his room, he saw rehearsals were starting for the chamber orchestra, who were struggling with their instruments in the fresh and vigorous breeze that was blowing down the terraces of the Inn, sending showers of tree pollen into the orchestra's faces and causing a rash of sneezing. Old blind Doctor Sheridan, whose ears were so sharp he could hear a pin drop at fifty paces, stood up as conductor, waving his baton ineffectually, and trying to make himself heard against the wind that blew the words from his mouth.

"And a one-two-three-four, and a one-two-three-four! Stop! Doctor Kristo, you've come in late again."

"I can't see you from here," countered Kristo, putting aside his battered old viola. "There's a r-rose bush in the way."

Doctor Sheridan snorted. "There's going to be at least two hundred people standing on this lawn and fifty of them will be attending the litter, so this is really the only place we can go. Waste of time, if you ask me. But ours not to reason why, and all that. Now, back to the *allegro* after the coda, and you come in after three beats, not four, Kristo. Ready? One, two, three. . .!"

Arlo watched, grinning, suddenly cheered by the change in routine. With everybody so distracted with preparations, he thought, perhaps it could be the perfect time to play a little trick of revenge of his own on Doctor Kane. . .

Usha shut the gate and started off down the stone-lined street that led to the barter-market, a bag of small trinkets for barter swinging from one hand. Auntie lived in the West Quarter, a once grand Middle-Citizen area, but its roads were now lined with similarly decaying, ramshackle old houses, their beauty rapidly fading into the dust. However, the location was still highly-regarded, for the West Quarter backed on to Central Square, the enormous stone plaza which housed the Academy, the Guildhall, the Founder's Medical College and the Inn of Court. As she passed the Inn's ivy-clad brick wall, she could hear snatches of chatter and a tinkling of plates.

February was nearly over, which meant that the convoys of winter produce from the pharms were already starting to dwindle as the seas around Genopolis dried up in the Heat. Since the introduction of the Food Laws, which strictly rationed the basic foodstuffs to a small amount of vouchers per Citizen for exactly this reason, any other provisions had to be gained for fair-exchange or barter. Auntie had once showed Usha some small pieces of metal (in gold, silver or bronze) that people had used in the old days, before the Apocalypse, to exchange for food. This had always seemed most illogical to Usha. How could a small piece of metal be worth anything? You couldn't eat it, you couldn't clothe yourself with it, so where was its value? Everyone knew that a potato or a carrot or a blanket were the most valuable things you could have, so much so that often the Higher or Middle Citizens would pay their tradesmen in crates of oranges for furniture and clothes. But apparently in times gone by the more of these pieces of metal you had, the Higher you were, so High sometimes that your pieces of metal were beyond counting and didn't exist apart from in people's heads. Usha hadn't really followed that part, but it all showed how well the system worked by comparison these days. At least you could see the value of an orange, a slice of bread, not just store it up where nobody could see it and still think it was worth something.

Unless you belonged to one of the Institutions like the Academy or the Inn of Court where you could get food and drink any time you wanted (people said), Middle Citizens like Auntie, who had no other family-unit apart from Usha, frequently had to resort to the barter-system. Auntie had rooms crammed full of antiques from before the Apocalypse; candlesticks, ornaments, pictures, crockery, statues. Sometimes Usha wondered at the beauty and delicacy of the ornaments that Auntie would send her off to barter with, but there was nothing for it. What good was surrounding yourself with beautiful objects, if you weren't alive to enjoy them? You couldn't eat metal or stone, no matter how lovely, could you?

In the middle of Central Square, she could see that the barter-circles were already starting to form. Directly in front of her was the first barter-circle, a fat Gemini-woman with a selection of linen shawls, trying to set up an arrangement with an old Citizen man dragging a sack of flour. The fat woman craned her head around as Usha passed.

"Hey! Sister! What you got there?"

Usha stepped into the circle, and brought out the two small ornaments from Auntie's mantelpiece.

"Well, them's no good to me," moaned the old man, "it's fruit I'm after."

"Hang on a minute," interrupted the fat woman,

"that boy's got a chest of plums! Come over here, Brother!"

One by one, other people joined the circle, bringing various objects with them, respectively, a chair, a wig, a crate of pears, a bag of plums and a box of bread rolls. You couldn't always exchange your property for exactly what you wanted. Often you had to change your mind and get a deal where the going was good. Although Auntie had asked her for a loaf of bread and some sugar, Usha eventually came away with the box of rolls and a few plums, having traded both her ornaments to the pear-seller, who had passed one on to the plum-seller, and another to the bread-boy. The fat woman exchanged her shawls for the chair, the chair's owner passed the shawls to the wig-owner, the pears went to the old man, who traded his sack of flour for the chair-owner, and the wig ended up in another barter-circle with the rest of the plums thrown in as a special deal.

All in all, quite a successful morning, Usha reflected, as she made her way homewards. She could hear the faint sound of the choir of the Inn of Court practising from the other side of the high wall, and she stopped a moment so that she could listen. As she did so, a hoarse voice spoke from her feet.

"Mornin', Sister. Spare some food, please?"

Usha glanced down. A small, thin, huddled form, swathed in a dark cloak, sat in the shade of the wall, its hand outstretched. A hood hung over its face, but she knew immediately that this was one of the disfigured beggar-children who would hang around the market, asking for food. Decent Citizens should always avoid or ignore them as much as possible.

"Anyfink yer 'ave, Sister?" said the figure again, pushing its outstretched palm towards her. With the other it started to pull off its all-enveloping hood. Usha gaped as she saw a cheek lined with a red scar and a rag covering one eye. . .

Quickly, glancing over her shoulder for watching Guardians, she pulled one of the rolls out and pushed it into the dirty hand. "That's it! That's all I can spare!" Without waiting to see the disfigured face beneath the hood, she started off at a brisk trot towards the welcome familiarity of the West Quarter, clutching the rest of Auntie's precious rolls and plums with all her might.

"Ssshh, boy," warned Arlo, as he tiptoed excitedly down to Doctor Kane's cramped little study at the back of the Laboratories, an excited Rem snuffling at his heels. He paused briefly and listened, but the corridor remained silent and empty, apart from the distant sound of the choir rehearsing in the Old Hall.

It was amazing, Arlo thought with a warm glow, how much life had changed since Rem had appeared. They had settled into a comfortable routine of chasing each other round the Inn gardens and it was already a common sight to see the dog hurtling down the drive, eagerly pursuing the sticks that Arlo threw for him.

Rem had taught Arlo how to steal ham from the pantry, how to find his way through a darkened oat-house to the precise cupboard where the sausages were stored, and how to tell the difference between a dish made with real eggs and one made from egg-flavoured nutrient powder. And better still, the dog seemed to know instinctively when Arlo was affected with the mood that Benedict called *melancholia*. When the sadness came on him, Rem seemed to feel the change in his master, and would lie on Arlo's feet or snuggle with his rough head in his lap until it passed.

The Laboratories themselves were out of bounds for Arlo, and had been since he turned five years old and able to wander around by himself and break valuable equipment, Ignatius had said tersely. Usually housing Doctor Kane's horticultural experiments and Doctor Phlegg's beetle collection, Kane's laboratory was really no more than a metal greenhouse protruding out from the end gable of the Inn. Flickering sunshine illuminated the glass with glancing reflections, making him more than once worry that he could see Kane pottering around inside.

After cautiously checking that this was not the case, Arlo pressed down gently on the doorknob. It was unlocked. Catching his breath at his good fortune, he pulled it open and quickly ushered Rem through the door. Once inside he stood still for a second while his eyes accustomed themselves to the light, squinting at the benches of plant clippings, the impaled arthropods and annelids in Doctor Phlegg's collection, butterflies skewered on pins and displayed in glass boxes, alongside the shelves of wires, fuses and general paraphernalia.

While Rem nosed around excitedly, Arlo searched through the cupboards and soon found what he was looking for. Doctor Benedict's basic chemistry lessons had been useful, he thought, grinning, but not in the way the old professor had planned. Unintentionally he had shown Arlo how to make a stink bomb.

If you mixed sulphuric acid with iron sulfide, then you would get a stench like rotten eggs, a sickening odour that lingered for hours. And if you poured it into the sink in the sluice-room it would run down into the pipes and stay all day. It could take Kane days to discover the source of the smell, he thought, snickering to himself. Yet, as he carefully lined up the ingredients on the counter, he noticed Rem stiffening as he stared at the corridor outside. Somebody must be coming.

Quickly Arlo ducked into a corner and pressed his back against the wall to avoid being spotted and questions asked. But as he leaned his full weight against it, somehow the wall seemed to open behind him and he staggered backwards to fall heavily and painfully against a large metal box of switches and wires. The beaker of sulfide and the vial of sulphuric acid flew over his head and crashed to the ground. Instantly the awful smell of rotting eggs rose up around him, almost suffocating in the tiny space. As he struggled to regain his balance, his sleeve caught on a lever and pulled it downwards, almost dragging the machine with it.

Through his panic, Arlo heard a voice start to speak in a calm and measured tone. He was really in trouble now, he thought anxiously to himself. He could hear Rem whining and growling outside the room but he could not reach him. Scrubbing his eyes clear, he turned around to see the speaker. Despite the hideous stench that now surrounded him, he stood still, his mouth open.

Projected on to the wall, flickering and yet still distinct, was the image of a small child, probably no more than three or four years old, running towards him. Again he heard the voice that he dimly recognized coming through the ancient recording system.

"This is the specimen at three Citizen-years and seven months during its three thousandth, one hundred and seventy-first Outbreak."

As Arlo watched, transfixed, the child tripped and fell heavily on to its knees. Instantly it screwed up its face and began to wail, the sound of its voice tinny and distant through the old recording. The next second, a Doctor whom Arlo did not recognize moved into the picture, patted it on the head and gave it a toy. As the child cried, a white box containing words appeared underneath its image.

STIMULUS – SIMPLE FALL
OUTBREAK – TEARS
EMOTION – DISTRESS

But it was not the words that Arlo found himself staring at in horror. Instead, he was transfixed by the toy that the child had been given, a small wind-up train with clockwork wheels, like the ones they had before the Apocalypse. . .

He knew that toy. It sat, gathering dust, on the mantelpiece in his room, broken in a long-distant and long-forgotten childhood accident. . .

And, in that moment he realized he was looking at himself.

When Usha got back from the market, she was surprised to see that the scissor-man, and Auntie, was already waiting in the reception-room for her weekly appointment. He flashed a light in her ears and throat, took her pulse and tapped her knee with a small hammer to make her foot jump, while Auntie watched her, beaming, from the divan.

Finally the scissor-man held out a small silver cup. "Drink this, please, Usha."

Usha took the cup obediently, but something in its bitter depths made her wrinkle her nose. "What is it, sir?"

"Nutrients for a growing girl. Need to make sure you eat properly. Not easy round here, with deliveries being stolen all the time. Down the hatch."

She held the cup and sipped cautiously.

It tasted better than it smelled, but she could not restrain a grimace as she wiped her mouth and handed him back the cup. Turning around to collect the tea tray, she suddenly swayed. The room seemed to have become dark around her. Confused, she tottered towards the door and put a hand uncertainly on the frame. Her vision had split, and she could no longer see the scissor-man and Auntie even though she knew they must still be within touching distance.

Her thoughts seemed impossibly slow and confused. Perhaps she should drink some water to rehydrate? But as she took the first step towards the kitchen, the ground abruptly tilted beneath her. She threw a hand out to catch herself but the floor became a slope, the slope became a precipice, and the next minute she toppled forward to crash heavily on to the flagstones.

For a moment the ceiling spun around her, before she managed to heave herself upright, clutching at the legs of the divan for support. Her arms and legs were rapidly becoming numb and strangely unresponsive, as if she was wading through treacle. Her mouth started to gush with water as a terrible sense of nausea surged up her body. Echoing in her ears was the noise of Auntie's voice exclaiming and the soothing tone of the scissor-man. She was hardly able to turn her face towards them before she was sick, copiously and unstoppably, all over the expensive shift dress that Auntie had given her for her eleventh Arrival-day present.

"I'm sorry, Auntie—" she tried to say, but before she could speak, the whirling darkness caught hold of her and dragged her down.

Arlo gazed at the flickering image in confusion, his heart thudding in his chest. Despite the stench of the stink bomb that still surrounded him, he could not leave. Panic crawled in his throat, and a horrid feeling of doubt rose up inside him. What *was* this place? What could this *mean*?

He stood inside a small alcove, one wall of which was taken up with a huge plaque of switches and dials. The image that he watched was projected by a beam of light from the front of a small black box whose lever he had pulled as he fell. It reminded him of the old cine-cameras that the Doctors sometimes used for study or to show some of the old films saved from the destruction of the Apocalypse.

Another wall was almost entirely covered in huge reels of celluloid film, each carefully labelled with a date and time.

Date: 44-6-3001/ Time: 6 Citizen Day-Hours.

With a click, the image changed and the child became a young boy, some years older, about seven years old. His arms were folded and his brows drawn together sulkily. Again the voice that he dimly recognized came from the screen.

"What's the matter, Arlo? What are you thinking?"

The boy on the screen shook his head, refusing to answer. Another voice broke in, cold and curt. "I think this Outbreak must have been caused by a rush of blood to the brain. Primary sign of anger. Cause of rage and violent attacks."

Bewildered, Arlo gazed at his own picture. In the tangle of thoughts that formed his brain at the moment, he searched out the memory of that long-lost day, when something had happened ... someone had broken something that he held very dear... What *was* it? *Why* couldn't he remember?

"I'm not thinking anything," sobbed the boy on the screen. "Why did you do that?"

Then the boy suddenly raised his eyes and gazed straight at him. On his face was an expression that Arlo instantly recognized, though he could not at first put a name to it. His eyes were wide, staring, his lips were trembling...

"Get out! Get out! What are you doing here?" cried a voice, and in the same second the image was abruptly switched off as if it had never been. Arlo jumped and turned around. Behind him stood Doctor Kane, his thin eyebrows drawn up almost to his hairline, pointing at him with a shaking forefinger.

"This room is out of bounds, boy! And what –" as he took in the stench surrounding them for the first time – "is that *smell*?"

Arlo gazed at him, memory suddenly flooding back to him at the sound of Kane's voice as the Doctor stepped forward and grasped him by his ear, pulling him out of the room and closing the door behind them.

"You're supposed to be in Doctor Benedict's office getting your Examination results right now instead of hiding in here! Yet you'd rather be making stink bombs than making something of your life, wouldn't you, you little—"

Something clicked inside Arlo. "It was you!" he cried. "I remember now!"

"What?" shouted Kane. "Do you dare to argue with me?"

"No!" cried Arlo. "You broke my train on purpose!"

Kane marched him painfully towards the door of the laboratory, kicking Rem out of his way as he did so. "That's enough! Get out!"

"What's going on?" cried Arlo. "Why do you have a film of me? Does Ignatius know about this?"

Kane drew himself away and gazed at Arlo with open distaste. "These are your medical records, boy! Everybody in the Inn has them, and because of your stupid escapade in the tree the other day, I was asked to review them."

Arlo stared back. Something in Kane's manner did not convince him, but, caught alone and out of bounds in his enemy's room, he was no match for the Doctor.

"But this is nothing to do with being in my Laboratory without permission! You are grounded, boy! Directly you have been to Doctor Benedict, you will go to your room and stay there, do you understand? I will speak to Ignatius myself, and we will work out a punishment that is suitable for you."

In a black fog, it was the darkness of the familiar dream that rose around Usha again, but this time she could not run.

Out of shadows she suddenly became aware of a tiny pinprick of white light, becoming stronger and stronger until she thought she could no longer see, swelling into a searing glare that slowly filled all her vision. Through the red slits of her eyelids the light danced and wheeled. Slowly she became aware of the echo of her own breathing in her chest, ragged and strangely uneven as if she had just run a race. As consciousness flowed back to her, she could sense that she was lying down on a hard bench, wearing a white surgical smock. She tried to move but her body was as dull and unresponsive as a lead weight. Something had been put in her nose and mouth, a bitter-tasting rubber tubing that made her want to gag. Around her rose a mutter of talk, but indistinct, as distant and faint as if heard through a wall. She listened, and presently the murmur divided into two voices, the scissor-man and Auntie, a mumbling conversational duet that faded in and out of focus the more she tried to listen.

" . . . And they say that Pharmopolis have refused to send any more food imports until Genopolis sends out a special force to attack the rebels who are holding the trade routes hostage. Did you ever hear anything like that?"

" . . . Ridiculous," returned Auntie crisply. "What else are we supposed to do? Last month there was no bread. Now there are no eggs. What next?"

"Terrible times," tutted the scissor-man, and there was a noise of silver tinkling against porcelain, "terrible times. In fact. . ."

With a great effort, Usha rolled her head slightly to the side and opened her eyes. Away from the glare of the light, the rest of the room was totally black in comparison, and it was a couple of seconds before she could see anything. But when the scene before her suddenly sharpened into focus, she gazed in disbelief.

A few metres away, on another bench, Auntie was lying down, on the same level as Usha, her face turned upwards, chatting amiably with the scissor-man, who stood over her, now robed from head to toe in white, with a mask covering his face. To his right hung a bracket of silver instruments that glinted in the light. He was calmly arranging clean sheets over Auntie's chest and legs, leaving her wrinkled belly bare and pale under the harsh glow of the light. A tube had been inserted into the vein of her arm, just at the point of the elbow, leading to a bag of fluid that hung suspended underneath the tray of instruments.

What was *happening*? Was Auntie all right? How had she *got* here? Usha's lips felt swollen and paralysed. She strove desperately to speak, but all that escaped from her mouth was a soft gasp. Her heart echoed in her chest.

Nonchalantly, the scissor-man raised his gloved hand and selected a large scalpel from the rack. Unable to move her eyes away, Usha looked on as the blade descended and, with unerring precision, cut a long sweep through the grey flesh of Auntie's stomach, from the base of the sternum to just above the pelvis. Through the incision bubbled a mass of yellow fat flecked with blood. Instantly the glistening fingers plucked swabs of cotton wool from an immaculate white roll, tucked them efficiently inside the edges of the bleeding gash to line it, and picked up a pair of forceps and a metal kidney bowl. The smell of blood caught at her nostrils, sickeningly warm and vaporous, with a tang like heated iron. Meanwhile Auntie's fingers drummed impatiently on the shiny table, her face impassively upturned. Usha opened her mouth, but nothing escaped from her lips except a breathless whimper. Her fingers twitched in vain as she tried to move, to pull the tubes from her face and leap from the table. But nothing worked. She could only stare helplessly as the scissor-man bent over the wound and opened a small clamp.

"I'm just isolating the arteries that lead to the liver, Miss Cybella," said the scissor-man chattily, "and then we'll be ready for your Transplants."

With Kane's bony hand digging into his shoulder, Arlo padded down the hall towards Benedict's office to collect his exam results, his head in a whirl and a rock of panic slowly growing inside his chest.

Doctor Benedict, MPA and Head of the Inn of Court, was one of the Inn's most proudly guarded treasures and author of the groundbreaking work *Emoticus Mensalis*, whose publication had ensured him a place in the scientific and literary history of the Inn and part of every Doctor's reading list. His work was also phenomenally boring, and Arlo had never got to the end of Chapter Four, which contained such fascinating topics as "Early Sensory Deprivation of the Infant Can Result in Formulation of Cool Logic in the Adult Mind – A Personal Theory".

On this occasion the Doctor was in his study, an elaborate set of scales arranged in front of a row of bottles. The tubular barrel was boiling furiously, drops of a pinkish liquid snaking down the inside of the U-neck to the bell jar where he was painstakingly measuring grams of a white powder taken from a silver box. When Arlo poked his head into the study, Benedict was so busy with his experiment that he had not heard Arlo's arrival, and he looked up with a start as Kane rapped loudly on the door to rouse him.

"Oh, hullo, you fellows! Did you want to see my new calculations on the psychometric medications?"

Kane coughed. "Actually, sir, I believe that you yourself told me that you had the boy's Examination results from the Academy's Education meeting yesterday."

"Oh yes, that's right," said Doctor Benedict cheerfully, uncorking a bottle of chorley that stood on the mantelpiece, totally oblivious both to Kane's sarcasm and to Arlo's worry. "Bored the pants off me, I can tell you. The number of times I have to listen to those old so-

and-so's banging on about education. Not worth the slate it's written on. Damned radicals. You want some?"

"No thanks," said Arlo. Chorley, an illicit drink brewed from berries and tree bark in the Inn's gardens by the cook's boy and various enthusiastic apprentices, made his head swim and numbed his tongue. But it was the drink of choice of the Doctors, who found they could talk and think faster under its influence, noticing none of the unpleasant effects.

Kane snorted. "Well, *sir* . . . after you have finished with him, I have told him that he should be confined to his room for the rest of the evening. I found him –" and here he paused dramatically – "looking at things that he *shouldn't have been looking at* . . . in my laboratory."

"Righty-ho," said Doctor Benedict, his jollity undimmed. "Let me have a word with Arlo first. Pop along now, there's a good fellow."

"And. . ." continued Kane, "he had the effrontery to make a stink bomb while he was there, as if he hadn't caused enough trouble already!"

"Interesting!" said Benedict enthusiastically. "Iron sulfide and sulphuric acid, was it?"

Rolling his eyes, Kane turned away and banged the door loudly after him. There followed an uncomfortable silence as Benedict searched the cluttered papers littering his desk as if looking for something.

"Sir?" asked Arlo, timidly, after a while. "Did . . . did I pass?"

"Hmmmm. . ." said Benedict, abandoning the search

of his desk and putting his arms comfortably behind his head. "Well . . . actually, no. You failed dismally after all our efforts. We all *knew* you would. Ignatius had hopes, but *I* was realistic."

Arlo sat motionless, his fingers curled underneath him, trying not to move a muscle of his face. Inside him he could feel the familiar churning as the weight within began relentlessly to grow and spread up into his chest. The prickling behind his eyes returned, and Doctor Benedict's face suddenly swam in front of him. Struggling to control his voice, he said, "But, sir, I don't understand what went wrong."

Doctor Benedict picked up a slate of scrawled notes and read from it, idly. " 'The subject did not achieve the recommended target of correct answers and demonstrated only a simplified lack of knowledge of the origins of the City . . . blah, blah. . . The questions were unfinished and—' "

Arlo broke in, "But I *answered* most of the questions. I did the essays fine. I wrote about Leuwenkind. I even remembered the dates that the City was founded. . ."

Doctor Benedict read on. " 'The subject demonstrated profoundly inferior intellect and ability to the average Citizen of the same age. In the other disciplines, mathematics and sciences were seventy per cent to the average Citizen's ninety per cent. History, English and philosophy were sixty per cent to the average Citizen's eighty-five. . .' Let's just say," said Benedict tossing the slate aside, "that it was the *way* you said things. It wasn't logical enough. There was too much scope for error."

A pulse thudded in Arlo's head. "But. . ."

"That's the problem," continued Benedict. "Your Citizenship exam was unfinished, and your mathematics exam was imprecise. And that's where you lost marks. As you know, anything that is imprecise is dangerous."

Arlo swallowed hard but now his throat was tightening, choking him, and his voice sounded giddy and unnatural.

"So, Doctor . . . does this mean . . . does it mean that I need to take the Examination again?"

But the Doctor had already lost interest in the conversation. "No," said Benedict vaguely, "no it doesn't. But it doesn't matter now. What's done is done. Now run along, Arlo. Kane says you're grounded for some silly reason or other, so go up to your room now, there's a good lad, and I'll get supper sent up to you on a tray."

As Arlo dragged himself out of Benedict's office, Kane was still loitering in the corridor outside, one eyebrow raised in a sneer. "Well, Arlo? Came top, did you, after all that study you've been doing? No? I bet even our Gemini servants could have got better marks than you!"

His heart pounding, Arlo ignored him and walked past quickly, but Kane followed him all the way up the stairs to his bedroom and held the door wide. "Now stay in there, otherwise you can't imagine the amount of trouble you'll be in. Don't set a foot outside until dinner!"

Too confused and bewildered to respond, Arlo flinched aside from Kane's cuff aimed at the side of his head. The next moment the door crashed shut behind him and he heard the sound of a key turning in the lock.

"I hope this won't take too long," said Auntie disagreeably, squinting up at the white light that swung over the operating table. "I'm expecting a delivery of cakes this afternoon."

A small spray of blood dotted the whiteness of the scissor-man's mask, and he turned away to mop his face. As he did so, Auntie turned her head and looked at Usha.

"Doctor! She sees! Her eyes are open!"

The scissor-man continued his work, without glancing across at Usha. "Impossible. The tranquillizer is too strong."

Auntie looked back up at the ceiling. "But I thought. . . My dear girl. . ."

"Now, Cybella," said the scissor-man, busy cutting with the scalpel inside the open wound, "you remember from last time that the donor must have a certain level of consciousness. The tissue must be live and the organs must be fresh for the Operation to be successful."

With a great effort, Usha managed to move her finger. The attempt was almost impossible. She tried to stir her hand, her wrist, but it was as if she was lying dead inside her own skin. Again she tried, and again, but to no avail. The paralysis was so consuming that now she could not even move her head away from the awful sight or close her eyes.

The scissor-man inserted the last clamp into Auntie's stomach and then, wiping his hands on a towel, came round to the table on which Usha lay. Efficiently he laid out a new row of metal instruments beside her, uncorked a flask of spirit and saturated a pad with it. He folded down the sheet that covered her stomach. She could feel a dull tickling sensation as he expertly swabbed her skin with spirit, and the smell of acid rose again in her nostrils, choking her –

"No! No!" Usha screamed silently.

Suddenly, the masked face loomed over her, bending down to her level so that he was looking straight at her. His eyes were pale green, rimmed with brown, like a muddy lake, just as she remembered from the unsettling vision two weeks ago. As she gazed at him, powerless, she saw them suddenly narrow with surprise. "Wait a moment." He lowered his scalpel. "She is. . ."

Over on the bench Auntie turned her head. "I told you! She is awake!"

Usha summoned all her strength in a last try. "Please," she whispered, barely able to speak. "Don't!"

With one hand, the scissor-man pulled off his mask and bent close to her. She could feel his hot moist breath on her cheek. He gazed at her in mock concern.

"But this is what you were chosen for, child. This is why the pharms bred you! To provide life for Mistress

Cybella in her old age, when her heart, spleen and liver fail. And this is your purpose, Usha. How can you deny it? This is your destiny!"

Sinking to the floor, Arlo leaned back against the locked door and sighed. So many thoughts were colliding inside his head that he could not think straight. How could he have failed? How could he have let Ignatius – and himself – down like that? What on earth was he going to do?

But then the questions that had been plaguing him since he had seen the cine-film of himself in Kane's laboratory suddenly rose above his remorse. What was the *real* meaning of the films in the cupboard? Did Ignatius know? By the stacks of neatly-labelled reels in the cupboard, it did not look as if the film he saw had been the only one. . .

But when and where had he been filmed? He remembered being deeply upset by the destruction of his train, but he was fairly sure that he did not remember a camera being present. Unless. . .

He looked over and froze. On the bare walls of his room, over the washstand, hung the mottled mirror. From where the mirror hung, it was angled to show the window seat of his room, the same window seat where he had sat that September morning, aged seven, crying. . .

With a sudden surge of anger he stormed up to the mirror, seized it with both hands and tried to wrench it off the wall. It remained obstinately fixed where it was. Furiously he tugged at it but to no avail. He raised his fist and smashed it into the middle of the mirror, realizing the next second in a sudden blaze of pain that this had been a very foolish thing to do. The glass remained unbroken but he hopped around, comforting his injured hand with the other, swearing furiously at Kane, Ignatius and anybody else that he could think of.

Finally, with curiosity at last getting the better of him, he walked up to the mirror, leaned in close and tried to stare through it. Only his own face, slightly dirty and streaked with tears, stared back at him from the cloudy depths where his breath had started to mist over the glass. He waved at it, stuck his tongue out, rolled his eyes up and giggled hysterically for a few minutes.

Nothing happened, although what exactly he was expecting to happen was uncertain. Feeling slightly foolish he stepped back. Perhaps he had been mistaken. Perhaps there was nothing there. Perhaps he had been too upset all along to notice that someone was filming him. . .

But then he noticed Rem. The dog was staring across at the mirror, muscles tensed, ears pricked. Anxiously, he stroked Rem's head, whispering, "What is it, Rem? What is it?"

Rem was already at the wall, nosing into the corner, his tail wagging excitedly. Curiously, Arlo pressed his ear against the wall and listened. There was silence, and he was just about to give up when he heard a slight sound. It was the noise of soft footsteps moving behind the wall. Something in the stealth of the movements sparked Arlo's attention. Somebody – or something – did not want to be heard.

Immediately the prickling along Arlo's neck brought him alive with a sensation that he had only experienced a few times in his life before; the night the oat-house had caught fire and he had been the first to smell the wisps of smoke, the day that Doctor Symmonds had tottered shaking into the library with his face blotched and sweating, and Ignatius had given the order for the Sanatorium to come and take Doctor Symmonds away; the time he had tasted something bad in the new food delivery from Pharmopolis and Kristo had instantly warned all the Doctors not to touch their plates –

It was the instinct that something was definitely wrong.

The difference between instinct and impulse, Arlo had been told, was this. Impulses – such as suffering an Outbreak when you failed your exam, wanting to hit Doctor Kane when he kicked Rem out of his way – had to be controlled. But instincts – the urge to pull back from a hot flame, to run to Rem's aid when he had a thorn stuck in his paw, to spit out a bad taste – should be acted upon, even when logic stood in its way. And despite Kane's logical explanation of the films as being Arlo's medical records, Arlo could feel instinctively that it was a lie.

Something was going on that he did not know about,

and Kane would not tell him. There was only one Doctor in the Inn whom he could trust to talk to now.

And there was only one way out of his room with the door locked.

Quickly, he cast around his room and discovered the black dressing gown worn by Doctors to prevent heat-loss on the rare occasions that Genopolis suffered a cold wind. Unfolding it to its fullest extent, he draped it over the mirror so that it was entirely covered.

He went over to the small casement window and unbolted it. Just outside his window two old lead pipes ran in long vertical lines down the wall, left over from the olden days when water was piped and not sold in barrels. He quailed before the steep drop down to the sharp, unforgiving gravel of the drive at the bottom. His bedroom was one of the highest rooms in the Inn. If the pipes proved too old to support him, if he made one wrong move and slipped. . .

But if Arlo had learned anything over the last few days, it was the dangers of thinking too much. Without allowing himself to realize properly what he was doing, he swung himself out and over the window sill, lowering himself down and to the left, to where his scrabbling toes could just feel the first pipe.

Shuddering with the effort, he managed to lodge his foot into the crevice between the two pipes, grasp the left pipe with his left hand and, after an agonized pause, let go of the window sill and hold on to the other pipe with his right. Now he was on his own. Clinging like a fly to a wall, he slowly began the descent, hand over hand, his toes feeling for whatever foothold he could find in the crumbling bricks or on the rivets that bounded the ancient pipes to the wall. Gritting his teeth, he willed himself not to think about the drop below him, and although there was a tricky moment about halfway down when one of the supports of the pipes suddenly gave way under his foot and left him kicking wildly in mid-air, he soon realized that he was past the tops of the cherry trees, and the next minute he was low enough to jump down with a soft crunch on to the courtyard.

Arlo struggled not to reflect on how much trouble he would get into if he was found out of his room after being grounded. Quickly checking that the coast was clear of Doctor Kane, he set out at a quick trot towards Ignatius's room. But as he entered the small arched passageway that led to his tutor's study, he heard raised voices from within. He had hardly enough time to dodge behind one of the old tapestries that lined the wall before Doctor Kane stormed out of Ignatius's study and paused for a second on the threshold.

"This is the end, Ignatius! You are a disgrace to the Inn and to science! You have been contaminated by your own Experiment!"

Arlo could not hear a reply from inside Ignatius's room, but Kane's fingers tightened on the door frame, his voice heavy with sarcasm. "Success, you say? You put all of us at risk! From now on, I refuse to be part of it. It is over, Ignatius! Both for the Experiment . . . and for you!"

Kane stamped down the corridor, elbowing the tapestry behind which Arlo hid as he did so. The door of Ignatius's study banged shut behind him. As the noise of Kane's footsteps faded, Arlo darted forward in a sudden flash of daring and applied his eye to the keyhole.

He could just about make out the old Doctor sitting behind his cluttered antique almond-wood desk, a steaming silver pot of chorley at his elbow. Ignatius did not seem to be alone. He could hear another voice coming through the thick oak door.

"We have been blind these last years, Ignatius. Too much attention to the Experiment, and not enough to the world outside. I blame myself for this. I should have seen it coming."

"We should not speak of blame," said Ignatius. "Blame is only for those who know the end beyond all doubt. And the world of men can still be changed in a single day. There are more powerful forces in Nature than we have discovered, Kristo."

"Kane has become irrational and personal," replied the librarian. "The Experiment has reached crisis point. We need to hide it before any damage occurs."

"I disagree," said Ignatius, speaking clearly. "I think that we should take this opportunity to tell Arlo exactly where he comes from. He deserves some straight answers, Kristo, about who he is and where he comes from."

Arlo had not realized that he had made a noise, rather, he felt that a noise was brimming and buzzing inside him until he was unable to keep it in any longer. Thoughts were flying around inside his head so fast that he was unable to breathe. It was as if Ignatius had read his most secret wishes, wishes that he had learnt long ago never to confess to Doctor Kane or Doctor Phlegg. . .

With the realization that he was on the brink of some important discovery he pressed his ear closer to the keyhole, only to topple forward as Ignatius wrenched the door open from the other side, and collapse on his knees in front of the astonished Doctors.

Staring up awkwardly, Arlo was astonished to see his old tutor gazing down at him intently with a small smile playing around the corners of his mouth. He scrambled clumsily to his feet, expecting a stern reproof, but instead Ignatius grasped his shoulder, pulled him inside the study and closed the door.

"Just in time, Arlo. We were wondering how long it would take you to discover our little secret."

Behind the scissor-man, Usha saw Auntie's old face illuminated in the white operating light, stretched into the kindly smile that she knew so well.

"Usha, darling. You are my future, my life. I chose you. I made you."

The girl stared at her, bewildered. "You made me . . . for *this*?"

"You are a Gemini, Usha," said the scissor-man, taking out a scalpel. "Remember your education. The first purpose of a Gemini is to serve a Citizen. We make you, and we unmake you. That is your place."

Suddenly with uncontrollable force, Usha's heels started to drum on the hard board of the bench. The scissor-man glanced down sharply.

"What is it?" called Auntie.

"The tranquillizer is indeed wearing off," said the scissor-man, turning around and making for the rack of instruments. "But that is easily fixed."

Quickly he selected a syringe and filled it with fluid from a small glass phial. Usha gasped. "Auntie, please. . ." Dimly she could see Auntie's face, smiling fondly across at her as she had so often done while telling Usha bedtime stories.

"Please. No. . . !"

The scissor-man came towards her, depressing the plunger of the syringe so that it shot a sparkling fountain of solution into the air. "Let me deal with this, Cybella. In a short while you will have again the life that you desire."

As he bent over her and pointed the needle at her arm, Usha closed her eyes, gritted her teeth, and swung her other wrist to dash his hand away. The syringe flew in an arc over him to smash into glittering fragments on the floor.

"Usha," shouted Auntie commandingly. "Stop that right now! This instant!"

But something had brought Usha alive again. Though weak in body and mind, a power greater than physical strength took over. Without properly knowing how it happened, the next minute she had rolled off the table and landed in a heap on the floor, bringing the scissor-man's instruments crashing down around her in a tinkling shower of scalpels, sutures, kidney basin and needles. She tried to scrabble to her feet, but her numbed legs refused to respond and gave way beneath her. Crawling on her elbows, dragging her paralysed legs, she made for the door, but in front of her lurched the scissor-man, cursing angrily.

Usha's fingers closed around the small silver scalpel that lay before her on the carpet. Yet before she could even raise her hand, the scissor-man's foot came down on the shiny kidney basin. It slipped from underneath his sole and sent him careening sideways against the bench on which she had just been lying. Flailing wildly, he sought to regain his balance, but tripped and fell forward over her in a vicious tangle of limbs. Usha rolled to one side, throwing up her hands to defend herself, but it was too late. Instantly he was on top of her, his weight crushing her, his fingers around her neck. . .

Winded from the fall, she did not have the strength to fight him. She closed her eyes, the room spinning around her, expecting the darkness to rise up around her again. However, after a few seconds, she realized that he was no longer stirring, and instead of throttling her, his arm lay heavy and unmoving across her cheek. Her right hand was trapped underneath him, and she shoved at him violently with her left, only to see his head flop sideways at a sickening angle. As it did so, she saw with horror that he had landed directly on the sharp blade of the upturned scalpel that was still clenched in her fist. The force of his fall had driven the knife so far into his eye that only a small portion of the handle still protruded from the socket.

Straining, she pushed at the heavy body until she could manage to struggle out from underneath. Slowly, with every movement seeming to take an age, she rolled on to her front and began to crawl again towards the hallway. Below her the floor moved and swayed, and several times she had to crouch on all fours, breathless, until the seizure had passed. Bit by bit, she hauled her leaden body over the carpet. As she drew level with the doorway, it seemed an eternity to summon up the strength she needed to make it across the short stretch of hallway.

Behind her came a choking cry. "Usha . . . please. . ."

Looking back over her shoulder, she saw Auntie, still lying helplessly on her bench. The old lady stretched one wasted hand towards the girl, the other clutching at her open stomach, now just a spreading mass of red that was starting to seep in scarlet trickles into the white sheet. Unbelievably, the old face twisted into an imploring smile.

"Usha . . . Usha . . . don't leave me. . ."

Slowly, heavily, Usha gazed one last time at Auntie. Then with a huge effort, as if a great weight was pushing down on her, she slowly turned away, and dragged herself, one hand over another, away and out of Auntie's parlour and into the cool, quiet darkness of the hallway.

Arlo stood, his fingers trembling, in front of the Doctors. "What's going on, Ignatius? Something's happening, isn't it? I saw the films in Kane's laboratory. What's going on?"

"Well done, Arlo," said Kristo, calmly pouring him a hot glass of chorley and offering it to him. Arlo backed away. "No! I don't want it! I just want to know what's going on!"

"I understand," said Ignatius, settling himself down on the sofa, one leg carelessly high-crossed over the other, and patted the seat next to him. "I think you deserve an explanation, and what I am about to say may come as a shock to you. For many years you have been the most valuable asset of the Inn, though you may not know it. Some of us here in the Inn have been engaged in one of the most important Experiments of all time. And that Experiment is you, Arlo."

"Concentrate now," said Kristo, gently. "What exactly did Benedict tell you about why you failed your Citizenship Examinations?"

The boy thought hard. "He said . . . he said something about my mathematics being imprecise. . .

He said that my marks were lower than the average Citizen's."

Ignatius chuckled. "Well, that may not be a bad thing, Arlo, and indeed one could say that this is predictable. Because you are not a Citizen, and never will be, no matter how hard you try. Though you were raised and educated as any young Citizen boy, your very identity is different to all of us. You are not a novice in training to be a Doctor. Actually, you are not even a Citizen. You are, in fact, a Natural."

Arlo stood up and took a step back, his head spinning. Inexplicably he had an uncontrollable impulse to laugh and be sick at the same time. He was a *Natural*? Ridiculous! Impossible!

He had studied Naturals in history, or heard the word bandied around as a term of abuse, or in the Doctors' endless political conversations. Since childhood he had always known he was different . . . but to be called a *Natural* . . . that was an insult, an embarrassment! He cringed inwardly at the thought of Doctor Kane's face if he ever. . . Did *everybody* know about him?

He was so lost in shock that he was almost unaware of Kristo calmly taking his arm and guiding him to sit down on the sofa next to his tutor.

"But you are the only Natural that is safe these days," continued Ignatius. "Naturals these days live wild outside the City, as you know, have no power or land, and live by ransacking the food convoys for things to eat. Inside Genopolis you are safe, Arlo, because on the day you were born you were delivered into our protection. We have looked after you all these years, because you, possibly out of all the world at this moment, carry the hope of the future in you."

Arlo was so shocked he could not answer. Kristo broke in. "Listen, Arlo. As a Natural, there is something very special and unique about you. Do you remember Question Two of your Examination? *What are the main differences between Citizens and Naturals?*"

Arlo began mechanically to recite his answer, but Ignatius shook his head. "You are correct, but also wrong. This is what you were taught, it is true. But the biggest difference we did not tell you, and have kept from you all these years, for the good of the Experiment. You possess something vitally different from us. It is this."

Briskly, Ignatius reached over and pulled one of his precious store of candles out of a drawer. He set it in the middle of a saucer, and brought out his tinderbox. Striking the flints together, he made a small spark and lit the wick. The glow flickered redly, an odd, unnatural sight in the late-afternoon sunshine. Kristo rose and pulled the shutters together so that deep shadow filled the room. His tutor turned to him and held out the candle.

"What would you do if I asked you to put your hand into the candle flame?"

The boy stared at him, astonished. Put his hand into the flame? Had Ignatius gone totally mad?

"I can't. . ." he stuttered, confused. "It . . . I couldn't do it!"

"Why?" asked Ignatius. "What would happen?"

Arlo struggled for words. "It would. . . It would . . . *hurt*. . ."

Ignatius nodded gravely. "Yes, it would hurt you. And yet, Arlo, I think you are the only one in the Inn who would not be able to do this. Watch."

His tutor leaned over to the candle burning on his desk, and deliberately held his hand in the flame for a few seconds. Despite himself, Arlo could not help crying out and pulling Ignatius's hand away. On the Doctor's palm a blackened scorch mark showed where the skin was beginning to blister, but his expression remained serene and unconcerned.

Arlo shook his head, horrified. "Ignatius! How can you *do* that?"

"Because the greatest difference between you and me, is that we Citizens have had the sensation of pain taken away from us," replied Ignatius. "When I put my hand in the candle – or even in more extreme danger – I feel nothing more than a gentle tickling. Yet you, who have not burned your own hand, can somehow feel it."

The boy gazed at him, horrified. "But how can you not feel *pain*, Ignatius?"

Ignatius smiled. "From your Natural History lessons you know that all living things are composed of tiny building blocks, called genes. These genes contain the codes of information that controls our bodies, whether we will have blue, green or brown eyes, grow tall or fat, be male or female. And, if changes are made to this coded information then our bodies change also. We Citizens have had our codes changed in a way that means we can no longer feel pain."

Arlo's head was whirling. "But who . . . *did* this to you, Ignatius?"

"We have always been like this," said Ignatius. "Our Founder, Leuwenkind, intended Citizens to be the new super-race, an invulnerable breed of people who could rebuild our shattered world. The only way we Citizens could withstand the extremes of the new world after the Apocalypse was by abolishing pain from our genetic code. Only if the element of suffering were removed from our people, could we manage to build a new City in this harsh environment.

"*Pain*, you see, is not an event outside us, or a sensation within our flesh, but is instead a recognition by the brain that something dangerous is happening to it. In our ancestors, the brain received a stimulus through nerve-endings from the skin that sent a message to the brain that it could be damaged. At that point, for self-preservation, the brain would instinctively cause its limb to move away from whatever was troubling it, the heat, the cold, the sharp object. So by removing that reaction from us, Leuwenkind intended us to be powerful, invulnerable against pain."

Confused, Arlo thought grimly of all the times that he had snatched his hand back from the blazing heaters and seen Doctor Kane laughing, of all the times that Kane had cuffed or pushed him roughly. . .

"But this very invulnerability actually made us weaker. Why? Because we do not feel pain, we do not react against it, so we are more easily controlled by our Rulers. There are still famines, wars and floods in the areas outside our City, but nothing is done because we do not *suffer* from them. People do not revolt against injustice, for we have no reason to. We have forgotten how it *feels*. We Citizens can live unperturbed by the droughts, the diseases, the instability of the outside world. Why? We do not feel pain, we do not feel discomfort; we feel as I do and have always done – a dim sense of well-being, and if things go wrong for us, nothing more than a mild irritation or indignation. We know the world is in disaster around us, but we can still carry on, regardless. Citizens can experience horrendous mutilations, starve to death, or die of terminal diseases and no longer experience distress. Medicines and operations? These can be carried out without anaesthetic."

Arlo shook his head, stunned.

"I understand your confusion," said Ignatius gravely. "For you, pain was so *natural*, that you never imagined that other people were different, like a blind man who has never known what it is to see. But it is crucial you understand how important you have been to us. You see, Arlo, we want to bring pain back to the world."

"But why on earth do you want to give pain *back*?" Arlo asked, incredulously.

"Because pain is important," returned Ignatius. "It was our ancestral defence system to alert us that something was wrong. Though pain was regarded as a weakness, it is actually our greatest strength. For, living in our safe, protected city, we Citizens are still dying, but from other, more hidden dangers. Children are born clawing their eyes to shreds when they rub their faces because they do not know the damage they are causing to themselves. Toddlers chew their tongues to pieces whilst being fed. Teenagers die because they are unable to feel the symptoms of a disease or the effects of a poisoned scratch. We check ourselves for bumps or scratches every day, we eat at set times, we calculate the amount of sleep we must have to keep us functioning properly. Yet hardly anyone lives to be over forty here. We have blind, dumb and crippled people. When we see our children, our companions, hideously deformed and dying, we feel nothing. It is a privileged world that we live in, Arlo."

Kristo suddenly got up and with a swift movement reached the door, opened it and looked out keenly.

"What is it?" asked Ignatius sharply.

"I thought I. . . Well, it all seems clear now, Ignatius."

Arlo caught at Ignatius's sleeve. "But, Ignatius . . . is that all I am to you – an Experiment?"

"No, Arlo," said Ignatius, and his face was suddenly alive with an expression that warmed the boy to the heart. "You are much more than an Experiment. It is because of you we have discovered something else. We learned something that is more incredible still, namely that you, who did not put your hand in the candle, could actually feel *my* pain, though I cannot feel it myself."

Seeing Arlo's expression, Kristo broke in. "You see, we have lost much more than pain, Arlo. Despite our Founder's good intentions, we have become robots inside our own skins. *'There can be no pleasure without pain'* – you've read Aristotle, that's exactly what he meant."

Ignatius put his hand on Arlo's shoulder. "At the moment, the average Citizen does not think of a Natural as human, because he does not understand him, he does not understand the suffering that a Natural endures. But through you, Arlo, I think – and Doctor Kristo thinks – that we have started to understand again. Yet within Genopolis this is criminalized as Infection by Emotions."

"But. . ." stammered Arlo. "What about . . . Doctor Kane?"

"Kane? Our learned friend was involved in the Experiment in its early days, but over the past years we have not been able to see eye-to-eye. Though he distrusts my approach to my research – er, *you* – he can never go against me. For the last fifty years the Inn has been bound by its most sacred code of honour, the preservation of knowledge. Even though he does not agree with me, to be a Doctor of the Inn of Court means to swear to safeguard all learning. Since our Founder built Genopolis, the Inn has been the voice of reason and research against those Citizens who, without empathy, mercy or guilt, have treated the Naturals – and themselves – appallingly."

Arlo's head was so full that he hardly took in Ignatius's last words, except the part about Doctor Kane knowing his true identity, a subject so sensitive that he could not bear to think about it at that moment. "So does this mean, sir –" he hardly dared ask – "that I . . . have . . . a family-unit of my own?"

Ignatius smiled. "Ah, well now, your personal history is quite a different story. And that might take a few day-hours more."

Many night-hours later, in the darkened parlour, Usha finally dragged herself to her feet. The anaesthetic that the scissor-man had given her had worn off enough to allow her to move, but her limbs still seemed distant and heavy. As she rounded the corner, she saw a pale form coming towards her. For a second she thought it was Auntie, but the next moment she realized that it was only her own reflection, white and phantom-like, trapped in the dusty hall mirror.

For a long time Usha stood motionless, her face illuminated by the ghostly beams of the evening light falling through the narrow window. Staring into the darkened glass, she loosened her braids, raised one of Auntie's silver-service knives in one hand, took hold of a lock of hair in the other and began to cut. Slowly, the pale strands floated down in drifts to form a rising pool at her feet.

At the same time, something else seemed to be falling away from Usha as well; the obedience that she had felt towards Auntie, the trust she had felt towards the scissor-man, her certainty of her place in Genopolis, her future plans and dreams. . .

Piece by piece, the reality of her life was sinking in.

Usha finally laid the knife down and gazed at herself curiously. She hardly recognized herself. Gone was the long straight hair that had framed her face. Instead, short uneven locks of hair fell untidily across her brow, curling up and fraying where the jagged edges of the blade had sheared. With her new crop she could look like a Citizen schoolboy, if it were not for her extraordinarily pale eyes – the same eyes of the other Gemini girls whose pictures lined the mouldering velvet walls around her. Slowly, she turned to look at their images, all smiling, laughing, frozen in time, all her age, with long pale hair, and unlined skin, all of them the very image of Auntie when she was twenty-one Citizen-years old.

From years gone past, identical faces stared back at her, never growing old, never fading. As Usha paced the walls, tracing each picture with her forefinger with steadily-growing realization, the old house seemed suddenly echoing with other voices, other long-lost laughter, footsteps running up and down the stairs. . .

Now she knew why none of the other girls ever came back to visit Auntie.

As if sleepwalking, she crossed the shadowy landing to Auntie's room. Without properly thinking what she was doing, she opened Auntie's closet door. The powerful smell of mothballs rose up around her from Auntie's old coats. She selected an old wool cloak from Auntie's earlier days, such as a Higher-Middle Citizen might wear, and a pair of boots for travelling in.

She was unsurprised to see that they were exactly her size.

Downstairs in the kitchen she methodically packed a small bag with the last of the week's provisions, the remaining rolls, a flask of water, a carrot and a few shrivelled apples. But Auntie's presentation tea-biscuits she left, lying in the crumbs at the bottom of the sweet-chest, next to the small bag of toffees that the scissor-man had given her.

Evening was darkening as Ignatius continued. Arlo huddled up on the sofa to listen to his tutor while Kristo stood watchfully at the door.

"In the beginning, Arlo, there were a few of us, all Citizens, all Doctors. At that time it was also – as it is now – very dangerous to be a supporter of Naturalism. We would meet in secret, because we knew the Governors would declare us heretics. Together we devised an Experiment, to research a Natural, and through our study, to understand scientifically what a Natural already knows instinctively.

"But a specimen was not easy to find. Naturals shunned us, or viewed us with mistrust. It had become a sign of their honour not to befriend a Citizen, and many times they closed ranks against us. All our forays had to be conducted without the knowledge of the Consulate, but their informers followed us everywhere.

"And then, as chance would have it, one of our number received word from an acquaintance of his, a Natural female. She was sick and in labour, and she needed our help. Our contact left the city secretly by night for an arranged meeting point. I do not know where it was, but he left by the west barrier, so I think that it was somewhere towards the swamps.

"In the morning, he came back, and to our surprise, brought with him a child – you. How he accomplished this I do not know. It may well have been –" and here Ignatius's voice grew suddenly gruff – "that something, probably food, changed hands."

Arlo flinched at his words. As Ignatius began his story, he had imagined that he might have had parents that he had read about in the dusty books in the library, real people, giving him up with sadness but also hope for his future, as if he actually meant something to them, not just something to be bartered. He did not trust himself to speak as Ignatius went on. "He never spoke of the details to me. It was safer that way, so that none of us could betray the others. All I do know is that you were brought to Genopolis on the morning of Midsummer's Eve, which the Naturals call the feast of Lithia, and that became your birthday.

"It fell to me to keep you. The Inn was the only secure place that – at least until recently – was independent from the outside world. With discretion, your secret could be kept for a long time. Doctor Benedict was one of our supporters, and as he was the head of the Inn, I was content that things would go as planned. And they have gone smoothly, for although you may not think it, you have had one of the most privileged existences that we have now in our City."

"Who were they, Ignatius?" begged Arlo. "Who were my family?"

Ignatius shook his head. "I am sorry, Arlo. I do not know."

"Then who was it?" insisted Arlo. "Who was the Doctor who took me?"

Kristo turned sharply, and Arlo saw the urgent flash of warning in the look he directed at Ignatius. Suddenly panic gripped him. "Ignatius! It. . . It wasn't Doctor Kane, was it?" Ignatius hesitated a fraction too long. The next second Arlo was on his feet. "No! Please! It can't be!"

"Listen, Arlo," said Ignatius, reaching over to take Arlo's hand, but Arlo pulled it away. "Not him! Anyone but him!"

Rage welled up in him and he buried his face in his hands, fighting to keep the awful feeling from bursting out. He felt Ignatius come to him and he pushed the comfort away roughly with his elbow, as if the least touch would shatter him. "Go away! Don't touch me!" He was aware of how squeaky and ridiculous he sounded but he couldn't stop.

His tutor's calm voice sounded in his ear. "It's getting

late, Arlo. You need to sleep. Everything will look better in the morning."

"I won't!" Arlo screamed, struggling to his feet. "You can't make me! Stop telling me what to do!"

Arlo tore himself away from Ignatius's grasp, ran over to the candle, took a deep breath and pushed his palm into the flame. "I'm not a Natural, Ignatius! I'm *not*!"

"Stop him! He'll damage himself!" Kristo ran over, but Arlo held on, gritting his teeth. "I'm a Citizen, Ignatius! I'm a *Citizen*!"

But his tutor was taller and stronger than him, and the next moment Ignatius's arms were round him, pulling him away from the candle, carrying him down the corridor towards his bedroom. In vain Arlo kicked and fought, but his tutor seemed unconcerned, although the boy's lashing fist caught him square in the face more than once. Finally, after much effort and only when Arlo's strength was finally spent, he was propelled through the door of his bedroom.

With a bark, Rem leapt up to meet him. Arlo threw his arms around the shaggy neck, dashing away the mingled tears of pain and fury. Ignatius stood in the doorway, his expression sober.

"I am sorry, Arlo. Let's speak more in the morning."

"I hate you!" screamed Arlo, mutinously. "Go away! Leave me alone!"

Flinging himself down on the bed he buried his face in the pillows, cradling his burned hand to his chest. He was so far gone with hysteria and tiredness that he was only dimly aware of his tutor pulling the blanket over him before a heavy, sickening sleep, born more of despair than pain, overcame him.

THE PATH THE DOCTOR HAD TAKEN

The baby's wails echoed around the rocky walls as Angus and the Doctor came back into the tiny chamber. Most of the ragged Naturals had vanished with the first mists of morning, and only Gea's mother and Kira still squatted in the corner, bending over the baby attentively. As Angus and the Doctor entered, the old woman jumped back nervously and laid the baby on the bed next to its mother. With the same movement she stuffed a small sharp object underneath her cloak to conceal it. As her mother slipped her hand around Gea's waist, Angus saw that her fingers were stained with a deep dye, a dark blue-black, almost purple.

"Leave us in private for a moment," said Angus wearily, rubbing his face with his hands. The old woman glanced at him sharply, before curtly summoning Kira and ushering her outside. Alarmed at his tone, Gea struggled up on to one elbow. Beads of sweat stood out on the chalky-white skin of her forehead and her lips had turned a purplish blue. She gazed at him in confusion.

"Angus . . . what. . .?"

The Doctor leaned against the doorway, seeming to fill the whole frame with his figure. Wrapped up in his dark coat and muffler, he watched silently as Angus sat down by his wife and reached out for her hand.

"Gea. . ."

The young woman glanced around, fear lighting her eyes, at the solemn faces in front of her. "No . . . Angus, no. . ."

She wrenched her hand back; he clung on her wrist, pulling her to face him. "We have to. We must. Gea. . ."

"Get off me! Get off him!"

"Listen! Please!"

"No! No!" Gea struggled away from Angus's grasp, clutching at the squirming baby that lay wrapped at her side. It started to bleat, then to howl, a thin tearing sound. Maddened by the noise, Gea hit out wildly at Angus, smacking at his face, ripping at his hair. "Get off! Get away! Get off him!"

"Gea . . . darling . . . please. . ." Angus gasped as her fist smashed into his cheekbone, then grasped her wrist tightly, restraining her. "Doctor. Quick! Now!"

The Doctor came forward briskly and picked up the infant, cradling it over his shoulder and drawing a length of his muffler around the tiny body.

"I knew it! I knew he would do this. I could feel it!"

Gea wrenched her hand free and threw herself at the Doctor, but Angus leapt after her and pinioned her arms from behind. Screaming and kicking she fought desperately with the last of her crumbling strength, but Angus clung on to her, weeping, his face pressed into her neck. Her cries followed the Doctor as he hurried down the alleyway and descended the buttress with surprising agility. As he picked his way over the drying river bed, he saw the old woman and Kira hastening towards him, alerted by Gea's screams.

But with a few strides he was already halfway up the cutting and a great gulf already separated him from the howling Naturals. His only thought was to get the child away, unharmed, as soon as possible. The sun was already coming up and he had no time to waste in returning to Genopolis.

But as he reached the top of the bank, the Doctor suddenly became aware of a prickling sensation on the back of his scalp. Turning, he saw the young girl Kira, silhouetted on the bridge of the viaduct, staring at him with a vicious intensity. Her mouth moved but he could not hear what she was saying. A sudden dismay came over him. Suddenly, he was confused, unsettled, disoriented. Around him the world seemed unfamiliar and perplexing. He could not see, he could not understand which way he should take. He swayed, momentarily, unsure of his direction. He could hardly remember who he was or what he came for.

Then the gurgling moan from the baby in his arms filtered through his confusion, rousing him back to life. He wheeled around and started to hasten up the track, his only wish being to put as much distance as possible between him and the girl's terrible, burning eyes.

The border was about three leagues away, a tall metalled barrier that cut through the forest and scrub of the outlying Regions. On the few main thoroughfares towards the City there were occasional small checkpoints patrolled by Guardian soldiers. After the night's storm the early sun drew steam from the saturated earth to form a light mist and from downwind the Doctor could already sense the tang of the campfire and smell the roasting of sausages before he saw them. The guards were fed well, but the bounty of supplies of food and drink was small reward for the difficulties of being billeted out in the Regions. It was an isolated occupation, in extreme weathers, and the soldiers welcomed the few travellers they saw, for there was almost no traffic in and out of Genopolis those days.

Whilst still out of sight of the checkpoint, the Doctor ducked behind a line of scrub and laid the baby carefully on the grass. He was amazed to see that despite all the noise and upset, it had somehow fallen asleep, its eyelids gummed together over its bulging eyes after its frantic wails earlier had led to no comfort save the rhythmic lurching sway of the Doctor's walk. Quickly he opened his crumpled medical bag and shook out the contents, unwound his scarf, wadded it up and lined the bottom of the bag. Then he lifted the sleeping child and gently placed it inside, leaving just enough room to pull the handles on each side almost closed. He stood up, taking the bag in one hand, deliberated briefly and then picked up the stethoscope in the other. Taking a deep breath, he stepped out on to the track and set out purposefully for the garrison hut and the barrier that blocked the path at the top of the hill.

The guards called him to halt while he was still some distance away. The Doctor set down his bag, and raised his stethoscope above his head. The officer who brought him in eyed his medical bag briefly but offered no comment.

"Terrible storm last night," said the Doctor lightly. "Went out to get some specimens and ended up trapped all night in the airbase."

"If you take my advice, sir, it's best to stay in Genopolis. It's getting worse outside. Floods happening all the time now. We've heard that most of the towns on the east side have been swamped. It's not safe anywhere else."

The Doctor filled in the entry questionnaire in the false name that he usually bore for such purposes. They chatted idly about the dreadful weather while the sweet smell of the guard's coffee filled the barracks. The Doctor was offered a hot drink but he regretfully had to refuse. It was a very Citizenly offer, but he had work to do and the storm had held him up all night. Finally, the guard swung open the barrier, saluted, and the Doctor stepped back on to Citizen territory. They shook hands.

"Everything seems to be in order, sir. I hope you won't need to come this way again," said the soldier, courteously.

Half a day-hour after the Doctor had disappeared into Genopolis through the morning steams, the guard's transmitter crackled. The soldier picked up his radio and listened to the voice on the other end, slowly stiffening to attention.

"Yessir. Nossir. Is that what the Doctor said? Naturals down by the old viaduct, are there? In that case, I'll send a unit down there right away, sir."

A few minutes later, a small file of soldiers in their camouflaged wilderness-fatigues were issuing swiftly and silently down the plain that led to the viaduct. As yet they remained unseen by the dark-haired girl, who still stood on the old bridge, looking towards the west, following with her eyes the path the Doctor had taken.

THREE

It was a glorious day for the Anointment Ceremony. The late-winter sun rose through a crystal blue sky, and flowering blossoms bobbed on the branches of the trees that surrounded the Inn. The diamond panes of the old library reflected the green of the gardens in a scattered mosaic of a thousand different fragments. A smell of baking drifted from the cookhouse and for the first time in living memory the four o'clock bell had not clanged to summon the Doctors to tea. Instead, all the Doctors were indoors preparing themselves for the Ceremony. In the deserted gardens, two gardeners laid the last of the white gravel up the main path to the Old Hall, over which the litter of the new Governor Regis would presently pass.

When Arlo had got back to his room after breakfast, the old mirror had already gone and been replaced by a rather unpleasant picture of Leuwenkind, complete with bald head and Doctor's robes, staring out of his frame complacently. When Arlo had removed the picture to check behind it, he had seen a tiny bump in the wall, as if someone had hurriedly replastered.

The Experiment was over.

Arlo leaned out of his bedroom window and surveyed the scene. It was odd, he thought, how much difference Ignatius's news had made to his life, and yet how little, as if deep inside him he had always, somehow, truly *known*. Little by little, all the missing pieces of his life were slowly clicking into place. Somehow that day, every Doctor in the Inn had seemed to know that Arlo had learned his true identity, and correspondingly, Arlo had grown to know theirs. Kristo had saved him a seat at breakfast, Doctor Sheridan and even Doctor Benedict had both been surprisingly warm towards him at lunch as if giving silent support, but Doctor Kane, Doctor Phlegg and a few others had seemed to take the revelation as a declaration of open war, and had not hesitated to try to needle and goad Arlo in any way possible.

But Ignatius himself had not been at table all day, and Arlo had not seen him since the events of the previous evening. Whenever he thought about what he had done he felt an unpleasant twist in his stomach. He should not have hit Ignatius physically like that, no matter how upset he had been. It made no difference whether Ignatius could feel it or not. Or did it?

From behind the door came a knock and the sound of Doctor Kristo calling his name. "Arlo! You'll be late for the Ceremony! Hadn't you better get changed?"

"Get changed?" Arlo pulled open the door in surprise. "I'm going to be at the Ceremony?"

"But of course!" Kristo returned. "Natural or not, you're still part of the Inn, aren't you? Go to the Robing Room, get dressed and get down to the Gatehouse quick as you can. I'll see you there."

Inside the Robing Room Arlo found his new novice's ceremonial robes hanging on a peg, gleaming black with a blue junior's sash. Admiring himself in front of the mirror, he slid the gown over his head and momentarily lost himself in its folds. From behind him, Rem yapped indignantly, his usual warning sign that a Doctor was approaching. Arlo pulled the robes down quickly and turned around, realizing too late that they were on the wrong way round. His heart plummeted as a shadow fell across the doorway. Doctor Phlegg and Doctor Kane stood before him, their faces a picture of resentment.

With one hand Arlo grasped Rem's collar to restrain his pet. Whatever happened, Rem must not be allowed to attack either of them again. "Sit, boy. Sit," he muttered frantically in Rem's ear. "Quiet now. *Sit!*"

Finally Rem subsided, obediently flattening his belly to the floor, but every line of his body remained alert and watchful, like a coiled spring.

"Ignatius has really gone too far this time!" spluttered Phlegg, his usually red face even ruddier.

"I told him," intoned Doctor Kane, glancing at Rem suspiciously from a safe distance behind Phlegg's ample frame, "I told Benedict that this wasn't to be allowed.

I said that Ignatius couldn't expect to get away with it."

"I mean," said Phlegg coldly, "the boy doesn't even *look* right. Nobody in their right mind could ever mistake him for a Citizen. With *those* ears?"

Instinctively, Arlo's hands crept up to touch his head. "Doctor—"

"Enough!" shouted Phlegg. "You're to go to your room immediately."

"But what about the Ceremony?" said Arlo, his colour rising.

"Forget the Ceremony!" crowed Kane. "You couldn't even pass your Examination, for goodness' sake! Why on earth do you think we want scum like you around?"

Rem rose slowly to his feet, quivering, lips pulled back over his teeth in a snarl. Arlo stood up and grasped his collar tightly. Phlegg stepped forward, his small eyes glinting triumphantly. As Arlo stared at the Doctors, from out of nowhere a thought came to him. *They're trying to provoke me. Phlegg wants Rem for his experiments. Don't rise to it.*

"Arlo *will* be attending the Ceremony," came Ignatius's voice testily from behind them, "so, gentlemen, I would thank you to keep your opinions to yourself."

The Doctors turned incredulously to face their new challenger. Arlo caught his breath as his tutor emerged into the dim light of the Robing Room. Ignatius's left eye was a great, shining purple.

Everyone stared at him in surprise and fascination for a few moments and Ignatius returned their gaze with a quizzically-raised eyebrow as if daring them to say anything. Abruptly, Rem sat down, his tail thumping happily on the ground.

"Arlo has been invited to attend the Ceremony personally by the new Regis," said Ignatius finally, with the tone of one settling an argument with indisputable fact. "And for that reason, Arlo will be present at the Ceremony in the same capacity as you or I – as a representative of the Inn."

There was a moment's silence before the two Doctors burst out laughing.

"Good one, Ignatius," said Phlegg. "You know, I really thought you'd lost it there. A Natural at an Anointment Ceremony? You'll be getting places for them in the Senate next!"

"I really think that you have misunderstood our new Overlord," said Kane evenly. "I have no doubts that he would like to see the Experiment and view the results for himself. But in the proper place and at the proper time, surely! It would be an insufferable insult to actually present the Natural at the Ceremony."

"Nonetheless," said Ignatius, his face calm and untroubled, "I sent a message to the Consulate yesterday informing them of our Experiment, and received the invitation back by return. Arlo is part of our community, and as such, he will be presented in no lesser circumstance. And as for his ears, Doctor Kane – you might wish to look to your own nose before you pass judgement on the features of others."

Despite himself, Arlo could not help laughing as Doctor Kane's hand went unconsciously to his face. But Kane's face darkened and the next second the Doctor was storming up the corridor in the direction of Doctor Benedict's study.

"Ignatius," said Phlegg, his chubby face assuming a look of wearied concern, "do reconsider. I mean *politically* speaking. Presenting a Natural at the Ceremony might send out messages that our scientific integrity is ..." Phlegg paused delicately, "... *compromised*. Some might even say ... *Infected*. Surely you wouldn't want *that*?"

"But the Inn's purpose is to protect the independence of knowledge," returned Ignatius. "Even our Founder was emphatic about that. Why should we allow the Governors to control us within these four walls?"

"But – the boy can't be trusted for five minutes!" waffled Phlegg. "Look what he's done to your eye! What's to say he's not going to ... fall over or ... bite the Regis or something? Or run amok if he drinks too much chorley? It's a liability, Ignatius! It's a security risk, and I'm not going to allow it!"

Ignatius smiled, and putting his hand on the shoulder of the fat Doctor, turned him round and propelled him forcibly towards the door. "I've spoken with Benedict, and he's of the same opinion as me. There's no sense hiding our Experiment now. If we are to rely on any of our rights, we need first to assert them."

Phlegg shrugged off Ignatius's hand like an irritating fly. "You say this, Ignatius, but things have changed now. Clinging to the old ways won't save you. Rights and rules are what we make them, or unmake them. The Consulate will not understand if you carry on like this. They will see it as treason."

Ignatius paused for a moment, and then answered pleasantly, "Then that is a risk that I will gladly take."

"So you are on your own," said Phlegg and, wheeling around on his good foot, he stumped out of the door and down the corridor. The door banged behind him with a clatter. Growling, Rem jumped up and planted his paws against the door.

Arlo turned to Ignatius, feeling the first tentative prickles of panic in his stomach. His tutor returned his stare gravely. "Good morning, Arlo. How are you feeling today?"

Arlo could only gaze at his swollen eye in embarrassed confusion. "Ignatius . . . oh, Ignatius . . . I'm so sorry. . ."

Unexpectedly, the old Doctor suddenly broke into a smile. "Good shot, Arlo. And given the shock you had yesterday, I imagine I probably got off lightly. But I think you need to control that temper of yours, don't you?"

"I won't do it again, sir—" began Arlo, but Ignatius was already beside him, hand on shoulder.

"Let's leave that behind us now, Arlo. We have the Ceremony to worry about now, and our new Regis to impress."

At Ignatius's matter-of-fact tone, Arlo felt suddenly weak as relief drained through him. Looking at his expression, the old Doctor grinned at him. "There's two things that you have to realize, Arlo. One, you don't have all the time in the world to change things. Two, sitting back and letting wrong things happen is as bad as doing them yourself. Kane thinks that by keeping his head down he'll escape danger. What he doesn't realize is that he will bring trouble on himself – and all of us." Ignatius smiled and ruffled the boy's hair. "But don't you worry. You're not alone. You've got me, haven't you?"

Arlo found no words to answer. It was impossible to argue with Ignatius when he was in this mood, no use to try to persuade him that things were not so simple. Couldn't he see the problems he was stirring up? Sometimes, for all his cleverness, Ignatius could be so *blind*. . .

He glanced up with foreboding at the old man's face as he stared unseeingly into the distance, bright with defiance. The sickish sensation of worry at the pit of his stomach threatened to overwhelm him, and he could not speak when Ignatius shook himself out of his reverie and slapped him on the shoulder.

"Right. First things first." Ignatius started to pick his way through the starched folds of Arlo's robes. "Let's get these on you the right way round, or Kane really will have something to complain about."

From her vantage point at the side of the Guildhall Square, Usha could see the carnival crowds gathering outside the walls of the Inn of Court. Brightly-coloured flags hung from the spires and distantly on the air she could hear the strains of an orchestra. In her Citizen's clothes and her hair covered by one of Auntie's best scarves, Usha could pass at first sight for a young Citizen-girl, as long as nobody looked at her too long or peered too deeply into her eyes. As she watched the scene two Gemini delivery-boys passed by with a candy-barrow, and in the process jostled her slightly. Immediately they apologized for the inconvenience and bowed respectfully at her feet. Usha turned her head quickly away until they had scampered off. It would never do to be recognized, even by a Gemini acquaintance.

Being outside and amongst normal Citizens again had put Usha into a practical frame of mind. Now the curfew had ended, she knew she must get as far away from the rambling mansions of the West Quarter as possible before the alarm was raised. Auntie had very few visitors, so the possibility of someone chancing upon the grim scene in the reception-room was remote. Nevertheless, the scissor-man would soon be sought for, and it would not take long for his movements to be traced. Usha knew the penalties for a runaway Gemini were severe. The first purpose of every Gemini was to serve a Citizen, and Citizens' lives were inviolable, everyone knew that.

All things considered, a crowd was the best place to be safe in, Usha calculated, and with brisk steps followed the crush of people thronging the pavement outside the Inn of Court.

The most important thing about passing for a Middle Citizen like Auntie, she soon learned, was to act like one. Holding your head up high and marching disdainfully past people seemed to have a miraculous effect and Gemini and Lower Citizens alike stepped aside from her path until the crowd became impenetrable. Slipping quickly into the cover afforded by the thronging Citizens, she heard the sound of sweet voices singing from somewhere in front of her, although she could not see over the heads of the packed bodies ahead.

"What's the occasion, Sister?" asked a golden-haired Citizen-woman to Usha's left. Usha opened her mouth to reply but the words stuck in her throat. Instead an old gentleman in front of her answered.

"It is the Anointment Ceremony of Governor Jano as Regis of the Inn of Court. The Maia are arriving. Listen. You can hear their processional song."

"What a damned nuisance," returned the lady sharply. "How on earth am I supposed to get to my dressmaker's through this lot?"

A shout went up and through the crowd Usha saw a file of brown-uniformed Guardian-soldiers pressing towards them. Roadblocks and patrols were common in parts of Genopolis, particularly the main squares, but usually you could avoid them if you saw them coming in time. But as Usha turned around to retreat, the swarm of Citizens around her suddenly tightened, and she found herself carried inextricably forward. Wary of tripping and falling under the feet of the crowd, she tried to force her way backwards, but the dense wall of bodies was unyielding, as more and more people packed into the square around her, singing, blowing whistles and waving flags. Brandishing his rifle, a Guardian bellowed above the noise of the crowd.

"Everybody line up to be searched. Please show your identification."

What was she to do? In a blinding flash, Usha remembered her identification token, lying on the floor of Auntie's bedroom along with her abandoned clothes. How could she have been so stupid? It was illegal to travel without a token, everybody knew that. To be caught without identification in a public place risked a fine or imprisonment. And if she told them that she had forgotten it, and if a Guardian escorted her back to the house to find it. . .

Directly before her, a row of Guardians were checking the tokens of the Citizens in front of her. No escape that way, and none behind. The next moment Usha found herself gazing into the eyes of a young soldier. He touched his cap.

"Token please, ma'am."

The bright tones of the orchestra were lost in another gust of wind and the gradually increasing rumble of the arriving guests. Around the Inn, the lawns were already starting to fill with Doctors and students alike in their black-and-white ceremonial robes, their vividly-coloured sashes denoting rank: blue for the apprentices, green for the acolytes, white for the Provosts and scarlet for the Doctors. Occasionally one might see the purple cloak of a visiting Dean, or the bejewelled chain of a Mayor. The Gemini garden-boys, unused to such large numbers strolling around their lawns, shepherded the company unsuccessfully to their places, only to have the guests ungratefully wander off again, spilling over on the cordoned-off sections for a better view, trying to swap their invitations for ones closer to the front, or crossing sides in an effort to gain a better vantage point.

Security was tight outside, however, and a file of brown-uniformed Guardians stood at the gates and manned watch-points around the approaching lanes, checking invitations and searching visitors quickly and expertly. One indignant (and doubtless important) guest complained loudly and vigorously about the ignominy of being asked to stand with legs apart and arms stretched, as a Guardian patted his voluminous robes in search of any concealed weapons. A captain stood apart, his rifle cocked, watching the guests keenly as they chattered their way down the gravel path. It was a big event, and you could never take too many precautions. You never knew what these rebel Naturals would do next to destabilize the City.

After securing Rem in his room with a large bowl of biscuits and gravy to keep him occupied, Arlo, feeling hot and bulky in his ceremonial robes, ventured cautiously down the long lawn towards the eddying crowd. He had no wish to bump into either Doctor Kane or Doctor Phlegg again, and he felt uncertain as to the effect his new attire might have on the other members of the Inn.

At the gates, there was an abrupt blare of trumpets, and the guests looked up expectantly with an excited ripple of chatter. Suddenly Arlo was aware of Ignatius leaning over from behind the bunting of the private box that separated the Inn's dignitaries from the rest of the milling crowd, and waving at him. "Jump in here, Arlo! You won't want to miss this!"

Arlo ducked under the boundary and climbed up beside his tutor. He tried to stand unobtrusively in the corner, but felt Ignatius steering him gently but firmly into the place by his side in front of the other Doctors. There was a low mutter of disapproval from the other inhabitants at his arrival and, behind him, Arlo felt Doctor Kane's eyes boring into the back of his head, but there was no time to worry about that now. Through the portcullis came two bright banners, and with it came a cheer that spread and multiplied through the crowd. The newcomers entered waving flowers above their heads and singing an anthem in voices that sounded like the choir, but with a tone much higher and clearer. Arlo strained to see properly, and as the procession came fully into view he was surprised to see that the hair of the newcomers was thick and full, whipping and fluttering around their faces in the afternoon breeze; the same wind that took their green cloaks and swirled them around their sandalled feet as they stepped lightly over the white gravel of the Square.

Ignatius's voice sounded low in his ear. "Some more learning for you, Arlo. These are the Maia. They have become more powerful over the last few years. Do you hear the singing? That is the song of reconciliation that represents them. The new Governor Regis has invited them here in the same spirit of reunion. But it has not always been like this. There was a time that they were not even allowed through our doors."

But Arlo's attention was fixed on the strange features of the new arrivals, unbearded and softer and smoother than those he knew, faces that he had never seen before, nor imagined. He could not tear his eyes away from the procession, gazing from one figure to the other as they walked singing and smiling and occasionally waving at the awed crowd. "Ignatius! What are the Maia? *Who* are they?"

Ignatius chuckled softly. "They are women, Arlo, female Doctors who have taken a vow of dedication to knowledge, just as we men have here in our Inn."

The boy stared, amazed, at the approaching procession. "But – but –"

Arlo felt a deep, rather unpleasant blush colouring his cheeks. He had read about women in the old books of the library, had seen pictures in the encyclopaedias, had known about them theoretically, scientifically; but this was the first time that he had ever seen one woman in the flesh, let alone a *hundred*. . .

A handkerchief was pushed quickly and discreetly into his hot palm. Dimly Arlo heard Ignatius mutter in his ear. "You might need this, Arlo. And try to keep your mouth shut. It's impolite to gape."

Embarrassed, Arlo mopped his face quickly as Ignatius continued.

"The Maian Scholars are particularly interested in the study of the Natural world, and ardent supporters of the rights of Naturals. Their Inn is not far from here, but you or indeed any man would not be allowed in without an invitation. Yet I have told their Abbess about you, Arlo, and she has lent her support to the Experiment. See her there, in the white cloak, under the banner."

The procession was now close enough for Arlo to see the range and difference of the arrivals, some features young and unlined, some older and greyer, some with fresh and full locks of hair, and others threaded with grey or shining silver, some bodies tall or slender, others fuller, more muscular or rounded. In front of them the Abbess of the Maia moved slowly, and with bent head, her long white hair swept up into a twist at the back of her head, and a light gauze over her face. As Ignatius finished speaking the Abbess raised her veil and gazed searchingly first at him, then at Ignatius. Arlo could see that she was very old, perhaps even older than Ignatius, but her face was alive with an intelligence and a wit such as few of the Doctors at the Inn could ever match. For a second her green eyes, clear but cold, rested on them. Then suddenly she too broke into a smile. At his side, Arlo felt Ignatius move slightly. Though Arlo could not see the older man's face, with a certainty born of another, far older instinct, he could tell without looking that Ignatius was beaming back at her.

The soldier leant forward to stare at Usha more closely. "Is there a problem, ma'am?"

Usha glanced around but there was no other escape. She would have to chance it, plunge through the first few rows of Citizens, keep her head down and hope that nobody caught hold of her. It was now or never.

She took a deep breath.

One, two. . .

From behind her, a deafening clash of cymbals rent the air and a shout went up from the crowd.

"The Regis! The Regis is here!"

Instantly, the throng suddenly erupted into cheering around her. From the left a group of eager young apprentices poured into the space between Usha and the soldier, craning their necks to see the procession. "There he is! See! See the Regis there, in the red litter!"

In the unexpected confusion, the soldier had been separated from her by six or seven students, all waving flags and shouting. During that brief second Usha saw her chance, and took it.

Ducking behind a fat Citizen woman who stood to the right of her, Usha dropped to her hands and knees and started to scuttle as fast as she could down the narrow shifting space between the rows of Citizens.

"You! Here! Come back!"

Dimly behind her she could hear the soldier shouting for her to stop, but she was out of his reach now, almost eight rows away, going strong. Around her all was chaos. Knees knocked against her head, feet trod on her hands, and more than once a Citizen stumbled over her, almost squashing her in the process. In the mayhem, the crowd was confused as to what was going on. From the back, Citizens were surging forward, keen for a sight of the Regis, and from the front voices demanded the back row to stop pushing. Between them, Usha scrambled frantically along on all fours, searching for a place to hide. Finally, fearing that she would be crushed beneath the crowd, she struggled upright and dodged between a burly Citizen and a Gemini balloon-seller, vaulted over a road-sweeper's cart and almost knocked over a Citizen schoolgirl about her age. Her Gemini-minder turned on Usha, hand upraised. "Hey! You! What do you think you're doing?"

His fingers tightened on her shoulder but she ripped herself free, leaving her collar in her assailant's hand, ducked through over-reaching hands and feet that kicked and voices that cursed. In front of her rose an apple-barrow, its crates piled high with ruby fruit. Desperately she wriggled through the narrow space between two crates, and with an effort, toppled one of the crates off the cart to splinter with a crash on the ground. Apples bounced everywhere and scattered themselves underneath the feet of her pursuers. In those few precious extra seconds, Usha dodged behind the back of the barrow but the blank east wall of the Inn of Court barred her way. From the other side of the apple-cart she could hear the soldier forcing his way through the crowd, loudly communicating on the radio.

"Back-up requested . . . over, back-up requested . . . South Third Street. Subject believed dangerous . . . over."

Usha beat her open palms on the wall, but it was no use. No escape.

Her luck was out.

Just as the last of the green-cloaked Maia disappeared into the Old Hall, the timpani stationed by the outer gates sent up a preparatory drum roll to signify the arrival of the new Master Regis.

From the other side of the Inn's walls echoed the cheering of a distant crowd, but inside, the stir caused by the arrival of the Maia was as if it had never been. The guests drew their cloaks around them and stood silent and respectful as the first sight of the crimson litter came into view through the gates, borne by robed Gemini bearers walking in rhythm to the hollow beat of the accompanying drums, one step, beat, another step, beat. The slow lurching sway of the litter seemed like some unearthly shambling creature, its heavy curtains with their gold fringing swinging from side to side to the rhythm like heavy locks of hair. One step, beat, another step, beat. The fascinated crowd followed its progress up the drive in absolute silence. As it approached a feeling of revulsion came upon Arlo and, as cautiously as he knew how, he retreated behind Ignatius, with a very strong feeling that, whoever the inhabitant of the litter might be, he had absolutely no wish to look at him.

The litter drew to a stop before the Doctors' box. A chaotic fanfare of trumpets sounded, and from the distant portcullis the black-garbed Gatekeeper raised his staff and cried aloud, "The Governor Regis has come. Welcome him."

"Enter into your Court and rule," replied the assembly.

From the side of the litter long fingers appeared through the velvet curtains, and after a seemingly-interminable wait, slowly pushed them open. There was a long silence, as the crowd took in the wasted, almost skeletal figure of a tall man, dressed in silken robes and headdress, poised on the embroidered cushions, the heavy chain of a Governor of Genopolis lying glittering around his neck.

Arlo shrank into Ignatius's side as he saw the skull-like face, the bleached whiteness of the skin like bone, the dark eyes like pools underneath the jutting cranium. The thin, pale fingers that clasped the velvet of the curtain tightened slightly as the bald head turned from side to side, scanning the crowd, and Arlo winced as the dark eyes fell on him, running over his hands, face and his ill-fitting robes. He was overcome by a feeling that was like the stench of something rotting; a taint so sickening that he could not believe that others could not smell it. He could not control the shiver that passed through him, nor the strange urge both to run for his life and to throw himself at the foot of the litter.

"Quick," hissed Doctor Phlegg through the silence, "clap! Clap!"

Hesitantly at first, and then rapidly, applause broke out, and several of the younger Doctors were heard to cheer, drowning out the trumpet fanfare that should have heralded the first overture of the chamber orchestra. Accordingly Doctor Sheridan missed his cue, the orchestra got off to a ragged start, and even from that far distance Arlo could hear the sound of Kristo's viola come in late again.

The litter-bearers started to pace again, and the heavy curtains fell back into place, masking the skeletal figure from view. As the litter passed amid the general cheers, hurrahs and rose throwing, Arlo watched it go with a dragging feeling of fear, until it finally turned and disappeared through the doors of the Old Hall.

Usha glanced around desperately. Immediately before her rose the sheer impenetrable stone wall of the Inn of Court. Each side of the apple-cart was stacked with crates of fruit, and behind them crowds of Citizens were straining to catch a glimpse of the procession. From the other side of the cart she could hear the ominous crackle of the radio, an inhuman, mechanical voice.

"Back-up approaching to apprehend suspect. Begin engagement."

It was all up. It was over.

Usha leaned heavily against the wall and sank to the ground, hiding her head in her hands. They would take her into the military station for questioning, they would discover she was a Gemini, then they would look her up on the Register and when they returned to the house to speak with Auntie. . .

From somewhere underneath her she heard a hoarse whisper.

"Oi! Sis! Look lively!"

A dream, thought Usha, without heeding, really it was all a dream. Dimly she wondered, without much interest, what would happen to her. Perhaps she would be sent back to the pharms, or maybe taken for Regeneration. . .

But again came the voice, hissing loudly, somewhere by her feet.

"Down here, Sis! Quick! Get yer skates on!"

With disbelief, Usha wriggled to one side and stared down at the ground. She had been slumped over a small iron grating, partially covered with debris. Underneath it, barely visible in the shadowy light, a thin mucky face grinned up at her, out of which one bright eye was shining.

"Come on! Bit slow, ain't yer?!"

Two grimy hands levered the grating downward from below, to reveal a dank, brick-lined tunnel, and beckoned to her. Usha hesitated. Behind the apple-cart the crackling of the radio grew steadily nearer. The eye glared at her.

"Sis! You comin' in or what, or you goin' ter wait out here till they make yer into toast?"

By the time the soldiers, rifles at the ready, sprang around the side of the apple-cart, the area was deserted. Only a few filthy pieces of rubbish, caught on the mid-morning breeze, flapped over the spot where their quarry had gone to ground.

The voices of the choir rose up to the high vaults of the Old Hall in the anthem that Doctor Sheridan had specially written for the occasion, *Let He Who Cometh With Knowledge,* which seemed to its audience to last as long as the three months it had apparently taken its proud author to compose. Already the heads of many Doctors and guests had tipped back, eyes slowly closing, and from more than one mouth a gentle snore emerged.

Leaning unhappily in his cramped corner at the back, Arlo gave himself over to brooding. Up until recently life had been so easy. He had known which Doctors to avoid and which to talk to, what to say and what to hide. The few crumbs of comfort that he had got from the other Doctors had been enough when he was younger. He could have got along just fine with the occasional smile from Doctor Benedict, a pat on the back from Ignatius, a word or two of commendation from Kristo. . . Not much indeed, but enough to keep him together. Until now. Now he had realized that this was not enough, had never been, and could never be enough again.

A clash of cymbals suddenly echoed around the Hall, Doctor Benedict's voice called out, "Hail to the Overlord Regis," and the crowd strained to see the cadaverous Governor Regis, his red robe hanging loose around his bony shoulders, limping up to the pedestal and taking his place upon the Judgement Chair. Behind the Regis followed a young boy, about nine Citizen-years old, a strange mix of curling fair hair and dark brown eyes, dressed in richly-embroidered clothes.

Arlo sat up in sudden interest and craned forward. Who could *that* be? The youngest of the Doctors in the Inn was over twenty-five Citizen years, and Arlo had rarely seen any Citizen children save (from a distance) the children of visiting diplomats (whom he was never allowed to talk to). As the boy took his place behind the Regis, he glanced in Arlo's direction and caught his eye. Showing a remarkable lack of respect for the Ceremony, he stared at Arlo for a few long seconds, his eyebrows raised, unblinking. Then he winked and mimed a yawn, as if he too was falling asleep. Surprised, Arlo felt his face and neck get hot, and instantly the boy's face crinkled into a cheerful grin. Arlo gazed back at him, the feelings of boredom and loneliness that had paralysed him suddenly evaporating into the stuffy air. Suddenly he felt alive and cheerful again.

As he leaned forward to see better, the thunderous roar of the organ trembled around him, and his view was suddenly blocked by the assembly rising to its feet and applauding. The Ceremony was finally over. Over the heads of the crowd Arlo could see the scarlet headdress of the Regis passing down the aisle, while all around him the Doctors were bowing deeply. Quickly Arlo bobbed his head in submission and ecstatically stretched his aching limbs that hurt from so many day-hours of sitting on the hard bench. It was time for the celebratory dinner, where he might be able to catch another glimpse of the strange boy who had so intrigued him, and who seemed so different from everyone around them.

In the shadow of the stinking tunnel, Usha and her unexpected rescuer stood pressed flat against the wall, his arm outflung against her shoulder, holding her motionless. Above them they could see the square grid of sunlight, flickering as the boots of the baffled soldiers tramped up and down overhead. Faint sounds of commotion filtered down into the dank hole.

"Find her! Find her!" the sergeant was bellowing. "Don't just stand there like a bunch of drooling halfwits! She hasn't just vanished into thin air! Get on with it!"

A hand yanked at the grating, but it had been expertly screwed back into position within seconds and held firm. The next second the light was blotted out as one of the soldiers knelt down and strained to see into the blackness. Usha stood rigid in the shadows, but breathed again as the soldier stood up and delivered his verdict.

"No way she could have got down there, sir. Bolted shut, it is. More likely she ducked back and got lost in the crowd."

"Oh for—" swore the sergeant, but the rest of his words were lost as he moved away, and the sunlight fell through the bars once more.

After a few seconds of silence, her new saviour judged it safe to speak. From what she could see of him in the dim light, he was a boy of about fifteen, curly-haired, thin and gangly and dressed in shabby clothes. But as he turned his face fully into the light, she could not repress a momentary flinch. His left eye was bound up by a piece of rag, and a deep scar cleft his cheek. For Usha, who had spent her life surrounded by clean and powdered Citizens, the effect was startling. But despite his fearsome appearance the boy grinned cheekily back at her as if he had known her for years.

"On the run from the brown-backs, are yer?"

Usha shook her head. "It's all a terrible mistake. I forgot my token, and—"

"Least you got a token," returned the boy. "When you get to looking like me, they take yer token away. Remember me, don't yer?"

Usha stared. "Remember you. . .? I'm sorry. I think you've got me confused with someone else."

"Confused? I might not look too pretty, but I ain't stupid. You work for that old gal, whatsername, Cybella somebody-or-other. On the corner. You've passed me many a time, but probably you was looking somewhere else. Even saw yer yesterday by the market, outside the Inn of Court, when yer give me that roll?"

"Oh!" said Usha in sudden recognition, as the memory of the beggar outside the barter-circles rose up before her. How long ago yesterday seemed!

"My name's Ozzie, by the way. Pleased to meet yer."

Ozzie held out a dirty palm. Her head in a whirl, Usha took it gingerly, but could not reply. She was saved from further speech as the boy turned away, beckoning to her to follow.

"Better not stick around here too long. Come down and meet the gang and have a cuppa. You look like you need it."

Laughter rang out from the white marquee that had been set up during the Ceremony, tethered like a great balloon in the gardens of the Inn. Underneath the shady canopy, long banquet tables had been set up and decorated with roses and candelabras. Arlo cast around for his seat, discovering with some relief that he was to sit at a table with a few old Doctors who no longer remembered their own names let alone anybody else's, Kristo, and Doctor Sheridan, who in polite dinner-time conversation had a disconcerting habit of taking his glass eye out and dropping it in a glass of water to refresh it.

But though the table filled up, Kristo's place remained empty. Arlo scanned the crowd but could not see him anywhere.

Up on the high table, the Regis and the Doctors were being ceremoniously shown to their places by attendant Gemini slaves. Cautiously Arlo looked over his shoulder at the tall figure taking the centre seat, shuddered and started to turn away. But then he saw two servants ushering in the boy he had glimpsed at the Ceremony and seating him at the right-hand side of the Governor Regis. As they entered, a buzz of chatter surrounded them and the elderly Doctors at the end of the table suddenly brightened up, pointing and gossiping amongst themselves.

". . . and that's the Regis's son, there. Corin, his name is."

His attention suddenly caught, Arlo craned forward to see. One servant knelt at his feet and reached for a footstool, the other hovered at his elbow. Unimpressed by their attentions, the boy waved them away impatiently, rolling his eyes, and as he did so, he caught sight of Arlo peering at him, grinned in quick recognition, screwed his eyes up and stuck out his tongue. The Regis glanced up and Arlo quickly turned around, shrinking down in his chair to make himself as small as possible. A few seconds later when he dared to look back, the boy had already lost interest and was idly using one of the Inn's spoons to catapult lumps of sugar towards the Maia table on the other side of the room. As he watched, one of the Maia suddenly jumped up, clutching at the back of her neck, and looked around. The boy quickly laid down the spoon and gazed up at the ceiling innocently. Arlo felt a chuckle rising in his chest, and quickly clamped his lips together. *Don't draw attention to yourself*, Ignatius had said. But how could he not laugh, when faced with someone who so plainly wanted to act the clown?

A blare of trumpets signalled the serving of the first food of the banquet to the high table. The two Gemini who had attended the boy stood close behind him and the Regis, bearing silver platters. Arlo noticed that for each dish that was served, a portion was given to one of the two Gemini to taste before either of them would eat. He puzzled on this momentarily before deciding that the Regis was so important that someone had to check that his food was well cooked before he was served. It was only after the feast that another, more sinister reason occurred to him.

A swarm of identical Gemini footmen brought in especially for the occasion dodged nimbly between the marquee tables, bearing with them platters of exotic imported foods and long-stemmed jugs brimming with unusual liquors that had certainly never been brewed in the chorley-barrel behind the cookhouse. Doctor Sheridan abandoned his knife and fork and ate using his fingers, tasted everything in his withered jaws and confidently pronounced its ingredients – hen stewed in white wine and parsley, sausage and walnut pie, quails with chestnut stuffing, hard-boiled eggs pickled in vinegar and spices, swan stuffed with peacock terrine, peas seasoned with mint. And there were poached pears in mulled wine, spiced apples baked in pastry, raisin and treacle tart and, most wonderful of all, an almond cheese, an egg-custard and a sherry syllabub. The arrival of the last dish caused a polite round of applause at its entry. Not many of the Doctors remembered the last time that fresh dairy milk or cream had been present at the Inn's table since the great Plague had claimed the life of the last beef herds. Though eggs still made occasional appearances at breakfast (fowls and poultry being easier to pharm than livestock) having milk produce at table was just the kind of thing that showed the importance of the occasion. The liquor that was poured into Arlo's glass was sweet like chorley but smelt of blossom and honey and other spices that he could not at first identify ("Anise and caraway!" deduced Doctor Sheridan), and to complement the meat and cheese there were pots of mustards, chutneys, balsamic herbs and compotes. Arlo helped himself to everything and refused nothing that the servants offered, happily accepting a third piece of almond cheese, a second helping of syllabub. The drink – Doctor Sheridan said it was called cider – went to his head and suddenly everything became warm and light. He felt flushed with excitement and inflated by the magnificence of the occasion. A hot glow spread inside him and he leaned back in his chair and gazed around the politely chattering, dutifully chewing assembly. How gracious Ignatius seemed, sitting at the left-hand of the Regis, and how beautiful the Abbess looked, laughing at his elbow. How lucky he was, indeed, to be sitting here with these good people; how blessed he had been that he had fallen into such good hands when his own family had so cold-heartedly traded him for food. How –

He was so lost in these thoughts and in the sweet tang of the sherry syllabub that at first he did not notice the waves of disorder starting at the other end of the marquee. There was a sudden chorus of raised voices and a small tinkle of glass that most of the other guests put down to an accident caused by the effects of the high-quality brandy. It was only when screams broke out and a table was overturned that Arlo's attention was caught. He looked up and felt his stomach clench. It was impossible to see the source of the trouble, but it could definitely be heard. A high-pitched, excited barking was echoing from the other end of the pavilion.

Arlo rose to his feet, but it was too late. Consternation had set in. Guests were pushing away from each other, knocking over glasses, bottles and pulling on tablecloths as they tried to get away from the phenomenon that had suddenly appeared in their midst. A visiting Mayor, his face purpling, tripped and fell heavily against one of the slender poles that supported the canopy. Instantly the right side of the carapace subsided and half of the guests were immediately enveloped in its white folds. The other half got to its feet, babbling in confusion and charged past the high table. Out of the drapes of material bounded

Rem in close pursuit, trailing a tablecloth, happily playing the game of chase that Arlo had so often played with him on the lawns of the Inn. A Guardian threw himself at Rem while two more quickly jumped either side of the Regis to protect him from the furry assassin. But the dog neatly dodged his pursuer and leapt up on to the high table, snatched up a piece of swan in his jaws and charged down the length of the high table, now dragging with him a garland of table flowers that had somehow become wrapped around his hind leg. As Rem reached the end of the table he caught Arlo's scent, yapped in joyous recognition and bounded towards him.

Rem had come to find his master. The next thing Arlo knew, the dog had dropped the meat, jumped up on to the table and was licking his face enthusiastically, his open-mouthed panting echoing the frantic beating of Arlo's own heart as he looked past the happily wagging tail at the chaos raging behind him. Wonderingly he passed his hands around Rem's collar and ran his fingers over the length of lead that he distinctly recalled tying with a tight knot that surely had not – *could not* – have unravelled by itself. . .

Gazing over in paralysed fright to the high table, all he could take in at that moment was the sight of Kane's beady eyes barely suppressing a gleeful smile, and the wide, shining look of innocence on Doctor Phlegg's face.

At the end of the slimy tunnel, Ozzie stopped in front of a heavy canvas curtain draped haphazardly from ceiling to floor. Reaching into a small alcove behind it he brought out a battered pewter bell which he rang vigorously. The echoes magnified sharply in the small tunnel and, as they died away, a voice came from the other side of the curtain. "Ooo's there?"

"It's me, yer fool," said Ozzie. "Open up, Toby."

"Password, or you ain't getting in."

"Stick yer password," returned Ozzie, pulling the curtain aside, to reveal the head of a spiky-haired boy of about eleven years old sticking out of a small trapdoor in the ceiling, his small face almost covered by an enormous pair of horn-rimmed spectacles, bound together in the middle by a length of sticking-tape.

"I'll give yer a clue, Oz. The one I taught yer the other day. Remember? *'People who live in glass houses. . .'*"

"In what?" repeated Ozzie, shaking his head.

"Glass houses. It's an old saying from centuries ago. 'People who live in glass houses *shouldn't throw bones*.'"

Ozzie groaned. "Just put the kettle on, will yer?"

Toby stared at Usha for a moment, and grumbling, retreated. "What's the use of 'avin' a password if yer ain't goin' ter remember it. . ." Ozzie swung himself expertly up into the hole. The next second he extended his arm down for Usha. "Come on, Sis. Big jump, now."

Usha took a step back at the smell that rolled down from behind the trapdoor. Now that the initial shock of escape was over, all Auntie's warnings about Infection were suddenly flooding back to her, and her situation suddenly struck her as very precarious. "Thank you very much, Ozzie, you've been very Citizenly, but I really think I should be going now."

"Going where? You'd be picked up within a day-hour. Never heard such nonsense!" scowled Ozzie, swinging forward to catch her wrist in his wiry grasp. The next moment Usha, with a shriek, was hauled bodily upwards through the trapdoor and deposited on the floor of the strangest place she had ever seen in her life.

Arlo sat, his heart thumping and his cheeks burning red, on a hard uncomfortable chair in the centre of the Old Hall. Before him, behind a large mahogany desk, sat the new Regis, one bony hand playing idly on its polished surface as if tapping at a piano, the other shading his ink-dark eyes from the glow of the lanterns. Whenever his black gaze fell on Arlo, the boy stared down furiously down at his boots, still smeared with grass and mud.

Around the walls at a respectful distance stood various members of the Inn's faculty, amongst them Doctor Benedict, Doctor Kane, Doctor Phlegg and Doctor Sheridan, his remaining eye swivelling grotesquely in its socket as he listened to the debate. To their left stood various dignitaries whom Arlo did not recognize from the Consulate alongside others he knew such as the Registrar, the Maia Abbess and the Dean of the Academy. Before him, Ignatius stood alone in the centre of the floor as if on trial. He was speaking but Arlo could not concentrate on what he was saying.

Confused images of the banquet kept surfacing into his mind. The circle of brown-uniformed Guardians who had fixed him and Rem with their rifles, shouting at him to put his hands up. A howling Rem being dragged away with cuffs and kicks. Ignatius remonstrating with them. A peculiar smile on the lips of the Governor Regis. The amazed, gleeful face of the blond boy, gazing at him over the shoulder of a burly Gemini servant as he was carried off to safety.

Arlo buried his head in his hands. His eyes started to smart. If they took Rem away for ever . . . if they never allowed him to see his dog again. If they. . .

With an effort Arlo pulled himself together and forced himself to listen to Ignatius. It was not the time for an Outbreak. He would not show everyone that Naturals were weak and cowardly.

". . . Through our Experiment," Ignatius was saying, "we have proved that *pain*, as our ancestors called it, is not a sensation itself but rather the interpretation of a sensation by a part of the brain called the thalamus. Pain is only recognized as such once it has been received by the thalamus and forwarded to another part of the brain called the somatosensory cortex."

"We know all this already," scoffed the Dean impatiently, "it's the whole principle that started the City of Genopolis. Do you mean to say that all this . . . *trouble* has been of no purpose whatsoever?"

"The Experiment was not an investigation into cortex reactivity," said Ignatius sharply. "What we were interested in was the chemistry of the Natural mind and its relationship to the limbic system — the part of the brain that gave expression to what our ancestors called . . . *emotions*."

The effect that his last word had on his listeners was marked. The Dean raised his eyebrows. Several of the Governors murmured amongst themselves. The Abbess stepped forward as if to move towards Ignatius, but Benedict caught her by the arm and stayed her. Only the Regis sat unmoved, staring at a fixed point above Ignatius's head as if entranced by the flickering motes of dust that danced in the candlelight.

"*Emotions?*" asked the Dean, his tone dangerously inviting.

"Emotions such as . . . Love," said Ignatius, "Loss. Loneliness."

"Aren't we getting all progressive suddenly!" remarked Kane. "Well, carry on, Ignatius, don't stop there."

Ignatius ignored him. "Only by understanding the past, can we progress to the future. What we have discovered is that through pain our Natural ancestors understood their limitations and their kinship. To feel pain was to realize that it should not be inflicted upon others. From pain came emotions such as compassion, kindness, mercy, empathy. These have largely disappeared from privileged daily Citizen life for more than a century, though good conduct and politeness are still looked upon as Citizenly values. But through our association – to use the long-dead word *friendship* – with Arlo, we have rediscovered *emotions*, and identified the chemical reactions in the brain that cause them. We need to bring back those sensations. Our society is fragmenting without them, and I predict that it will not continue for more than ten years."

Arlo blinked in confusion. The assembly rose to its feet indignantly, but Ignatius moved quickly forward, holding up a hand. "Continuing the Natural Experiment is vital for the salvation of all Citizens. Our aim was, and has always been, to further our knowledge for the good of the City. Who knows what we might have discovered? We could have raised a viper in our bosom. We might have proved what many Citizens believe, that Naturals are uncontrolled, unreliable and dangerous."

"Then I must congratulate you on the success of your Experiment," said Doctor Kane, drily. "For you have proved beyond doubt that this is indeed the case. Failing examinations, hitting you in the face, unreported Outbreaks, setting his dog on all of us – all classic subversive behaviour if you ask me."

"Academic ability is not everything," said Ignatius swiftly, "and the Natural has demonstrated better Citizenly conduct and good intentions than many real Citizens. It is through observing him that we have gained an understanding of the true differences between

Naturals and Citizens, and on the basis of our research formed a proposal."

"A proposal for what?" sneered Doctor Phlegg.

"To build a world which Naturals and Citizens can both share."

There was a sudden uproar at his words, with the various Doctors – with the exception of Doctor Benedict – all staring at each other and shaking their heads vehemently.

"Poppycock!" Phlegg was chortling. "Never heard anything like it in all my days!"

In the corner, blind Doctor Sheridan could be heard bleating, "Give it to 'em, Ignatius! Give it to 'em!"

Doctor Kane stepped languorously forward, waving the others to silence behind him. "In my considered opinion, the Experiment should have been terminated a long time ago, and its resources Regenerated to worthy Citizens. Now that the subject Natural is of full age, I suggest that the Experiment be consigned to history."

Arlo gazed in confusion. What on earth were they talking about?

But Ignatius's next words drove all further doubt from his mind. "His name is Arlo," said Ignatius, "and I refuse to treat him as an object to be disposed of once he has served our purpose."

Usha was almost too astonished to speak. She sat in a hot, dusty underground cellar beneath Central Square and the Inn of Court, lit by a flickering orange light siphoned off from the Inn of Court's private supply. In its dull glow she could see, suspended from the ceiling, a strange and tattered assortment of objects: a string of onions, a lady's silk dressing gown, an old Guardian's uniform, a battered tin kettle, ropes and grappling hooks and, oddest of all, about fifty pairs of socks, ranging from tiny embroidered slippers to enormous, saggy stockings. And crouched in the darkness, on heaps of dirty coats or blankets, a group of about ten huddled children, the youngest a boy of perhaps four or five years old, the oldest a girl of about sixteen. Usha glanced around, and from the shadows, scarred and bandaged faces stared back at her, taking in her well-dressed but dishevelled appearance.

"Who's this?" hissed a voice out of the shadows suspiciously. "What you bringing *her* in for, Ozzie?"

"'Ow we goin' ter feed 'er?" complained another. "We ain't had no luck this week even fer ourselves!"

"Shut up, you lot," said Ozzie tersely. "Usha ain't got no injuries. She'll pull her weight all right. Toby, come and show yer manners ter the lady."

Toby grinned toothily and pushed a battered iron mug of black tea and a piece of hard biscuit into Usha's palm. Ozzie snorted. "You can do better than that, Brains."

"Pleased ter meet yer," said Toby, shyly, extending his hand. Usha hesitated, but as politely as she was able, shook and promptly dropped it as she noticed that the third and fourth digit fingers of the boy's withered right hand were missing and only stumps remained. With private misgivings she looked around the circle of faces. Surely she wasn't expected to shake hands with *all* of them? But apparently she was, because Ozzie brought her over to a girl of about twelve, a veil covering her face. "Now this piece of trouble's called Nanda. Say hello to Usha."

Nanda stood up and removed her veil. Usha took a step backwards and wrenched her hand away. For a moment she could not believe her eyes. Nanda's face was disfigured by a deep burn that ran from chin to forehead, and the left side of her head was mottled where the hair had been singed down to the scalp. The eyes that stared back at her were blank and blind.

Amazed, Usha opened her mouth, but no words came out. She had never seen anything like it in her life. Even the poorest beggars in the Square did not have disfigurements like this. Who *were* these people? What was going *on*?

Ozzie noted her reaction with a sharp eye. "Ah, come on now, Sis. Ain't yer going ter be a good Citizen, now?"

"She ain't even a Citizen," shouted another, bending close and gazing into Usha's pale eyes. "Made-to-measure Gemini, that's what she is!"

Usha glanced behind her, but the trapdoor was closed, and Toby now stood on top of it, looking at her unpleasantly. "Something wrong, Sis? Don't yer know not ter judge a book by its colour?"

"No," stammered Usha, "nothing's wrong, but. . ."

"Never seen anything like us before, have yer?" sneered Ozzie. "We're invisible, ain't we, people like us?

Don't want ter see us, so yer don't see us. Until yer on the wrong side of the law as well, then you ain't any better than we are! Do yer want ter go back ter the soldiers? I can arrange it if yer want!"

Usha gaped, totally lost for words at the boy's fierce Outbreak. She had never seen any Citizen act like this in front of her, and it left her totally confused. "I'm so sorry, I just wasn't—"

"I can't see any more, Usha, but I know what I look like," said Nanda quietly, sitting back on the heap of rags. "I was cooking chips and it all blew up in my face. My family-unit couldn't hide me. The neighbours would have talked, and the Guardians would have sent me for Regeneration."

"Yeah, but they still kept the chip-pan, didn't they?" muttered Ozzie darkly.

"My name's Mindie. I haven't walked since I got hit by a pharm-wagon when I was eight," put in a tiny girl sitting in a battered chair with wheels roughly bolted on to it. Usha glanced down and saw with incredulity that both her legs were missing. "They said I couldn't earn my keep, but I don't know why they said that. There's nothing wrong with my hands, or my brains."

"And Toby?" cried Ozzie. "The soldiers came ter take him for Regeneration but he ran out the back door to hide, thinking he'd have more of a chance down the stinking sewers, like all of us!"

"Stop it, Ozzie!" cried Mindie. "She understands now. Don't shout like that."

Ozzie aimed a kick at the battered old oil drum. "Takes the biscuit, it does! Bleeding cheek! *She* should be the one getting down on her knees in front of *us*!"

"Mindie's right, Ozzie," cut in Nanda, feeling for Usha's hand and gently guiding them both by touch towards the heap of rags that served as a couch in the corner. "You've had your say. Now show *your* manners and get out some of that food you've been hoarding and let's have a proper, Citizenly talk."

"I would like to hear," said the Dean stiffly, "the opinion of the Regis on what should be done with the Natural."

The Regis got up, drawing his crimson cloak around him, and walked with a measured, slightly limping tread, to a shelf bearing a couple of crystal decanters behind his desk. As he poured a sparkling amber stream into a tumbler, Arlo's nostrils caught the sharp smell of real brandy.

"You talk of preserving knowledge, Ignatius, but knowledge is a dangerous thing. Knowledge is pain, Ignatius, and pain is knowledge. Imagine the upheaval that this would cause if people started to *feel* again. It could only upset the delicate balance of our Paradise."

"But this paradise is something that only Higher Citizens know," said Ignatius, calmly. "Better a real Hell than an imagined Heaven. There is no purpose in believing that life is bliss if under our feet the foundations of our world are crumbling."

The Regis looked into the candlelight and took a long swallow from his glass. "But that is the beauty of living in Genopolis, that the outside world is of no consequence to us. As Milton says in *Paradise Lost*, 'The mind is its own place, and of itself, Can make a Heav'n of Hell, a Hell of Heav'n.'"

Ignatius turned to him. "Yet just because we do not feel something does not mean it does not exist. We are on a sinking ship, but we do not see our danger, we have lost our bearings, our internal compass, the barometer of our instinct. We are at the mercy of our corrupted Nature, we have taken her, abused and destroyed her, and she has turned upon us. Go outside, any door, any direction, and you will see the decay underneath the beauty of our buildings, the crippled Citizen children that roam our backstreets, the winds and tides that ravage the remaining land, while we remain, ageing lepers who feed on the blood of captured Naturals and pharmed Gemini."

"Really," broke in the Dean, "it sounds like Ignatius himself has become Infected. I think I've heard just about as much as I can take of all this."

"And there is danger to us so long as we continue to persecute the Naturals," pursued Ignatius. "The Regeneration Experiment is nothing short of wholesale murder of people – yes, *people*! But now – we see nothing wrong in taking a hundred Natural lives for one Citizen."

Arlo's thoughts were in a whirl. *Murder?* A hundred Naturals for one Citizen? Suddenly all the small scraps of talk that he had heard fell into place and he saw his true situation with a clarity that he had never seen before. Doctor Kane, in a sense, was right. He was not one of them, never could be one of them. With new eyes he suddenly saw the Citizens around him as false and unreal, and felt as if with one push he could break their world open, wipe the polite smiles from their artificial faces, rip out a dark instinct from deep within him, and with its force destroy the very stones upon which the Inn rested. And in that second he realized that he was not, and was glad not to be, a Citizen.

"You ignore the Naturals at your peril," agreed the Abbess, stepping forward to Ignatius's side from the corner where she had been listening unobserved. "The Naturals live in the cracks of the ruined world outside our borders, and try as you might you will not find, nor exterminate all of them. Though we have lost the sensation of pain, they still retain it. If we prick them, they will bleed; and as long as we make them suffer, they will take revenge."

"All the more reason to kill them off quicker!" said a Governor, punching the air. This suggestion was met with a rumble of approval and clapping. The Abbess and Ignatius exchanged glances. Arlo's knuckles whitened as he squeezed his fingers together, the roaring feeling inside him swelling to an uncontrollable crescendo. Just as he thought he could contain it no longer, the Registrar stood up.

"I suggest, m'lord, that we adjourn this hearing u

tomorrow morning so Your Lordship can ponder the facts to make a decision on the future of the Natural."

"But what about the animal, this . . . *dog*?" asked the Dean, disdainfully.

Doctor Phlegg nodded briskly. "It is held in the Garden Laboratory, sir, where it will be absolutely secure until tomorrow."

The Dean sat back down at his desk and banged his gavel. "Case adjourned until tomorrow."

Arlo bit his lip, screwed up his courage, and put his hand in the air.

"Excuse me, sir? Can I say something?"

Ozzie ladled out a second steaming portion of onion soup into Usha's tin mug, Citizenly once more after his previous Outbreak. "You all right there, Sis? Get some of that down yer and yer'll be right as rain soon."

It was strange, Usha thought, looking around the small cellar, how quickly you could get used to things. The Kids (for so they referred to themselves) were the closest that Usha had ever come to a real Citizen family-unit. Though some of them still eyed her suspiciously, the mood of the group had gradually changed over dinner towards curious friendliness or at least a grudging tolerance. It was clear that all of them looked out for each other, and each ~~~ber of the group had their own tasks to do, whether ~~~ooking, mending or begging. Inwardly Usha ~~~hat only a few day-hours ago, she had never ~~~ked to a beggar, or seen any injuries worse than a scratched arm, and here she was surrounded by some of the strangest disfigurements she had ever seen, *and* already starting to see it as normal.

Not for the first time Usha wondered how she could have walked past children like this before, without even noticing, or being so repulsed by their condition that she did not really see them. Moreover, none of them seemed the remotest bit held back by their circumstances, instead having found ingenious and creative ways to get by without an arm, a leg or a foot. All in all, they seemed to have been living fuller lives than she had ever lived, thought Usha soberly. She marvelled as she watched blind Nanda skilfully handle the ladle of the food, and run her fingers over anything that she needed to examine with far more dexterity than Usha had ever managed. And tiny fragile Mindie, dependent on others to carry her or push her chair around, cheerfully sang, cooked and managed the den, able to scold the older kids for not washing their hands, spoon-feed the younger ones and brush their hair all at the same time.

As she drained the last of her soup, Toby brought out the question that Usha had tried to avoid.

"So, Usha. What made *you* come 'ere, Sis?"

Usha took a deep breath and pushed aside her mug.

"Well, it's a bit of a long story so I hope you're all sitting comfortably. . ."

What prompted Arlo to do it, he could not understand, but as he stepped forward and raised his hand it was with desperate resolution tempered with a realization that for him, at least, things could not get any worse.

"Excuse me! Please, sir?"

At the sound of his voice, heads turned towards him incredulously. The Dean's face was a picture. Even Ignatius seemed taken aback.

"I . . . listen, sir, I mean Regis . . . could I talk to you for a second?" quavered Arlo. "In private, I mean. . . ." he added unnecessarily.

"Be careful, sir!" cried Phlegg. "You don't want to end up with a shiner like Ignatius, do you?"

But the Regis ignored him, and turned to Arlo. Dark eyes bored into his, and again Arlo felt a shiver of revulsion, as if he had uncovered a rotting, wormy apple in a basket of shiny fruit. It was an effort to keep from trembling. Though the man inclined his head politely, his face remained cold and mirthless.

"Ignatius's Experiment indeed. How intriguing to see such research in the flesh for once. And how fitting, some might say, to talk with it directly. Give the boy water and rest, and tonight show him to my study, where we will talk more. Then I alone shall decide what is to be done with him."

"TIE HIM UP AND LET'S GET GOING!"

As the evening steams rose out of the baked earth, tall columns of vapour drawn into the darkening sky by the movement of the cool evening air, Angus sat motionless, head bowed, and waited for death to come to him.

Around and above him, the day had come and gone. He had ignored the hot bars of sunlight that soon dispersed the early mists and the gritty afternoon dust-winds that razed the exposed hills and the old viaduct where he crouched. He felt numb and hollow, as if something deep within him had been burnt away, as if he was a shell inside which voices still echoed.

"Why! Why did you do it, Angus? I trusted you!!"

Gea's voice, raging, crying. He flinched at the memory. She had thrown herself at him like a wild animal in its last dying frenzy. There had been a tussle, and she had smashed a stick into his face, bloodying his nose and splitting his eye. As the world wheeled around him, he had fallen backwards on to the rocky floor like a limp rag. He had lain there, feeling the blows land on him, without raising his arm in his defence, strangely uninterested in his own pain. She was hitting someone else, someone far distant from him, someone whom he was rapidly forgetting. . .

"You gave our son away so that he could live? Fool! He's as good as dead now, don't you know that?"

But the wall around Angus had been too thick for him to be able to speak. It was as if solid glass had risen up between them through which he watched her screaming silently, beating on the invisible barrier that he could not pass. As she finally sank to the floor opposite him, too weak to cry, her old mother Ira knelt down beside her urgently. "Listen, my daughter. Grieve later. Kira has seen movement from the City. It is not safe to stay within sight of their walls."

As if waking from a dream, Gea rubbed her eyes, reached up her hands like a child and allowed Ira to help her outside to where Angus's niece Kira waited on the marshy river bed. Kira sobbed as Angus followed them, looking at him with shocked, hate-filled eyes.

"You can't come back with us, you know," she spat, bitterly.

Angus did know. There was no mercy for a Natural who betrayed another, these days. A mother had been hung from a tree for three days and nights after her aged father had wandered off into the wilderness alone to die. In vain she had protested that her father had asked her not to follow him, but the blame fell on her. For the law of the Region was absolute. No exceptions. Extreme laws passed by the Citizens had given rise to extreme laws in the Regions.

Yet it was even worse than that, he cursed himself silently. He had betrayed Gea, their son and himself. He had purposely given their own blood into the hands of the Citizens. Even talking to a Citizen was an offence severely punished, though many Naturals disobeyed secretly for the small advantages that a Citizen could provide, such as food, water and medical assistance.

Gea turned briefly to look at him and Angus's heart leapt in hope, but there was no mercy to be found in her eyes, just a cold sadness. "You'd better watch out," said Gea softly, "this is a tribal area. If they find you. . ."

Gea's warning was well-founded. There were some Naturals that said that even capture by Citizens was preferable to capture by some of their own, lawless kind. But the most terrible knowledge for Angus was that he would not be able to go back to their Region. To be cast out of a Region was as good as death. If you were not a Citizen, nor in a tribe, you were as good as dead, prey for one and an outlaw for the other. He could not even bear to watch as the small party made their painful way through the darkness of the viaduct and back home to the wild Regions beyond.

It was the first snap of a twig under a soldier's boot that finally woke Angus from his stupor. Suddenly wide awake, he gazed around in the creeping dusk, uncertain from which direction the noise had come. On either side of him the stretch of blasted tarmac that formed the road of the viaduct disappeared into the overgrown brush of the neighbouring hills. The steams had formed the beginnings of a heavy fog that blew in ragged clouds over the treetops, and filled the gulf below the viaduct so that the bridge appeared to be suspended in the white cloud. Although he could see little through the vapours, Angus knew, with a deep gulping certainty, that he was surrounded.

Slowly backing away, he turned and tried to walk casually down the battered causeway in the direction of the Region. Perhaps if they saw him leaving, and carrying nothing, they would not bother pursuing him.

Step by step he moved slowly to the opposite side of the viaduct, his feet dragging as if he were wading through mud. He was surprised at the rush of emotions suddenly flooding his chest. Only a few hours previously he had held his life of no account; now the fear that he might actually lose it had reawakened him to its value. The memory of his newborn son seemed to be pouring back life into his veins. It was painful, but it was the pain of blood slowly flowing back into a numbed limb. Taking a deep breath, he took the last step off the viaduct and prepared to disappear amongst the shadowy trees on the hill. He would go back to the Region. He would beg Gea to forgive him. He would do whatever penance she asked. Then he would form a group and follow the Doctor to Genopolis; they would get their son back, by force if necessary. . .

The butt of a soldier's gun caught him, expertly, on the side of the head as he rounded the first grove of trees. Angus saw dark soil rushing up to meet him, and then, as the soldier's boot connected with the back of his neck, everything dissolved in an explosion of blackness.

"Idiot!" snapped Captain Hacker, springing out of her hiding place and bending over Angus's limp form, lying crumpled on the damp earth. "What did you do that for? Now we won't get anything out of him for ages."

The soldier who had knocked Angus unconscious flashed

his torch into their captive's face. "I didn't hit him that hard, ma'am. I think he's faking."

Hacker shook her head, taking her helmet off and running her hand idly through her short fair hair. "They're not able to cope with it. You know that. Naturals aren't able to pick themselves up and just get on with it. Dirty weaklings."

Another soldier from the patrol arrived up the bank of the cutting at a steady trot and saluted. "Excuse me, captain, but we've checked out the area of the viaduct and there's no sign of any tribal Naturals there."

Hacker frowned, her grey eyes disconcerted. "Nothing at all?"

"Looks like it's been deserted for a while, captain. But there were footprints on the river bank that go upstream, probably no more than a day old. They probably scarpered when they saw us coming. The Doctor reported seeing their campfire, remember. There's certainly none of them left around here."

"Apart from this one." Hacker looked down at the limp body and pursed her lips. "Doesn't fit the usual pattern. These people, they stick together. You wouldn't usually find any of them wandering around alone."

"Maybe he's sick, captain. Perhaps they left him here to die, or to Infect us!"

The soldiers all took a step back. Warnings of illness had been drummed into them during basic training. Despite all the advantages of their super-breed, there were still some things that could kill and harm, unseen and unheard, and a man could carry the seeds of death in him unknowing for many months. During that time he could Infect many others, and, until the signs of illness were clear to the trained eye (or not) he was a danger to himself and all around him. Some believed that sickness came from the mere contact of a Natural, another reason to despise them.

But Hacker had served her time as an Inspector before her stationing in the border patrols, a background with enough medical knowledge to separate fact from fiction and was unimpressed by old wives' tales. She examined the unconscious man's vital signs and the colour of his skin, eyes and mouth. Finally she straightened up and delivered her verdict.

"He's not sick. Nor yet dead enough for my liking. But there's something odd about him being out here alone that I can't pin down. At least he's not a tribal Natural, you can tell that by his Mark." She pointed out a tiny blue symbol like a three-pronged wheel, almost obscured by blood and dirt, tattooed on the Natural's shoulder. "That shows at least he's from a Registered village in the East Regions. But then why is he out in the Borderlands and why are there other footprints heading back upriver? If there's any funny business going on —" Hacker checked her timepiece quickly — "we've not got long. Tie him up and let's get going."

FOUR

Out of a deep sleep, Usha felt someone shaking her. Confused, she opened her eyes to see Ozzie and Toby standing over her, dressed in outdoor clothes.

"Stir yer stumps, Sis! Don't want to be late for work, do yer!"

"*The early bird catches the germs*," quoted Toby, knowledgeably.

Usha heaved herself up on one elbow. "What in Genopolis are you talking about?" She glanced at the timepiece which read two night-hours. "It's not time to get up yet!"

Ozzie winked. "Night shift, Sis! Some of us can't go to work in the daylight looking like we do, can we?"

"But the curfew. . ." objected Usha, faintly.

"Stick the curfew," returned Ozzie roundly. "No point wasting good time indoors when yer could be working!"

Nanda passed Usha a dark coat with a hood. "You can wear mine if you want, Sis. I'm not working tonight."

Wondering, Usha got dressed. It seemed that only she, Ozzie and Toby were to be sent on this particular errand, as the others were still sleeping, some turning over faintly to mutter, "Good luck!" or, "Put the bleeding light out!"

"Right! Are we all sorted?" Ozzie pulled on his own dark coat and unhooked a length of rope from the wall. "Mindie! What's the shopping list?"

"We need apples, more onions, some beans, another blanket and more biscuits," recited Mindie. "But don't bother going back to the place that you got those last ones, they was horrible."

"Apples, onions, beans, blanket, biccies, gotcha," said Ozzie, stowing the ropes and hooks into a small backpack. "Ready to go, Sis?"

Toby swung himself out of the trapdoor and down on to the tunnel floor. Usha followed, and finally Ozzie, who switched the light off and closed the trapdoor quietly. "Them lot are the day shift," he explained in response to Usha's question. "It's only strong ones like us what usually go out at night."

One thing had been puzzling Usha. "Ozzie," she murmured, as they made their way down the tunnel. "Why are you doing this? You don't know me at all apart from I'm a Gemini, and yet you've fed me and looked after me better than anyone. Any other Citizen would have turned me over to the Guardians and collected the reward. Why didn't you?"

She could not see Ozzie's face in the dark tunnel, but she heard him chuckle. "Like I said, Sis, yer ain't injured, and that means yer'll be able to help get us food and supplies no problem. Anyhow, we're all at the bottom of the City heap right now, couldn't get any worse unless we was dirty bleedin' Naturals! Nobody else to look after us, so better we look after ourselves. Toby told me a word for it the other day, from before the Apocalypse. 'Friend', they used to call it."

"Friend," repeated Usha curiously. "What does that mean?"

"Well, I'm not exactly sure," said Ozzie, "but it's kind of like what I'm doing to yer, treating yer well, like, and if you treat me back well then yer a friend as well. Anyway, that's how I understand it."

Usha shook her head. Auntie had treated her well, better even than a good Citizen should treat their servant, but she had most definitely not been a friend, not like Ozzie. "No, I think it's something more than being Citizenly. But I can't say exactly what I mean."

But Ozzie had already lost interest. "Right, now 'ere's the back door. Quiet now. I'll go out first, and if it's all clear, you come up after me double-quick, and keep in the shadows. Right?"

Arlo pushed open the heavy oak door of the study allocated to the Regis and entered, to stand blinking in surprise at the sight that met his eyes.

An enormous table occupied the centre of the room, staggering under the weight of hundreds of tiny plants, as if a small forest had suddenly sprouted unlooked-for out of the polished grain. As he looked closer, this revealed itself to be a thicket of miniature trees, oak, elm, birch and laburnum, all tiny, but exactly in scale. Small blossoms hung from the trees, and finely-sculpted branches entwined themselves into their neighbours'. A set of gardening tools, scissors, shearing knife and digging fork lay nearby. Whoever had created that miniature woodland had clipped, pruned, stunted and repressed the natural growth of the plant, so that each tree remained a small, beautiful, but tortured replica of its full-size self.

Despite himself, Arlo drew near to examine the tiny forest, and was so taken up in observing it that he did not notice for some minutes that the Regis, now dressed in a silk evening robe and carrying a small pair of silver secateurs, had entered from an antechamber and was standing quietly watching him.

Arlo jumped and opened his mouth, but at the sight of the hollowed face he found himself stammering stupidly. Unconcerned by his confusion, the Regis walked over to the table and fastidiously bent over to trim a minute seedling from a tiny bough, curved into a faultless arc by means of a small, heavy weight suspended from its end by a shining wire.

"Nature, wild and untamed. By the hand of man, perfected, by the hand of man destroyed." The Regis gazed ruminatively at the plants. "Under our care, who knows what wonders can be created, the powers of the natural world harnessed to their full potential?"

Arlo opened his mouth, but he could no longer even remember the words he had planned to say. Up close, the Regis was as gaunt and pale as he had appeared at his Anointment, the skin white to the point of translucency, stretched as if to breaking point over the sharp bones so that his face seemed to be all planes and angles. His deep-set eyes seemed always to be darkened in the shadow of his brow, and tiny veins showed blue and thread-like on his hairless temples. How old he was Arlo could not even come close to guessing. He would once have been a tall man, but something had produced a change in him that ran deeper than usual ageing.

"But enough about my hobby. Why did you request to see me, Natural?"

Arlo glanced away under the intensity of the other's gaze. "Please, sir. I'm really sorry about . . . messing up the Ceremony . . . when my dog got out. . ."

The Regis raised his hairless eyebrows, a wrinkle of skin curving along his bony forehead. "*Your* dog?" he murmured. "You did not secure it properly?"

"Well, actually I think he was let out on purpose," said Arlo truthfully, "but anyway, I wanted to say that I was sorry. You thought he was going to attack you, but he wasn't. He was playing a game." He waited for a response, and when there was none, he looked up and was surprised to see a slight smile playing on the Regis's lips. "Please don't hurt him. He doesn't deserve to be locked away and drugged. He isn't a danger to anyone."

But the keen glance was sweeping his face again, deaf to Arlo's entreaty. Recklessly, the boy ploughed on, "If you give my dog back, I'll keep him out of your way. I promise. You won't need to put any guards on him. In fact, you'll never have to see him ever again."

"A bold request. It is clear that you are more concerned with your creature's safety than with your own!" mocked the Regis. "Tell me, Natural, what will you give for him?"

Arlo did not stop to think. "Anything. Ask anything, and I will give it." It was the truth. He could not bear to think of any more days without Rem, his sole reason for living. "Just tell me, and I will do it."

The Regis nodded absently as if Arlo's promise was of no importance.

"Interesting. Anything at all. What do you think a Natural can provide that a Citizen would want?"

Arlo did not know how to answer such a statement. He could only gaze at him in despair as the Regis continued.

"Yet, there is something that I want. And you, Arlo, are possibly the only person who can provide it."

Though Usha had seen Genopolis by moonlight from Auntie's roof many times, nothing had prepared her for actually walking through its deserted streets. Swathed in Nanda's dark coat, she followed the Kids as they moved soundlessly through the shadows; first Ozzie creeping ahead to scout the way, then Usha, and then Toby bringing up the rear. Once they had nearly bumped into a party of Guardians, taking a quick break to pass around a flagon of chorley behind the wall of the Academy, but Ozzie's remaining eye was razor-sharp through the gloom – able to spot a grain of sugar in a pot of salt, he'd informed Usha proudly – and he beckoned them away from the danger in time. Like shadows they followed him, creeping through the backstreets of the South Quarter, down squalid paths that Usha had never known existed.

Here was a vastly different world to the one she came from. Downtown, the roads that led to the docks where the food deliveries arrived from the pharms were small and winding and littered with stinking debris. Vents of steam blew white into the night air, in great belching bursts, as the massive turbines that powered Genopolis rumbled below their feet, as if they were tiptoeing over the belly of a sleeping giant.

Genopolis was its own ecosystem. The climate that surrounded it, the air and water that flowed around it, were controlled by the massive subterranean generators supplied directly from Genergis. The City itself stood many feet above sea-level, and the port below was heavily guarded by a military marina, but the storage-houses were set up on the sheer slope that descended downhill to the docks. From where they stood, they could just see the tops of the warehouses and storage kilns below them. Great cranes and winches stood motionless, their pulleys strapped down with chains and cables as if to stop the mighty machines from raising their huge pincers to their full height.

Down the slope the Kids flitted like faint shadows, keeping to the shade of the huge piledrivers and gantries stacked with empty crates and pallets. "Duck under here, Sis," muttered Ozzie, tugging at the hem of Usha's coat. "Sit tight. The three o'clock watch'll be around any minute."

Usha squeezed into the small space between the diggers. Sure enough, a few minutes later, a Guardian wharf-patrol came marching around the corner, flashlights blazing through the darkness, and almost immediately disappeared. "They don't like it here," muttered Ozzie in her ear, "they're always expecting ter bump into us. They won't be back till four-thirty, now. Time enough ter do what we need ter."

Usha looked at him. "What are we going to do?"

Ozzie opened his satchel and took out the grappling hooks. "Why, ain't you a soft one. Think food's goin' ter drop out of the sky?"

He rose to his feet, but Usha barred his way.

"You're not going to . . . *steal* it, are you?"

Her face was a picture. Ozzie stared at her. "Come on, Sis, what d'yer think I saved yer for? How else we goin' ter feed ourselves?"

"But. . ." Usha objected, unable to find the words she wanted. Stealing was un-Citizenly, everybody knew that. Fair trade or barter was allowed, but *stealing* was one of the worst things you could do to your fellow

Citizens. Regeneration was the usual penalty, but even the lowest Citizens preferred to trade rather than steal. "We can exchange my coat and my headscarf if you want! They'd bring in a lot of food."

But her words were like water off a tiled roof to Ozzie. "Well, Sis, us dropouts here ain't got your high-and-mighty standards. We ain't taking much, just a few bits and pieces here and there, otherwise they'll notice and stop us coming back, see? Nobody'll ever know. Now, hang on ter this and let it out gently when I say so."

He pushed the coil of rope into her hand and padded up to the first scaffold, threading a small hook on to the end, stepped back, whirled it slowly round his head and threw it up. The hook flew through the air to fall on top of the gantry. He pulled it gently back until there was a dim scraping noise and then a clunk as the hook caught fast. Ozzie hauled experimentally on the rope, judging its strength, before shinning up it with the ease of a spider. Usha had hardly time enough to take breath before his head, a small dark spot against the night sky, appeared silhouetted over the edge of the gantry, and an apple thudded down on to the ground in front of her.

In confused surprise, Arlo stared down at the ground. He had not actually thought he could persuade anyone to release Rem. The urge to confront the Regis had been more of an instinctive desire to defend his pet, rather than a conscious strategy. And now the bargain was so easily forthcoming he felt bewildered rather than elated. Something was wrong. Suddenly uncertain, he began to walk towards the door. Perhaps he should have tried to find Ignatius first. Perhaps. . .

At that moment he felt, soft as a drift of dust, the swish of the Regis's robe immediately behind him, and the next moment a touch on the back of his neck, just behind the ear. In cold shock he turned round and put his hand up in anticipation of a blow. The Regis towered above him, and along Arlo's arms and the back of his neck his hairs stood up on end as if charged by a dangerous current.

"Tell me, Natural. Where do you have your Mark?"

Arlo gazed at him, confused. "Sir?"

"Your Mark. Where is it? Your neck? Your shoulder?"

Leaning back, Arlo eyed him in dismay. "I don't have any mark! I don't know what you're talking about."

Unexpectedly, the intense look fell from the Regis's face, to leave a pale, cold mask that gazed at him stonily. "You have no *Mark*? No stain, no scratch, nothing?"

"No, sir," said Arlo desperately, confused. It had been a mistake to come here without at least Kristo to help him. "I don't know what you mean!"

The Regis blinked, and stepped back, his lips suddenly contracting over his yellowing teeth in an awful rictus which Arlo realized must be laughter.

"A great jest indeed! Eleven years as a Citizen, and one day as a Natural! But who *is* this Natural? Where did he come from?"

Arlo felt the atmosphere change abruptly as if a switch had been flicked. Suddenly all business, the Regis pushed a sheet of parchment on to the table, as if his sudden Outbreak had never happened. "Sign here, at the bottom, if you please."

The boy looked puzzled. "Sign?"

"Your name. Just here."

Arlo looked down. The language was a strange one, full of curlicues and flourishes, containing few of the letters that he knew. From his lessons with Kristo he thought it was probably the ancient official tongue of the Consulate, but then he had never managed to pay much attention to, or been particularly good at languages.

"But I can't read it, sir," said Arlo, anxiously. "What does it mean?"

"That is of no consequence," said the Regis calmly. "Your name is all I need."

Arlo regarded the bony face with mounting suspicion. Instinctively he felt a twinge from his gut. Something was definitely wrong. Most Citizens wrote on writing-blocks or slates which could be cleaned and reused, so anything written permanently on parchment or paper had to be extremely important. Standing up, he pushed the manuscript away. "I'm not sure, sir. I think. . ."

An emaciated hand shot out and gripped Arlo's wrist. The next second he found himself face down with his cheek pressing on the table as his arm was twisted around and to the side with punishing force. He felt the cracking in his muscle as his arm was forced slowly upwards behind his back. Pain ripped through his shoulder to his chest. It was hard to breathe. He tried to struggle, to cry out, but he was held fast, while the hot breath of the Regis tickled his ear.

"I think, Natural, if you wish to see your . . . *creature* again, then you had better sign that paper. Otherwise . . . I will be forced to do something that I fear *you* will regret."

It took all Usha's strength to lower the bundles of stolen food sent by Ozzie down hand over hand on the rope without letting them tumble to the floor. After they had finished the third warehouse, Toby checked his battered old timepiece, squinting to make out the time through its cracked front. "Best be going, kids," he hissed softly through the shadows. "Four-thirty watch'll be around in a minute."

Even as he spoke, they could see the distant approach of flickering torches through the silhouetted cranes that lined the docks. There was no time to lose. Usha rapidly collected the last of the oranges and put them in the sack slung between their shoulders. Together they strained against the weight of the growing bulk of provisions, which was almost heavy enough to pull them over, and began to make their halting way up the steep track away from the warehouses. In the same moment Ozzie came shooting down the rope, unhooked it and stowed it away in his bag.

"There yer go, Sis, that wasn't too hard, was it?"

Abruptly, just as Arlo thought he could bear it no longer, the Regis released his vice-like grip on his arm. Arlo slowly straightened up, gasping for air, flexing his elbow. As the Regis moved towards him, he shrank away, expecting worse. But the older man only sighed, wearily, proffering the manuscript to him once again.

"Do not disappoint me, Arlo. Like all Naturals, are you really so stubborn, and yet so weak?"

"Please," begged Arlo, his breath hoarse in his chest. "I'm sorry!"

But the dark eyes were implacable. "Again, I ask you. Sign here."

Shaking from the pain of his injured arm, Arlo knew only that he would do anything, say anything, than suffer the man to touch him again. Slowly, as if he had aged eighty Citizen-years during the last night-hour, he dipped his pen into the ink and laboriously began to write. The wrecked banquet seemed a hundred years ago.

As he finished, the Regis reached over and took back the document. He studied Arlo's signature with silent satisfaction, and then tucked it into a fold of his silk robe. The dark eyes glazed and seemed to be looking at something that was not directly before him. It was as if he no longer saw that the boy was still in the room. Fearfully, Arlo took one step back towards the door and then another, anxious not to disturb his reverie or do anything that would cause the man to turn on him once more. Finally, with one hand safely on the doorknob, he paused and moistened his dry lips.

"Sir? When will you . . . give me back my dog?"

Turning, the Regis shook himself out of his trance and, coming towards Arlo, grasped him firmly by the collar. A triumphant malice was burning in his eyes.

"Today is a special day, Arlo. Rules are changing around here. And believe you me, *everything* is going to change from now on." He opened the front of an elaborate golden timepiece that hung from his sash and checked the hour, nodding in satisfaction. "In fact, the changes should already be in motion. Why don't you come down to the gardens with me, and see for yourself?"

Half-led, half-dragged by the Regis, Arlo stumbled out into the grey morning light and stopped dead in amazement and fear. During the night-hours they had spent in the study, an enormous mound had been built up on the soft lawn of the Square. A teetering pile of crates were stacked around a metal pole, all containing something that looked like fluttering paper. As he watched, two Guardians came out of the Library, each bearing a box on their shoulders, and threw the contents roughly on to the heap.

Drawing closer Arlo saw to his disbelief that the growing pile was made almost entirely of books, the spines ripped and torn, covers scarred and tattered, their pages spilling out over the green grass. Yet another Guardian came and dumped more volumes on to the swelling mass, and another. Stray pages caught by the warm morning breeze blew around the courtyard and fetched up in the guttering, some typed, others handwritten, some old rolls of vellum parchment, yellowed manuscripts of music, the maps of the Old World from the Geography Room, volumes of geometric equations, chemical formulas, poetry verses. . .

Confused, Arlo stood and looked at the scene, his head whirling. What was going on? Why were they clearing the books? Where was Kristo? How could he be letting this *happen* to his beloved library?

He cast a horrified glance at the Regis, and saw a smile of pleasure on the bony face. "You see, Arlo. Books are lies, and all writers, liars. Books are the chains that hold us to the past. Only through their destruction can we fully go forward to the future. It is my purpose to destroy this evil way of life!"

From the Gatehouse there came the tolling of the entry-bell, and the noise of boots briskly marching up the stone path. Arlo turned around to see a small unit of Inspectors tramping in formation towards the Square, their black uniforms and gold piping announcing their high status. With a sense of horror gradually rising in his throat, Arlo watched as the unit wheeled to a stop and saluted the Regis, who stood next to the unlit bonfire.

"Good day, Brigadier Hacker," said the Regis evenly. "You have come at a good time. The Cleansing of the Inn of Court is just beginning."

It had been a successful shopping trip. As they made their way back through the last shadows of the backstreets of the East Quarter, they passed smaller, shabbier houses than those in Auntie's area, with tattered gates and barred windows. Most people living here were Lower Citizens, usually assigned to the menial jobs in Genopolis, and definitely unable to afford the expense of a Gemini-servant. Usha had never ventured into its winding streets, for though there were cheaper barter-markets there than outside the Guildhall, Auntie had never thought it safe for her to go there alone. For safety, they had taken the long way round from the South Quarter back to the Kids' basement.

"Always go back a different route ter what yer came," Ozzie whispered in response to Usha's mystified question. "Sometimes yer might get followed, or they lie in wait and catch yer red-handed when yer come back with yer shopping. Besides, I grew up round here, there ain't nothing I don't know about these streets."

Usha looked at him, amazed. "Really? Where did you live, Ozzie?"

"Don't matter, dunnit?" muttered the boy, shortly, stepping forward to hold up the dragging bag of provisions. "Didn't count fer anything before, still ended up here, didn't I? Live for the moment, that's me. No sense thinking about the past."

No, thought Usha, perhaps there wasn't any sense thinking about the past, but sometimes you couldn't help it, even so.

To rid her mind of the image of Auntie's face she peeped over a low fence to her left, and saw an embroidered shawl hanging up over a length of line that ran from one end of the yard to another. Lower Citizens washed their clothes themselves, and this had obviously been hung out to dry overnight. She couldn't help imagining how beautiful it would look and how well it would insulate her, and despite herself she slowed her pace as they passed.

Ozzie looked over at her face. "Do yer like it? Do yer want it, Sis?"

"I . . . no, Ozzie, I. . ."

"Well, if yer like it, what's ter stop yer taking it?" Ozzie swung a foot up and over the fence, and before Usha could stop him, vaulted nimbly into the yard.

Usha gesticulated wildly at him. "Ozzie, stop! Put it *back*!"

But Ozzie had already tugged the shawl off the line. "We got little enough, Sis, why yer so against taking what yer can when yer can?"

"Leave it! Let's go, Ozzie!"

But in her haste Usha leaned too heavily on the fragile fence. With a crack it split. Grabbing wildly but ineffectually at the supports, she pitched forward, straight into a stack of small pots just inside the yard. With a splintering crash, they rolled in all directions and smashed. Toby froze, staring up at the house. In the quiet of the night curfew, the noise seemed deafening.

Ozzie frantically motioned to Usha to stay still, but it

was too late. Upstairs, a window opened and a male voice shouted something. Ozzie came sprinting towards Usha, dragging her up by the shoulder, hissing loudly. "Get out of here! Go!" Behind them there came the noise of doors crashing and the next second the shrill sound of a whistle cut the air.

"Patrol!" called Toby in a hoarse whisper. "Quick!"

Ozzie swore, tugging at the food-sack. "Come on!"

"Leave it! We can't run with all this!" argued Toby.

"We ain't leaving nothing! Pull the bleeding thing! Now!"

But as they grappled with the sack, Ozzie wrenched too hard and the bulging seam was suddenly rent by a deep gash. Food cascaded into the gutter, burying them ankle-deep in squashed apples and hard, rolling beans.

For a second they stood motionless, aghast, before Toby's urgent pleading broke through to them and they realized the true seriousness of their situation. Turning with one accord, they ran for their lives, the whistle blowing quicker and nearer to them every second and the sounds of pursuit echoing down every alley.

As the Brigadier stepped forward towards the Regis, Arlo's mouth fell open in shock. His stomach heaved but he could not tear his eyes away. One side of the Brigadier's face was a melted mess of flesh, as if a hot iron had been held against the face and had dragged its folds down to the jowl. Her eye protruded, bulging and lidless, from the scoured socket, and from forehead to neck the skin was a virulent purple-red. As the Brigadier raised an arm in salute, a glint of metal protruded from the black folds of the uniform, and instead of a hand, a finely-tuned mechanized claw slowly emerged from the cuff, flexed itself and retracted again inside the sleeve.

Scarcely believing what he saw, Arlo inched backwards towards the shadow of the door. As the Brigadier conferred with the Regis, Arlo saw the other side of her face, a face that had once been both a Citizen and a beautiful one, with fair skin, grey eyes, long nose and a thin mouth. Strands of colourless hair still protruded from the part of the wrinkled scalp visible underneath the cap, and the white silk scarf denoting her high military rank was drawn around the scarred tissue of her neck. He gazed at her arm, transfixed by the polished metal protruding from the ruined flesh. But even as he stared, he knew, without looking up, that the stony grey eye of the Brigadier was fixed on him.

From across the lawn there was a metallic jingle, and another unit of brown-clad Guardians appeared, escorting at gunpoint a line of Doctors chained from head to foot into the main Square. The old Doctors gazed in shock and confusion at the towering stack of books on the green grass. Against the kitchen wall stood the remaining Gemini servants, their heads lowered, eyes downcast, a Guardian standing before them with rifle at the ready.

Arlo's mouth dried as he saw that Doctor Benedict

walked amongst them, his wrist bound to the neighbouring soldier with a metal chain. Doctor Benedict raised his head, a frown of dignified indignation contorting his features.

"What is the meaning of this, Governor Regis? Surely you have not come to destroy everything that you have inherited?"

The Regis laughed, and his voice was calm and deadly. "No indeed, Doctor Benedict. We have come to save the Inn from falling into the chasm of treason. Infection is now rife in the Inn. Emotions are now contaminating many of you! Brigadier Hacker, Veteran Protector and Chief Inspector of Genopolis, has come to personally oversee the destruction of your library of unauthorized knowledge and ensure that the Inn meets the highest possible standards of the Inspectorate. She will be interviewing you now and will pass sentence on you presently."

As the Brigadier marched away, the Guardians prodded Benedict after her towards the open doors of the Old Hall. Arlo took a step backwards, his legs trembling so violently that he thought they would hold him up no longer. But as he turned to slip away, the Guardian at the door swung his rifle at him and released the safety-catch. On hearing the sound, the Regis spoke without turning his head.

"Where do you think you are going, Arlo? Stay with me here, and watch the new Order come to pass."

Usha skidded on the loose stones as they pelted around the corner, and would have fallen if Toby had not been close behind her, dragging her upright. Searchlights blazed in their eyes as the whistles blared the alarm, and the staccato rat-tat-tat of a rifle sounded somewhere behind them.

Ozzie was ahead of them and twisted his head back to shout frantically, "Back door, Toby! Quickly! Go ter the *back door*!"

Usha had no idea what he was talking about, but Toby responded immediately, abruptly turning off from the main street and pulling Usha with him. At the same time Ozzie swerved down a small passageway in the opposite direction. Behind them, the pursuit faltered momentarily as their prey separated, uncertain as to which group to follow. In that brief second of reprieve, Toby pushed Usha down a blind alley between two houses, braced his back on the end wall, bent his knees and put his hands together to form a stirrup. "Put your foot here! Now!"

Auntie had never let Usha so much as climb a wall in her life before, but there was no time to protest. Obediently she put her foot on Toby's hands and reached for the top of the wall. Toby heaved, and the next second Usha was boosted violently up and over, to fall on the other side with a crash.

For a minute she was stunned, unable to move, the taste of dust in her mouth nearly choking her. Dimly she saw Toby jump nimbly down next to her, get to his knees and tug at a grating in the corner, to expose a small black hole underneath.

"Get in! Usha! Get in!"

But as Usha put her hands down to push herself upright again, her left arm suddenly sagged underneath her like a wet sleeve. Helplessly, she fell forward, clutching with her good hand at the wall to pull herself up.

"Toby – help – I'm –"

In that moment, she realized why Auntie had never let her most valuable possession climb walls or trees.

Arlo stood in the centre of the Square with the Regis, a Guardian standing behind him with rifle cocked. All eyes were fixed on him. He looked down, unable to return their glances. What was happening? Where was Ignatius? Where was Kristo? A pulse beat behind his eyes and he felt sick and giddy. His body seemed faint and insubstantial, as if he were no more than a ghost in the early light.

Old Doctor Sheridan, his white hair and beard blowing in the breeze, stepped forward, his blind eyes rolling angrily.

"This is a disgrace! For what end do you come here? Delight at the destruction of learning? You and your kind will not triumph, Regis. You take knowledge from the hands of men, but you will not succeed in wiping it from history. There are things greater than your position, and there are powers greater than those you enjoy."

Arlo felt a wrench in his stomach at the old man's words. He turned to the Regis, an appeal for the Doctor already starting on his lips, but it was too late. A Guardian stepped up behind Doctor Sheridan and hit the old man with the butt of his rifle. Doctor Sheridan toppled forward on to his face. Either side of him the Doctors stared straight ahead as if they had not noticed. Arlo turned away, a crushing pain in his chest. Beside him the Regis laughed, raising his voice.

"You old Doctors and your eternal dedication to books and manuscripts and centuries gone by. Fools! All knowledge is temporary! Men die, other men are born, knowledge is lost, other learning takes its place. Kingdoms rise and fall, civilizations grow and decay, wars are fought between followers of one truth and another.

"But now I declare the dawn of a new age. No longer will our kind live just a tiny cycle of years, a brief second in the light only to die at the first dusk. The progress of our scientists has brought about a new beginning. In place of death and deterioration will come a new race, of Citizens that no longer die, who do not wither, and for whom there will be one knowledge, one truth, one belief.

"This new beginning is the New Renaissance, the Regeneration Project. Our Citizens will be strengthened, enlightened, revived by the life of lesser beings. At the beginning of our Order, victory over pain was the first triumph against Nature. Pain had restricted us, bound us, held us back from fulfilling our ultimate potential. Now our final victory over Death is at hand."

Arlo heard the Regis's voice but as if from a great distance. Around him the air seemed too hot, too close. He swayed on his feet, his mouth dry. It took every ounce of strength to keep standing upright.

"Wait!" came a commanding voice. "Are you insane, Regis? You do not know the extent of what you propose!"

With the rest of the assembly, Arlo turned in surprise to see Ignatius, irritably marching up the path, one hand manacled to an Inspector, who was trying unsuccessfully to restrain him.

"In seeking victory over death you will only find the curse of your own mortality, Regis, along with that of thousands of others. The Regeneration Experiment is doomed to failure. Murder of Naturals will not sustain dying Citizens. There is only one way to preserve life, and that is by valuing both life and death as part of Nature."

The Regis stepped forward to face the Doctor, dropping his voice low to a sneer. "Interesting, Ignatius, that you set so much store by Nature, when Nature itself is our enemy. Nature is not *fair*, Ignatius! Nature depends on strength alone, putting the weak under the powerful, woman under man, man under storms, fire and earthquakes. But our City of Genopolis has ensured that all Citizens are equal, whether they are Higher or Lower, man or woman, strong or frail. Are you saying that you would wish a return to Nature's savage law, Ignatius?"

Ignatius opened his mouth to respond, but at that second there was a curt interjection from behind, and the Brigadier strode up to stand next to the Regis.

"Doctor Ignatius, enough of this talk. You stand accused of high treason against Genopolis."

"What proof do you have?" asked Ignatius calmly. "Even a Brigadier cannot make an accusation out of nothing in front of hundreds of witnesses."

The Brigadier held out two scrolls. "Depositions testifying to your treachery signed by Doctors Kane and Phlegg, loyal servants of the City."

Ignatius laughed scornfully. "I can produce a thousand testaments to the contrary. Any investigation will reveal Kane's personal dislike of my Experiment, but this petty disagreement alone will not serve to convict me."

"Indeed," said the Regis with smooth delight, and the bony hand slid out of his silken robes to show a roll of manuscript that looked alarmingly familiar to Arlo, "then perhaps this will. Your own pet Natural has today signed a document that personally reinforces your perfidy. Now, by your own beliefs you stand convicted."

Arlo felt as if a fist had been slammed into his stomach. For the first time, he could see shock in Ignatius's eyes. The old Doctor turned his head and looked at him.

"Oh, Arlo. . . What have you *done*?"

The boy shook his head, confused. "No, Ignatius, it wasn't like that. . ."

"What was it?" pressed Ignatius, urgently. "What did you sign?"

Arlo felt a hot flush welling up inside him. "But he *hurt* me, Ignatius, and. . ."

"And then he put his name," said the Regis with calm satisfaction, unrolling the scroll that Arlo had signed earlier. "He traded the life of his dog for your neck, Ignatius. For the life of a dirty hound over yours. By your own hand created, by your own hand destroyed."

Ignatius shook his head, amazed. "This is absurd, Regis."

"Absurd?" laughed the other. "An advocate for the rights of Naturals calling this absurd? By his own mouth you stand condemned, along with Doctor Benedict."

"No," begged Arlo, frantically. "I didn't mean it! Take me, not him!"

"You?" mocked the Regis, haughtily. "You cannot give what you do not have, Arlo! You already belong to me, as Regis of the Inn of Court. And accordingly I will take you now – for my *own* Regeneration."

At the other end of the courtyard, the Gatehouse doors swung open and a small platoon – four sweating Gemini-slaves and two female soldiers, their battledress crisp and pressed – marched briskly up the gravelled drive, pulling with them a wagon covered in a green tarpaulin. They stood in a line and saluted Brigadier Hacker. Their captain stepped forward.

"Special Guard to accompany the Natural captive on your orders, ma'am."

"At last," said the Brigadier, nastily, "you've finally made it. Good. Take the Natural back to the Regis's palace and make sure it is secured. The Regis and I will be there in a few day-hours, but until that time you are personally responsible for his detention. Do you understand?"

"Yes, ma'am." The soldier stepped back and raised the rifle to her shoulder with a swift movement, aiming coolly between Arlo's eyes. "In the wagon, Natural. Look sharp."

In the dark of the Kids' cavern, Mindie was tending to Usha's wrist, gently straightening the Gemini's arm and feeling the movement of the bones beneath. Toby stood close behind her, still panting from the breathless chase and the exertion of dragging Usha down the passageways to safety. Round her, the Kids, slowly wakening from their sleep, crowded to see. "What is it, Mindie? What's she done?"

Mindie examined her wrist with care, feeling its awkward twisted position where Usha had landed on it with all her weight. "Can you move it at all, Usha?"

Usha tried, but her hand hung down dully from her arm. "I *can't*. I'm *trying*."

Mindie took two of the larger socks hanging off the ceiling and slit them open with a knife to make a long length of material. With one she bound Usha's wrist tightly, and the other she knotted in a circle to form a large loose sling, slipped it over Usha's head and carefully levered her lower arm into it so that it was supported and immobile. "I think it might be broken, Sis. You need to keep it still while it mends itself together."

Toby squatted down next to her, his eyes huge through his thick spectacles searching Usha's face. "Oh, Usha, I didn't mean to, I never thought—"

"It wasn't your fault," said Usha composedly, but inside her thoughts were a whirl. *Broken?* From what she knew and had seen, this was the beginning of the end. You had an injury, and little by little it got worse. You couldn't see it deteriorate but it did. Infection could set in, or it would heal badly and be only partially useful (if at all) or you might even lose it altogether. And once you had one injury, it was much more likely that you would get another.

Mindie saw her face and rushed to offer support. "Don't think like that, Usha, we've all been through this. Just make sure yer don't move it and it'll heal all right."

Nanda suddenly broke in. "Where's Ozzie got to?"

Toby looked at Usha. "He went the other way about half an hour ago. You don't reckon they've got him, do yer?"

But at that moment there was a clatter from the tunnel and Toby ran to pull the trapdoor back. Ozzie's head, covered in grime and filth, appeared through the aperture, the stolen shawl from the East Quarter still slung across his shoulder. "Stupid rubbish chutes," he grumbled. Then, catching sight of Usha and her sling, he raised his eyebrows. "All right? What's goin' on here?"

"Usha broke her wrist, Oz," said Toby. "Fell off the wall by the back door."

But if Usha was expecting any sympathy from Ozzie, it wasn't to happen. Ozzie swung himself up into the cellar, threw down his bag of grappling hooks, and casually dumped the shawl on top of her.

"Welcome to the gang, Sis," he said shortly. "Looks like you got sworn in quicker than we thought."

"Ozzie. . ." started Nanda, but Ozzie was having none of it.

"Well, after that stunt yer pulled, Sis, yer ain't going out fer a while anyway 'cos all the brown-backs'll be looking high and low fer us outside, and thanks ter you we ain't got no food fer a bleeding week anyhow."

Turning his back on them, he lay down brusquely, pulling the blanket up and over his head as a sign that the conversation was over. "Now put that stupid light off and let's get some kip."

Arlo stared down the barrel of the soldier's gun, then glanced at Ignatius, terrified. "Ignatius – but—"

"Do as they say, Arlo," said Ignatius, and there was a look on his face that Arlo had never seen before. "No heroics now. Go quietly."

"I can't," gasped Arlo, the beginnings of an Outbreak starting to brim in his eyes. Ignatius's face, distorted, swam in front of him. "I'm sorry. I'm so sorry."

Uncomfortably, the soldiers glanced at each other. The Brigadier raised a contemptuous eyebrow.

"There is nothing to be sorry for, Arlo," replied Ignatius. "It is no shame for an honest heart to be tricked to another's ends."

"I didn't know, Ignatius. I didn't realize. . ."

"Pull yourself together!" said Ignatius briskly. "This will not last for ever, I promise you. All things come to an end."

"Oh, get the stinking Natural in the truck!" rapped out Brigadier Hacker sharply. "I've had enough of this. And you," turning to one of the Guardians that stood over Ignatius, "get on with that bonfire. And quickly!"

A cold cylinder of metal prodded Arlo in the back of his neck, and he moved forward dully. But as he trudged, heart sinking, towards the military wagon, a great cry went up from behind him. He turned his head and immediately felt as if a sharp knife had been thrust deep into his chest. Doctor Benedict, manacled by his hands and feet, was being led by the Brigadier to the metal pole that protruded from the centre of the heap. All around the Square, the lines of Doctors swayed and retreated as they struggled against their chains and shouted their protest. More and more Guardians were coming into the Square, keeping the old men back with the butts of their weapons, and the soldiers surrounding Ignatius pulled him towards the Old Hall at gunpoint.

"The first ruling to be passed is on Doctor Benedict," declaimed the Brigadier over the tumult. "Already found guilty of authorizing treason within the Inn and sentenced to destruction along with the fruit of his crimes."

Rooted to the spot with shock, Arlo watched as Benedict was forced on to the pyre, resisting his aggressors until a vicious blow in the face temporarily stunned him. At once a chain was wrapped around his arms and chest and padlocked. A Guardian stepped forward and thrust a lit taper into the bottom of the pyre. The next second a red strip of fire caught the heap of papers and flickered upwards with a sudden rush, wreathing Benedict in fire to the waist.

"No! Stop! Doctor!"

Without thinking, Arlo broke away from the guards and sprinted towards Benedict, only for the soldiers to leap after him and roughly drag him back. From the pyre a shower of sparks filled the air as the rest of the paper and tinder suddenly caught fire with a terrible roar. As the blaze shot up around him, Benedict raised his face to the sky. For a brief second Arlo could see him mouthing words, but he could not hear what he was saying. A bitter smell filled the air, and the next moment the old Doctor became a dark silhouette at the centre of the encircling flames.

Dazed with revulsion and grief, Arlo covered his face. The agony of the fire seemed to have taken root in his own bones. He could not breathe. The ache in his chest was overwhelming. A sharp blow to his temple dazed him and he sagged helplessly to one side. Immediately he felt himself being lifted up and a stunning jolt as he was thrown in a heap on to the floor of the military wagon. "Quickly!" shouted the Brigadier. "Take the Natural away! Immediately!"

Boots landed painfully on his legs as the soldiers leapt inside the wagon. One grabbed his wrists and lashed them behind his back. His head smacked against the boards as the wagon skidded along the stony path. The next second he felt the change of the ground underneath the wheels as it rolled out on the smooth stone of the City road. As the gates clanged shut behind the wagon, the clamour of the Doctors slowly receded, and was overtaken by the harsh, heaving sound of his own tears.

From behind the high walls of the Inn, the smoke from the bonfire rose like a tall stain spreading into the early morning sky, its bitter smell carrying on the wind for many miles. As the wagon disappeared rapidly towards the North Quarter along the deserted City street, charred fragments of parchment were already starting to flutter down on the breeze, falling like blackened, brittle snowflakes which shattered into ashes the moment that they touched the earth.

"I PROMISE YOU"

Morning in the Regions was a cheerless, cold hour during which the dim sun struggled to break through the dark fog that lay thick in the valleys. One Citizen-hour before sunrise, Captain Hacker took one last glance at the huddle of huts and mounds lying down the slopes in front of them, and turned to her men for a briefing. With the aid of their standard-issue thermometers she checked the temperature of each Guardian soldier and prescribed a dose of chorley for those who seemed in danger of hypothermia. Although the patrol was highly fit, they needed to be checked regularly for warning signs of illness, and Hacker was sharper than most at spotting if something was wrong.

"Now listen," said Hacker, indicating the sleeping village behind her. "There's a thousand registered inhabitants in Region Three. We've got back-up from the air for an Inspection on site. What we'll do is isolate this village from the others. It needs to be short, sharp, and effective, otherwise if the rest of 'em get down here we'll have a whole riot on our hands. Understand?"

The patrol nodded eagerly. This was their first stint of action for a few months, and for some it was the first real mission they had been on since enrolment. Hacker nodded in approval. "You know what to do. Now let's go!"

One hour later, the round-up had been completed, as quickly and efficiently as she had wished, without disturbing *the rest of the Region. Hacker peered with satisfaction at the lines of huddled Naturals that stood shaking before her. To her left stood the men of the village, mostly old and toothless, dressed in the rags that they salvaged from the debris of the river that poured out from the sewers of Genopolis. To the right were grouped the women and girls – why was it that there always seemed to be more women than men? – almost unrecognizable as female under their tangled hair and ragged clothes fashioned out of pieces of sacking. Surrounded by sharp bayonets at their backs, they stared hopelessly at the ground as the Guardians carried out the routine search of their houses. The noise of breaking and splintering drifted across the hushed square as the soldiers flung over beds, poked guns up into the rafters and overturned cupboards. Hacker paced through the silent lines, peering into faces to search for a clue, an expression, a movement that would betray the secrets of the abandoned man in the borderlands. She had been trained in the Inspectorate to look out for rapid blinking, shortness of breath, pallor, involuntary movements, twitching. Hacker knew the codes to Natural behaviour. These people were transparent when they had something to hide.*

Passing down a line in the female section, Hacker heard a slight intake of breath, so slight that it almost disappeared in the early morning wind. Turning slowly, she found herself face-to-face with a young woman with long tangled red hair. Underneath the shadow of her hood, her chin quivered slightly. It wasn't much, but it was enough. Hacker bent forward and stared into her face.

"Bring this one forward."

Two soldiers obeyed her request. Wisely, the girl offered no resistance, and instead hobbled, supported by the soldiers, to kneel, head bowed, in front of the lines of villagers. Hacker scanned the rows of frightened faces. It was rare that they operated alone. There would be an accomplice somewhere.

Her eyes rested on the old woman standing in the row behind. Though as decrepit and muddy a creature as the others, her rags were clogged with a thicker, darker mud. Hacker leaned forward and sniffed the air. There was no mistaking it – the dank, marshy smell of the river bed underneath the viaduct. She gazed at the old woman searchingly, and was rewarded by a mocking smile, the bright eyes staring back with a hint of malice. Despite herself, Hacker felt a sudden tremor. How dare the old Natural stare at her like that? She motioned over a soldier, who prodded the old woman forward with the butt of his gun until she tottered over to where the girl knelt, still gazing impassively at the earth.

"They don't look like a raiding party to me, captain," muttered the young corporal in her ear.

"Be quiet," snapped Hacker. Spies were spies, nonetheless. And Natural women were no less dangerous than men. But she could not control a flicker of doubt as she called forward a couple of corporals to search the captives. It was true that they didn't seem the type to be trained in explosives or mines, much less possess the physical capacity of the raiding parties from the lawless Natural tribes that attacked the goods carriers entering the City every week. As they knelt shivering in front of her, something about the guarded, limping way the young woman had moved pricked Hacker's curiosity.

"What's your name?" she asked the girl, squatting down in front of her.

The girl stared impassively back. "My name is Gea."

"Address and Natural registration number?"

"Third Region. Registered Natural 24971. I live here, in Scar Valley."

"Who is your family-unit?" asked Hacker.

The girl glanced at the old woman. "This is my mother."

"Who else?"

"Nobody," said Gea, looking down. "I have no one."

Hacker put the point of her baton underneath the girl's chin and tilted her face up again.

"Don't tell me lies, now. Are you married?"

Gea swallowed nervously. "No."

"What were you doing out in the Borderlands yesterday?"

"I wasn't in the Borderlands, ma'am."

"Why were you there, then?" asked Hacker, turning to the old hag next to her.

"She cannot speak, ma'am," said the girl. "She is deaf."

"What was your mother doing in the Borderlands, then?" pressed the captain.

The girl closed her eyes and shrugged. Hacker sighed.

"There's only one way to get to the bottom of this. Bring him out."

In a black daze, Angus felt himself being grasped by his bound legs, tugged painfully over the tussocked grass and thrown in a heap. The bag covering his head was wrenched off, and his first instinct was to clutch at his eyes to shield them from the light. From all around there rose a dull murmur as the villagers took in his bloodied and battered appearance for the first time, and right next to him he heard a soft gasp in his ear.

Looking up through his fingers, Angus saw Gea kneeling above him, the muzzle of a rifle pointing at her head. As their eyes met, she recoiled as if stung by a wasp. Next to her, Captain Hacker smiled slightly.

"You know him, then?"

Gea swallowed, her eyes panicked. The soldier next to her pushed her with the barrel of his rifle, demanding an answer.

"I do not know him, captain."

The next minute Gea crumpled as the soldier's rifle slammed into her side. She doubled up, retching. Without thinking, Angus threw himself forward to catch her, but the posse of soldiers surrounded him and dragged him away.

Hacker watched as the soldiers rained down blows and kicks on the foolish Natural. What else did he expect? She looked down at the sobbing girl at her feet, bent over, clutching at her stomach.

"Get me the medic," she growled at the corporal. "There's something here that I can't put my finger on. But I'm going to get to the bottom of it, no matter what."

Gea was examined inside a small earth hut that the soldiers had commandeered for any prisoners. Almost immediately the medic was able to make a report to his captain.

"A Natural pregnancy, ma'am. She would have had the

baby no more than twenty-four hours ago, carried to full term. I don't know where they've hidden it though. Killed it for food, most likely."

"No," said Hacker thoughtfully, "these people don't eat their children, rats though they are. And if it were born dead, why go all the way to the Borderlands to hide it? No, it's something else. I think they've sold it on the black market."

"Sold it? To whom?"

"That's what we've got to find out," said Hacker, "and fast. These three aren't just looking at the punishment for avoiding Registration, they're looking at the penalties for treason."

Hacker turned on her heel and set off at a brisk march towards the small hut where the rebel Naturals had been imprisoned. The soldier trotted after her.

"Why treason, captain?"

Hacker sneered. "Naturals are kept for the wealth of the Citizens, not for Naturals to profit by. Any child should have been Registered and delivered up for Regeneration. Anything otherwise is a betrayal of the City, and it's the duty of good Citizens like you and me to uphold it."

"What's going to happen to them now, captain?"

The soldier could not see the expression on his superior's face, but he heard the satisfaction in her words. "Oh, we'll get the truth out of them soon, don't you worry."

Inside the little hut it was pitch black and the stifling darkness made panic lurch in Angus's throat. He moistened his lips and for the first time was aware of the deep sunburn along the side of his face from his day spent in the open. A length of rope bound his arms to his sides, and the agony from his bruised ribs was a reminder of the brutal kicking the soldiers had given him.

A hand touched his arm, moved up his shoulder, and rested on his cheek. Angus turned, unbelieving, and felt Gea's thin body lean against him as she leaned over and kissed his forehead.

"I'm sorry," whispered Angus, into the darkness.

Gea pressed her lips to his forehead again. "Ssshh. Don't talk."

"It wasn't right," sobbed Angus. "We're a family. I shouldn't have done it. Please forgive me."

"There's nothing to forgive," whispered Gea. "There was nothing you could do. It was his only chance. I understand."

"I don't understand myself," muttered Angus. "But I promise you, Gea. If it's the last thing I do, I will find him again, I promise you."

FIVE

Arlo lay face down, his cheek pressed against the squeaking boards of the wagon as it swung sickeningly around yet another corner. The barrel of a rifle was still pushed into the back of his neck by the soldier who stood over him, but he was almost past caring. The horror of the Cleansing seemed to have paralysed him. He had not eaten anything since the banquet of the day before, and now an acid, burning sensation rose up in his throat, making him gag. Panicked, he struggled uselessly. His wrists were tied behind his back so tightly that his stomach was crushed against the floor of the wagon. He was going to be sick. He was going to choke –

Instinctively he tried to struggle, to turn his face to the side for air, but at that moment there was a sudden crunch and the wagon came shuddering to a stop. Abruptly the pressure on the back of his neck was released, and the canvas covering of the wagon was thrown open, shedding a splash of bright sunshine over him. Arlo screwed his eyes shut against the dazzle, but two soldiers were suddenly beside him, pulling him upright and turning him into the full glare of the midday sun.

"Easy now, easy!" a familiar voice was saying. "Let him get some air. Hasn't anybody got any water?"

Arlo squinted up at the speaker in disbelief. Directly in front of him, dressed in the same Guardian battledress as the others but with his fair hair hidden by a white commander's cap, knelt the librarian Kristo, a standard-issue Guardian carbine cocked over one arm, his shy stammer replaced by a crisp accent. "Arlo? Can you hear me?"

The soldier who had held him at gunpoint knelt next to him, unscrewed the stopper of her hip-flask and turned to Arlo. "Drink this, Natural."

Metal clinked against Arlo's teeth as the rim of the flask was pushed into his mouth. He choked and coughed, so confused that he did not register that his numbed and aching hands had been relieved of the cruel handcuffs. But the taste of the water in his parched mouth revived him and he gulped it down greedily.

The soldier who had forced him into the truck took off her cap and shook out a mane of curly brown hair which had been piled up underneath. Behind Kristo, Arlo could see, kneeling with their faces to the wall, a group of gagged and bound figures, stripped to their white underclothes and their arms behind their heads.

Over them stood another young Maian woman, also dressed in the brown Guardian uniform, a rifle trained on their backs.

"How long have we got, Sofia?" Kristo was asking the curly-haired soldier.

"About three day-hours before they return to the Palace and discover the disappearance of their Special Guard. But all is not well, Kristo. Doctor Benedict. . ."

Arlo struggled to speak. "Kristo – they killed . . . they killed –"

Kristo turned questioningly to the soldier Sofia, who nodded. "They Cleansed the Inn, Kristo. Doctor Benedict was burned for treason, and every book of learning along with him."

The gun clattered from Kristo's hand. "They *what*?"

"They killed him. I saw it with my own eyes."

"And Ignatius?" prodded Kristo urgently.

Sofia shook her head. "I do not know, Kristo. They took him away in chains. I did not see what happened."

Arlo could contain himself at the girl's calmness no longer, and burst out bitterly, "But why didn't you save Benedict too, then? Why didn't you take Ignatius? And why didn't you let me bring Rem?"

Sofia stared at him, puzzled by his words, and glanced over at Kristo uncertainly. "My orders were to disguise ourselves as Guardians and bring the Natural to safety, sir. The Abbess said that was the only mission. I knew of no other."

"That was the only mission," said Kristo shortly. "But

it appears that they had plans that we did not realize. Listen, Arlo. We do not have time to talk. Let me get you away from here, and then I will explain everything."

Kristo held out a hand. Arlo took it, too bemused by the past events to protest any longer. He struggled down the tailgate and saw that they had pulled off a deserted stretch of road into the cover of a group of ruined warehouses. A second wagon, the type that usually carried barrels of water from door to door, was parked next to them, with two Gemini wagon-pullers and a female driver sitting astride the helm. "Right Arlo. In you go. There's a small place at the back where you can sit."

Arlo had trouble getting past the two large water-barrels. There was only just enough space for him to squeeze around the side of the first, but as he reached the second, he saw that it was only half a barrel, a shell that had been bolted into the floorboards, an ingeniously-contrived hiding place providing a small niche where a person could secrete themselves unobserved – to a casual eye. But there was to be even less space than he had imagined, for the curly-haired soldier leaped nimbly up beside him, sliding her slender body in the tiny space opposite him. Kristo rearranged the canvas covering over both of them and the barrels, and leant in for one last word.

"Arlo, my comrade Sofia will now take you to the Inn of the Maia, where the Abbess is waiting for you. I will rejoin you there very shortly. But in that time, you will obey Sofia in everything. Do I make myself clear?"

Arlo nodded, dumbly.

"And the Special Guard, Kristo?" whispered Sofia, nodding towards the group of bound and gagged Guardians who were now being herded at gunpoint into the wagon that Arlo had arrived in. "What is the plan for them?"

"I will take care of them," said Kristo, shortly. "Give me one day-hour."

Usha lay awake, blinking into the stuffy darkness of the cellar, the soft snores of the Kids rising around her.

How could she have been so *stupid*? Everything had been going so well, until she had tried to stop Ozzie taking the shawl. Why hadn't she just gone along with it? Why hadn't she managed to just keep her mouth *shut*?

And now they had no rations for the day, and no hope for any more during the rest of the week, because, as Ozzie had said, it was all her fault that the Guardians would be watching out for them now. From the pile of smashed food that they'd left in the East Quarter, the patrol would have traced their steps back to the warehouses of the South Quarter, maybe even seen the small marks of their presence – forced lids of crates, scrapes and scratches from the grappling hooks – and lie in wait for them the next time they returned. "Nobody's to go out at night for a while," Mindie had ordered them, firmly. "It's not worth it." Now they could only rely on the day-shift's begging and scavenging, with all its accompanying dangers and difficulties of being arrested for the tiny amount of food that this would bring in.

Usha sat up, and instantly felt her injured wrist slide awkwardly out of the sling. Carefully, with her other hand, she supported and guided it back into position, but even then she could feel the bones grating against each other underneath the skin. She could see clearly enough that the hand was bent outwards and no longer lay straight with her arm. This was serious. She couldn't go on like this. Even if her wrist eventually healed, her hand would be twisted so badly out of shape as to be unusable.

Rubbing her forehead with her good hand, she tried to think logically. Despite her condition, there must be some place that she could find food. She owed it to the Kids, at least, after spoiling their expedition so catastrophically. Usha reached for her tin cup of water, but someone had already drunk it, and the water-barrel in the corner was dry and smelly.

Then she remembered her idea of the night before. The Citizen's coat and headscarf that she had taken from Auntie. Surely they would bring in a little food, at least enough to tide them over until they could chance another run down to the docks?

It seemed to take an age for her to get to her feet, with only one arm to balance herself, and pick her way over the slumbering forms that surrounded her to where her coat and scarf lay hooked on a nail. As she did so, Ozzie turned in his sleep and muttered something. She froze for a second in case he woke up and saw her, but then the regular sound of his breathing reassured her. Stepping over him gently, in another moment she reached the trapdoor, slid it open quietly, and dangled her legs down the hole.

It was a difficult manoeuvre to swing herself down only half-supported, and she stumbled on the slimy floor of the passageway as she landed. Straightening up, she checked herself over quickly, but nothing further appeared to be wrong. As she walked, she found that with her injured arm, her sense of balance and space had also been affected. She was bumping against the walls far more often than before.

Finally, she found herself by the back door grating, and after a slight struggle, managed to unhook it and heave herself up and out into the early sunlight. As she straightened up unobserved in the shadow of the tower, she heard the first rumbles of the trader-carts rolling up and down to the grimy barter-markets that lay deep in the heart of the East Quarter.

In the jolting darkness of the tiny water-wagon, Arlo sat with his knees drawn up to his chin, his face sullenly downcast. Opposite him crouched Sofia, swaying to the rhythm of the wheels, her face thrown into half-shadow underneath the long locks of hair that flowed down over her stolen battledress, a rifle laid carelessly across her knees. From beneath his lowered eyelids, Arlo observed her cautiously, taking the opportunity, despite the darkness, to look carefully at the first woman he had ever seen at such close range.

As if feeling his eyes on her, Sofia turned and looked at him sharply. "What is it, Natural? Why are you looking at me like that?"

"I'm not looking," lied Arlo, a feeling of warm blood rising unexpectedly to his cheeks and neck. For the first time he was grateful for the darkness of the wagon so that the Maian could not see the colour of his face. Suddenly the yawning hole in his stomach opened. "I'm just tired and hungry."

"Tired and hungry. . ." repeated Sofia, cautiously, as if she were unsure of the words. "You mean you must nutrate and rest?"

"Yes," said Arlo, hiding a smile. He had not realized how odd his everyday routine must sound outside the walls of the Inn and the luxuries of the Doctors. He felt a sudden pang as a picture of Benedict's face rose up before him, and he blinked it away determinedly.

Sofia looked puzzled, checking her timepiece. "But it is not yet the breakfast hour by my watch."

"Oh, I don't need a timepiece to know when it's time to eat," said Arlo, his hopes of food slowly subsiding.

The Maian looked at him, interestedly. "Naturals must have many advantages, or so it seems."

"I suppose so," answered Arlo, confusedly, although he could not see the intense hunger that was ravaging his insides as an advantage by any means.

Suddenly the wheels jolted to a stop and a command rang out from the other side of the canvas. "Halt! Who goes there?"

Instantly, Arlo found himself pushed into the curve of the false water-barrel, his arms over his head. Next to him there was a soft click as the Maian released the safety catch on her rifle, and took careful aim at the rear of the wagon. "Stay down, Arlo," murmured Sofia.

The Maian driver who had been guiding the wagon raised her voice. "We have urgent water-supplies for the Inn of the Maia, brother. We have already been delayed and the Abbess is expecting important guests. We beg you of your Citizenly goodwill, not to detain us further."

"Special Orders, I'm afraid," said the voice, and there was the sound of iron-heeled boots marching briskly towards the wagon. "Big crackdown on traitors going on this morning. Can't leave anything to chance."

The next second a bright crack of sunlight split the darkness of the water-wagon, and the outline of a Guardian's head appeared at the rear of the wagon. He looked around each side, tapped the nearest barrel with his gun, and listened to the sloshing of the contents inside. Shaking with fear and fatigue, Arlo's teeth began to chatter and he quickly pushed his hand over his mouth to still the noise. During the inspection of the wagon, the Maian's rifle was steadily trained on the oblivious soldier, watching him intently from the shadows as he leaned over and pushed idly at the false barrel behind which they lay. Bolted into the floor, the barrel did not move, but apparently the soldier understood this as being full, for he grunted in satisfaction, leaned back and let the flap of the canvas fall back into place. He gave the tailgate a slap and turned away. "All in order, Sister. Drive on."

Inside the wagon, Arlo's breath, held for thirty agonizing seconds, exploded in a great sigh, as the wagon began to move again. But he noticed that all the time, the Maian's hand had been rock-steady on the trigger of the gun, and remained so as she watched through the flaps of the canvas even as they drove away and through the gates of the Inn of the Maia.

A stench of sour vegetables and old cooking oil hung heavy in the streets of the East Quarter. Though the sun was barely up, Lower Citizens were already dragging their bags of belongings to barter. Here it was much less organized than outside the Guildhall, noted Usha as she followed them, there were no proper Citizenly barter-circles forming, instead people seemed already to know who to look for and who to exchange with. A lot of the trading seemed to be taking place behind doors and away from public view; people carrying sacks of possessions briefly disappeared down alleyways, to return triumphantly bearing boxes of provisions and stowing them craftily in covered wagons that were dragged hurriedly away.

As she passed through the crowd with her coat and headscarf draped over her shoulder to hide her sling, dirty wizened faces gazed back at her suspiciously. This area rarely saw a stranger, and when it did they remembered it. Her colouring and hair clearly marked her out as a Middle Citizen, and although many of those present might never have encountered a real living Gemini, there was something about her eyes that made them look twice, and it would not be long before they put two and two together. Perhaps it had not been the best idea to come here, thought Usha confusedly. These people looked the sort to blow the whistle on you, and if the Guardians were already out looking for the gang of kids who had raided the warehouses, or if they had heard that a runaway Gemini was on the loose in Genopolis, or if they managed to trace the coat and headscarf back to its original owner. . .

No time for thoughts like these, she told herself sternly. Think logically. There are more important things at stake here than you.

Pulling herself together, she approached an old man standing behind a wagon full of boxes of egg-powder and politely held out the coat for his consideration. He blinked, and wrinkled his nose up at it in disgust.

"What d'ye want me to do wiv' that?" he asked scornfully, poking at the fine weave with a dirty forefinger. "Waste of me bleeding time."

"But it's real wool," said Usha encouragingly, "one of the best fabrics in Genopolis. You could trade this up at Central Square for three boxes of potatoes."

"Then why dontcha bleeding go up there, then," said

the old man sourly, turning away and leaving Usha standing bewildered on the pavement. An old woman, huddled on the corner, clutched at her hem.

"Ah wouldn't a-go up ter Central Square, if ah was you, Sister. They say there's all sorts of trouble goin' on at the Inn of Court this mornin'."

Usha considered. For the first time in her life, all her logical decisions had come to nothing. Things were getting desperate, but she had little choice. If she went to Central Square she would be twice as likely to be recognized as the fugitive from yesterday. If, as seemed likely, the scissor-man had been reported missing, then her time as a free Gemini would be running out. But whether she had days, hours or minutes left, she could not tell.

Quickly she turned and made her way down the nearest alleyway.

The wheels of the wagon skidded on uneven stone, and drew to a stop. There was a creaking noise and a clang of heavy gates shutting.

It was a haunting smell that first caught Arlo's attention as he struggled stiffly down the tailgate into a small cobbled courtyard, a faint, delicate scent like honey blown on the breeze. He stepped down into a gatehouse courtyard, smaller and darker than the Inn of Court. The two Gemini, their tunics stained dark from their exertions of pulling the wagon, stood at attention. Behind them, two Maia, dressed in green ceremonial cloaks, pushed a heavy caber across the doors to bar them. Arlo breathed a sigh of relief as he stretched his aching body and stood taking in the silence around him, a sudden oasis of peace in the whirlwind of the last twenty-four hours.

Like its counterpart the Inn of Court, the Maian Inn was an ancient building built around a central courtyard and gatehouse, but from there, any resemblance ended. Where the Inn of Court rambled in all directions in a motley collection of stone, brick, leaded windows and ivy, the Maian Inn was smaller, built of dove-grey marble polished to a gentle gleam, its stones laced with darker streaks that threaded through it like veins. Around the courtyard, tall graceful pillars with ornate wreaths of flowers and fruit chiselled at their crest ran in an open colonnade where two could walk together. But it was the centre of the courtyard that caught Arlo's attention and his breath, for he had never seen anything like it before.

Sunlight glittered on a wide, circular pool of water, bubbling out of a white-stone rockery covered with green moss. From its centre shot jets of water, sometimes blown on the wind and arching high into the air where they fragmented like a shower of beads, sparkling jewel-like in the sunshine before falling back into the pool beneath. But it was also the noise that stirred something in him, the tinkling splash of the falling droplets forming a music that he seemed to have heard somewhere before, once, many years ago. As he took a step towards it, he caught again the smell of honey blown on the wind, and saw that the rockery was entwined with tiny white flowers that bobbed and swayed, releasing their delicate scent into the breeze. Arlo had never seen so much water in his life before, let alone water for pleasure alone. Back at the Inn they had been rationed to one small bowl a day. He walked closer for a better look.

"It is called a fountain," said a low voice from behind him. "We have the good fortune to have a secret clear-spring bubbling at its source in our gardens. In times gone by to be near running water was seen to be healing to the soul."

Arlo turned, and saw the Abbess who he remembered from the Anointment Ceremony, straightening up from a flower bed where she had been kneeling unobserved. Exactly as yesterday, her long white hair was swept up on top of her head, and her green eyes smiled across at him in recognition. Yet now she dressed humbly in a long, patched shirt and shapeless trousers, and her old fingers that held a basket of seedlings and a small trowel were stained with crumbs of earth.

Arlo thought of the Regis, with his clippers, wires and weights, bending over his tiny captive forest, and could not repress a shudder. Yet here the flowers of the Maia grew where they would, either drooping like rain from baskets hanging from the colonnades, or rambling around the fountain and the borders of the grassy courtyard in sprinkles of white, gold and purple.

"Welcome, Arlo," said the Abbess, gazing at him with the same searching look. "It has been a long time, hasn't it?"

Arlo bowed awkwardly, in the same manner that he had seen the Doctors greet the Maian procession, but in his fatigue and dizziness he lost his balance and nearly fell flat on his face in front of her. From over his shoulder he could hear a ripple of quiet amusement, and as he quickly straightened up, he saw that the colonnades were now thronged with slender, long-haired figures, draped in the same mossy green as yesterday, gazing at him and murmuring amongst themselves. Again he felt the blood rush to his face and his neck felt hot. He bit his lip.

"Have a care, Sisters," said the Abbess, raising her voice to the crowd. "Our young visitor is in need of food and rest and I would like to see him shown the hospitality of our table. Grant him the courtesy of privacy also, for he has seen in two days what many do not see in a lifetime."

Obediently the crowd dispersed to their business, though a couple lingered curiously, pretending a sudden interest in the fountain or the clear sky overhead, but soon the rippling music of the fountain echoed uninterrupted across the courtyard once more. There was something about its tone that touched a spring deep inside Arlo, releasing a feeling of such peace and comfort that he felt that he could throw himself down next to the honey-blossoms and almost forget about the terrors of the morning.

The Abbess noted his face with a sharp eye. "I see that there is much that weighs on your mind. But first the body must be refreshed before the tongue can speak. Eat first, and we will share our troubles later."

"The table is ready, Natural, hurry up!" called Sofia from behind him, opening wide a door that led down a shady stone corridor.

"His name is Arlo," said the Abbess, gently yet reprovingly.

The younger Maian bowed her head, accepting the rebuke. "Your pardon, Arlo. Please follow me."

"When he has quite finished, show him to my study," said the Abbess. "We do not have much time, and there are still many things that Arlo must learn before the next stage of his journey."

Usha was almost back at the grating when she heard someone calling behind her, a deep voice that was garbled and distorted as it echoed down the narrow alleyway.

"Sister! Sister! Wait!"

She turned and saw a man waving at her from the shade of an overhanging dressmaker's awning. He smiled and took a step forward so that the weak morning sunlight caught his face. Unusually for a Citizen, he had a beard and slightly long hair. He used two strips of cord to keep his trousers up, over which his fat belly hung, peeping out of his shirt, which was grimy with ancient stains.

"Hear you've got summat ter barter?" he said. His accent was a strange one as well, its syllables roughened and over-articulated, as if the language of Genopolis was not his native speech. "It's difficult to exchange round here. People only want to barter with 'oo they know."

She took a quick glance round, uncertainly. The alleyway was deserted, and only the cries of the traders echoed faintly through from the neighbouring streets. The man took another step towards her. "Maybe I can help you, yes?"

Usha considered. No harm in trying. She walked towards him, still holding the cloak and scarf, but as she drew near they slipped to the floor, revealing her sling. The man raised his eyebrows slightly at the sight of her injured arm.

"If you are having . . . difficulty, I know someone who would be pleased to help you . . . for a price."

"No thank you," said Usha shortly, bending down awkwardly to pick up the clothes, but at that moment a shadow fell over her as a third person joined them. The man turned and smiled. "Let me introduce you to my sister, Zenna, an experienced scissor-woman. But she also has a good head for business, if you prefer to barter."

Usha looked up and caught her breath. A woman stood there, tall and slender, with delicate, slanted features, and long hair so black it seemed almost blue. She stared as the woman knelt down gracefully next to her to gather up the fallen clothes.

"These are good quality," she said in a clear voice that

was tinged with the same accent as the man's. "You are expecting a high exchange for these, yes?"

"Yes I am," said Usha firmly, although she had secretly little idea what value clothes like this would command. "I am asking for three bags of potatoes, or any other vegetable or fruit."

Zenna smiled, and her teeth glinted white in the strengthening sun. "How unfortunate. We have only two large bags of dried nutrient powder. And you seem so very sure that nothing else will do."

Usha deliberated, torn. Dried nutrient powder was the staple diet of much of Lower Genopolis. Some Lower Citizens existed only on powdered food, mixed with water into an unappetizing, if nutritious, soup or drink. Each Citizen was supposed to have a daily ration, containing exactly the right amount of vitamins and other minerals to keep them healthy, but it had a bitter, corrosive taste if eaten dry and as such was the lowest unit of barter in Genopolis. At Auntie's house she had blended the powder in Auntie's tea or soup, and although Auntie had always insisted that Usha also take a daily portion, it made the food taste so gritty that Usha had usually ended up chucking hers out into the garden. On reflection, it might have been this which had made the shrubbery grow so thick and wild. . .

But even nutrient powder was better than nothing, and how could she turn down such an offer when there was nothing else?

Slowly, she nodded. Zenna folded the clothes over her

arm with satisfaction and turned away, beckoning Usha to follow her. "Excellent. Come with me now. Our quarters are very close to here. It should only take a few minutes."

Heaped on the plain white-wood trestle tables of the Maian dining hall was a plate of scrambled eggs, a bowl of porridge (which Arlo pushed away), white cakes and honey, a large jug of lemonade and a bunch of purple grapes. Despite his tiredness and sorrow, Arlo sat down and ate ravenously. But even in the middle of his hunger he was embarrassingly conscious of Sofia sitting opposite him and observing him as closely as he had looked at her in the wagon. To prevent himself from blushing again, he looked around the bare white walls to where a huge wooden plaque was raised upon the wall, nearly five arm-spans in each direction.

At first he thought it must be an enormous timepiece, or perhaps a sundial, but on closer inspection he could see that it was a circle divided into eighths around a central point. At each quarter it had engraved GREATER SABBATS, and halfway between each quarter there was a small division entitled LESSER SABBATS. Around it were carved flowers, fruits, animals and symbols.

Sofia followed his puzzled glance. "That is our Wheel of the Year, Arlo. In ancient times, centuries before the Apocalypse, the Celtic Naturals regarded it as their calendar, whose seasons – *sabbats* – followed a cycle of death and rebirth. They worshipped the fertility of the land and the body, for the land meant life. Later beliefs, though, placed man in dominion over the land and saw nature's fertility as a menace to be tamed and suppressed. And it was not as now, where nothing grows save in the laboratories of Pharmopolis, whenever it is commanded to. There was a time for planting, and a time for reaping, a time to die and a time to be born. These days everyone remembers those Naturals as the destroyers of our world, but there was once a time when the word Natural meant exactly the opposite."

Arlo gazed closer while Sofia spelt out and explained the names that he did not recognize. As it was early March, they were still in Imbolc, the season of spring, germination and new growth. From the first day of May would come the season of Beltane, the summer season of fertility and birth, whose summer solstice was celebrated as Lithia, or Midsummer's Day, the longest day of the year.

His birthday! Something tugged deep inside Arlo, but he showed no sign and listened intently as Sofia read on, welcoming the attention of her young listener. After Beltane came the harvest season of Lammas, while the last quarter of the wheel was Samhain, the season of winter, of darkness and death, and the long sleep of the land until it awoke again with the first buds of Imbolc.

A bell rang and Sofia roused herself and stood up. "You have eaten enough, Natural? I mean, Arlo? The Abbess is waiting for you."

In a street full of barred and shuttered doors, the foreign woman stopped in front of a dark archway, reached inside and unlocked a metal gate.

"If you can wait here one second. . ."

"No thank you," said Usha firmly. Long experience of bartering had taught her well. If they thought that she would just stand there patiently while they ran off with her goods, they could think again. She was no fool. "I can come in and help you carry the bags, perhaps."

"Good idea," said the man, holding out his hand to her. "You are very cautious. May I have the pleasure of knowing your name before I leave?"

"U. . ." began Usha, and corrected herself hurriedly. "Um. . . My name is . . . Cybella."

"Pleased to meet you, Sister Um-Cybella," smiled the man. "My name is Zadoc. You will be safe in Zenna's hands. I am sure that she will give you the value that you deserve."

Usha shook his hand and gladly dropped it. As Zadoc moved, a smell like sour onions came from beneath his stained shirt. She was so keen to see him leave that she waited until he had turned the corner before she followed the woman through the metal gate and into a small stone courtyard.

But there was no one there. She paused momentarily, perplexed.

"Over here," Zenna's melodic voice floated from a small passageway, almost invisible behind a thorny briar. "First turning on your left."

Cautiously, Usha rounded the corner, but all she could see was a narrow, shadowy lane passing between two high walls. Zenna was nowhere to be seen. "Hello?" she called, uncertainly.

"Just down here, Usha," continued Zenna. "Go to the end and take the first doorway on your left."

Puzzled, Usha started forward, then hesitated. Something was not as it should be, but she could not put her finger on it. "Where are you?" she called, and her voice bounced back to her, fragmented and jarring, from the high walls overhead.

"Come inside," echoed Zenna's voice softly. "Two bags of nutrient powder, didn't we agree?"

As Zenna spoke, Usha spied the corner of a small grey sack of powder leaning against a door-jamb. As she picked it up, no easy task with only one good arm, she quickly checked that the Pharmopolis seal and cord were still intact around it. They were. "But, Zenna? There's only one bag here."

"The other's here," came Zenna's voice. "Just come behind the door."

But as Usha took two paces more into the shadows, something thick and heavy descended over her head and face, choking her. She tried to cry out but the smell of sour onions was suddenly all around her, making her gag. Immediately her legs were swept from under her and a pair of strong hands seized her, pinioning her arms to her sides. Before she fully realized what was happening, she found herself dumped unceremoniously face down on the dusty floor, while strong fingers gripped her kicking ankle and fastened something cold and metallic around it with a click. The next moment she was abruptly released, and through the all-enveloping folds of the sack, she heard the clang of a gate closing and the noise of a heavy bolt slamming home.

The study of the Abbess was empty when Sofia showed Arlo in. It was a long low room, open on one side to a balcony that overlooked the courtyard and fountain beneath. But where Ignatius's study had been full of books, and Benedict's full of test-tubes and scientific apparatus, the Abbess's study was bare, save for a desk, and a circle of chairs, though the walls were painted with a fine and delicate mural of shapes, both human and animal, running around the study.

As he passed to the balcony, he could see right down into the bubbling source of the fountain. The next second he caught his breath. A dark shadow had curved into the bowl of the fountain, flickered in the sunlight, and just as quickly, disappeared. Arlo straightened up in surprise, and saw the Abbess entering the study. Almost lost for words, he could only point. "Look! There's something in the fountain, and I think it's alive!"

The Abbess smiled, joining him at the balcony rail. "They are called *fish*, Arlo. Sometimes, when the hour is right, they come to the surface to bask in the sunshine. Do not let your shadow fall over the fountain, or you will startle them."

A second curving shape broke the surface of the water, leaving a small pop of bubbles in its wake, and Arlo could see the glitter of a skin that seemed both hard and yet rippling, propelled in a swift, darting motion by small feather-like shapes that fanned out from the centre of its body.

They watched the fish in companionable silence for a while until a bubble of memory rose up from Arlo's past, and the words that she had said at his first entrance to the Inn rang in his ears. All the strange recollections since he had entered the Inn – the smell of honey, the sound of the falling water – suddenly fitted together.

"Didn't you say," he asked the Abbess, "when I arrived, that it had been a long time? Because there's something about this place that I remember, something about the way it smells." He winced as he realized what he had said. "I didn't mean it like that ... I just thought ... I feel I've been here before, somehow, sometime."

"Indeed you have," said the Abbess, smiling. "It has been more than ten years since I first held you on my knee next to this fountain, Arlo. I remember it as clear as if it were yesterday. It was the only thing that would stop you from crying, and of course, nobody could understand what was causing such an Outbreak. I must admit, when our small circle first had the plan to look after a baby Natural, we had little idea how difficult it would be. Our Citizen babies have a routine; we can care for them by the hour, give them the right foods and the right amount of water, but you were different. Though you were fed, clean and healthy, you still cried, illogically, we thought. None of us had any sleep for weeks. But in time, we learned your needs, and along this courtyard you learned to take your first steps and say your first words."

Arlo gazed at her entranced. "And . . . and who gave me my name, Abbess?"

"I named you, Arlo," said the Abbess, smiling. "Your name means *homestead,* or *fortification* in the ancient tongue of the Celts, and it was my hope that you would be one day able to find your true home.

"When you were nearly two Citizen-years old, Doctor Benedict arranged for you to be brought to the Inn of Court, where Ignatius had been preparing your arrival. I have never forgotten how you screamed as the litter took you away and how small you looked. But during all this time I have never stopped thinking about you, and of course, Ignatius has always kept me up to date with your doings."

At the mention of Ignatius, the black cloud flowed back over Arlo again, and suddenly the hope seemed gone out of everything. But the Abbess noted Arlo's face. "Sofia has told me what happened to Ignatius and Benedict this morning, Arlo. But you should not blame yourself. Benedict did not suffer, Arlo. In fact, you bore his pain for him."

"But it was my fault," said Arlo dully. "I betrayed them."

Before he realized what he was doing, he found himself telling her all about the Regis and what had happened in the study. The eyes of the Abbess were gentle and understanding, and did not flinch even when the long-expected Outbreak started to happen. As Arlo blew his nose, she took his hand in hers.

"Pain is your greatest weakness in times like these, it is true, Arlo. But there is a way to conquer pain, and the fear of pain. In centuries gone by, some Naturals achieved a state of concentration so deep that they could even walk over hot coals without feeling it. Would you like me to show you how?"

All around Usha was blackness. The thick rag that had been tied about her head had totally blocked out her sight, and another fold had been forced around her mouth, gagging her. Coughing and choking, she tore at the material that stifled her and managed to pull it free from her mouth so that she could breathe freely at last. Where was she? What did they want from her?

With the tips of the fingers of her good hand, she reached out cautiously and touched a metal bar. Less than a hand-span apart came a second bar, and a third, all riveted deep into a plank. She got to her knees, and traced the bars upwards until they joined a rough ceiling, only an arm's length above her. Usha needed no more to tell her that she was lying in a small cage, not even large enough to stand up in.

Slowly, pace by pace, she crawled from one side to

another. At her feet there was a soft clink, and the metal brace on her ankle tightened. She was able to crawl only four paces in any direction, before she came up against the bars. Around her the air was rough, cold and slightly wet as if she was underground, much like the inside of the cellar where the Kids lived. At the thought of the Kids, an odd sensation moved in Usha's stomach, but there was no time to think about them now.

Through the all-enveloping folds of the cloth, she could hear the distant sound of voices coming closer.

"Twenty boxes," said a rough voice. "Twenty boxes, and that's my final offer."

"Come on now, Merco," replied a silky female voice that Usha recognized as Zenna's. "She is fit and young. She is worth twice that!"

"I bid twenty-five," drawled another, genteel male voice, which Usha noted in surprise, had a Higher Citizen accent. "Twenty-five, and first option for the second."

"Twenty-five boxes! How very generous, Governor!" replied Zenna, sweetly.

"But she is already spoiled," said the first man who had been addressed as Merco, sullenly. "Her left wrist is broken. She has only half the use."

"That will heal," countered Zenna, and to Usha it sounded almost as if she were laughing. "Surely you cannot be too worried about injuries, in *your* line of business?"

"If you are uncertain, Merco, I will increase my

offer," said the second voice, smoothly. "The Regis has authorized me to go up to thirty boxes."

"Forty boxes then, Zenna," snapped Merco, "and you patch that wrist up."

Zenna coughed delicately. "Governor Angelo? Can you match our honourable acquaintance's offer?"

"Unfortunately, I cannot," said the Governor, scornfully. "For that price, the Regis could get a fresh Gemini straight from the pharms."

Usha shrank into the floor and buried her head in her arms. But there was a short pause before Zenna spoke. "Well then. Forty boxes and the wrist repaired? I think that we have a deal, Merco."

"Put her in the warehouse," said the gruff voice, "along with the other cargo that you sold me earlier. I'll be around to collect them shortly."

Arlo gazed at the Abbess. Learn how to control pain? Was this *possible*? But from her expression it did not appear that she was mocking him.

In the furthest corner of the study stood a stone alcove lined with bricks, and on its floor lay a heap of black rocks. The Abbess took his hand and led him to kneel before it, produced a small vial and drenched the rocks in a sweet-scented oil. From her dress she took a tinderbox, struck a flame and dropped it on them. Suddenly the rocks began to glow red as a flamelike a candle flickered around them. Arlo looked on in amazement. Stones that burned – which he remembered used to be called coal – were so rare these days that only once had he seen something similar burning in Benedict's study. The flames grew so strong that the boy could feel the flickering heat on his face. The Abbess put her hand on his shoulder.

"Kneel down, Arlo, and look into the fire. Concentrate on your breathing, and count very, very slowly. Clear your mind of everything else."

Arlo gazed at the centre of the fire, fascinated. As he counted, the room around him seemed to become dark and, as he looked at the glowing cavern, he felt suddenly tiny, as if he was hovering in space over a strange world made of liquid fire. From far away he heard the Abbess speaking.

"Now put your hand into the fire."

Unthinking, Arlo obeyed, stretching his hand out in front of him. Incredibly, the fire felt cool, not hot. He felt as if he was standing at the edge of a long curved tunnel, whose walls rippled around him, but whether with fire or water, he could not say. Hesitantly, he took one step, and then another down the fiery path. Melting rivers coursed along the floor in front of him.

A third step, and then a fourth. Now he could hear the sound of his own heart beating loud and echoing in his chest. It seemed as if he was completely inside the fire, but still cool and untouched.

Then, from what seemed like a long way away, he smelt a faint smell of burning. Suddenly he realized that what he was doing was impossible, and a terrible fear overcame him. He could hear a voice speaking at first distantly, and then urgently. Something grabbed him by the wrist and he was spun sideways into the dripping wall.

Arlo screamed, and wrenched his hand away from the blazing coals. Instantly he realized that it had all been a hallucination, a trance. He was still kneeling in front of the fire, but his palm felt like a hole had been drilled through to the bone. Dimly he was aware of the Abbess holding his wrist and pressing a pad of something cold against his hand. Her voice broke soothingly through his pain.

"It's all right, Arlo, I'm here. Breathe deep. Do not worry."

Arlo couldn't manage to answer. Sweat poured down his forehead and he sobbed convulsively.

"It will pass," said the Abbess, gently tending to his palm. "Let me give you some more ice. For a moment, you managed to override centuries of Natural learning, that fire burns, so keep away. Yet you managed to change the perception of your brain and withstand what should have been great pain for almost three minutes!"

Eventually Arlo felt a comforting numbness seeping through to the pain in his hand. Around him the swirling room reassembled itself into the familiarity of desk, chair and the Abbess, watching him carefully.

"The thing that impresses me," she said, her eyes sparkling with excitement, "is the extent to which you, a

Natural, were able to bear quite severe pain. In fact, if I am not mistaken, it was only when your fear started to rise that you could not manage to keep it under control. Your mind can control your body, Arlo. It is the most powerful tool you possess. If you practise this, then no Citizen can ever control you."

Arlo examined his palm. The skin had been reddened, but contrary to his imagination it was not charred or black. What if the Abbess was right? What if he could become just like one of those Citizens?

What if he could become even *better* than them?

Usha flattened herself against the rough bottom of the cage for support as she felt herself being lifted up. Helplessly she slithered against the bars as the cage tilted suddenly to one side. Where were they taking her?

"Wait!" came Zenna's voice. "Help me, Zadoc. You're going too fast."

The cage rocked to and fro before it was steadied and balanced by Zadoc's muscular arms. Again his smell of sour onions rose around Usha, sickening her. She buried her nose in her sleeve.

"But, Zen, we were meant to go back to the pharms tonight," grumbled Zadoc. "Why d'ye have to go window-shopping now of all times?"

"We must take opportunities where we find them," said Zenna, puffing as she strove to keep pace with him and keep up her end of the cage. "In any case you must collect the payment from Merco. He already owes us for the other cargo we have in storage, and I do not propose to leave without it."

"Can't we collect it on the next trip?" argued Zadoc. "Merco isn't going anywhere. We know where the Circus is, well enough."

"You shall wait another day in Genopolis," said Zenna, authoritatively. "Tonight I will leave by barge from the south-eastern cove by the port at three night-hours when the tide is high. I am a businesswoman, Zadoc, and my time is precious."

Usha lay quiet, but inwardly her mind was spinning. *Smugglers!*

Auntie had often warned her about smugglers from Pharmopolis, but she had never thought of ever encountering one . . . or two. Though authorized food only came from the pharm barges that sailed into the docks, tales abounded of cheaper (and worse) produce heaped in grimy barges that punted quietly over the shallows to the City's south-eastern side. Often you would make what you thought was a good bargain in the barter-circle, only to discover later on that your exchange was actually partially rotten, or a reject, or damaged in some way. "Always try to make a good bargain, Usha," Auntie used to say, "but beware of bargains that are too good to be true – because they probably are."

But it seemed that the smugglers were bringing in things other than food to the City, and even trading to Higher Citizens, if Zenna's words were true. And who exactly Merco was, or what Zadoc meant by the *Circus*, Usha had no idea.

The cage jolted wildly as her bearers crashed through two enormous doors that swung shut behind them with a boom. From the echo around her and a thin breeze blowing from one side Usha judged that she had been taken into a large, cavernous space. The next moment the cage-bearers dropped their burden with a jarring crash on the rocky floor, and Usha was left alone in the shadows, listening to the sound of their receding footsteps.

The Abbess touched his shoulder gently. "Listen now, Arlo. Events have moved quicker than we thought. I have summoned the members of our Circle here for a secret meeting to decide what must be done. You need not fear anyone you meet here. They have been part of the Experiment even before your birth, and many of them know you, though you do not know them. They are the other members of our Circle of Learning, a group dedicated to knowledge, but now called the traitorous Resistance by the Governors of Genopolis."

Half an hour later, the Abbess's study seemed full of people. Arlo crouched in wonder by the fire as one by one the members of the Circle entered and were introduced to him. Apart from the Abbess and Sofia, four other Maia ranging from young to old; two respectable-looking supply-merchants from Pharmopolis called Tariq and Sasha, both Middle-Citizens; a dark-skinned schoolmaster named Tutu from the Academy, a female architect named Tarissa; two scientists, brother and sister, the first Citizen-family that Arlo had ever seen, named Yoshi and Yuma; and finally an older, rather rumpled-looking gentleman called Sir Herbert whom everyone else seemed to treat with the greatest Citizenly respect. Some – the men especially – stared at him with fascination as they were introduced and cautiously extended their hands to shake his in the polite Citizen-gesture as if they thought he might bite. Others – the Maians and Yoshi and Yuma – seemed to know him already, and greeted him enthusiastically with a warmth he had never known, even in the Inn. It was bewildering to feel himself part of their group. If only Ignatius, Benedict and perhaps even Doctor Sheridan could have been there. . .

Suddenly the door flew open and Kristo, the last member of the Circle, entered, now almost unrecognizable in nondescript Middle-Citizen clothes. Gone was the mild-mannered persona of the stammering librarian of the Inn, and in its place was a stern-faced man whom Arlo hardly recognized. With a few curt words he called the meeting to order and outlined the events of the previous night, including the murder of Benedict, the capture of Ignatius and the rescue of Arlo to the horrified Circle.

"But Ignatius, Kristo?" called Tutu. "Why couldn't you save him too?"

Kristo shook his head. "Ignatius was convinced that someone must stay and counter the Regis on his own terms, stand up for the Experiment in public, not sneak away like a thief in the night. Yet they moved faster than us, to find a way of condemning both him and Benedict with treason in the meantime.

"Now, my fellow members. We have very little time to decide. I am glad that we have all had the chance to meet Arlo and see the cause that we have been fighting for. Some of you have been involved in the Experiment from the very beginning. Others have joined us because their paths have led them here. But ultimately, it is because we believe that without reintegration with Naturals, our society is doomed. Here we have a Natural who has been raised like a Citizen, educated like a Citizen, thinks like a Citizen, yet retains the essential instinct and self-preservation that is vital to human life. Arlo is the most precious thing that we have, real proof that Naturals are not at heart sadistic or destructive, given to tribal or un-Citizenly conduct, or below Citizen intellect."

Arlo thought guiltily of his exam results and tried to stop himself blushing.

"But why do they think the Natural – *Arlo* – is so dangerous?" asked Tariq, one of the Pharmopolis merchants.

"What we discovered," said Kristo, now speaking carefully, "is that emotions, as written in ancient books, of love, anger, fear, are not yet dead in all of us. Through association with Arlo, Ignatius discovered that such emotions still lie dormant, awaiting the spark or trigger to set them off. Arlo is that trigger, and observation of the changing characters of the Inn of Court since his arrival has proved it. Some of us – myself included – have felt a warmth towards Arlo that we cannot otherwise describe. Others have developed an antipathy – what the ancients used to call *hatred* – towards him. In no case has anyone who has had prolonged contact with Arlo remained ambivalent. In other words, he is the catalyst that can help bring our Citizens into the real world again, and other Naturals as well. It is this power that is the most special thing about our Experiment."

Arlo shuffled his feet. Was Kristo really talking about *him*? How many times he had felt that the Doctors had never really understood him! But perhaps they *could* understand, even if only a little. And yes, this would explain the look in the eyes of Kane and Phlegg as they stared at him, and why they had let Rem out on purpose. . .

The Abbess broke in. "But the most important thing we have to decide is this. I leave Genopolis tonight to travel to the North and petition the Senate. All things willing, within a week I hope to have gained the protection of my mentors there, who alone can afford us support and a safeguard against this radical new Order. Until then, Arlo must remain in hiding and safety."

A discussion then ensued as to what should be done with Arlo, almost as if he was not there, he thought bitterly.

"I would have him stay here," said the Abbess, "but I believe that this is the first place that the soldiers of the Regis will look once they discover the abduction of their Special Guard."

"He is welcome to come with us to the Institute," said Yoshi and Yuma instantly in chorus, and at the same time Tutu and Tarissa spoke up. "We can take him to the Academy and place him with the pupils there."

"This will not work," said Kristo tersely, leaning back in his chair. "The sympathies of Yoshi and Yuma are well known and the Institute will be the second place they will look. We cannot risk that, neither for their sake nor Arlo's. And hiding Arlo at the Academy with Tutu or Tarissa will fool no one. Naturals are as different from Citizens as the sun from the moon, and he will stick out like a sore thumb in the Academy too. No, the only place that he can remain safely is in a private house, the house of someone the Regis will not think to enter. Sir Herbert, your home is the only place where Arlo may rest securely."

Sir Herbert, who had been spending all this time gazing myopically at the ceiling, twisted himself upright to stare in surprise at Kristo.

"But, my dear fellow, I can't possibly. Surely there must be somewhere else he can go?"

"I am sorry, Brother," said the Abbess gently but firmly. "There is nowhere else. But it may be only for a few days."

"But my children are back from the Academy for the

school holidays!" stuttered Sir Herbert. "How on earth am I going to explain it to them?"

Tariq immediately stood up, tossing a Citizen identity-token on to the table in front of him. "You may tell them that he is the son of a visiting diplomat from Pharmopolis who is visiting the City for a few days. Here is a token to prove it. They will not know the mannerisms or speech of Pharmopolis and it need only be for a short time."

"And if the Abbess takes longer than expected?" said Herbert indignantly.

"We shall cross that bridge when we come to it," said Kristo quietly. "Unfortunately I am already sought after and very soon my face will be known everywhere. I must go into hiding, but very soon I will be in touch with news. Until then, Arlo must remain in your house in safety. Do you understand?"

Herbert gazed round the row of faces turned to him and looked as if he were about to object again, but something stopped him. He sighed, pulled on his cloak and stood up. "In that case, I will arrange for my litter to come for Arlo. I just hope that in the end, it will be all worth it."

Somewhere, down in the murky depths of the cage, something was stirring.

Through Usha's dazed senses, a familiar, dreadful smell rose around her, a musty, bitter reek that clogged her lungs and sent her mind reeling. Even though she could not see through the suffocating darkness, she knew, with a certainty that was greater than sight, that something terrible was in the adjoining cage, almost touching her, something snuffling with curiosity, moving so close she could even feel the heat from its body, its rank odour choking her –

It was the smell from her dream.

With an effort, she struggled to a sitting position, trying to catch her breath. Almost immediately she froze as a low growl sounded from the other side of the pen.

Surely, *surely*, thought Usha, she must be dreaming again. . .

But as she tried to move, the chain tightened around her ankle, and reminded her that this was no dream.

Instead, the thing of her nightmares was now real, and a mere few feet away, separated from her only by a few metal bars.

"STRING THEM UP FOR THE CROWS"

It was the strange stillness – or perhaps more precisely the absence of movement – that Angus first noticed in his uneasy sleep. In the suffocating blackness of the little hut, he and Gea had dozed on and off for what he drowsily estimated must have been most of the morning. Still parched and nauseous, he woke at last to find that he was still lying painfully on the floor with his shoulder and neck pressed against the inner wall, his arms and hands numb from the constricting ropes that strapped them to his sides. Gea still lay against him, just as she had fallen asleep, with her head resting against his shoulder.

It was hard to tell exactly what was wrong, or what instinct had called him to wakefulness. Her position had not changed, but her slight body suddenly felt deeply heavy as if saturated with water, a cold, dead weight that bore down upon him like the pressure of earth. And there was something else – the darkness was silent. Too silent.

Panic rose in his throat and he struggled to breathe, to push her off him, spitting out her hair that lay in dry strands across his mouth. Struggling against his bindings, he vainly tried to jolt Gea to consciousness again, hissing her name quietly to avoid the attention of the guard outside.

"Gea! Gea! Wake up!"

She did not answer him. With mounting fear he pushed against her with his shoulder, once, twice, three times, calling to her frantically, his terror of the guards outside as nothing compared to the horror that lay lifeless against his chest.

"Gea! Please! No! Gea!"

But still she remained limp as a rag doll, her head lolling on his chest as he shook and urged her to wakefulness, as cold as a stone as he curled his body around hers, trying to bring some life and warmth back to her, as blank and unresponsive as a wall to the echo of his voice as he wept and begged her to open her eyes, over and over again.

"What on earth is that noise?" muttered Captain Hacker, laying down her clipboard in a commandeered hut, where she had been checking the Registrations.

At that moment her orderly put his head around the door. "I'm sorry, captain, but you need to come and see the female prisoner."

"The female prisoner is making that kind of a din?"

"No, captain, it's the male prisoner. The female – well, you'd better come and see for yourself."

Hacker threw down her pen and stalked after him. These kind of things always happened as soon as you got your hands dirty dealing with Naturals. Immediately after she got back to the billet she would apply for a transfer, far from the isolation, the storms and the unpredictability of the Regions.

Rounding the corner towards the prisoner's hut, Hacker could see that they were in trouble. A few of her men stood defensively with the safety catch off their weapons, warning off a steadily-growing crowd of Naturals who were emerging up the slope. Outside the open door of the prison hut lay the motionless form of the female prisoner, covered with a sack. Beside it the male prisoner lay, suffering an intense Outbreak of weeping, curled almost double as his suffering racked him with jerking spasms. As Hacker approached, he retched and started to keen again in the same horrible, high-pitched, broken sound.

"Someone shut him up, quick," snapped Hacker as she quickly loaded her rifle from the ordnance box carried by her assistant. It didn't do to let them carry on like this too long. "Look at them. Like iron to a magnet. The next thing you know, we'll have a riot going on. Get him back inside, and look sharp about it."

Hacker was right. More and more Naturals were emerging from their huts as if drawn unstoppably to their fallen comrade by the sound of grief. Following her orders the patrol dragged the prisoner back inside the hut and barred it, but the damage had been done. Within minutes the captain and her unit stood gazing on a grim-faced crowd that far outnumbered them and returned their glances with a fixed and stony stare.

Though calm herself — how many times had she been in a similar situation with these creatures? — Hacker could see several of her newer recruits begin to look uncertain. She shot a quick glance upwards. With a clear morning and no harsh winds, the airship should have been here by now, along with the support team that she had requested as they first marched to the Region village, almost fifteen hours ago.

Trust the City to leave them alone and outnumbered, thought Hacker, those fools at the Consulate needed to do a stint of duty out here in the Regions, then they'd have a better idea of what their soldiers needed.

"Wait a minute," she said suddenly, scanning the rows of faces, "there's more of them than there should be. There should only be two hundred. Now there's more than five hundred. The rest of the Region are coming!"

The patrol raised their rifles and adjusted their sights. A shudder passed through the crowd, but they did not give ground at the sight of the guns. Gazing at the tense, swaying movement, the captain had an uneasy premonition, unusual for her, of a coiled snake about to strike. In the silence there came a series of staccato clicks as the soldiers flicked off their safety catches and squinted through their sights.

"Don't be ridiculous," said Hacker quickly, "you can't take them all on. You might kill a few but they'd rush you before you could reload. Hold your fire. Let me talk to them."

Hacker pushed her way in front of the patrol and faced the swaying mob, who gazed back rudely. Raising her voice so even those at the back could hear her, she held her rifle at the defensive and spoke.

"At this moment a military airship is on its way here. If you raise a finger against us it will retaliate against you. We are Guardians of Genopolis, and any refusal to do as we say will be taken as proof of rebellion."

The pack looked back at her, unmoving. A few of the more timid ones scanned the clear sky warily. Hacker rolled her eyes. Did they doubt her power? She looked over the haggard faces, so recently bewildered, cowed and timid, now suddenly and inexplicably hardening into sullen resentment, eyes narrowed, arms folded.

"You have three minutes until the airship arrives. Anyone remaining outside in the open after the three minutes are up will be killed. You have three minutes."

A slight mutter of unease flickered through the ranks, and at the back, Hacker could see a few people slip away and back into the woods, but by and large the crowd stood firm. Hacker set her lip. So they were going to play her, were they?

"You now have two minutes. If you do not leave now, the airship will bomb your village and burn it to the ground. Is this what you want?"

The crowd moved slightly, and Hacker breathed again. Finally they were going to disperse. It had been a difficult situation, but as usual, it was all bluster. But whether they went peaceably or not, she already knew what orders she would give to the airship when it finally arrived.

But the movement of the crowd continued until the front row parted, and to Hacker's surprise the old woman prisoner hobbled through, leaning on a stick and supported on the other side by a young, black-haired girl of no more than eleven Citizen-years, bearing a dirty strip of white rag as a crude flag of truce.

"What's all this?" asked Hacker in disbelief, turning to the orderly. "I thought I told you to put her in with the other two prisoners?"

"I know you did, captain, but she was so old, and she

wouldn't get up, and I really couldn't see what harm it would do to let her go. I mean you can't say that she's dangerous. She can't even walk properly."

"Oh yes," said Hacker grimly, "she's dangerous all right. You don't need to be strong to be dangerous."

She threw the old hag a look of contempt mixed with mistrust. Had the old woman come to parley with her? Did they really think that they were in any position to bargain?

"Captain," muttered the soldier who was manning the communicator, "I've had word through from the airship. Estimated time of arrival ten minutes."

Hacker shot a quick look towards the blue, open sky. It was a small window for the airship to arrive. In an hour the dust winds would start to squall and make visibility impossible. But there was nothing she could do with such an inflammatory situation on her hands. Playing for time and relying on her military training, she lowered her weapon with theatrical deliberation to demonstrate good intent to the rabble, but wisely left the safety catch off, and turned to the young girl. "Name and Natural registration number?"

"She is my grandmother, Ira, mother of my aunt Gea, Registered Natural 3837, Region Three, Scar Valley. I am her granddaughter, Kira."

"What do you want?" rapped Hacker.

The girl looked back at her. "Ira has a request to make, captain. She wishes to take her daughter back for burial."

Whatever Hacker had expected, it certainly was not this. Barely controlling a snort of laughter, she shook her head and said, "I'm sorry. This is not possible. The female Natural is the property of the City, and as such must be returned to them."

The old hag started mumbling again, passing her hand in the air. The girl looked anxiously at her and started again. "Grandmother Ira requests her daughter back for an honourable burial. She says that to refuse her this request is an offence against Nature."

Hacker blinked. An offence against Nature? The Natural's speech left her almost speechless with the thought of such downright treachery. But, consummate professional as she was, Hacker nodded slowly, as if considering this ridiculous request. "I understand. But I cannot make this decision. We need to wait for the airship to arrive, and then I can put your request to them. Let us wait some time."

"No," said the girl with quick intensity. "You must decide now."

"Otherwise?" said Hacker, trying to keep the sneer out of her voice.

"Otherwise you will die," said the girl calmly. "Ira has prophesied this."

Hacker shook her head. "I will not decide."

The next second, there was a light and almost imperceptible touch on Hacker's cheek which could have been no more than the settling of a fly. Her soldier's training told her that it was more than it seemed. Raising her hand to her face, she felt a tiny, sharp splinter no larger than a bee sting, embedded in her cheek. The next second she felt the same sensation in her forearm, and another in her neck. Turning to her unit, she could see their faces studded with similar small black pinpricks. One soldier raised his hand to his eye, bewildered.

"Get back," cried Hacker urgently, "get back. They've got darts. Cover your eyes. No, don't rub them off, you fool —" one soldier was starting to paw at his face — "you'll spread the poison. Back off, and cover me!"

Her unit held the crowd at bay while Hacker sped down the slope, stabbing frantically at her communicator, but as soon as the soldiers took their first step back, the crowd let out a wild whoop and charged. One look at the mob hurtling towards them, and the Guardians turned and ran for their lives. Like a huge wave breaking on the shore, the horde of Naturals bore down on the running patrol. The soldiers were still short of the cover of the forest by some hundred yards, when the first soldier tripped and fell sprawling. Immediately the rearguard wheeled round defiantly and took aim. Rifles cracked. A few Naturals stumbled and fell but their comrades swept undaunted over them in their headlong charge.

"Don't shoot, don't shoot," shouted Hacker breathlessly over her shoulder, "there's too many of them. Run! Run!"

But it was too late. Three of the patrol were swallowed up by the surging mass while they scrabbled for more ammunition. The next minute a great cheer, terrible to hear in its savagery, rose up from the mass and the broken bodies of the three soldiers were tossed in the air over the heaving sea of the crowd.

Hacker turned to flee but something was wrong. Her body suddenly seemed strangely stretched and remote. She opened her mouth but she could not speak. Gagging on her tongue, which suddenly seemed large and swollen, she took two unsteady footsteps forward, and sank to her knees. She was aware of her men staring at her curiously, but then the same thing was slowly happening to them. It was as if time had slowed to a standstill. She could see one soldier trying to fire his rifle, but his limp hand kept dropping from his gun. The other was shouting silently to her, his movements exaggerated and slow-moving. As the paralysis swept up her body Hacker could not even move her eyes. Instead, as her muscles began to stiffen, she doubled over with a slow, inexorable finality, until her cheek was resting on the rocky floor. Her last sight was of the pebbles directly in front of her staring eyes, beautiful crystalline stones which now crunched beneath the ragged boots of the Naturals who were emerging from the forest to stand over them.

"What shall we do with them, Ira?" asked one of the Naturals.

It was the voice of the old woman, once so mumbling and ancient, that now replied coldly. "Take them to the gibbets and string them up for the crows."

SIX

It was early evening by the time Sir Herbert's litter, borne by four burly Gemini-carriers, drew up at the west-wall of the Maian Inn. Quietly a door opened and two shadows slipped quickly out and behind the heavy drapes of blue velvet.

It had cost Arlo an effort to leave the Maia, especially the Abbess. As she had kissed him farewell, he had struggled to contain an Outbreak of tears, reluctant to show any sign of his Natural weakness in front of a group of people that seemed to prize him so highly. As she drew back and stroked his face, she covertly slipped a small wrapped parcel into his arms, whispering in his ear.

"Listen, Arlo. I know that you have many questions. When you are ready to know who you are, then open this book and read it, for it contains many answers. But in the meantime, do not fear to take with you whoever you may find on your journey, for there are others here who are also in need of help, and whose help you may be glad of, in your turn."

Beside him and Sir Herbert in the darkness of the litter sat Kristo, patting Arlo's shoulder in the old gesture as he had when Arlo was younger, but Arlo could not even feel it. Events had happened so fast that he was bewildered and confused. All he wanted to do was lie in the shady darkness of the Maian courtyard and talk to the Abbess. Instead, Kristo was muttering in his ear.

"It will only be for a few days, Arlo. Your Pharmopolis name will be Torin, the son of a diplomat visiting the Consulate for a conference. If you should meet the children, or anybody should ask you any question about Pharmopolis, then use what you studied in your Natural History books. They won't know any better, and they won't be half as educated as you. Do not leave the house. I will come to you before the first week is over to let you know progress. Do you understand?"

Arlo nodded, unable to speak. The litter drew to a stop and Kristo cautiously poked his head from between the drapes, checked that it was clear, gave Arlo one last squeeze on the shoulder and was gone.

Left alone with Sir Herbert in frosty silence in the litter, Arlo had the distinct impression that he was not pleased about the new arrangements, but even so there leaped a small spark of excitement inside him. He was going to see the inside of a real Citizen house, but best of all he was actually going to meet a real Citizen family-unit – and a girl and boy his own age – for the very first time.

Usha opened her eyes again to blackness. A light flickered somewhere in the distance, and she strained to see. She felt as if she was lying at the bottom of a dark well, looking through its rippling surface to the faces of her captors. Above her, Zenna and Zadoc stared down at her. Their lips moved but she could not hear what they were saying. There was a slow rushing in her ears and everything in front of her swayed, merged, and fragmented like oil poured on water.

Usha felt grit underneath her bare feet. She must be back at the pharms.

Directly in front of her stretched a long corridor, bounded on both sides by wire cages. Through the cages stretched withered arms, clutching at the bars, forming a narrow causeway through which to walk. At the end of the passageway was a door, light radiating dimly through the crack around it. As she walked forwards, she heard the low growling sound again, as if something large and heavy was pacing back and forth behind it.

Slowly she reached out to the doorknob, but something was wrong with her arm. It wouldn't move. She felt her bones grinding and moving against each other, as if her arm were being twisted in a great vice. . .

Then Ozzie was beside her, slumping across the door

frame, morosely running a finger along the edge of his knife, sucking his teeth.

"I dunno, Sis, looks like you got us in a bunch of trouble here."

Usha spun around, but she could not see his face clearly in the shadows. "I'm sorry, Ozzie. I didn't mean. . ."

"Something's wrong with Mindie. I think she's sick. We don't have any water, Sis. What we going ter do now? Eh?"

Ozzie moved towards her, but now he was limping with the same shuffling tread of the scissor-man, his right leg dragging slightly, and the knife that he held out in front of him shone like a scalpel.

Usha glanced wildly around, but there was nowhere to run, save through the door. As she hesitated, from behind the door came a knocking, and Auntie's faltering tones, pitched high in entreaty.

"Usha? Usha, my life, my own. . ."

The scissor-man came forward into the light, Ozzie no longer. What little light there was glinted on the silver handle of the blade that now protruded from his left eye. A black trickle of blood snaked down over his cheek.

"Aren't you going to help Auntie, Usha? She's calling for you. She needs you. Don't you remember your first purpose?"

Usha gazed around, and suddenly the cages were full of the same fair-haired, grey-eyed girls of Auntie's pictures, all clutching at her, calling, *Usha . . . Usha. . .*

Ablaze of light such as Arlo had never seen before heralded the front gate of Sir Herbert's mansion. At first he thought he was entering another large building such as the Inn of Court, but as he gazed up at the ornate façade he realized that it must be all one great house. The North Quarter housed the stately homes of the governors and rulers of Genopolis, and Sir Herbert, as a retired chief law-maker of Genopolis, was no exception. As Arlo followed Sir Herbert up the long flight of stairs to the entrance, it appeared that the whole Gemini staff had turned out to meet them, dressed in white and bobbing their heads respectfully as their master passed.

Inside, the house was even more impressive. A great winding staircase came down in a graceful helix to a front hall carpeted with shining glass and tiles – Pre-Apocalyptic Mosaic, pointed out Sir Herbert proudly – and statutes and pictures as rich as any he had seen in the Inn of Court hung on the walls or stood watchfully in alcoves. Arlo stood for some minutes and gazed, slightly dazzled by the richness of the house. A great chandelier was suspended from the domed cupola of the hall, and sparkled with colour. It was a few seconds before he realized that Sir Herbert had fetched two Citizen children, a boy and a girl, both staring at him with ill-concealed surprise.

"Children, this is our new guest, Torin from Pharmopolis," said Sir Herbert, vaguely, ushering Arlo forward to meet them. "Ar . . . er . . . Torin, these are my children, Clarence and Cecilia. Now, children, Torin is a very special guest, and we are going to show him the very best of Genopolian hospitality, aren't we?"

The boy was around the same age as Arlo, but taller and sturdier, similar to Kristo in his fair colouring and build. But there was no trace of Kristo in the pale, rather glassy blue eyes that were turned to him as the boy looked Arlo up and down.

"Father, you're not going to make me *share* a room with him, are you?"

"Well, I rather thought. . ." began Sir Herbert, but the girl sneered.

"Well, he won't be sharing with *me*, Father, I can promise you that."

She was around two years younger than both the boys, her blonde hair twisted into two pigtails above a round, pudgy face, and there was something in her manner that reminded Arlo of Doctor Phlegg. "Nobody from school has friends from the *pharms*. They'd rather be seen dead than go around with people like *that*!"

"Now, now," replied their parent mildly, "it'll just be for a few days. Why don't you all run along and play, or something? I'm sure there's lots of things that you'd want to show our guest."

Clarence stood, his pale eyes fixed on Arlo, saying nothing, as if weighing him up in silence. Arlo returned the stare in frank amazement. He was eager to find out more about the first Citizens that he had seen at close quarters, but something about Clarence's manner seemed to forbid any familiarity. Behind him Cecilia coughed nervously.

"Clarrie, we can't stand here doing nothing. If he has to be here, then why don't we show him the playroom?"

Sir Herbert coughed gently. "Oh yes, that's a wonderful idea. Right then, I'll . . . leave you to get acquainted."

Arlo watched the old man's retreating back with dread as Sir Herbert shuffled quickly away and shut the door firmly behind him.

Hours later, Usha woke and found herself lying in a narrow cot in a darkened cell. Around her all was noise, voices barking orders, feet running to and fro and gates clanging. In sudden panic, remembering the snuffling creature of her nightmares, she shook herself awake and gazed wildly around, but the room, apart from her small cot, seemed empty and deathly quiet. Dim light fell in a criss-cross pattern over her face, like dusty beams falling through wire.

She sat up and tried to swing her legs off the bench, but a chain on her ankle and a heavy weight on her left arm prevented her from moving comfortably. Her left arm, from the tips of the fingers nearly to the elbow, was encased in a hard, shell-like substance, similar to the plaster with which she had seen Gemini repairing the outside of houses, hardened so that she could not move it at all. She rapped on it gingerly with the knuckles of her other hand, and it rang dully.

"Idiot Gemini," came a voice from the other side of the cell. "Trying to undo all my good handiwork?"

Usha jumped and gazed into the shadows. Zenna, her hair twisted into a long snaking plait, was standing wiping her hands on a rag. A bowl of whitish putty and a roll of bandages lay on a bench before her. She returned the girl's gaze with a sneer. "You should leave that well alone. Don't you understand that this is your one chance of letting your wrist heal properly?"

"What have you done to me?" asked Usha, feeling with one foot for the ground, which was covered with grit and small stones. "Zenna?" Then as she touched the damp, dripping wall behind her, "Where *am* I?"

"You are in the Circus," replied Zenna, calmly shaking out a sack and putting her materials inside.

"What is the Circus?" asked Usha warily, trying to edge her other foot to the floor, but a chain tightened around it, pinning her to the bench.

Zenna smiled. "You will find out, soon enough." Gathering up her final tools, she glided over to the bed and stood over the girl. Usha smelled vinegar and soap, and a slight whiff of mould, like the toadstools that sometimes grew wild on Auntie's lawn overnight. She leaned away as Zenna bent forward over her, her breath tickling Usha's face.

"You were lucky that you managed to end up here, Gemini. Even a living death is preferable to Regeneration. But do not even think of trying to escape. I have heard that Merco treats his gladiators with no mercy."

With her leg still chained to the bed and one arm out of action, there was only one thing she could do, and, mustering all her spit, Usha gave it her best shot.

The playroom was enormous, with white walls and large windows hung with heavy gold curtains. Heaped all around the floor were piles of toys, rocking-horses, tops, dolls, footballs, tennis racquets and small swords. Arlo found it hard to keep his eyes from popping out of his head as he followed the children inside. Yet all of these toys had been broken or disfigured in some way, the pictures had been scribbled on, the dolls had their hair cut or burnt off, and pieces of the games had been strewn everywhere. Unconsciously he found himself slipping his hand inside his shirt to check that the book that the Abbess had given him was safe and untouched.

Clarence was eyeing him closely with a faint look of suspicion on his face. "What's the matter, pharm-boy? Haven't you got these kind of things where you come from?"

"Not quite like this," said Arlo truthfully, as an image of the Inn's library rose before him. Turning hastily aside in case Clarence could see his face, he picked his way over to where a large purple baize table, covered with small figurines of warriors with swords and shields, stood in a corner. "What are these?"

Cecilia, her pigtails flying excitedly round her head, joined him. "They're the new Circus gladiator-figures.

See this one? That's Bjarn. He's Clarence's favourite. But this one," and here she picked up a small figurine dressed in silver armour with black plaits, "this is Talia. She's lasted five seasons and she's a silver medallist."

"Four seasons," corrected Clarence, idly sifting through the other warriors.

"All right, four seasons, but she's still got a shot at the gold this year."

Arlo searched for a way to join in the conversation, his mind racing. "What . . . what's the Circus?"

"What's the *Circus*?" mocked Cecilia. "You mean you don't have Circuses where you come from?"

"No," said Clarence nastily, "they just ride horses all day, don't you, pharm-boy?"

"Horses?" said Arlo, puzzled. He had read about horses in the old books in the library, but he had never thought of real *living* horses before.

Clarence's next words made his heart sink. "Yes, *horses*, stupid, or do you spend all your time sitting indoors all day? Mind you, if you did, you might not be such a skinny little shrimp. How old are you, anyway?"

Arlo bit his lip. He had endured similar muttered insults from Kane and the other Doctors who had disliked him, but coming from someone his age it was very hard to take. Slowly the realization grew on him that his main danger that evening might not, after all, be from the Regis.

Keep calm, he told himself, keep calm.

"I'm eleven and a half Citizen-years old," he said in as

friendly a way as he could manage. "How about you?"

"Eleven and a half!" sneered Clarence. "They're sending babies over from Pharmopolis now!"

"But, Clarrie, you're only—" started Cecilia, but Clarence cut her off, his face bright with excitement.

"Ceci, I've just had a brilliant idea."

Arlo didn't like the sound of this, but Cecilia caught up on it instantly. "Tell me! What is it?"

"Tonight's the Grand Opening of the Circus, isn't it?"

Cecilia looked dubious. "Yes, of course, but Father already said no. . ."

Her brother grinned. "But if we're entertaining *such* an important guest from the pharms –" and here he shot Arlo a condescending look – "then he can't really refuse us again, could he? It wouldn't be polite. It wouldn't be *Citizenly*."

Arlo shook his head. "I'm not sure. . ."

But Clarence was already pushing past him to the door, his high nasal voice bleating loudly. "Father! Father!"

"No, Clarence –" began Cecilia, but there was already the sound of footsteps in the corridor and Sir Herbert's voice came again.

"Oh, Clarrie, do be quiet, there's a good boy. You're making the whole house noisy and it's time to rest."

"But, Father, Torin said that he wanted to go to the Circus tonight," lied Clarence, his blue eyes wide. "And *you* said that we needed to look after him and show him how we do things here in the City."

Sir Herbert's surprised gaze rested on them for a moment, and Arlo did his best to return a look that mixed polite ignorance of what Clarence was jabbering about with a desperate hope that Sir Herbert would not, after all, take him to the Circus. Sir Herbert did not recognize any of this, of course, and after a second replied in a hushed tone, "Well, Torin, I hope that you do not find us wanting in manners, but I do think that your Citizen-parents will need to be consulted. And I am sure that you will first need to rest and sleep after your long journey, wouldn't you say?"

There was little else that Arlo could do but grin in a casual way that he hoped would please everyone. All he really wanted was to be alone and read the book that the Abbess had given him. He was starting to come to the conclusion that Citizen children were not for him after all. Whereupon Sir Herbert, evidently concluding that the matter was settled, patted his offspring vaguely on the head, nodded to Arlo, and retreated.

Arlo was expecting Clarence to be displeased at this, but he was unprepared for the ugly light that suddenly shone in the boy's pale eyes as he walked up to Arlo and glared at him. Cecilia looked at her elder brother, biting her lip. Suddenly, Clarence's arm shot out and pushed Arlo in the chest, forcefully. As Arlo stepped back, his foot slipped on a small ball and he tripped over, bringing a shower of toys down with him in a crash. Cecilia let out a shriek.

"My doll's house! He's broken it! Hit him, Clarrie!"

Arlo struggled backwards as the older boy waded over the sea of broken toys towards him. He opened his mouth to shout but the next second the wind had been knocked out of him by the force of Clarence's punch sinking into his stomach.

I mustn't scream. I mustn't cry. I mustn't show them I feel anything, he thought desperately. The pain made him feel sick. He shook his head dizzily and the room whirled around him.

Then, in a calm voice at the back of his head, he dimly heard the voice of the Abbess, counting down the numbers to zero. Almost magically, the ache in his stomach began to recede. Still crouched on top of the heap of shattered toys, he started to breathe deeply once more, still concentrating, fighting to regain his balance.

From the corner of his eye, he saw Clarence raise his fist again –

Zenna stood quite still for a moment, the gleam of Usha's spit still trickling down her pointed cheek. Then slowly, disdainfully, she turned away and moved gracefully towards the cage door. As she unlocked it and prepared to leave, the light caught her pointed white teeth, curved in an unpleasant smile.

"Tonight the Circus opens and I will get my barter-worth out of you, Gemini," she said, as she pulled the cage door shut and turned the key. "And believe me, I will enjoy watching every minute of it."

As soon as she had disappeared down the narrow corridor, Usha wriggled with what skill she could manage to the end of the cot, placed one foot on the cell floor and hopped forward so that she could just about touch the bars, craning to see the strange new place that she had been left in.

Through the front of her cage, she could see a long corridor of similar cages, and at the end, a dull speck of evening light, from where all the clanging and shouting was coming. As Usha watched, men wheeled barrows and carts to and fro, pulled cages and strewed grit over the floor. Puzzled, she watched them. What was this place? Why had she been bartered here?

Then, from the other side of her there came the waft of a familiar rank smell that chilled her to the marrow. Turning, she saw, on the opposite side of the passageway, a cage thrown into dark shadow, inside which she could just see the outline of something large and heavy stirring. Beneath the clatter and bangs around her she could hear a low rumbling sound, as of deep snorting breaths, coming out of the darkness, along with the smell from her nightmares. . .

"Zenna!" she shrieked, shaking at the bars. "Zenna! Come back here, you dirty thief! Don't leave me here! Zenna!"

But it was not Zenna but Zadoc who finally heard Usha's screams, and came down the long corridor towards her, chewing lazily on a long strip of dried meat.

"Something bothering you, Miss Um-Cybella?"

"Please," begged Usha, reaching through the bars towards him. "Please! I'll give you anything you want! Please don't leave me here!"

Zadoc stood out of her way, a beady light glinting in his little eyes.

"That is a shame, Mistress Um-Cybella, but I think you are actually very fortunate, no? Only this afternoon came the news of a lady who had been found murdered in the West Quarter along with her surgeon, while her missing Gemini-companion is nowhere to be found. Perhaps you know of where she might be, yes?"

Plainly enjoying the effect of his words on Usha, Zadoc turned away, wiping his greasy hands across his belly as though it were a napkin. Carelessly yet deliberately he tossed his chewed rind just in front of the bars of the opposite cage. Immediately something – too fast for Usha to see – shot out, grabbed it, and dragged it inside. Out of the darkness came a hideous noise of ripping and tearing.

Usha was struck dumb, staring at the cage, as Zadoc sauntered away.

"You should be grateful, Miss Um-Cybella, that you still have your life. I suggest you enjoy it – while it lasts."

Arlo ducked Clarence's punch and rolled sideways, sending the taller and heavier boy crashing forward on to the heap of toys just where Arlo had been lying. Scrambling quickly to his feet, Arlo dived on top of him and together they fought, kicking and punching, encouraged by Cecilia's screams and the kicks and blows that she aimed at Arlo, but which more often than not missed their target and hit her brother instead. Though Arlo was smaller, he was also lighter and quicker than Clarence, able to duck and dodge and judge by instinct where the older boy was aiming at. The punches, when they landed on him, were painful at first, but even as he fought he kept up the rhythm of his counting in the back of his head, and this helped to dull the impact of Clarence's glancing blows.

And there was an advantage, he thought confusedly, over feeling pain when the other person did not – it gave you a sharp instinct to protect parts of your body such as your nose or stomach and to dodge punches in those areas. Whereas Clarence just threw himself forward, fists swinging wildly, with no idea of defence or strategy. Arlo had already landed several clear blows on his face, and now Clarence's cheek had started to swell so that he could no longer see his opponent out of his left eye. As long as Arlo kept moving, Clarence was unable to pinpoint him closely enough to punch. But Arlo himself was nearing exhaustion, and it was as much as he could do to keep his distance from the stronger boy, while Cecilia fired an energetic volley of dolls, teddy bears, balls and jigsaw pieces directly at him.

At last Clarence held up a hand and staggered to the side of the room, where, apparently aware of the injuries on his face for the first time, he dabbed at his nose and peered at it with his good eye in the mirror.

"Well, pharm-boy, good round. You certainly know how to fight out there."

Cecilia had already gone running for some ice, which she brought back from the kitchen and pressed on her brother's swollen face. She did not offer any to Arlo, and neither did Arlo ask for it. Panting from the scuffle, he sat down awkwardly on the shattered remains of the doll's house. For some reason he had been oddly cheered by the fight – not by the punching and kicking, that had all gone rather by instinct – but by the prospect of actively striking back at the people who had hurt him. Yet, as he looked at Clarence's battered face, his cheeriness died abruptly. Though it was the other boy who had pushed him into it, he did not feel at all pleased at what he had done.

Abruptly the door was flung open and Sir Herbert stood in the doorway again, his eyes travelling over the wreckage of the children's toys on the floor. "Oh," he said with mild surprise, "been playing, have you? Did you have a nice time?"

"Wonderful, Father," said Clarence sarcastically, ducking behind his sister.

"Clarrie, what have you done to your *face*?"

"Fell over, Father," said Clarence, his voice muffled from the pad of melting ice. "Nothing, really. "

"Yes, but, Clarence, you *know* you're not allowed to fight. Look, you've gone and damaged yourself."

"Really, Father," said Clarence smoothly, "it'll be better in the morning."

"Well, it's rather a shame because . . . well I'd wondered if you still wanted to go to the Circus, you see, and you can't really go out looking like that. . ."

Cecilia and Clarence suddenly leapt up, cheering. "I'll be fine, Father," assured Clarence, earnestly. "I'll put a hat on."

"Yes, well, you'd better go and get dressed then. . ." said Sir Herbert, vaguely, but was drowned out by the whoops and screams of his children as they flung open the door and went crashing down the corridor to the clothing-room.

Directly the noise of their departure had faded, Sir Herbert grasped Arlo's shoulder with surprising strength, and pulled him down a passageway into a small bare room. He closed the door and put a finger to his lips. It was as if the cloak of mild ridiculousness had suddenly fallen away to show the sharp, urgent mind hidden beneath. Arlo gazed at him, amazed at the transformation.

"Listen, boy. I have bad news. The Regis is on your tail, and the Guardians have been given orders to search every house in Genopolis to find you. They have been through the West Quarter first, and they will reach us in a couple of hours. I cannot keep you here, but neither can you leave alone because they would find you, and they have ways to make you tell them all you know. None of our Circle would be safe. There is only one chance, to take you out to the revels at the Circus, where we can lose ourselves in the crowd."

Stunned, Arlo nodded, feeling sick again, as Sir Herbert continued. "I have tried to get word to the others, particularly Kristo, and I am hoping that he will be able to meet us there and bear you away to another place of safety. Until that time, I ask you to stay quiet and keep close to me. Can you do that?"

Arlo nodded again and Sir Herbert rested a hand on his shoulder. "Good lad. My litter will be at the door in twenty minutes."

As Arlo made to leave, something caught his eye. The room in which they were standing had no furnishings, save one. In an alcove next to the door hung a portrait of a woman, as richly dressed as Sir Herbert, her long tawny hair wound with jewels, returning his gaze with a sweet and steady stare, the corners of her mouth slightly upraised in the beginnings of a delighted smile.

"Who . . . who is she?" asked Arlo, awed.

"She was my wife," replied Sir Herbert.

Something told Arlo he should ask no more questions but somehow he could not help it. "But . . . where is she now, sir?"

"She died in the great Plague ten years ago," replied Sir Herbert, and on his face was a look that Arlo had never seen on the face of a Citizen before. "Losing her was one of the reasons that I joined Ignatius's Circle, for I could bear to be alone with my thoughts no longer. For both she and I had committed the crime of Love, which made us outlaws in our own city, secret criminals under the same laws that I administered and the same judgments that I passed. And for my punishment, I now have nothing, not a lock of hair, not a touch from her hand, nothing save this painting, which I must keep under lock and key, lest the servants talk and the Guardians discover that even after ten years I am still Infected – perhaps for ever.

"For if you are Infectious, Arlo, then I was Infected on the day that I met her, and I sicken still. We Citizens are not made of stone, Arlo, we only sleep, until such time as something happens to awaken our emotions. But sometimes I fear that this awakening will be beyond my lifetime, and perhaps my children's lifetimes too."

Arlo could think of no words to answer him. Together they gazed in silence at the portrait, and he could see a smile beginning to dawn on the face of the old, broken man, before a bell rang downstairs and Sir Herbert roused himself, clapping him on the shoulder.

"Out of the frying pan and into the fire, Arlo. Now we must trust to luck."

A key screeched in the lock and Usha looked up quickly, roused from her stupor and momentarily forgetting her useless arm. In the doorway stood Zadoc and a small gaunt man, dressed in a close-fitting riding coat and high boots. His yellowy-white hair was sparse and pulled back into a lank ponytail. Two pale eyes bulged from his jaundiced face as if they were being squeezed from his skull. Strangely for a Citizen he had a rambling line of hair growing over his top lip and running down each side of his mouth in a cascade, waxed into two long points. Usha had seen old pictures in Auntie's house – Auntie had told her this was a *moustache*, and the effect would have been comical, had the man not, in his square fist, held a long whip, and motioned towards Usha with it. With his first words, she recognized his voice as Merco, the man who had bargained with the Governor in the smugglers' hideout.

"Rest time over. Stir your stumps and let's get moving."

With the butt of Merco's whip prodding into her back, Usha walked slowly out of the line of cages and emerged into a huge, open space. She caught her breath.

In front of her was an immense, circular arena, strewn with grit and dust. It was pitted with large troughs dug into the ground and great boulders lying so haphazardly that she could not see in a direct line from one side of the ground to the other. All around the area ran an immense stone wall, etched with rough carvings of running and fighting figures, as though crudely scratched by a giant child with a knife. Huge grids of metal, such as the one they had just passed, were set into the wall at intervals like great doors. Above the carved boundary wall, she could see tiers of stone seats, separated by walkways, rising up in ever-larger circles, and stretching higher and higher into the air until they disappeared against a small glimpse of the reddening evening sky. It was the highest building she had seen in her life.

Yet, though Usha was not to know it, the whole amphitheatre had been carved into the belly of a disused quarry. Far from being a tall building, the topmost part was at ground level. As she stared upwards, a distant smell wafted down to her, a salty, slightly fishy smell, stirring a dim memory in her. Forgetting the spear at her back, she stopped and sniffed the air eagerly.

Merco regarded her critically, cleaning his long nails on a jagged tooth. "This one looks like trouble, Zadoc."

Zadoc tutted. "I thought trouble was exactly what you wanted from your gladiators, Ringmaster?"

Merco walked around Usha, gazing at her, slit-eyed, poking at her with the butt of his whip. "I told you not to bother getting Gemini. Crowds won't pay to see them. Not like real Citizens."

Zadoc shot Usha an evil look as if to say being a Gemini was all her fault. Not liking the way the conversation was going, Usha tried to move forward again. But this time Merco had other ideas. He stepped aside to a smoking brazier and pulled out a long metal poker from its bowels. Turning towards her, smirking, he held up the glowing iron so that Usha could see that the tip was embossed with a sharp raised ridge in the shape of a *G*.

In the bitter evening night-wind of the south-eastern side of Genopolis, Sir Herbert stepped out of the litter, followed by a chattering Clarence and Cecilia, and after a short pause, Arlo, a scarf wrapped around his face. A great stream of people was swarming by and it was easy to slip unobserved into the crowd. All around them were similar family-units, dressed in their best clothes, chattering and eating a strange, spun-sugar substance that Clarence badgered his father to barter his handkerchief for and offered cheerfully around. Arlo accepted, slightly surprised. Despite the pad of ice, Clarence's nose and eye had swollen up considerably, yet he did not appear to blame Arlo for it in the least. No trace remained of the pale glare that had transformed the other boy's face during the fight. Clarence now seemed the very image of a cheerful schoolboy on his way to take part in the revels of the Circus. Cecilia too was chattering happily away. Only Sir Herbert's eyes occasionally met Arlo's, and beneath his genial, foggy stare, Arlo could sense a real and very strained anxiety.

"Look!" Clarence caught his arm and pointed upwards. "Fireworks!"

Arlo had no idea what he meant, but he looked up obediently and his mouth fell open. Screaming upwards in an arc above them shot small rockets of smoke and sputtering fire which seemed to dwindle to nothing before exploding in a shower of gold and silver, lighting up the early night air in flickering sparks. Another and then another blazed across the sky, this time exploding in a cacophony of purple and orange like a huge flower. Clarence eyed Arlo with amusement.

"Don't have fireworks where you come from, do they, pharm-boy?"

"No," replied Arlo, unthinkingly. "I mean, not as good as this," he corrected himself hurriedly.

Some Citizens, Arlo noticed, were carrying damp-looking bags from which an unholy stench was rising. Cecilia sniffed as she saw Arlo looking at them curiously. "Lower-Citizen scum. They carry rotting food to throw at the fighters they don't like. I'm so glad Father managed to get us our box. Last time we came late and we had to sit on *ordinary* seats next to that lot. Clarrie nearly got a rotten lettuce in his face."

As they neared two enormous stone pillars that rose up out of the stunted grass, Arlo felt Sir Herbert pull him discreetly aside. "Listen, Arlo. Here are the Gates. On the other side, there should be a green litter waiting for you with four female Gemini as bearers. Talk to no one, look at no one, just pull aside the curtain and get in. They will take you to where the Circle has decided will be your next hiding place. Here we are, now. Go, with best fortune."

Sir Herbert held his hand tightly for a moment, then put an arm around each of his children, and pushed them gently forward so that Arlo could fall behind unobserved. In a few seconds he was separated from them by a group of Citizens in bright cloaks munching on toffee apples. Quickly, keeping his eyes casually fixed on the ground, he stole off as the crowd streamed through the Gates. Slipping quickly through the mass of people, he turned right as the crowd bore left, taking with them Sir Herbert and his family. With his heart beating rapidly in his chest he walked slowly around the left pillar and stopped dead in his tracks.

There was no litter there.

Still struggling, Usha was thrust into another chamber by Merco's bony arms, and the metal grid clanged back shut behind her.

Her eyes straining to see into the blackness, she ventured slowly down the dark corridor towards a streak of lamplight gleaming from underneath a pair of large double doors. From behind the doors came the sound of raucous laughter, crashes and some very loud, ribald singing, as if Usha had wandered into the lowest kind of chorley-house.

Creeping slowly round the door, she saw a group of about fifteen men and women clustered around a table, tankards of frothing drink and the remains of a dinner scattered around them. Two of them were swaying together, singing, and another proceeded to leap up on to the table and perform a wild kind of dance. Almost instantly he tripped and fell off the table in a clatter of plates, whereupon the others broke into whooping and cheering and drummed on the table with their palms and on the floor with their heels. Usha watched, wishing only to be left unobserved, so that the strange and terrible new world into which she had been forced might leave her alone.

"Look!" called a voice, and the crowd suddenly looked over its shoulder and took in the young Gemini cringing at the door, her stained face and pale hair streaked with dirty cobwebs. A young woman of about eighteen Citizen-years sat with her feet carelessly up on the table, one arm behind her head while the other waved a flagon of chorley in time to the discordant singing. "I see we have another visitor. Come in, Blondie, and make yourself at home."

Usha sidled round the door, unwilling to approach the company too closely. The girl she could see was dressed like a Citizen man in trousers and loose-necked shirt, and with boots that reached up to the knee. Her skin was black and her dark hair was plaited into thin braids that reached to her jaw, falling untidily into her eyes as she swept them lazily away.

"So!" grinned the girl, not altogether pleasantly. "What brings you here, Blondie?"

"I don't know," said Usha, lost, and it was the truth.

"You must've been doing *something* pretty bad, else you wouldn't have ended up here," retorted the girl, with unassailable logic.

Zadoc's words about that morning's discovery in the West Quarter flickered through Usha's head and she looked down at the floor, unable to return the other's gaze. Curiously, the girl swung her legs off the table, sauntered slowly over to Usha, and peered into her face. Usha flinched away, but the girl gently raised the sleeve of her dress, looked at the charred *G* burnt into the flesh of Usha's upper arm, and turned away.

"Gentlemen!" she addressed the crowd, and here the rabble raised their drinks and cheered. "We have a new

281

addition to our illustrious company." She threw an arm around Usha's neck, not unkindly, and pulled her along to the table. "Come and sit down, Blondie, you're just in time to catch the party."

Usha sat down on a rickety stool opposite the girl. A few scraps of meat and a crust of bread were tossed in front of her but she could only stare at them blankly. She could not reply to the few questions that were put to her, and, gradually losing interest in their silent newcomer, the crowd returned to their bawdy songs and dancing again, this time with much laughter and joyful smashing of plates against the rocky walls. She looked up to see the other girl watching her closely, as she drained the last of her flagon of chorley. "Come now! No point sitting there with a face like a wet Wednesday! Eat, drink and be merry, Blondie, for tonight. . ."

"Usha," corrected Usha firmly. "My name's Usha."

"Whatever you say, Blondie," grinned the girl. "I must say, though, I'm pretty curious as to why you're here. What did you do?"

Avoiding her stare, Usha nibbled cautiously on the crust and tried to make her voice sound casual. "I . . . I ran away."

"You ran *away*?" sneered the girl disbelievingly. "From what?"

Swallowing the crust was difficult with Usha's dry mouth, and despite herself she reached for a dirty cup of frothing chorley which had been pushed at her elbow and took a gulp. The bitter taste rose up her nostrils and made her sneeze, so that it was some minutes before she could reply. Yet, before she knew it, she found herself relating the whole story as if she could not stop.

"Aha!" said the other, smiling. "Running from one death to another. Well, I suppose that at least now you've got a fighting chance."

Usha looked at her sharply. "That's what Zadoc said. What do you mean?"

"Have you been living under a stone all your life? Tonight is the night we go to the ring and fight for our living while the great and the good of Citizen society come to watch us for their pleasure." With the same movement she pulled out a long, narrow-bladed sword from a sheath at her hip and laid it on the table. "Let me introduce myself to you, by the way. My name is Talia, four times champion of the Circus, *and* silver medal last season."

She sat proudly, seemingly waiting for Usha's congratulations.

"But you could die!" said Usha, amazed.

Talia snorted. "So? To be a gladiator means to make a pact with death."

"But don't you ever want to escape?" asked Usha.

Talia blinked in surprise. "Escape to what? Here we get our food and as much chorley as we can drink, somewhere to sleep and all we need to do in exchange is fight. I'm good at my job, and all of Genopolis knows my name. Talia the Tormentor, they call me!"

None of this seemed to make any sense to Usha. Why would anyone wish to stay in a place like this? Armed and dangerous as they appeared, surely a group of such keen fighters as this could manage to fight their way out of captivity?

She tried to say as much to Talia, but the other shook her head. "You got to be kidding, Blondie. What else do you think we'd be doing in the City? Outside they'd put most of us up for Regeneration! Bjarn here sold his freedom for three years to pay off his barter-debts," she said, pointing at a powerful-looking, bearded man in the corner. "And this likely lass —" she motioned to a tall girl slouched in the corner gazing at her chorley-cup in cross-eyed fascination — "ran away from her Citizen-husband because she didn't want to marry him. Now *there's* un-Citizenly conduct for you!"

"So," said Usha shyly, now that she seemed to have an ally in this disturbing world that she could confide in, "what did you do, Talia, to get put in here?"

Talia glared at her, slammed down her goblet and got up from the table, making a few practice passes with her sword so that it cut gleaming whirls through the smoky air. "None of your damn business, Blondie."

In panic, Arlo stared this way and that, trying to see over the bobbing heads of the crowd around him. He could see no litter, no Gemini servants, nothing. Only a never-ending stream of Citizen family-units with balloons and candy that shoved past him, sending him stumbling in all directions. Finally he managed to gain the relative safety of one of the pillars where the crowd thinned out and leaned against the rough stone. The energy of the last few hours was rapidly draining out of him. What had gone *wrong*? Perhaps Kristo had been intercepted, or perhaps he had not even got the message. Perhaps it was forbidden to park a litter right at the Gates? If he could not find Kristo, what on earth was he going to do?

From behind him he heard the coarse banging of a gong and a voice shouting. "All down for the Circus! Five minutes to curfew! Hurry along, there!"

Arlo bit his lip. He could not stay alone in the shadow of the pillars for long. Even the laziest Guardian would not believe his story of being Torin, a visiting diplomat's son, and his vague knowledge of Pharmopolis would not stand up to close examination, despite his token. Already the Circus attendants were pulling at the iron gates in preparation for closure, and with a last desperate glance over his shoulder he made his decision. He could just see Sir Herbert's blue cape loitering by the left-hand pillar of the Gate, and started to push his way back through the crowd towards them.

". . . but he can't be lost! He must be here *somewhere*!" he could hear Clarence complaining petulantly.

"Tough luck! So he'll miss the show," Cecilia shouted back, pulling at her parent's arm. "I'm sure he'll find us, won't he, Father? Come on!"

But as Arlo tried to reach them, the last of the audience, herded by the Circus attendants, moved in front of him in a great surge. Frantically he waved and called, but his voice was drowned in a hubbub of excited schoolchildren who ran cheering in front of him. Before he knew it, Sir Herbert and his children had disappeared and the rest of the rabble was swarming down through the Gates and into a yawning cleft in the rocky ground that opened like a mouth in front of them.

A hand lay on his shoulder and he jumped. A Circus attendant was motioning at him. "Oy! Brother! Are you coming to the Circus or not?"

Reluctantly, he nodded, and the man gave him a push on his shoulder. "Go on then. Down the staircase and keep to the left."

There was nothing that Arlo could do but follow the last of the crowd down the winding staircase, keep his hood over his face, and watch the show . . . alone.

Through the huge metal grid that separated the gladiators from the main arena came a smoky, reddish light and the hum of a vast crowd arriving. With the clash of metal and the singing of the gladiators ringing from the chamber behind her, Usha ventured down the passageway, feeling her way with her fingers.

The gladiators' quarter was divided into a number of small dark rooms: one a communal sleeping-area with hammocks slung up in rows; another an armoury with metal breastplates, shining tunics made of silver rings, slit-eyed helmets, tridents and nets; another a stinking toilet, just a hole in the ground. Usha turned away, overwhelmed by the stench and the futility of her situation. Leaning her back against the rocky wall, she slid to the ground, her face resting against the slimy stones.

Suddenly a light was shining into her face. Rolling over, she looked up. The Circus guard had thrust a torch through the huge grid, and was hissing at her urgently.

"Oi! You! Over here, and look sharp."

Usha struggled to her feet and approached him warily. As she reached the grid, the guard turned to someone behind him and held up a warning hand. "Two sacks of grain, you said? You've got them right here?"

The figure nodded, its drooping hood almost obscuring its face, and pushed a bulkily-wrapped bundle into the guard's arms. The guard grunted and moved away. "Two minutes then. Not a moment longer."

Usha stared, too dazed even to believe what she was seeing. Below the hood of the arriving stranger she could just make out a thin, sharp nose, and a piece of grimy rag that covered most of a face, including the left eye. . .

"Oh!" she gasped, clutching at him through the bars with her good arm. "Ozzie! However did you find me?"

"Dammit, Sis," muttered Ozzie in her ear, almost stifled from her embrace. "What was yer thinking of, going down East Street with the whole of Genopolis looking for yer? Are yer bleeding mental?"

"I'm so sorry. . ." began Usha but Ozzie cut her short while he glanced warily behind him.

"Look, Sis, we ain't got much time. Soon as I woke up and saw yer gone, I knew we was in trouble. Asked around and some old gal had seen yer going down past the bridge with them smuggling scum. When I heard that, I knew what they'd do with yer. This is where most people who're on the run end up.

"Listen up now. This place you're in, it's actually a pit dug out of the ground, see? It's meant to stop people like you escaping because the only entrance is up top, but there's some underground pipes and sewer-lines running around down here on both sides. Toby reckons he's found the sewer pipes that come out of this place, and I think we could break it open again from outside 'cos it's loose stone from the mining. Toby's back there now, working on it, but it'll take a couple hours more, I reckon."

Usha followed little of this. "But why can't you take me now, Ozzie? That guard's gone, and you could open the grid for me. . ."

"Look, Sis, I got in here 'cos I promised the guard two sacks of grain, and I'm hoping he don't realize I've given him gravel! Even if I got yer out, I couldn't fight me way out against two hundred Citizens, but thanks for the belief anyway. No, it's the only way, Sis. It'll be smelly, but you got to put up with that. Be by the toilet-hole in three night-hours, and we'll be with you as soon as we can."

Over his shoulder, Usha could see the guard approaching and clung to the boy as hard as she could. "But, Ozzie –"

Ozzie disentangled himself with some difficulty and thrust her back beyond the grate. "Come on, Sis, don't have an Outbreak on me, keep it together now!"

As he walked away his final words floated back to her through the reddish light of the flickering torches. "All you got to do is last the night out, Sis. You can do that, can't yer?"

As he emerged into the seats of the Circus pit along with the last stragglers, Arlo took in the amazing sight before him. Almost five hundred feet below him lay a vast arena, dug with trenches in the form of a maze and scattered with rocks. Tiny figures moved across its surface like ants. All around him were rows of seats, all with the same dizzying view of the cavern, rapidly filling up with a happy rabble of Citizens, all chewing spun-sugar, elbowing each other aside and pushing to get the best places. But Arlo was herded into one of many large stalls along with a motley crowd dressed in shabby clothes, who heaved and swayed, clapping their hands in time to a rousing song. Once inside the stall, the stench of chorley-fumes nearly knocked him over as a dripping flask was handed around. Arlo made his way to a corner and craned to see Sir Herbert and his children, but there were so many faces in the auditorium that it was hopeless.

From below came a hoarse blare of trumpets, and instantly the entire crowd burst into cheering and ragged singing. Through the applause Arlo could see people nudging each other and pointing to a great, carved balcony directly opposite. As if in response, a golden curtain was pulled back to a sudden fanfare. He froze. Far opposite, behind the ceremoniously-carved awnings, servants were bowing and ushering into place a man and a curly-haired boy. He could not see the man's face, but he caught a glimpse of deep-red robes and the sparkle as the chain of a Governor caught the light of the burning torches.

Instantly he was pulling the hood over his face and moving behind the burly Citizen next to him. Then through the brief silence he could hear two voices that he recognized floating down from the balcony above.

"Who's that in the Victor's Box?" Cecilia was asking her brother.

"Some big cheese or other," replied Clarence contemptuously. "If it hadn't been for him, Father'd have got us in there."

Arlo glanced up and saw that Clarence and Cecilia were excitedly craning over the edge of the box above him. For a moment he considered trying to make his way up to their balcony to find Sir Herbert, but he would be in full view of the Regis all the while. And there was another reason. The same pale light of destructive delight that had flickered in Clarence's eyes was now reflected in many of the other faces present. He scanned the ranks of Citizens from the safety of his hood. If Sir Herbert was indeed right that emotion was dulled and sleeping in the Citizens until something awoke it, then something had definitely managed to bring the crowd temporarily alive again. Seeing the evil sparkle in the eyes of most of those present, he shivered to think what that emotion could be.

"Here, boy!" sang out the plump and chorley-soaked Citizen carousing next to him, passing over a pair of thick glasses that looked like the spectacles that some old Doctors at the Inn wore. "Look through these!"

Not knowing what else to do, Arlo accepted them and held them over his nose. All of a sudden the tiny ant-like figures in the arena beneath sharpened into focus and he could suddenly make out a small, thin man, dressed in red coat and tails, standing in the centre of the ring. On his head was a golden top hat and in his hand a long gleaming whip. As he raised his arms, he cracked it savagely and the lash swung around him in a great curving plume.

"Ladies and Gentlemen! Welcome to the one and only . . . *Mephisto Merco's Mutant Circus!*"

In the gladiator's chambers they were drawing straws for who would be up first. The merrymaking had turned to fierce skirmishing, as the group practised their sword-strokes against each other. Usha, as the youngest and with one arm in a cast, was the only one to be excluded from the ballot, and she watched silently as the others queued up to learn their fate. Most were no more than twenty. Some, like Talia and Bjarn, the man she had pointed out to Usha previously, her rival challenger for the Championship, were already confidently performing stretches, limbering up and oiling their swords. From outside came a strident blare of music and the noise of a great roaring and stamping. Usha had never heard anything like it in her life.

"That's the crowd, Blondie," said Talia, smiling, and in her eyes Usha could see a glitter of wild enjoyment. "Hear them? They know we're coming. They know our names. Every one of them is here, just to see us."

Usha swallowed, trying not to keep glancing down the tunnel towards the toilet-room, from which she was almost sure she could hear the muffled sound of banging. . .

But the next second she realized that it was Merco, now dressed in a red fitted jacket, white boots and a large top hat over his hideous head, who strode down the corridor, beating a gong as he did so.

"Oi! You! Gemini!!"

Usha looked up with a start. "You're up in the final Game," said Merco. "The others'll tell you when."

"But, Merco," objected Bjarn, turning to him, "she's only just joined us. She hasn't trained, and she's only got one arm. It's not fair."

Merco ignored him. "Now listen," he said, thrusting his face into Usha's. "I've got ten thousand tickets sold for tonight's show, and we're one gladiator short for the big one. You get a damn sword and you get on out there. Hear me?"

With all attention riveted on the arena below, no one paid Arlo a bit of attention. At first, he had kept as far behind his neighbours as possible, but he soon realized that the Regis had no eyes for the crowd, or indeed any of the spectacle, sitting slumped in his box with his hand shading his forehead. It was his son who leaned excitedly over the balcony, alternately shouting encouragement to the fighters below or standing up to wave to the crowd.

Slowly, Arlo let the hood slip from his face and rested his burning cheek on his fist. Far below him, the Circus had begun, with much cheering from the watching crowd. First of all there had been a boxing match between two large, well-muscled Gemini which had been greeted with much jeering and booing, then an archery tournament by a couple of female warriors who shot blazing arrows through hoops. The audience had become impatient by this time and a clapping and stamping echoed around the auditorium. In the box where Arlo stood, a few of his neighbours had hurled a few rotten onions at the pit, but the rest appeared to be keeping their vegetables in reserve.

"Next bit's my favourite," said his neighbour excitedly, elbowing him in the side. "Give me back those glasses, Brother, will you?"

A drum roll rent the air and instantly the riotous crowd were hushed. In the middle of the pit,

Ringmaster Merco stood, a megaphone to his lips.

"Gentle Citizens. Tonight ... the Circus brings you ... the event that you have all been waiting for ... the dark ... the dangerous ... the deadly ... Labyrinth!"

Talia gave Usha a furious shove. "That's us! We're on!"

Up rolled the enormous grid in front of them and the glare of the arena dazzled her. All around was confusion and cheering and as she stumbled forward with the small group of gladiators, she knew that behind the flaming torches there was a vast audience hungry for blood. "Stay close to me, Blondie," muttered Talia, before she strode forward, holding her sword aloft in response to the hurrahs of the crowd. "Remember what I told you. Otherwise you won't survive."

"But. .." began Usha, but Talia was already leaping forward down into the shallow pit that fell before them and there was no time to ask questions. Usha clambered down the gritty bank behind the other girl, looking watchfully over her shoulder, replaying in her mind the brief instructions Talia had given her back in the gladiator's cavern.

Down in the labyrinth of troughs and boulders, they were lost in a maze of wandering paths and dead-ends. Up above, the audience must have a fine sight of what was going on, thought Usha, but down here they were effectively blinded, unable to see around the next corner unless they turned it. As Talia had told her, she looked for the first tall boulder that she could find, pressed herself back in its shadow and drew her sword.

"And hunting our brave warriors," proclaimed Merco's voice from above her, "are some of the most fearsome . . . dreadful . . . loathsome creatures that the pharms have ever produced. Gentle Citizens . . . I give you . . . the Mutants!"

A terrible noise rose about them, of roaring, bellowing and screaming that made Usha drop her sword and cover her ears, not so much from the noise as from the sudden realization that she was shortly about to confront the thing that had been haunting her nightmares ever since she had Arrived at Auntie's house.

"Creatures such as you have never imagined. . ." continued Merco's voice, echoing around the auditorium, but Arlo's attention was suddenly riveted on the forms that had been released from one of the metal grids. They streaked hungrily along the side of the arena to the screams and cheers of the crowd. First came two lithe, golden-striped creatures, long fangs gleaming from dripping jaws as they snuffled and picked up the scent of the gladiators who had run into the Maze. From above, he could hear Cecilia let out a muffled shriek.

"Sabre-tooths! Look, Clarence, they've regenerated live sabre-tooth tigers!"

"Shhh!" argued Clarence. "Last time they had a *mammoth*. This is *nothing*."

Arlo gazed as the striped forms padded their way down the steps and loped their way through the maze towards the crouching gladiators, who could see and hear nothing of their approach. In horror, both of what could happen and of the evident enjoyment of the crowd, he momentarily forgot his own danger and seized the glasses back off his neighbour, in time to see one of the tigers stealing around a boulder, muscles quivering, as it prepared to spring on a small, fair-haired gladiator, who cowered in the deep trough of the Labyrinth, her sword on the floor at her feet.

A flash of orange plummeting towards her and the ringing sound of steel were all that Usha saw before something caught her on the side of the head and she found herself knocked flying into the gritty sand. Crawling to her feet, she dazedly took in the form of a giant creature slumped at her side like nothing she had ever seen before, four-legged, its hairy skin striped with an orange and brown, its jaws open and bloodied. Her mouth open, she looked up at the figure of Talia, standing astride it, unsheathing her sword from deep within its chest in one swift sharp motion.

"What the hell are you playing at, you Gemini moron!" shouted Talia over her shoulder. "Don't just stand there like a lemon!"

Usha tried to speak but her tongue was dry and the words stuck in her throat. Raising a shaking hand she pointed in the direction of the dark tunnel-mouth.

"Talia . . . be careful, there's something else coming, something really bad. . ."

But Talia picked up Usha's sword and pressed the hilt into her hand without listening. "Shut up, Blondie. Of course there'll be more mutants coming, just you see. Keep sharp or you're going to let the side down. Now *move*!"

As the cheer that had greeted the slaying of the first tiger died away, Arlo sank back into his corner, weak from relief. For the second time in his life he had seen someone – even if it was a Citizen – close to death, and he seemed to be the only one who was not taking pleasure in the experience. Above him he could hear the sound of Sir Herbert's two children cheering and laughing.

"Talia! Talia!" chanted Cecilia, punching the air. "First blood to Talia!"

"Bjarn'll get his," snorted Clarence in response. "Ah, look, there he goes."

A bearded gladiator had dodged the second tiger mid-spring, and beheaded it with a single stroke. Clarence clapped and cheered. "Right. First round to the Champions. Let's see what they bring out next."

But, as the metal grid rumbled open and the expectant crowd drew in its breath, Arlo sprang to his feet, staring incredulously at the next creature that issued from the tunnel. Far below him, though almost unrecognizably thin and his hair matted and caked with dirt, slunk no other creature but . . . Rem.

Goaded by attendants with long pikes, he was being forced down into the labyrinth where desperate armed men and women waited to fight for their lives, gentle Rem who had never hurt a Citizen in his life, and who would approach them with no fear, only wanting to play. . .

A blind instinct overcame Arlo and he was up on his feet, pushing past the other Citizens. He stumbled out of the stall and down into part of the common seating where the crowd sat riveted on the spectacle before them. Blundering down the steep steps that led down to the ringside, he shouldered his way through groups of Citizens and left a trail of protests and shouts in his wake.

Clarence's voice rang out clearly from behind him.

"Look, there's Torin! He's made it! Hey! Where're you going, you silly pharm-boy? You're not meant to take part!"

But all that Arlo could see, as he pelted wildly towards the wall that surrounded the arena, was the image of Rem being torn away from him at the end of the Ceremony, lunging and barking as he was dragged off. He would not abandon his dog again, better they be together against a thousand monsters than left alone with the Citizen rabble or Clarence and Cecilia . . . All the fury he had felt towards the Doctors, the way he was passed around like a parcel, came to the fore. For once, he would make his own decisions. He would choose his own way.

He was hurtling down the steep steps so fast that the attendants who lined the walls had little time to hear his approach. The rough masonry of the wall could be easily climbed, and, lodging the toe of his boot into a crevice, he pulled himself up with his fingers. As he struggled up on to the top, there was a sudden cry and attendants ran to seize him. Pulling himself up and out of their reach, Arlo stood upright on the wall, searching for a glimpse of Rem below. But at that angle, the huge trenches and boulders formed a perfect maze, inside which the gladiators and animals were hidden. All Arlo could see, as he stared wildly around, was the distant form of the Regis, staring down from the Victor's Box far above, and beside him, the curly-haired boy, pointing excitedly down towards him. . .

Then a shout broke out behind him and, turning, he saw the distant but unmistakable figure of Kristo on the stairs above him, shouting at Sir Herbert.

"Where is he! Where's Arlo? What have you done to him?"

Arlo turned in shock towards him. "Kristo!" he called. "I'm—"

The next second, a well-aimed rotten cabbage, thrown from the singing Citizens above, caught him squarely on the side of the head. He lost his balance and, before he knew it, he was falling head first through the air, limbs flailing wildly, while the roar of a great crowd boomed and echoed around him.

Usha steadied herself, the sword drooping at her side. Her blurred eyes took in the scene. Padding towards her was another creature, though not as huge as the others. Thin and dejected, its ears drooping, it gazed at her and uttered a small whine. Even though Usha had never seen such an animal before, she could see that it had been treated cruelly, it looked half-starved and tufts of bloodied hair on its back showed where it had been beaten. As if it was too weary even to carry on, it flopped on to its stomach, its tongue lolling, and raised its sad eyes to hers.

Confused, Usha lowered her sword. Even in such danger as she was, she could see that the creature meant her no harm. She took a deep breath.

From behind her came the sound of Talia yelling, "Kill it, Blondie! Kill it, you imbecile, or I'll have to do it for you!"

"Hold, Talia," called Bjarn from behind them. "Let Usha earn her first blood."

But as Usha reluctantly raised her sword above her head, she saw something plummet from the encircling wall, hit the gritty sand above the trench and roll down the bank directly in front of her.

Usha could only stand and gape. Through the dust blown up by its arrival, she could see the object lying still as if stunned by its tumultuous arrival. Incredulously, she made out that it was a thin boy of about her age, dressed as a Citizen, lying on his back, his reddish-brown hair covered in dust and sand from his descent.

The next moment, the wild creature in front of her suddenly struggled to its feet, bounded over to the boy and started licking his face.

And then, to Usha's utmost surprise, the boy suddenly stirred, came to, flung his arms around the animal and started hugging it tightly.

THE ROARING OF THE APPROACHING FIRES

The woods were burning. Above and below the valley bright streaks of fire ran their vivid course along the treeline, the flames that licked the green leaves causing a thick plume of smoke to eclipse the dell where the village had once stood. The Naturals had fired their own land to create cover, and the lone airship that had finally responded to Hacker's distress call now buzzed around the thick column of fumes as ineffectually as a moth against a candle.

Down on the ground the heavy smog had turned the sky dark and threatening. With the winds picking up and the dryness of the summer bracken it was only a matter of time before the whole area became an inferno.

But in the village something essential had changed. A new mood of urgency was in the air. With the force of a dam breaking, the group feeling had moved from cowering and timidity to reckless courage. After the rout and victory over the Citizen patrol, the men and women of Region Three had gained confidence, walked taller, talked with a new vigour. The soldiers' rifles and uniforms had been distributed amongst their leaders, and the rest had armed themselves with axes, poles, knives and whatever tools they could find. As word of the rebellion spread, more and more people from the outlying Regional villages were pressing into the square until almost a thousand milled excitedly around the clearing, their weapons clutched in their hands. There was work to do.

In one hour, the flimsy wooden huts of the village had been almost totally demolished, and in the midst of the clearing, a tall funeral pyre had been built with their wood. On the summit Gea was laid, covered with a green shroud and decked with flowers. Those who passed her touched their foreheads as a mark of respect.

Supported by Kira, the old woman Ira limped forward so that she could gaze upon the face of her daughter.

Gea's expression was now peaceful as it had never been while life illuminated it. At the sight, Ira shuddered, and for a second the world spun around her. She could not think, she could not see, she was almost stupefied by her huge loss. It felt as if she had been blown apart, as if without warning the natural laws of her universe had turned in upon themselves, making everything that had previously been real suddenly collide, break apart and float; it was as inconceivable and grotesque as if a tree had sprouted legs or a fish could fly. If a parent could lose a child, then nothing could be impossible; nothing could be more ugly, evil, wrong –

A voice beside her was saying her name repeatedly. "Grandmother. Grandmother. Are you all right?"

Ira fought against the weight of fear pressing down on her lungs. The touch of the small hand that gripped hers became her only anchor in a heaving sea. The hand pulled gently and slowly she became aware of Kira beside her, her thin face sweating and mud-streaked, her eyes watering in the smoky light.

Ira gazed at her granddaughter, the only living relation still left to her. Gea — she could not mourn her now. Now was the time for revenge, not reflection. Her people needed a leader, not a mourner. With one hand she grasped Hacker's rifle, in the other a flaming torch, and climbed up on to the pyre beside her daughter. A single shot fired into the air was all that was needed to bring the crowd's attention. All heads turned to see her where she stood, outlined against the rolling clouds of smoke.

"Hear me. Today is the longest day of our year. It is also the day that marks the end of this age. On this day we shall set such a fire in the flesh of the Citizens as they will long to be rid of it. Those who feel nothing will come to be in eternal pain."

The crowd roared its approval.

"From the miserable, the downtrodden, comes the second Apocalypse. Too long have they rested on our suffering. The well-fed and comfortable Citizens are rotten inside their own skins. They do not know their own bodies or their own souls."

As Ira spoke, the torchlight flickered on the faces of friends, strangers, men, women, some weathered and scarred, some young and pale. Together they pressed round her, angry, confused, frightened.

"He came to us, the Doctor, promising us aid. We entrusted him with our dearest secret. And he took our love, our future, our hopes. He took everything we had, and we received nothing but lies, betrayal and treason.

"And that was our weakness. The weakness of love blinded us to our danger. Now we stand before our destruction. But the death of my daughter will not go unremembered. The kidnapping of her son – our heir – will not be permitted. Our lust for revenge will be stronger than any Citizen!"

A huge shout of rage answered her, and a clashing of metal as the ragged troops beat their weapons together in a crashing wave of sound.

Ira raised her voice higher over the clamour. "On this day we renounce everything that we have had from the Citizens – our shameful names, our fear of their brutality, the pain they use to control us. We become true unto ourselves and we shall march to take back what is ours. Today is the day of uprising. We march on Genopolis!"

Ira threw her torch on to the pyre, bent briefly for the last time to kiss her daughter's forehead, and leapt down into the crowd. The next second the oil-soaked tinder took fire, and with a whoosh shot blazing sparks into the blackening sky. A kind of frenzy took the crowd as Ira passed through them. They parted around her, caught her up on their shoulders and took up step in her wake, cheering and chanting as they passed out of the clearing and into the woods.

As he lay bound and exhausted in the dark and suffocating hut, Angus listened to their passage, feeling the turf shake underneath him with the stamp of their marching, and the roaring of the approaching fires.

SEVEN

Arlo buried his face in Rem's neck and breathed in the familiar dog-smell. His senses still reeling from his fall, he could only kneel with his arms around his pet, feeling tears well up and soak into the coarse hair. As he stroked the rough pelt, he felt the dog wince as his fingers uncovered the deep gashes left by a Circus whip."Oh, Rem . . . Rem . . . what have they done to you?"

But Rem only whined with delight and licked his face.

Slowly, Arlo's head cleared, and from the shadows above came the screaming of the enormous crowd. Down thudded a rain of rotten vegetables, exploding into foul-smelling mush, as the crowd, bursting with excitement, threw into the pit anything they could find. In front of him he saw a small group of amazed gladiators clustered in the shadow of a boulder, staring at him. One of them, the fair-haired girl who had narrowly escaped the tiger, was gazing at his embrace with Rem in disbelief. Now that he was closer, he could see that one of her arms was wrapped in a sling, but in the other quivered a sharp-looking sword.

Arlo pulled Rem towards him and wrapped his arms protectively around the dog. "Please! Don't hurt him!"

Another female gladiator with black plaits, the very image of Cecilia's figurine in the playroom, stepped forward incredulously. "What on earth are you doing? Where did you come from? Where's your weapon?"

Immediately an exclamation broke from the fair-haired girl's lips, and despite her plain fear of Rem, she started towards him eagerly. "Are you from outside? Are you part of Ozzie's gang?"

Arlo stared, confused. What weapon? Who on earth was Ozzie? He opened his mouth to speak but the fair-haired girl was suddenly blazing with excitement at him. "Did you break the lavatory wall down? Talia! Listen! It must be open. . ."

Arlo shook his head, bewildered, getting to his feet and feeling for Rem's collar with his left hand. "No! I don't know anything about Ozzie. And I'm not a gladiator! I had to come. He's my dog, you see." He glanced at their faces, blank with incomprehension, and pointed up in the direction of the amphitheatre from where he had jumped. "They're coming after me. We need to escape!"

"Escape?" sneered the gladiator. "Escape is for cowards."

"No, wait!" cried the fair-haired girl. "I know how! Talia, listen, if we. . ."

But the expression on the older girl's face silenced her, and Talia turned the sharp point of her sword towards them. "Don't even think about it, Blondie. No gladiator runs away from the Labyrinth and lives to tell the tale. If you fly, you die."

The fair-haired girl stared back at her, mouth open, lost for words. Arlo noticed that her eyes had suddenly clouded over to a dark slate grey, dull and unseeing. She was gazing over his shoulder, at something he could not see. . .

He felt a prickling at the back of his neck.

Then, as if in answer, a great bubbling roar issued from the mouth of the tunnel behind him.

A blackness rose up around Usha as she heard the roar thrill down the corridors of the Labyrinth. Dimly she could hear her fellow gladiators murmur and draw back as, through the dark passageway formed by two huge boulders, came a great horned shape, outlined against the evening dusk, and with it the musky stench that she knew so well from her nightmares. The strange boy who had fallen into the Labyrinth suddenly caught sight of the creature, and stumbled backwards, pulling the wild creature to him protectively.

From far above them, the Citizen crowd drew its breath as it took in the beast that approached the small group of gladiators. It had seen many a mutant, bred from ancient animal genes in the laboratories of Pharmopolis and sent in to the Circus for hunting and killing, but this was something deeper and darker than anyone present had ever seen before.

Above them, Merco's voice rose proudly above the gasps. "The Circus . . . presents you with . . . the new Mutant of the Age. I give you . . . the Minotaur!"

The shape moved forward and the flickering rush-lights that illuminated the tunnels revealed its form. Aghast, Usha turned to face the beast for the first time.

It seemed human, and yet not human. It was about the height of a normal Citizen man, with a body and four limbs, but there all resemblance ended. Squat and brutish, the body was covered in stinking rough hair, while the head was huge, grotesque, swollen out of all proportion, weighed down to one side by its bulk. Two great horns bulged from the top and swelled out to pointed rings behind. Its eyes, slanting and lit with a red glare, were stretched on either side of its head, and the flared nostrils pulled the nose back in two great arcs, so when the creature moved the echo of its breathing rasped in the momentary silence.

For many years the scientists of Pharmopolis had worked to combine exactly the right combination of man and beast for the delight of the Citizen crowds. At last they had produced a thing that walked upright as a man with the head of a bull, thinking and sensing as a creature of the wild, yet distorted into a vicious killing-machine.

And Usha, trembling, felt a deep and unhealthy recognition of the creature that had been created and bred alongside her, in the pen that bordered hers, an early nightmare which most Gemini had been conditioned to forget. . .

She tried to back away, but her legs failed to respond. Now she understood. She had seen this beast once before. Long ago at the pharms, before she had been brought to Auntie's house with her brain washed clean and unsuspecting, she had seen it breed and grow. And, somehow, she had always known that she would see it again.

We were created together, she thought, gazing at the shape, *in the same place at the same time. But for luck, they could have made me into something like this.*

And at the same time, the Minotaur caught her scent in its curling nostrils, and hesitated. It remembered her. For a split second the hunters and hunted stared at each other. Then, without warning, the mutant charged forward, head lowered.

But Talia and Bjarn, seasoned veterans of the Labyrinth, were ready. Springing forward they dealt a double stroke, on each side, on the rough hide of the monster, and just as quickly leapt back. A screaming bellow from the beast rose up to delight the ears of the crowd as it recoiled from the wounds dealt by the two gladiators and set off at a blundering run towards Usha.

"Blondie!" roared Talia somewhere to her left. "Get behind him, you lazy Gem! Get your sword up! Fight!"

But Usha still could not move. Horror darkened her mind and made her stand, helpless and hypnotized, as it thundered towards her. It was all over. It had come to nothing –

Something was tugging at her arm, insistent, dragging her out of her black despair. Confused, she turned. The strange boy was pulling desperately at her while the creature yapped at his heels. "Come on! Quick! Quick!"

Grasping Usha's wrist, he pulled her violently to the side and away from the beast – not a moment too soon. With a crash, the Minotaur collided with the boulder in front of which she had been standing and savagely gored it with its horns.

The trance was lifted. Usha's feet could move again and she gripped her sword. Roaring, the Minotaur wheeled to face them, blood streaming from its gashed tusks. They took one look, and then with one accord, turned and ran for their lives.

Sprinting down the narrow corridors, littered with stones and slime, they dodged and jumped, conscious all the time of the pounding beast at their heels. Openings branched off in all directions and the older, fleeter gladiators, knowing their paths, quickly disappeared until it was only Usha and the strange boy who had saved her life pelting blindly along the Labyrinth with no sense of direction. As they wheeled round a corner, Usha stopped short with a cry.

They had turned into a dead-end.

Images of Ozzie waiting for her in the gladiator's chambers flashed before Usha. They had to get out. Scanning the rocky wall that rose up in front of them she shook her head. Even if she could climb it with one wrist in plaster they would be seized and brought down by the Minotaur before they had gone more than a few arms-lengths.

Behind her there was a stumble and a cry. The boy had slipped on one of the many treacherous rocks that lined the floor. As he tried to pull himself to his feet, the corridor echoed with deep rumbling breaths as the Minotaur lumbered into full view around the corner of the tunnel and fixed them with its red glare.

Usha raised her sword and flung it at the beast like a javelin. It pierced the hide and dark blood spattered down the animal's haunch, but the wound was not deep and the sword clattered harmlessly to the floor. With her last weapon gone, Usha could only watch helplessly as the blade was splintered beneath the iron hoof of the Minotaur, as it moved closer and closer towards them.

But Rem had seen his master fall. The dog wheeled about and ran back to where Arlo lay, barking furiously at the approaching monster. Puzzled but undaunted by the small creature, the Minotaur came to a halt, and lowered itself to all fours, fixing the dog with its bloody stare. Scrabbling behind him on the floor,

Arlo's hand closed over a small rock. Even as Rem lunged at the beast's ankle, he pulled himself up, took aim and flung it hard between the creature's eyes.

As the Minotaur reared up, bellowing, Arlo saw a bearded gladiator, his sword flashing, leaping out of the shadows and hewing at its back leg. With a roar of pain and rage, the Minotaur wheeled to face its new challenger, who stepped backwards but lost his footing and fell. Instantly the beast was on top of him, but not for long. Behind him was Talia, who, seizing the moment when it was distracted by its prey, raised her sword and delivered the final death-stroke. A swathe of blood spattered her cheek as she drove the blade deep into the mutant's neck.

Flinging itself against the walls of the tunnel, howling, with dark blood streaming down its hide, the Minotaur staggered a little way towards them, its little eyes clouding over. Then, like the toppling of a huge boulder, it slumped to the floor with a crash, bringing Talia down with it. A momentary silence filled the trench as the bloodied, dust-covered fighters glanced at each other, and then at the huge form that lay motionless before them, almost blocking the maze with its bulk.

"Well fought, gladiators!" muttered Talia, stirring, as she lay in the dust.

Arlo felt a hand grasp his shoulder, and he turned to see the small fair-haired girl, her eyes now open and clear, pointing wildly at the top of the Labyrinth.

"You still want to escape, boy? Then come with me! Now!"

Yet, as Arlo turned dazedly to follow the girl, a shot whistled above his head and buried itself in the wall of the tunnel. Another shot followed, and then another, peppering the Labyrinth and the bewildered gladiators with bullets.

"What's happening?" cried the fair-haired girl. "What's going on?"

Arlo glanced up at the arena walls and saw a troop of brown-uniformed Guardians climbing down into the Circus pit. In that instant he realized what was happening. The Guardians had been called once the Regis had glimpsed him, and now that the Minotaur had been slain, they had gained courage to approach. He could see rope-ladders unfurling into the arena, and hear orders being shouted at a distance. Instantly, he threw himself into the shadowy overhang of a rocky wall, pulling the girl with him, speaking through great heaving breaths.

"The soldiers . . . I think they're after me. . . ."

In front of them, the bearded gladiator scrambled to his feet, sword upraised. "Why are they shooting? They cannot do this! It is against the laws of the Circus!"

"Bjarn, please!" begged the girl. "Shush! They'll kill you!"

But it was too late. A line of guns swung in the gladiator's direction, and there came the sharp crack of a rifle. Bjarn's sword suddenly clattered to the ground.

With disbelief in his eyes, Bjarn turned to look at his shattered right hand, blood streaming from where the bullet had passed clean through his flesh and buried itself in the rocky wall of the tunnel.

"Bjarn! Quick! Escape with us!" called the girl, wildly.

The man turned his head and Arlo was close enough to see the darkness in his eyes. "I do not think I can go," he said. "Where is there for me to go after this? The sewers? Regeneration? This is the end for me now. After all that I have seen, and all that I have conquered, it is over. There is nobody waiting for me."

"That's not true!" implored the girl. "You can come back with me. . ."

But Bjarn shook his head. "My life was here, child, and it stays here. But you are young, and all life is before you. If you will go, then go now, quickly."

"No!" cried the girl, but Bjarn was already sprinting away from them, holding his sword in his left hand, drawing the sights of the soldiers away from the two children who still crouched in the shadow of the rock. "Stop shooting!" he roared. "This is madness! The fight is over!"

"Watch out!" cried Arlo, but it was too late. A second bullet ripped through Bjarn's throat, picked him up, spun him round and slammed him against the rocky floor, just inches from where Talia had fallen as she dealt the final stroke against the Minotaur. The female gladiator gazed at the sight in horror.

"Bjarn! Bjarn!"

But the only answer was a trickle of blood that snaked out from Bjarn's limp body, to mingle with the dark puddle that welled from underneath the Minotaur.

Talia crawled to her fallen comrade, tugging at him dazedly, in full line of the guns, too confused to see the danger. "Bjarn! What are you doing! Get up!"

"Stop it, Talia! They've killed him!" cried the girl. "And if we don't go, they're going to kill us too!"

Arlo was surprised to see such an Outbreak from a Citizen. For a moment her face was turned towards him fully, and he saw something in her grey eyes that made him remember the Gemini servants that attended him in the Inn.

Surely she couldn't be a. . .

But the next second the idea was swept from his mind by the huge rumble of gunfire that leapt up all around them. There was no more time to argue. It was now flight or death. Grabbing Rem with one hand he leapt forward, following the fair-haired girl, who took off at full pelt down the corridor, ducking low to avoid the whine of the bullets and leaving the others where they lay.

Usha sprinted out of the tunnel and emerged into the bright glare of the auditorium, the strange boy and the creature running hard on her heels. As she ran, she could see a battalion of Guardians issuing into the arena, a huge net strung between them. As soon as they leapt out, they were seen, the alarm was given and instantly a group were racing towards them over the dusty ground.

"Quick! This way!" Usha dodged beneath a metal grid towards the chambers, the boy and his creature stumbling in her wake. Inside the tunnel, a few of the gladiators waiting for the next fight crowded round them, attracted by the sounds of commotion. "What's going on? What's happening?"

But at that moment Talia came sprinting into the tunnel behind them, her face alive with a fierce energy. With her left hand, she reached up and pulled down the lever to shut the grid, ducking in quickly as the heavy metal gate thudded to the ground behind her.

"Where are the others?" cried Usha, but Talia only had eyes for the boy, shouldered her way through the others and slammed him against the rocky wall. Rem lunged for her ankle but the gladiator kicked him aside and he dodged into a corner, snarling. Unfazed, Talia unsheathed her dagger and held it inches from Arlo's face.

"What the hell is going on? You're getting good gladiators killed out there!"

"No!" Usha pulled ineffectively on Talia's sleeve. "It's not his fault!"

"I had to," gasped the boy, desperately. "They were after me. . ."

"I don't care!" barked Talia, threateningly. "You got my partner killed and you've blown the championship for me now! Tell me why I shouldn't just kill you here and now!"

"I'm sorry about Bjarn," gasped the boy, as well as he could through her choking grasp. "But if they catch me, they'll kill me."

"Yeah?" sneered Talia. "Who'd worry about dirtying their hands over a little piece of muck like you?"

"It's the Governor Regis of the Inn of Court. He's got his soldiers with him, there's the chief-of-police called Brigadier Hacker and they've burned Doctor Benedict and imprisoned Ignatius and. . ."

Talia recoiled from him suddenly, and the boy slid to the floor, coughing. On her face was a look of shock that Usha had not seen there before. Slowly, the hand holding the dagger fell to her side. In the sudden pause, the sound of a voice hissed through a small crack in the wall.

"Oi! Sis! What you playing at in there!"

Usha swung around and pressed her face gladly against the stone. "Ozzie! We're out," she gasped, "but there's some soldiers coming and started firing, they'll be here in a moment!"

"Well quit quarrelling and get yer gang ter help us then!" rejoined Ozzie, and suddenly a loud banging started from behind the wall. The strange boy scrambled to his feet, seeming to grasp the situation instantly, seized a rock from the ground and vigorously attacked his side of the wall with it.

"Are you coming?" cried Usha to the other gladiators, but they shook their heads and hurriedly retreated down the corridor into the chambers.

"Bjarn thought like you and now he's dead!" cried Usha after them. Chancing a quick look around the corner she could see and hear the soldiers discussing how best to break through the metal grid. "You've got to come with us! Otherwise you're going to die!"

But within seconds only Talia, Usha and the strange boy with his animal remained in the tunnel. With great deliberation, Talia spat into the dust. "Great. Thanks for nothing, Blondie. You and your little boyfriend here have gone and wrecked my chances. Regeneration's the only place for a failed gladiator. So I reckon I've got no choice but to be coming along with you, then. But you put one foot wrong, you hear, and I'll make you sorry you were ever Created."

Arlo banged frantically at the wall with the jagged chunk of rock. He knew only that his one chance of escape seemed to be with the fair-haired girl and the voice on the other side of the wall. Sweat poured down his forehead and he could feel his fingers numbing with the repeated blows. Around him Rem dodged and yapped, filling the whole cavern with his shrill barking.

All of a sudden the wall seemed to waver and ripple before his eyes.

"Whoa! Mind out!" came the voice.

Quickly Arlo turned and ran but not quickly enough; the bricks had already begun to topple and the falling masonry narrowly missed him and smashed into the toilet chamber, sending a wave of foul-smelling liquid over everything. Arlo crouched against the wall and felt his stomach heave as he shielded his face with his arms. Through the crash of the rubble he could hear a voice shouting incoherently. Looking up, outlined in the hole in front of them by the flickering light of a guttering torch, he saw a boy a few years older than him, his eye bound up with a strip of rag, gesticulating frantically at him.

"Where is she? Where's Usha?"

"Who?" shouted back Arlo, now totally confused, but at that moment the fair-haired girl dashed past him and flung herself headlong at the other boy. "Ozzie! Ozzie! Thank you!"

"Come on!" growled the boy, pulling her arms away from his neck. "We got to go now, Sis," and, shooting a look towards Arlo and Talia, "Where the hell do yer think *you're* goin'?"

"They're coming with us, Ozzie!" started the fair-haired girl, but the one-eyed boy cut her off abruptly.

"Time enough to sort that out later, Sis. Just get moving otherwise we'll wish we'd never bin born."

At that moment Rem pushed his head inquiringly between Arlo's knees and Ozzie leapt back with a muttered curse at the sight. "Come on now, Sis, we can't have no Circus animals coming with us! They'd eat us soon as look at us, they would!"

Arlo opened his mouth to speak but the girl tugged desperately at Ozzie's arm. "The animal's not dangerous, honestly, it didn't touch anyone, and they saved my life back there, Ozzie, so let's just *go*, can we?"

"I have slain wilder creatures than this before," broke in the female gladiator abruptly, "so if it attacks anyone I shall kill it instantly."

Ozzie turned with a muttered curse and stormed down the sewer-tunnel. Arlo pulled Rem protectively away from Talia, but she ignored the dog and merely pushed Arlo sharply on the shoulder. "Get in there."

Once through the jagged hole in the wall, the floor of the tunnel was sticky and slippery, forcing them to slow down and pick their way with difficulty, the noise of their many feet muffled and echoing down the slimy walls. Ozzie led the way, confidently navigating his way in the dark and often doubling back to lose any pursuers. Behind him came Usha and then Arlo, holding a straining Rem on the leash. Finally, Talia brought up the rear, glancing repeatedly behind her at the enveloping dark. Whenever Arlo looked back at her, he could see her staring at him with a strange look on her face. Ahead, Ozzie's torch burned low to a smouldering red, and finally extinguished itself. As they forged their way deeper into the blackness, the sound of their breathing seemed to reverberate and multiply down the long pipes until all around them it seemed that the air was full of clustering ghosts that muttered and whispered around them.

Finally, just as Arlo could bear it no longer, Ozzie slowed down and signalled for them to stop. In front of him a tiny match flared, and Arlo could see in its dim light Ozzie and Usha standing at a small crossroads where the tunnel had divided into two. From the left-hand passage flowed air that smelt sick and sulphurous, from the right, a cleaner, thinner breeze. But although the left tunnel was broader and cleaner, the right-hand tunnel was barely more than a few feet in any direction, and its mouth was scattered with stones from a recent rockfall.

"I don't understand it!" Ozzie was saying. "I told 'im to wait right 'ere!"

"Are you sure we're in the right place?" began Usha, but Ozzie had raised his voice and started hissing down the left-hand tunnel.

"Toby! Toby! Where are yer, yer idiot?" He looked around, grumbling. "Just gone off and left us, he has!"

"Look!" cut in Talia brusquely. "What's wrong with the creature?"

Arlo stared at Rem. The dog had his nose down at the entrance of the left-hand tunnel, and was standing stock-still, bristling, a low growl emanating from his thin belly.

"What is it?" breathed Usha. "What's happening?"

Arlo felt a cold chill. Rem was acting in the same way as he had in Kane's laboratory, or in his bedroom when he was gazing at the mirror. . .

"Wait!" called Arlo. "There must be danger there. It's not safe."

Ozzie wheeled to face him. "Not safe? I grew up in

these tunnels! I know every bit of 'em like the back of me hand! You ever lived here?"

"No," stuttered Arlo, feeling ill-at-ease beneath the older boy's stare. "But I've a feeling that something's wrong, and so does my dog."

"What's a feeling?" started Usha, but Ozzie thrust her rudely aside.

"Ah, well, if yer don't *feel* like it, then yer can just go the other way, can't you, and so can anyone else who *feels* like you do. . ."

The fair-haired girl tugged at Ozzie's sleeve, her voice raised and echoing down the tunnel. "Stop it!" she protested. "Ozzie, he saved me back there—"

"Yeah, I'm sure he did, Sis," returned Ozzie shortly, stepping back, "but we can't take people who challenge the way I do things, you know? Only room for one boss here, get me?"

At that second there was a small but distinct sound from the left-hand tunnel, a brittle jingle of metal on stone. Instantly Ozzie waved them all to silence and blew out the match. They froze, apart from Talia, whose hand went swiftly to her sword. They stood, holding their breath. Not a sound could be heard in the tunnel.

"I thought we'd lost them?" whispered Usha as quietly as she could.

Out of the darkness of the left-hand tunnel, footsteps echoed on the stony floor, and a voice spoke coldly.

"No. You are the ones who are lost."

The group spun round in sudden panic as a small

lantern was unsheathed. In the dim light a posse of soldiers strode forward from the left-hand tunnel where they had been crouching. Another group emerged out of the shadows of the tunnel behind them. Arlo could not see the face of the man who spoke, but the voice he knew well, and it turned his blood to ice in his veins.

"My dear children, do you really think that you could escape us? Our eyes and our ears are everywhere. Young vermin, you live in our sewers and consume our garbage because we suffer you to. Gladiators, you fight in our circuses to entertain us before your ultimate Regeneration. But the idea of escape, from our City, is sadly impossible. All ways, all exits are guarded. We see all, we hear all."

As the voice of the Regis hissed around the chamber, Arlo felt himself backing slowly away, one hand clutching Rem, the other feeling for the dark right-hand passageway down which the stream of cleaner air flowed.

"Yet, even now, poor and desperate as you are, I offer you a bargain. I will offer you your freedom in exchange for the red-haired boy amongst you that I seek. He alone I want, and will take, if you surrender him to me freely."

Talia gazed at the Regis suspiciously. "Why? What's he worth to you?"

The Regis laughed, a horrible, grating sound. "Nothing, if you are thinking of barter, though to be sure it has cost me a certain amount of trouble. But if you must know, he is a fugitive Natural, *less than human*, who has escaped from the laboratory that has housed him and evaded arrest from our loyal Inspector, Brigadier Hacker. It is the duty of all good Citizens, such as yourselves, to keep the City free from the taint of such creatures."

With a feeling of dread, Arlo saw the faces of the others turn towards him slowly, and in a flash he understood what would happen. They would give him over to the Regis, they could not help it, there was no other choice – but the Regis would not keep his side of the bargain, just as he had not kept it in the study with Arlo. It was a trick, a way to keep them talking as the soldiers inched ever nearer –

"He's lying!" he burst out, suddenly. "Please! Don't believe him!"

"Why would they believe you, Arlo?" taunted the Regis. "Dressing in Citizen's clothes, eating their food, and breathing their air cannot make you more than you are, a Natural. You are not worth the dirt under a Citizen's feet."

Ozzie turned to Talia and Usha, muttering softly, "Come on, Sis, it's a no-brainer. He's a bleeding Nat! I knew as soon as I seen him that there were something wrong. Just give him over and let's be on our way."

"But, Ozzie, listen to yourself," Usha hissed back. "I'm not a proper Citizen, and neither are you, now! Look how they've treated us! You're going to betray someone to go back to a life of crawling in the sewers?

Don't you remember what you said? It's not *fair*!"

"Ah, a dissenting voice from a Gemini, of all people," said the Regis, calmly. "Then perhaps I should make my request and the bargain clearer. If you refuse my request, I will kill you. If you run, I will hunt you down until the ends of the earth, and I will make sure that nowhere in Genopolis will be safe for you."

Around him Arlo could feel the group shift uneasily. Ozzie looked at him mistrustfully, but it was Usha who spoke up again. "He saved me in the Labyrinth, Ozzie, and if it wasn't for him I wouldn't be here now."

Ozzie dug his elbow into her. "Shut *up*, Sis. . ."

The Regis sighed. "Then let me show you another way in which you might be persuaded. A life for a life, perhaps?"

At that moment there was a choking gasp, and the Regis stepped forward into the light, his bony arm hooked tightly around the neck of a small, spectacled, spiky-haired figure, struggling weakly to stay on his feet. The other hand held a small shining dagger, the blade of which was turned against the boy's throat.

"Toby!" cried the fair-haired girl, and Ozzie swore terribly.

"What's going on! Let him go, yer bald creep! Don't yer touch him!"

"I'm sorry, Oz," gasped Toby. "I didn't see 'em coming! I'm sorry!"

The Regis started to draw his dagger mockingly against Toby's neck but Talia was faster. With one lightning motion she bent to the floor, picked up a rock and flung it at the lantern with all her strength. It hit it squarely, shattering the glass, and throwing an arc of blazing oil up and around them, to fall in fiery clods on the uniform of the soldiers and the cloak of the Regis. Instantly all was turmoil as the flames caught hold and the soldiers staggered back, beating at their blazing clothes. With a cry the Regis released his hold on Toby, and Ozzie leapt forward, caught him by the scruff of the neck and dragged him away.

But Talia, veteran of many fights and Circus champion, was totally in control. "Run! Run!" she cried, pushing the group into the tiny right-hand tunnel. As the last of the children disappeared, she ducked after them, driving her sword uep into the earthy roof. A small heap of rocks and a large drift of earth cascaded down into the mouth of the tunnel, nearly swamping her. Talia did not wait to see more, but followed the others at full tilt. From behind her she heard the groan of the rocks as the mouth of the tunnel started to subside, sealing them off from the pursuit and the distant howls of the Regis.

Slipping and sliding, the group flung themselves down the narrow earthy tunnel as it slowly caved in behind them. In places it got so narrow that the children had to crawl on all fours, often through inches of muddy stinking water. Just when Usha, leading at the front, thought that they would be buried altogether, the tunnel suddenly opened out and she stumbled into the night. She felt slime underneath her hand and breathed in a lungful of warm, salty air that reminded her of the port. Through the blackness she saw that they had crawled out into a small, open-sided cave, whose rocky floor led down to an enormous expanse of dark, rippling water, larger than anything she had ever seen.

One by one, coughing and blinking, the runaways emerged into the salty air, to regard the scene before them in bewilderment.

"What is it?" breathed Usha.

"It's the sea, you stupid idiot," snapped Ozzie, as he crawled out and leaned against the wall. "What the hell are you thinking of, Usha? We had a chance ter go free, yer know? And yer threw it all away for a bleeding *Natural*?"

Usha wheeled to face him. "Shut *up*, Ozzie! I need to think!"

"Better think real hard, Sis, 'cos you just lost us the last chance we had. That bloke ain't going ter rest till he finds us again. I seen it in his eyes."

Toby dragged himself to the wall, where he sat, wheezing and coughing. "His breath stinked something awful. I was afraid he were going to stab me, but then I thought I could die from his pong instead."

Yet Talia, covered with earth from the tunnel, emerged jubilant, as if the skirmish had somehow revived her. Usha could see once more the satisfied glitter in her eyes as she cleaned her dirty sword against the side of her boot. "Fight for their pleasure because they allow us, indeed? They're lucky I let them go alive!"

Ozzie flung himself down and covered his remaining eye with his sleeve. "Where are we going ter go, Sis? Yer so clever, what the hell we going ter do now? We can't go back, and there's only the sea in front of us, and we ain't no fishes."

But it was the Natural boy who spoke up. "Don't speak to her like that! She was only trying to help!"

Ozzie gazed at him sharply. "Yeah, Natural? Was I talking to you?"

"Arlo," said the boy, with a sudden flash in his eyes. "My name's Arlo."

"Whatever," sneered Ozzie. "We're all in this mess 'cos of you, you know that?"

"Ozzie, don't be so un-Citizenly," reproved Usha, but the Natural had already turned on his heel and headed down to where the black water lapped at the shore. Hesitantly, Usha followed him.

He was crouching at the waterside, holding on his lap a small dark parcel. His dog lay at his feet, tail twitching. Usha sat carefully down on the other side, as far from the creature as she could get.

"Ozzie, you know, he says a lot of things that he doesn't mean, so don't mind him," began Usha, after a while, glancing shyly at the Natural. He had a nice face, she thought, although a bit odd and thin, and up close he was much younger than his rich clothes and his posh accent had first made him appear. He reminded her of the Higher Citizens she had seen around the Academy or the Inn of Court, or the Governor who had tried to bargain for her from the smugglers. . .

Thinking of it made her shiver, and she pulled her cloak closer around her. She had heard of Naturals – who hadn't, these days – but she had never thought of meeting one in the flesh, much less one who had risked his life to pull her away from the Minotaur. As with all things that people said, the reality was so different from the story. Auntie had always complained that Naturals just made a nuisance of themselves and stopped decent people getting their weekly cake delivery on time.

But the boy paid her no attention, still staring undecided at the parcel that he held. Cradled in his hands was a sheaf of parchment, bound between a leather cover. It looked very old, and Usha had never seen anything like it, even in Auntie's house. "What are you doing?" she asked. "What is it?"

"It's a book," said the boy softly, stroking the cover with one forefinger.

Usha peered at it interestedly. "What's that?" she asked.

"What's a book?" The boy turned round and stared at her. "Oh, of course," he said, almost contemptuously. "I forgot Geminis can't read."

"Of course I can't," answered Usha, taken aback. She

might just have well have been asked if she could fly. "What's the use of reading?"

"Well. . ." said the boy, surprised, "if you can read books, they can tell you things that other people have forgotten. They can remember things that happened many years ago, and tell you about it as if it was yesterday."

"But Auntie says reading is dangerous," objected Usha. "It can put other ideas into your mind."

"It's not like that," answered the boy. "This book is different. It's about me."

Usha caught a slight quiver in his tone and craned forward, suddenly fascinated. "Really? So what does it say then?"

"I don't know," he answered. "I haven't read it."

"Why not?" she scoffed. "I thought you could?"

"It's not that," he said, so quietly that she almost couldn't hear him. "I'm scared."

At the first sight of the book, Arlo's heart had risen into his mouth. It had cost him a great effort to bear it through the trials of Sir Herbert's house and not read it, but something that he could not name was holding him back. For the first time he was holding the key to his history, but the idea of learning who he was and where he came from was strangely frightening.

Next to him the fair-haired Gemini leaned over and leafed through the pages, looking at the scribbles curiously. "What's that? What does it say?"

Arlo held the page up to the moonlight and squinted

at it. Instead of being printed and bound like most books he had read, it seemed to have been handwritten on some stiff paper and a thick piece of leather roughly stitched over the outside as a makeshift cover. Inside, the ink was patchy and faded, scrawled as if the writer had been in a terrible hurry, with misspellings, blotches and incomplete sentences. He examined the first sentence, and with perseverance, made it out.

" '*A Manifesto Concerning An Experiment for the Advancement of Genopolis. The Natural Equation.*' "

"What does that mean?" asked the girl.

Arlo shook his head. "No idea," he said, but the girl was not to be so easily put off. "Read on!" she said, pushing the book at him. "Don't you want to know about *you*?"

Arlo took a deep breath. " '*We, the undersigned, being members of the Inn of Court and the Maian Inn, do hereby swear the following Manifesto. . .*' I can't read it after there. It's too dark."

"Try!" insisted the girl and Arlo scanned further down the page.

" '*For these reasons, we decided to procure a baby Natural. Some of our members had contacts in Region Three, a small, Citizen-controlled Natural reserve, situated in scrubland towards the east of the City of Genopolis, and one Natural family in particular stood out for their suitability. The father, Angus, was in his twenties and had previously befriended our contact during a research mission. His wife, Gea. . .*' "

Arlo's voice trailed off as a lump rose in his throat. For the first time ever, he was looking at the names of his mother and father.

"Go on," prodded the girl, and Arlo blinked away the water that blurred his eyes.

"*'His wife, Gea, was with child for the first time. Yet the monitoring of childbirth in the Regions had become stricter. It was almost definite that the child would be confiscated once born. Angus asked our contact to take the baby with him for safety. He hoped that if it was raised in the City, far from the sickness and poverty of its homeland, then the child would be safe. For these reasons we judged the child to be eminently suitable for the terms of our Experiment. . .*

"*'Yet the child's mother was reluctant to let her baby go, and showed great distress when our contact attempted to take the child with her. It appears that so great was the bond between Naturals that she was caused emotional pain at the thought of being separated from him. Once our contact had extracted the child, and brought it back secretly to the City, a disturbance began in the Regions. A great. . .'*"

Arlo broke off as he turned the page, his head spinning so fast that he could barely take in the facts and turn over, but when he did, another shock met him. The next few pages had been torn out roughly in the middle of a sentence, leaving only a feathery clump of scrap-paper attached to the spine.

"That's it. That's all there is," he said, disappointed.

But the girl's attention was on a small piece of paper that had slipped down unobserved and lay at the ground at his feet. "What's this? Is this part of the book?"

Arlo unfolded it. At first sight it seemed like a sprawling mess of ink and scratches of a pen in no particular order. Puzzled, he turned it this way and that, until the blurred words suddenly separated into clarity and he could read "Region III" in the corner of the parchment. The next moment it all made sense.

"It's a map," cried Arlo. "Look!"

"What's a—" began Usha, but Arlo was on his feet, suddenly transformed, his face blazing with joy.

"A map's a picture, a list of directions . . . to where my family-unit live. Not in Pharmopolis, not in Genergis, but even further, in a land over the water."

"A land over the water?" croaked Toby from behind them, where he had been listening. "You mean there's other places outside the City?"

"There's a whole world outside the City," said Arlo, and Usha was amazed at the sound in his voice. "It's my home," he said happily, stroking the dog's head with his other hand. A smile broke out over his thin features, quite transforming him.

Usha blinked. *Home* was something that she had never properly understood. It was a word that she had used when living with Auntie, but it had been Auntie's house that it described. Ozzie had had a real home once but that had all ended once he had lost his eye. Though Usha had never known such a thing, a *home* seemed a very precious thing to those who had lost them, or who were searching for them.

All the same, she was strangely impressed at his idea of escaping from the City. To leave this place of stone and bricks, where she had never been anything other than a servant, and never would be anything other than a Gemini, was enticing. How many times had she sat on the roof of Auntie's house and wondered . . . wished . . . to find somewhere that the City did not reach, a place where you could no longer see the Consulate towering over everything. . .

Thoughtfully Usha got up and wandered to the edge of the cavern. The water had risen up the rock face even while they were talking and the huge expanse of sea stretched away on every side, glimmering in the beam from the distant lighthouse.

"Don't go up there, Sis," called Ozzie. "That way goes south-east to the port, and there ain't no way out from there."

The port! Usha stopped dead, turned and ran back to Ozzie, swinging him round to face her.

"Ozzie, did you say that way goes to the port?"

"Yeah, Sis, but there's guards all over there. . ."

Usha hardly heard him. For an instant she was back in the cage, by the two smugglers, listening to Zenna's voice ringing in her ears.

"I will leave by barge from the south-eastern cove by the port at three night-hours when the tide is high."

Usha ran back to the bedraggled group, pointing furiously behind her.

"If we're on the south-eastern side, Ozzie, there must be a cove around here, a place that the smugglers use to come in and out of the City. What's the time now?"

Ozzie looked at her incredulously. "It's nearly three night-hours, but yer not thinking of bumping into them again, are yer, Sis?"

"Come here, everyone!" cried Usha. "Listen to me! I've got an idea!"

Down a darkened passageway, Zenna hustled along, her eyes flickering in the dim glow of the candle that she bore aloft. The smugglers' paths that wove through the bowels of Genopolis were dark and intricate, and known only to a few. As she descended into a narrow cove, she could hear the sea lapping at high tide. At the water's edge the dim bulk of her boat moved against the rocky jetty with a grating sound, borne on the gentle swell of the rising waters. She paused briefly and listened over her shoulder. The hubbub of the events in the Circus was deadened through many layers of rock, but Zenna's sharp ears could have sworn that she heard the soft pad of footsteps following her, and which stopped abruptly when she turned around.

Setting down the candle on the shore so that its faint glow illuminated the small cave, she took hold of the painter and started to unwind the boat from its moorings. Suddenly a shadow moved behind her and she froze.

"Where do you think you're going, Zenna?" asked Usha coolly, stepping out of the darkness of the rock behind her.

Zenna stood up and moved back from the girl, recovering her composure, even laughing a little.

"Well, Gemini! You nearly startled me there."

She was taller and stronger than Usha and her hand strayed warningly to her waist, where the handle of a curved knife rested.

"Where are you going?" repeated Usha, and in her eyes there was a quiet confidence that Zenna had not seen before.

"I'm going back to the pharms," replied Zenna with a sneer, backing away from her and towards the boat.

"Really?" said Usha softly, moving forward.

Zenna pulled out the dagger and held it in front of her. "Stand back, or I swear I'll slit your throat," she snapped. "You cost me more than barter this evening. Thanks to you, I've got a reputation to make up."

"And where do I go?" asked Usha.

Zenna shrugged. "Live or die, it's all the same to me. You won't last long in the streets. You'll get taken by someone else or hunted down or die of starvation before the month is out."

Something nudged Zenna in the back and she turned around to see a small group of desperate runaways, a gladiator's sword pointed at her throat. A hand fastened around her wrist and removed her dagger. Zenna did not resist. Though defiant, she was not stupid. She was outnumbered.

"What do you want?" she asked haughtily.

"We want to escape from Genopolis," said Usha.

"Impossible," snorted the smuggler, gazing at them contemptuously.

"Not impossible," returned Usha sweetly, "because you are going to take us."

Through the dark waters that swirled around Genopolis, a boat sculled quietly. A small, wide, flat-bottomed barge, it was used for frequent consignments of illegal cargo, and cut its way smoothly through the choppy waves. Zenna stood at the bow and plied the long paddle that propelled the barge forward. Behind her, Talia stood on guard, holding her notched sword inches away from the back of Zenna's neck. Usha, Ozzie and Toby sat in the middle of the boat and Rem and Arlo in the rear.

Arlo sat quietly enough but his heart was pounding with excitement as he strained his eyes into the night. In his hand he still held the small book that the Abbess had given him, with his finger tucked into the map. There was now no light to see by, but he needed none to see the route that he followed in his mind's eye.

Despite the success of their escape, there were still problems. Though mindful of the danger posed by the Regis, Ozzie was adamant that he would not leave the City. "Our only home's here, Sis, and what'll the others do without me? I can't leave Mindie there on her own with all them lot to look after!"

Usha shook her head, dubiously. "I don't think we can go back, Ozzie," she said, choosing her words with care. "It's too dangerous."

Ozzie folded his arms mutinously. "Look, Sis, if yer don't want to come with me and Toby back ter the Kids, then that's yer own lookout. I don't know why yer want ter dash off on this crazy idea of going ter the Regions. Why, everyone knows that nothin' good comes from there."

"It's not that, Ozzie," muttered Usha. "They've found out about Auntie, and if I go back there I'll be Regenerated, and perhaps you too."

But Ozzie would not be moved and convinced Toby, despite Usha's pleas, that the Regis could never discover their well-concealed hideout. After much discussion, they had finally agreed to take the boat up the east side of Genopolis, away from the port and the lighthouse in the South Quarter. Once clear, they would pull in and let Ozzie and Toby out to find their way back to the other Kids. So it was that Usha had ten minutes to make up her mind what she would do.

Talia however, had no such qualms. Ever since the fight, she had seemed invigorated, refreshed with new purpose. After Arlo had shown her the book and explained his history, she had, surprisingly, offered him her support on his journey to the Regions. "I met Naturals before in the Circus," she said shortly, prodding Zenna in the back with her sword as if for emphasis. "They fought bravely, but they are weak. I don't think I will have any trouble out in the wilderness."

"But they ain't yer people, Talia," countered Ozzie, earnestly. "Yer don't know what yer getting yerself into."

The gladiator sniffed. "There's nothing else left for me here, thanks to you lot," she said, so coldly that Ozzie was silenced. "But now that I have somewhere to go, then go I will."

Ozzie suddenly sat forward, riveted with excitement. "I recognize yer now! You're Talia, ain't yer? I seen you on the posters! Talia the Tormentor!"

"Yeah. That used to be my name," said Talia, brushing him aside, but Ozzie was not so easily put off, turning to Usha.

"Yer know who she is, don't yer?"

"Ozzie. . ." Talia turned towards him warningly, but Ozzie was bubbling with enthusiasm. "She were the fastest sprinter at the Games a few years back, *and* the best javelin thrower, weren't yer?"

Usha gazed at her in wonder. "So you weren't always a gladiator, Talia?"

Talia's face was a stony picture. "Shut up –" she began, but in that moment, her attention had wandered. Sensing her chance, Zenna shoved roughly at Talia, knocking her against the deck, scrambled to the side and leapt into the black seething water with a resounding splash. Surfacing, she started to flounder her way back towards the cove.

"Zenna!" cried Usha, heedless of Talia's attempts to silence her, but the smuggler turned her dripping head, now safely out of reach, her teeth bared in a smile of fierce triumph, holding the dripping barge-paddle in one hand.

"You thought you could outwit me, Gemini? You wanted to escape? Escape then, fools! Go where the wind and waves take you!"

What happened next, Arlo could barely comprehend. From the black water behind Zenna came a flash of gleaming wet shapes with sharp fins that crested through the foam of the waves. They briefly circled the oblivious smuggler and then plunged underneath her. As she laughed at the fugitives in vicious delight, something suddenly surged up underneath her. Even in that brief second, Arlo could see that there was something wrong with Zenna, although she herself did not yet know it; twisted sideways like a snapped doll from Cecelia's nursery, the bottom half of her body seemed to be missing. . .

The next second Zenna disappeared as if she had been dragged down to the depths from below. A boiling plume of bubbles rose to the surface and then once more the waters were black and empty.

The children craned to the side, breathless.

"What was that?" gasped Toby.

"I think it was a fish," said Arlo, sweat breaking out over his forehead. From his brief glimpse the shapes had reminded him of the fish that darted in the fountain of

341

the Abbess at the Maian Inn. Yet these had been much bigger, much more sinister and vicious, as comparable to the fish in the fountain as the sabre-tooth mutants at the Circus had been to Rem. For the first time he felt a prickle of uneasiness as he realized how much he still had to learn about the Regions and the place he was taking them. How many other, more sinister creatures might there be out there, of which they had no knowledge, and which might even now be stalking them?

But a sudden shout from Ozzie alerted him to more immediate problems. The steering-pole to guide the barge now floated on the bloodstained waves only a few feet away, but it was still out of arm's reach. Without it, the barge floated directionless on the surface of the water. Even Talia, the tallest, tried craning over as far as she could, but without success, and no one wished to put their hands in the water to paddle the boat any nearer.

"We gotta get the bleeding paddle, Tobe!" cursed Ozzie. "Otherwise we'll end up going to the bleeding Regions with this crazy lot!"

"I don't wunna go, Oz!" cried Toby. "I don't wunna go near no Regions! Stop it! I wunna go home!"

"Shut up, you snivelling brats," broke in Talia. "There's nothing we can do."

For, as she spoke, a stronger current had already taken their small barge, bearing it away from the faint lights of the City and out into the darker sea beyond.

*

Hours passed. The immediate outcry that had followed the runaways' desperate plight had subsided in the face of their helplessness. No one spoke. A pale moon rose, shedding a silvery trail over the black waters. Gratefully, Usha raised her face to its light, sat up and looked around her.

The Natural boy had fallen asleep in the stern, his head resting on the hairy flank of his dog. Usha shuddered at the sight. Unused to animals, their smell and appearance appalled her, and the idea of the huge fish cruising in the waters beneath them made her even less comfortable. Ozzie sat, lost in his own thoughts, still gazing out to where the last glow of the City had disappeared into the horizon. For the past hour he had not responded to any attempts to talk to him. In the bottom of the boat, Toby snored loudly, his glasses askew, mouth open, dribbling.

Usha could not see Talia's face in the gloom but the sound of her breathing made it appear that she was still awake.

"Talia?" she asked shyly. "Why, if you were such a good athlete, did you end up in the Circus?"

There was the sound of an exasperated sigh through the blackness. "You ask too many questions, Blondie."

But Talia's tone was kinder than her words, and to keep her mind off their danger, Usha decided to dig a little. "Ozzie said you were the champion of sprinting and javelin a few years ago. You didn't tell me that."

"Yeah, well. I *was* the best," replied Talia, with calm

assurance. "I was the fastest, the swiftest, the best shot in my year. I could have retired early. I was only a couple of years away from City Champion."

Usha didn't follow. "So what happened?"

Talia took a deep breath, as if her next words were hard to say. "I started losing, Blondie."

"Started losing?" said Usha, remembering the statues that lined the Consulate, so like Talia in physique and attitude.

"Yeah, Blondie, all right, don't rub it in. Five years ago I was the top-class sprinter in my section and I had the highest patronage a sports-Citizen could hope for. I won three golds in a row for the javelin. But I started losing because I wouldn't take the injections when they made them compulsory. It wasn't good enough to be as fast as I was, I had to be faster, you know?"

"I think so," said Usha, doing her best to understand. She had often heard of the latest exploits of the athletes at the yearly Consulate Games, but Auntie had never let her follow it properly, calling it vulgar. "Wasn't there a prize for the best athlete every year?"

"There was indeed, kid, and I was shortlisted for it. I had one final race to win, and I was against sprinters that I knew I could beat. But in order to compete I had to have the injection the night before. I refused. I'd seen other athletes in the peak of health killed from taking it. It might do you good, or it might do you bad, understand?

"So I didn't take it. I took the race, and won. But they disqualified me because I hadn't conformed with the rules. I was nearly dropped, but the patron gave me one more chance – provided I took the injection. I know I should have refused again, but I was desperate to be City Champion. So they gave it to me the night before the race. . .

"Blondie, I've never known anything like it. They said it was genetically-enhancing, but I would call it the worst thing a Citizen could ever live through. I thought my body was falling to pieces. I couldn't think straight. I couldn't move one of my legs and I couldn't see more than two feet in front of me. The scissor-man who came to see me, he thought I'd never walk again."

Talia paused. Usha put out her hand and found Talia's, but the gladiator pushed it away impatiently. "Anyway. . . It took me nearly a year to get over the effects of the injection, and then the only job I could find was cleaning the racetrack after the Games were over. One night, I was working late and I saw the patron passing by with two Gemini bodyguards. I don't know what happened to me. I walked over and then it all goes black. I woke up the next morning in prison."

"In prison?" asked Usha, aghast.

Talia grinned. "I didn't kill anyone, Blondie, but apparently it was pretty close. They said I was temporarily out of my mind – which was true – and that rather than

Regenerate me, I should be put to some use where the patron could make some barter-worth out of me. So I was put in the Circus, and there I stayed. Instead of City Champion, I became the Circus champion. People heard of me again, some of them came especially to see me. And do you know what? It was the best thing that ever happened to me."

"But in a place like *that*?" gasped Usha. Talia spat over the side of the barge.

"Winning's winning, kid. Don't you forget it. And now I've lost it all – again."

"So who was the patron?" asked Usha. "Who was the man you nearly killed?"

"Not a man, Blondie, a woman. Brigadier Hacker, her name is. Tough old boot, war-veteran and everything. She owns most of the athletic schools in Genopolis. When they put me in the Circus I never thought I'd hear of her again. So imagine my surprise when this Natural here shows up with some tale that she's after him?

"I mean, after what happened to me, I'm with anyone who says they're against the Brigadier. I suppose you could say that I realized that there still might be something to live for if I can get even with her again. Mind you, that might be easier said than done. She seems to have nine lives, 'cos word was she was nearly killed once before, out in the Regions, in the Natural mutiny eleven years ago."

"Natural mutiny?" said Usha cautiously, but Talia

had suddenly lost interest, stretching out in the bottom of the boat and closing her eyes.

"Give it a rest now, Blondie. We've got a Natural here to vouch for us, and that's as much as we can hope for, given the fix we're in."

Little by little, the rocking of the boat and the gentle snores of the others lulled Usha gradually to sleep. Caught on a current, the boat drifted silently out into the wide disc of the world beyond Genopolis until the whole universe seemed to be made of dark water. Still they all slept, as slowly the moon faded and the sea paled around them in the first breeze of the early morning, drifting helplessly into the unknown.

"FIND HIM SOON"

It was late in the evening before the ragged procession bearing the last of their weakly-flickering torches reached the viaduct that overlooked the plain of Genopolis. Sweat trickled down Kira's forehead and stung her eyes, the heat and pressure of the day giving her a dull headache. Over her shoulder she still bore the tattered remains of the white flag.

The sun had fallen low on the horizon, a sullen red ball barred by black streaks of cloud. The evening steams caused by the arrival of the cooler night air had started late, and now the first fogs were starting to descend, stinging their nostrils with a bitter, ashy smell. The last rays of the sun slanted through the gathering fumes and the huge hulk of Genopolis seemed to crouch like an iron beast on its hill.

Quickly, Ira marshalled her troops along the viaduct and on the bridge between the great ruined posts at the edge of no-man's-land. In front of them stretched the plain with its shattered railway, and through it the snaking gulf of the river bed, now baked dry by the blazing heat of the sun until it had cracked in a crazed web of craters like the patterned skin of some enormous lizard. To both sides rolled the last thorn-trees and scrub of the Regions, cut through by the thin metalled line of the distant border that gleamed redly in the dying sun.

The area was unnervingly quiet, and Ira felt the first stirring of apprehension. She had not expected this. The smoke and dust-winds of the day had given them cover against the reconnoitring airships, but she was not fool enough to think that their march from Region Three had been unobserved. For all that the Citizens treated their own people as disposable, she had no doubt that the ambush of the soldiers had been reported, and that their approach had set off furious activity in the defences of Genopolis.

Squinting through her fingers, she gazed searchingly at the sky, and identified the tiny glints of light that signalled the distant airships hovering discreetly above the City awaiting orders. The only wonder was that they had not been attacked earlier, but she knew that after the rout in Scar Valley, the Citizens would be waiting to engage them in the open, far from the cover of the hills and scrub.

Another hour would bring darkness, much needed for their cover, but still too late for their purposes. Already her company was tiring and the vigorous fury and outrage that had fired them to tramp all day through the blazing heat was rapidly evaporating. Some were complaining of the pain in their feet, already others were looking fearfully at the mighty fortress in front of them and a few even murmuring timidly about the possibility of returning before things "got too bad". Hearing a child's halting voice begging for water, Ira looked back at her ragged followers with a pang, scarred men, limping women and their children, all carrying some weapon or other, all with the same desperate, pinched look that she had so often seen on Gea's face —

"Grandmother," said Kira, and her voice was trembling, "everyone is frightened. We want to go home. We need to leave now, before the Citizens come."

Ira gazed over at Kira and the murmuring troops behind her with a savage smile. "Go home? What home would that be? We have come here to take back our home! If we leave now, we go to certain death, hunted like creatures without dignity, with no hope.

"It is true, that many of us will not outlive this day. But to live one day in the pursuit of human dignity is worth a thousand years crawling on our bellies. If you doubt me, think of the many husbands, wives, fathers and mothers that they have taken from us. Think of the countless tortures and humiliations they have visited on our children and our future, Kira. Think of Gea, your mother's sister, and your baby cousin, whom they have taken from you. And I promise you this. From this day onwards, the feast of Lithia will not dawn, but the world shall remember our name."

No answering shout to her words this time – the border was too near – but Ira sensed the movement, the intake of breath along the ranks, the restless limbs tensing to silence. Every man, woman and child was once again looking at her with a dark intensity, their faith restored. With that power, they could storm the walls, Ira thought. With that heat in their minds they could overrun a thousand Citizens, if only they could sustain it.

Looking down the river bank and up again at the shadowing dome of the sky, she saw more of the airships' glints of light align over the City and start to drift towards the viaduct. There was no question about it. This was it.

"Quick," she shouted to Kira, "they're coming. In another second they'll be bombing the river. Tell the others to follow me. We're going in."

The next second Ira was racing across the huge, sun-baked flats of the dried river bed and past the shattered hulk of the old railway train that lay embedded in the cracked mud, the bright spark of her torch gleaming in the dusk. With a cheer, most of the crowd followed her. The few remaining dithered, caught between the fear of being left behind and the terror of the approaching airships.

They were only halfway to the foot of the City when fire strafed the group from above. A sheet of scorching flame slashed the column of advancing Naturals in two, the impact bringing with it a hot whack of heated air that burned and shrivelled all around it. Trapped at the back of the crowd, Kira felt the wave of heat searing against her eyeballs, nostrils and mouth, as if she was breathing in hot iron. Immediately all around her was chaos. Instinctively she threw herself down and shielded her head to avoid being crushed in the stampede as people fled from the conflagration. Sobbing, she lay still, straining her eyes to see a glimpse of green through the fiery dusk. She could no longer see her grandmother's torch.

At the front of the column, Ira and her troops were propelled forward by the blast. Some, their clothes blazing, blundered past screaming, beating at their clothes or rolling madly on the ground. With no chance of retreat through the *fiery wall, those who still could stormed forward to the enormous rocky staircase that led into the underbelly of the City. A dull thud-thud-thud echoed around the narrow arena from the hovering airships. In front of her, Ira saw the bodies of men tumbling like bundles of rags back down the staircase. Around her women and children were crumpling and falling and the thwack-thwack sound of the bullets spat fiercely, as they ricocheted off the rock to bury themselves in deep holes in the granite.*

From all around, their people were scattering, running here and there wildly. The attack had become a rout. Desperately Ira raised her torch and tried to rally them. "Forward! Forward!" But the terror and the carnage were too much. Within minutes she was left alone on the smoking ground. As she turned to mount the first step a bullet deflected from the tunnel mouth caught her in the neck and she fell.

From where she crouched, Kira had seen her grandmother fall. In an instant, she was up and stumbling through the smoke and flames towards her, dropping on her knees beside her and trying to pull her away from the burning soil.

Roused slightly by her touch, the old woman squeezed her fingers gently.

"Listen to me. You must continue the fight. But lie low. Strike and retreat. Dig deep. Bury yourself in the cracks underneath their feet. Attack them at night and fade away in the morning. We are no match for them in force or weapons. But as the ghost in the night, with the tripwire, the poison, the silent arrow, with these things you may fight

them. *Nothing else. Go now, or it will indeed be all for nothing.*"

Kira buried her head into her grandmother's neck, unable to move, smelling the familiar scent of basil and wool now mixed with sweat and the unfamiliar odour of blood. With her last strength Ira moved to push her granddaughter away, but her arm fell on empty ground, and she realized with relief that Kira had already gone.

It was early morning before the last survivors of the uprising reached the remains of Region Three.

Mist and the last of the smoke of the burning lay heavy over the valley and the sun's early rays still struggled to penetrate the smog. A thick, raw, sweetish smell lay over everything, the smell of charred wood mixed with scorched rubbish and soil. The clearing was hardly recognizable. Huts, bushes and trails had all gone. Instead, tall poles of trees loomed up through the mist like bones whittled to sharp points, their branches and leaves stripped by the fires. Drifts of white ash lay in the hollows, diluted into thick grey mud by the night-rain.

Through this nightmare landscape stumbled Kira and a handful of others, mostly young Naturals who had held back during the attack on Genopolis. Too tired, too traumatized and too confused to speak, they seemed more like tottering phantoms than living people. Faces were stained, burned, bloodied; their clothes were ripped and charred. They had not drunk water for twenty-four hours but they were not thirsty, they were exhausted but could only wander aimlessly, staring at the ruin all around them of everything they had ever known.

"We can't stay here," muttered Kira. "We need to disappear. They'll be coming. They'll hunt us down like rats."

But her words fell on deaf ears. A few sat down, stupidly, or tried to paw through the carbonized remains of the funeral pyre. Others stood in a daze or desperately tried to drag some shattered remains of their homes from the ashy debris.

Suddenly Kira let out a scream. They looked up to see her running over to the charred skeleton of the hut where Angus had lain, still jutting upright from its turf foundations. "Uncle! Uncle!"

For a moment her cry jarred them awake again and even the dullest of them looked up briefly. "What is it? What're you about?"

Kira had dashed over to the blackened and roofless hut, pulling at it desperately. "He was here!" They looked up uncomprehendingly as she threw herself against the burned, crumbling walls. "He was here! Inside! And we left him!"

Roused but puzzled by her desperation, they joined her as she fought through the carbonized posts that had once supported the doorway. A girl murmured, "But he was a traitor. Was his fault that this all started. Best to be rid of him."

Kira turned her face to them and tired as they were the group flinched at the naked grief on her tear-stained face. "No! He was my family! He was all I had left!"

One of them stepped forward into the wreck and cast

through the debris on the floor. A quick search, and the truth was certain. "There's nothing there any longer, lass. Don't distress yourself."

Kira stared. "But he was there! I don't understand!"

"Well, he's not there now. No bones, no teeth. Escaped, most as likely, though he won't have got very far. The fire or the fumes will have got him, mark my words."

A little later, when the Citizen extermination unit arrived, no Natural alive or dead remained in the clearing. The only bodies there were the six blackened corpses of the Citizen soldiers hanging on the iron gibbet, which still swung, creaking, in the early morning breeze.

"I think we're too late, sir," called one of the white-coated unit to another. "Those filthy Naturals have killed them all."

"We might as well leave them here to rot," added another. "They're no good even for Regeneration in this state."

"Stop that talk!" cut in their commander. "We're to take everything we find here back to Genopolis. Special Orders."

But, as they moved to take down the first body from its gibbet, they sprang back as it moved slightly. "Commander! This one's still alive!"

They could hardly make out the charred face that stared back at them, but they recognized the voice that rasped from deep within the smoke-stained lungs and through the melted lips.

"Where are they? Where are the Naturals?"

The commander ran forwards. "Captain Hacker!" he cried incredulously. "You are alive!"

But the eye that stared back at him was harsh and impassive.

"It will take more than a trifling riot by Naturals to kill me, commander. Now cut me down from this tree immediately. We are losing valuable time."

The commander stared. Such dedication by a soldier to the cause should be generously rewarded. As the soldiers took Hacker's ruined body down from the gallows and laid her on a stretcher, he raised his arm and saluted. "Captain! I will see that you shall be promoted for your loyal service to Genopolis!"

Hacker sneered. "Promotion may wait for me, for I have waited for it long enough. First I seek the prisoner that I imprisoned in that hut. Where is he?"

"There is no one left here, captain. Most of the Naturals are dead, and we will undoubtedly catch the last of them before nightfall—"

"Then I will seek him with you," rasped Hacker. "He is the key to a treasonous plot against the City of Genopolis."

"But, captain—" began the commander, but Hacker silenced him with a deadly stare.

"When I find him and discover the child that he has given away, and to whom he sold it, then I vow that I will give him and his conspirators a long, slow and living death. I do not care how long it takes me. But find him I will, and find him soon."

EIGHT

The first that Arlo knew of the Regions was a grinding underneath the barge as the keel drove against a sandbank, sending the rear of the boat swinging around violently and causing all those who were asleep to fall in a heap in the bottom. Jolted awake, Arlo struggled to his feet amid the sleepy protests of the others, and saw that they had drifted into a wide and shallow river and become lodged in a stiff cluster of reeds that grew out of a tangle of knotted roots on the water's edge.

Were these the Regions? Had they arrived?

Shielding his eyes from the early morning sun – which seemed vastly hotter and brighter than it ever had in the City – he swung a leg over the side into the water. It sank nearly to his knee, but his foot felt a rocky bed underneath his sole, and the river was slightly warm if a bit musty-smelling. Despite his soreness and hunger, Arlo splashed his way excitedly to the shore and pushed his way through a canopy of ferns, Rem panting at his heels.

The sight that met his eyes was a strange but magnificent one. For almost as far as the eye could see rolled an undulating plain, rippling with grass, dotted with bushes and scrub. Yellow blossom was flowering on some of the plant-forms that thronged the river-scrub, and small insects droned through the early-morning air. Yet as he took another step forward on to the strange new land, his foot sank into slime. Glancing down, he saw a glint of water beneath the grasses and understood. This paradise was no solid ground, but a swamp, built on the snarled roots of plants and other river debris, and in the heat of the early summer, the teeming plants had burst into open flower.

Usha pushed her way through the reeds after him, gasping. "Arlo! It's so beautiful! Oh!" Her foot also sank deep into the mud – and after her, Ozzie, mightily suspicious of the sudden expanse of sky and water around him, trod as carefully as he might in a particularly dangerous sewer of Genopolis. Behind them, Toby stood up, trying to clean his smeared glasses, while Talia, rubbing her eyes from sleep, took in the view of the early morning.

"It's so big. . ." murmured Usha in awe, and she spoke for all of them, Gemini, Citizen and Natural alike. Never had any of them seen a place so vast and empty of human habitation. In the City they had never been far from a road, a building, a food-wagon or the noise of hundreds of Citizens talking, bartering, working and going about their daily business. Now the horizon lay blank and bare in a shimmering haze of shining water behind them, and the great bulk of Genopolis was nowhere to be seen.

"It smells different. . ." Usha faltered. "It *feels* different. . ." But just what she meant by that she could not properly explain, though the others seemed to understand, gazing mesmerized at the view before them.

Arlo himself was lost for words. The first sight of his homeland had bewildered yet excited him. The colours and smells were overwhelming to begin with, but as he looked around him and breathed in the morning air, each new thing seemed as familiar to him as if he had known it in a former life. Somewhere out here, he thought as they took their first steps through the swamp, was the place that his family-unit had lived, twelve years ago. As they passed a flowering bush garlanded with deep red spines, a swarm of delicate blossoms suddenly burst out of the scrub and fluttered around them, making them jump and scatter momentarily. After he had got over his surprise, Arlo could see that they were huge butterflies, vastly bigger and more colourful than those Doctor Phlegg kept impaled on pins in the Garden Laboratory. And with that memory came the cheering thought that Doctor Phlegg, and Genopolis were now many miles behind him.

With no compass and only the vaguest idea of the

swampy peninsular along which they were heading, the map that Arlo held was of little use. From the position of the sun in the sky, he calculated that they were heading north-east, but more than that he could not tell, unless they came across a landmark marked on the map. Also, the map had been drawn up more than ten years ago, and perhaps the swamp had not even existed then?

"I wunna go *home*. . ." started Toby but this time Ozzie cuffed him into shape.

"Shut up now, Tobe. We can't go home, 'cos we ain't got no paddle and we ain't got no idea of where we are."

"It's going to be all right, Toby," comforted Usha. "We're going to get to Arlo's family-unit, and then we'll be fine. Just hang on a little bit, can't you?"

After almost an hour's travel, sweat was streaming into their eyes from the morning sun, and Arlo called a halt. With the fiercely mounting heat, a sickening smell had started to rise up from the marshes and every time they pulled a foot free, the swirling gas made them giddy and faint.

"It's time to eat," he told them, feeling the familiar gnawing sensation in his belly that the Citizens had not seemed to notice. None of them carried a timepiece, and without knowing the hour to eat or sleep, they were at a loss. They found a small ring of boulders that rose through the mud and shared round the last of the provisions found in the bottom of Zenna's barge while Rem ran off to nose in the undergrowth. Stale bread and raisins seemed delicious to Arlo that morning, and he ate ravenously, but when he saw Usha stoop for a drink of water from the swamp, he stopped her.

"I don't think we can drink from here, Usha," he said quickly. "It smells bad. I think we should wait until we find water somewhere else."

Usha stared at him doubtfully, but surprisingly Talia came to Arlo's assistance. "I would listen to him if I were you. The Naturals I knew at the Circus could tell whether food was poisoned or a wound was infected before we could. They have a sense that we do not."

At Usha's side Ozzie shifted uneasily. "I don't like it here, Sis," he breathed softly in her ear. "I don't like it here one bit. It's not safe like solid bricks and stone, or good honest roads and walls. Nothing seems like what it is, if you get my meaning."

In the silence, Ozzie's words, quiet as they were, fell like a thunderclap. Arlo felt a blaze of impatience. Was this stupid Citizen always to find fault with all Natural things? Had he brought everyone here only to listen to complaints and dissatisfaction?

"Stop moaning!" he cried, waving his arms wildly. "You want to go back to Genopolis after all they've done to you? This book shows the way to my people! They'll understand! They'll take care of us!"

"What?" sneered Ozzie. "Yer going ter take us all this way just 'cos of a bleeding book?"

"Too many books spoil the broth. . ." chimed in Toby, helpfully, but this was the last straw for Arlo.

Instead of answering Ozzie, he turned on Toby.

"It's too many *cooks* spoil the broth, Toby for goodness' sake! Stop pretending you're some kind of brain-box know it all! It's so *stupid*, the way you carry on –"

Directly the words were out of his mouth, he felt a sudden wave of regret. Toby stood looking at him, his mouth open. "I'm sorry, Toby," Arlo started, "I didn't mean. . ."

But the next moment a shrill barking from Rem made Arlo spin around, and as he did, he became aware that a group of small, thin men dressed in drab grey and a carrying bristling, vicious-looking spears had swiftly and silently surrounded them.

Delight and wonder filled Arlo's heart as he looked on the faces, bruised and weather-beaten, as unlike the smooth and regular features of Citizens as he could have wished. These must be his people! So great was his joy that he did not see the strange glint in their eyes as they gazed evenly back at him.

"Are you—" began Arlo breathlessly, but the tallest of the group, though not even up to Talia's shoulder, stepped forward and made a quick movement that Arlo did not see. But he felt it. Pain exploded at the back of his head, the sky and sea whirled around him and he fell limply on to the ground.

Usha tried to move her bound hands behind her and pull herself upright but with no success. She was lying on the earthy floor of a small low cave that had been hollowed out underneath the great bole of a tree. Its thick roots plunged into the soil like bars and a giant creeper had been woven around them to block any light. At the front of the cave, dimly glimpsed through a sheet of woven grass matting, stood a Natural, his spear at the ready.

Next to her lay the slumped bodies of Talia, Ozzie and Toby. Usha wriggled uselessly in her bonds and tried to remember clearly. After Arlo had been knocked unconscious, the Citizens had been totally outmanoeuvred. Though Talia in particular had put up an enormous fight, laying at least three of the men out cold, the leader of the Natural tribe had used his cunning more than his fists. Unhooking a net from his belt, he had carefully circled the gladiator as she fought, and with a flick of his hand sent the net whirling soundlessly up and over the top of her head. Encircled in its folds, she stumbled, tripped and crashed to the ground, to be rolled up like a parcel by their other attackers. Ozzie, though swordless and outnumbered four to one, had flung himself on them, shouting hoarsely over his shoulder for Usha and Toby to run, but as they turned to flee, the oldest of the Naturals had caught them and held them fast. The only one of them to escape was the stupid dog, thought Usha, who had dodged all attempts of capture and raced off into the wild. Overpowered and beyond reach of any aid, they had been dragged for some three to four hours through the evil-smelling swamp, and unceremoniously dumped in their present location.

From what little Usha had seen on the journey, they had been brought into a small encampment on the margins of the swamp, built from woven grasses and creepers. But the village, if that was what it was, seemed rough and unfinished; hammocks were suspended from the small wiry trees and campfires flickered in charred hollows. Woven rush and grass matting hung down every structure to camouflage it, and even if Usha had passed within one mile of the settlement she probably would not have seen it unless she knew what she was looking for. A more hidden place she had never seen, and its inhabitants were equally secretive. Though she had caught movements of people watching their arrival through the brush, they had remained silent and wary, fading away through the rambling jungle as soon as she turned her head to see.

The matting covering the doorway was abruptly twitched aside and Usha caught her breath. Through the opening shuffled an old man, stooped almost double, dressed in the same drab grey tunic and hood as the others. His face was weathered and bronzed into a maze of grooves and wrinkles and his blue eyes stared down at them from underneath an overhanging brow. His long white hair was tangled and pulled back in two long plaits and his arms, muscled and wiry, were clasped with burnished metal bracelets. Usha had never seen a man with long hair or jewellery before, and shrank away against the unconscious bodies of her two companions as he came towards them.

But the old man simply squatted down and gazed into her eyes for a moment with a clear, almost compassionate gaze.

"*Gun-zel*," he muttered, and from a small bowl took a white, clay-like mixture, and daubed it on the faces of her unconscious companions. Ozzie groaned at the touch, and for a moment Usha hoped he would wake up, but although his eye flickered open, he did not seem to see her and only quivered and lay without speaking. As the old man bent over Usha, she summoned all her courage to speak.

"Please. . ." she whispered, so that the sentry outside could not hear her, "please, we're not here to harm you. We are . . . friends, at least the Natural boy with us is your friend, and I don't know where they've taken him. . ."

But the feeling of the cold white clay on her face silenced her. "*Gun-zel*," muttered the old man once more, and crawled backwards out of the hut, leaving her huddling next to the other Citizens in the darkness.

At the same time, Arlo knelt on a rocky floor in a small clearing, his hands also bound behind him. His head swam from the blow and if he closed his eyes he could feel the world start to rock gently as if he was still in the barge. His thoughts were in a whirl. Why were they acting like this? What had they done with his friends? Where was Rem?

In front of him, on a kind of chair built of rocks and

creepers, sat a large man, tall for a Natural, although not the size of a full Citizen. Unlike the others he did not wear the grey cloak, but instead despite the day's heat, wore over his shoulders a hairy, stinking garment that reminded Arlo of the smell of the animals from the Circus. As if sensing his unspoken question, the man pulled his cloak around him, and Arlo could see the lifeless head of a grey, doglike creature hanging from its side, lips drawn back over sharp fangs and eyes rolled heavenward in its skull. The man's head was almost totally bald, swathed in a dark cloth against the heat of the blazing sun, and around his neck there were dark cords from which dangled white objects that looked like teeth or bones.

As Arlo, haltingly, finished telling his story, the man paused for a long time as if thinking it over. The eyes that looked back at him were opaque and brutal, and the accent was so thick and hoarse that Arlo could barely understand him. "So that is your story is it, child? You are a kidnapped Natural from the Dead City, seeking your real family?"

Arlo nodded eagerly but the man cut him off before he could continue. "Your Mark, then, child. Where is it?"

Confused, Arlo looked warily at him. The request reminded him of the Regis and the seemingly long-ago time that he had spent in his study. "I'm afraid I don't have a Mark," he stuttered, "and . . . I don't really know what one is?"

The man stood up, belched and wiped his mouth with the back of his hand, his face suddenly transformed with a sudden, almost fiendish light. "Don't know what a Mark is?" he jeered. "A Mark is your bloodline, it shows your stock, your breeding, your ancestors, your family. A Mark is more than you are, child, a Mark *is* you! Search him!"

Two Naturals instantly came to Arlo's side and tore at his clothes roughly. He tried to fend them off but he was tied up and outnumbered. Humiliated and sobbing, he had no choice but to submit to the examination.

"Not a Mark on him, master. I've never seen a Natural like it."

"Apart from this piece of wood," added the other, and threw down the book that he had found tucked into Arlo's shirt. Arlo realized with a weary wave of thankfulness that none of those present had any idea of what it was.

Goren raised his hairy brows, suddenly all solicitude. "A Natural with no bloodline? An orphan? A blank slate? Who will look after you now, boy? Who will protect you?"

Clicking his fingers he summoned an old man with long white hair held back in two braids, holding a water-pitcher. The old man scuttled forward and held the container to Goren's lips; but he staggered slightly under its weight and a small trickle of water cascaded down on to his lord's tunic. Instantly, the old man stepped back, shaking, but Goren was quicker, with two mighty blows he cuffed him each side of his head and sent him out of the clearing, flinging the pitcher after him with a snarling curse. Then casually, as if nothing had happened, he turned to Arlo and said, "And the Citizens, child? What do you propose we do with them?"

Arlo gaped at him, deeply frightened. Despite the old man's distress, nobody had moved to help him, as if Goren's superior strength somehow forbade it. A sick feeling rose in his stomach. This was a very different, primitive, violent place where force ruled over all. A thudding in his head reminded him of his danger. He had to calm down, think clearly.

"Well," he stuttered finally, "they're my . . . friends, and. . ."

The man laughed, a great, braying roar of amusement. "Friends, indeed! You call such walking corpses from the Dead City friends? *Gun-zel*, we call them in the Regions, which means dead-flesh, and we do not suffer them to come amongst us.

"But to you I can offer this choice. You, though unclaimed and unprotected, may stay with us and become part of my tribe. But the dead-flesh that came with you must be sacrificed. Life for life. Flesh for flesh. That is the law.

"Tonight the Great Feast will take place, and through the death of your friends will come your new life in the tribe of Goren, the Wolf-son. Otherwise you will face a living death with the rest of your group. Name your choice now, child, for I have work to attend to."

Arlo shuddered and everything swam in front of his eyes. *Goren*. He had heard the name before. With it came the sickening realization that he and the Citizens had strayed right into the hands of the bloodthirsty, tribal warlord about whom tales were told in the safety of the Inn, back in the time when any news of the wild Regions were just adventure stories, like the books in the old library. . .

But as to the choice that Goren had given him, there was no choice to be made. The other Citizens had not given him up to the Regis – largely because of Usha – and there was no question of him now sealing their fate. Yet how they could escape the grasp of this savage, whose swamp-craft and hunting was far superior to theirs?

Slowly, with as much conviction as he could muster, he nodded. Whatever happened, Goren must not suspect the truth. Only if he was left to wander free and unobserved could he find his friends and escape with them. Taking a deep breath, he choked down the nausea in his stomach and smiled up at the man.

"Yes, master. I will join you."

Goren grunted, as if he expected nothing else, and called back the old white-haired man with a motion of his hand. Arlo noticed that the man's nose was bloodied and he was trying to staunch the flow with his ragged cloak. "So it will be. Take him away, Onofre, and prepare him for his initiation into the Wolf-men."

As the old man motioned to him to follow, Arlo gathered his clothes together and with them the tattered remains of the book that lay ignored in the dirt at his feet.

It seemed many hours later that Usha was pulled roughly from the hut with the other Citizens and forced to her feet. She wondered why she was so dizzy, and then realized that none of them had had anything to drink for nearly twenty-four hours.

"Water," she murmured to the Natural who was pushing her along at spear-point. "Water. . ."

But she was ignored. Instead mocking laughter rippled around the clearing. Suddenly the encampment seemed full of Naturals, their toothless, dirty faces gaping stupidly at the Citizens as they were marched helplessly along. Fingers and spear shafts poked and prodded them hilariously, as the tribe made fun of the dead-flesh that walked in their midst. A spear left a long red scratch down Ozzie's back accompanied by whoops of encouragement; Toby's glasses were knocked from his nose and smashed on the ground, and Talia was tripped to her knees as the Naturals mocked the odd-looking girl who dared to carry weapons and fight like a man.

"If I just had *one* hand free," swore Talia through gritted teeth, "I'd show these barbarians a lesson they wouldn't forget in a hurry. . ."

But the Naturals called back, "Go back to the cooking-fire, girl, go back to your weaving and sewing. Little girls shouldn't go hunting! Know your place, woman!"

What kind of savages were these? What had they let themselves in for? Where on earth was Arlo? In the midst of the crowd, Usha twisted her head around, desperately searching for Arlo but she could see him nowhere. Now that they had discovered he was a Natural they must have taken him in. A fine friend he was, thought Usha. As soon as they found his tribe he abandoned them. Where was he now that they were in trouble? *And* she had spoken up for him in the darkness of the tunnel, helped him when they had the chance to give him up for their freedom, helped him find his way back to his homeland, *trusted* him. . .

"That bleedin' Natural!" Ozzie was swearing. "When I get my 'ands on 'im I'll teach 'im a bleeding lesson!"

Abruptly they came to a small cliff that rose out of the swampland and Usha could see, in the evening dusk, a swampy culvert in the river where a tall clump of trees, hung with creepers, stood against the last glint of the evening sky. A stink rose off the flatbeds of mud and as they drew nearer they saw that the whole tribe was gathered on top of the cliff opposite the trees, their faces daubed with streaks of white clay. Some beat crude drums made from dried animal skins stretched over hollowed-out gourds, and their dull thump throbbed through the air. Others were singing, a wailing, tuneless scream that reminded Usha of the noises of the animals in the Circus. As she turned to look at Talia and Ozzie behind her, a Natural holding a spear pushed her violently in the side and she stumbled, falling face down on to the very edge of the drop.

"Usha! No!" Instantly Ozzie tried to dive forward to help her but the rope binding his arms to his side was yanked back and he fell to his knees helplessly. Beside him Toby let out a wailing shout. "What's happening, Oz! I can't see!"

Staring over the side of the cliff, all Usha could see was the three trees and behind them a long, writhing shadow that rippled through the swampland with a strange, hypnotic motion. The Natural who had knocked Usha over uttered a squealing moan of delight.

"Prepare to run, dead-flesh, for they eat anything they can catch!"

The spearmen at her side pulled Usha down a small winding path that snaked down the cliff and dragged her over to the foremost tree. One of them pulled a creeper down from the branches and the other lashed her securely to the tree trunk with it.

"Help!" she called desperately. "Talia!"

But it was Ozzie whose voice she heard through the dim light. "Don't yer worry, now, Sis. We're coming. We've got out of worse in our time, ain't we?"

Talia did not outwardly react, but her eyes glowered and behind her back her left hand began to work up and down on the knot that held it.

A strange wailing and thumping through the air drifted into Arlo's exhausted sleep. Though the sound was totally unfamiliar to him, something about it made the hackles rise up on the back of his neck. Instantly he was fully awake and struggling out of the hammock in which he had been left to rest, and saw Onofre standing over him, his face bruised and cut, and a knife shining in his hand. Arlo flinched away, but the old man simply laid down the knife and motioned for him to sit on a small stool bound with skins.

"Come here, child, and prepare for your rebirth. Do not fear the drums, for they beat for the Great Sacrifice of the dead-flesh tonight."

Arlo trembled as he sat down, willing himself to breathe evenly and keep still. Whatever happened, he needed to keep a grip on himself. They were hopelessly outnumbered and the only possibility was pretending to play along. However, it would be no easy task. These were his own people, as sensitive to deception as he had been in the Inn, and they would be quick to spot anything curious.

The knife flashed before his eyes and a lock of his hair fell down on to the floor. It was a rough and painful sensation but Onofre seemed not to care, twisting Arlo's head this way and that as he cut his hair. Arlo gritted his teeth and thought about Rem. Where was he now? Had he been killed by the Wolf Men?

"You come from the Dead City, you say?" Onofre asked at length, in his strange accent. "How did you come there?"

Arlo briefly related the story that he had told Goren, ending cautiously, "But the Citizens that came with me, they were good Citizens, not dead-flesh. They helped me escape. . ."

Onofre shook his head. "We can make no exceptions. The dead-flesh do not pity us, so we do not forgive them."

"But these Citizens are different," began Arlo desperately.

"Criminals, handicapped, slaves, I know." The old man nodded. "Yes, when one first experiences hardship, one realizes how it must be for others. Yet they do not know *pain*, and because of this they will never know how it is to truly love, lose or suffer. They are dead to themselves and dead to us."

"But that's not true! Some Citizens are learning how to feel again, but they think that it is Infection. . ." Arlo began, but Onofre had suddenly stopped, staring at the back of his head, just behind his left ear. At the same time the blade of the knife was now pressed against his neck. When the old man spoke, his voice was hard.

"Child, you are a traitor. You are deceiving us."

Arlo gaped. "No, sir, really, I—"

"What is this?" insisted Onofre furiously. "What is this Mark?"

Confused, Arlo raised his hand to touch the back of his head. "What. . .?"

With a flick of his wiry wrist, the old man sent Arlo

flying into the dust. In one bound he was kneeling on top of him, holding the knife-blade warningly in front of the boy's terrified eyes so that it glinted in the last rays of the dying sun.

"Tell me no lies, now, child. Why did she send you? Why?"

"Who?" gasped Arlo, pinioned underneath Onofre's savage grasp. "What? I don't understand what you're saying!"

"You are from her tribe!" spat the old man angrily. "You are a spy! Confess now for a merciful death, or you shall see how Goren treats his outsiders!"

There was nothing that Arlo could do but shake his head wordlessly as he struggled desperately for breath. When he could not drag any more air into his chest, something in his expression made Onofre slowly lower his knife from Arlo's throat, staring at him thoughtfully.

"I do not understand, child. There is no lie in your eyes, but the Mark says otherwise. How can it be that you bear the Mark of the Orphans, and yet have no knowledge of it?"

From his tunic he pulled two battered silver discs. Perhaps they had once been plates but they had been beaten so smooth and flat that in their murky depths Arlo could dimly see his own face. The old man held one in front of him and the other tilted so that Arlo could make out the back of his own head, his hair cut right down to the pale skin. He caught his breath.

Behind his left ear, inside the hairline and hidden for nearly twelve years, there was a dark, spreading tattoo, in the form of a three-pronged wheel, dulled through time and age but visible nonetheless.

Bound to the tree, Usha gazed at her powerless comrades. Despite their struggles, the Wolf-men had overpowered Ozzie and Toby and tied them to the other trees, and now Talia was being forced towards them at spear-point down the winding track from the cliff-edge.

"Didn't I tell yer?" Ozzie was shouting. "Didn't I tell yer that Nats were nothing but trouble? I bet they got something really nasty lined up!"

A Natural holding a wide gourd containing a shimmering, sweet-smelling liquid stood in front of Usha, and daubed the sticky contents over her feet and ankles.

"Hey! What you doing ter her?" spat Ozzie from her left, and the Natural chuckled and moved over to him, trickling the contents over him and Toby. "A sweet revenge, dead-one, for your last Anointment. With honey we lead a trail to their nest."

"What're they doin', Oz?" whined Toby.

Usha could not see behind her, but she could hear a rustling noise, as though many small pairs of legs were crawling through the undergrowth behind her. What was it? What was this formless creature that the Naturals said ate flesh?

Suddenly, a shout broke through the air and she saw

the slackened bonds fall from Talia's wrists. Instantly Talia was pounding towards Usha, skidding to a stop and tearing at the creepers that bound her.

It had all happened so fast that Usha could only stare at Talia, amazed. The gladiator snorted impatiently. "Get . . . a . . . damn . . . move on, Blondie!"

Yet, as Usha wriggled out of her bonds and ran to help cut Ozzie and Toby free, there came a whistling thud through the air and Talia suddenly slumped against the tree, the shaft of a spear protruding from her shoulder. In shock, Usha dropped to her knees beside Talia and saw that a spear, thrown from one of the cliffs above, had passed clean through the warrior's shoulder, pinning her to the trunk. In vain she pulled at it but it would not budge.

"Filthy Natural," cursed Talia, wrenching uselessly at the spear-shaft. "Let me do it, Blondie. Go untie the others."

Yet even as Usha unwillingly rose to her feet and started to tug at Toby's bindings, she saw that the ground around Talia seemed to be swarming and rippling underfoot. In horror Usha gazed about her and saw that the earth was suddenly covered with hundreds of small bugs, like the beetles she had sometimes seen around Auntie's house, but larger with black shells and great upraised pincers. Turning around she stared in amazement as out of the undergrowth issued a huge black column of insects running, falling and clambering over each other in a confusion of legs, shells and wings.

As she watched, a couple of them swarmed on to her foot and ankle where the sticky stain of the honey lay, and nipped at her fiercely. A streak of blood ran down her skin where the beetle had bitten her and she kicked it away furiously, but more and more came, eddying towards them in a great, undulating wave. As she stared, almost hypnotized, frantic shouts came from Ozzie and Toby.

"Sis! Get us out of here! We're going ter get eaten alive!"

As Arlo finished reading his story from the book, Onofre stared with troubled eyes at the knife in his hand. "Then it is true, the tale they told."

"What tale?" asked Arlo.

The old man shook his head. "The story of the Orphan tribe from Region Three. Your tribe, or so it seems."

Arlo looked at him, his heart thudding in his throat. Casting a furtive glance behind him, Onofre crept closer and whispered in the gathering gloom.

"I was not always part of this tribe, the Wolf-men. My own tribe came from a fishing village south of here. We had heard of other Naturals forced to live in Regions under Citizen control, which were regularly harvested for the blood, flesh and bones that would be provided for the City. We despised the Region Naturals, with no backbone or spirit, dependent on the Citizens, dying in a living cage, like animals.

"Yet it was one of these very Regions that started the revolution on Midsummer night, eleven years ago, during the feast of Lithia. Region Three rose up and marched on the City – for it was countryside then, not this shallow sea. They said that a Natural child had been kidnapped from there by a Citizen and taken to Genopolis."

"And then?" murmured Arlo.

"They were destroyed. Crushed by the Citizens. The area was burned to a crisp and later flooded by the rains. Out of the stinking mud grew this swamp, and my people could no longer fish. Then the Wolf-men came, led by Goren's father, took our women and children and forced us to join their tribe or die. There was nowhere else for us to go, and I have been here ever since."

"But what happened to the Region people?" questioned Arlo, urgently.

"Some escaped, led by one of the survivors, herself little more than a child. Wandering from shore to shore, they are called the Tribe of Orphans because they have no ancestors of their own, no land, no kin, no place to call their own. And the mark of the Orphans is the same as the mark of that Region – a three-pronged wheel . . . the Mark you bear, child."

"Then where are they?" asked Arlo, barely containing his eagerness. "Where are the Orphans now?"

Onofre shook his head. "They were last heard of in the north of this estuary, child, but you will not get there. For the Orphans are the sworn enemy of Goren, and their leader is his mortal foe. When he sees your Mark, he will not hesitate but to sacrifice you with the Citizens, thinking as I did, that you are a spy."

Arlo sprang to his feet. Suddenly the mention of the others had brought back to him the thought of their very real danger. "Where are they?" he cried urgently. "Where are they? What is Goren doing to them?"

"They are down at the mudflats for the Sacrifice. You cannot go in there alone and unarmed. It would be certain death."

But there was a glint in the blue eyes that reminded Arlo suddenly of Ignatius, as the old man sheathed his knife and turned towards him. His old body seemed suddenly taller and stronger, as if the cares that he carried were falling away.

"But if you give me your promise that you will help me in your turn, child, I will try to help you rescue your friends and find your tribe. All I ask is that if you find them, you will speak for me and allow me to join also. Goren's rule is cruel and unjust. My own tribe was not like that. My wife and child are long dead, and I stay here because I am old and weak, for no one else will have me, now that I bear the Mark of the Wolf-men. But if you will take me with you, then it may not be too late."

His answer reminded Arlo strongly of Talia. *If I have somewhere to go, then go I will*, and with it came a sudden realization that Naturals and Citizens were more alike than either would care to admit. And how different was this old man, at the end of his years, to the gladiator

Bjarn in the Circus, who threw his life away whilst in the prime of it.

Arlo turned and held out his hand. "You have my promise," he answered sincerely.

But instead of a hand-clasp, a white robe and a curved knife with a wickedly-shaped hook were thrust into his arms. "We have a deal then, child. Take this knife and hide it under your robe. Now listen carefully to what I tell you."

Usha struggled desperately with the creepers binding Toby's arms and feet, trying in vain to get the spearhead to cut them, but with one arm weighed down by plaster the other could not reach up far enough to get a satisfactory grip. "I can't do it, Toby!" she gasped. "I can't reach!"

"Yer can, Sis!" encouraged Ozzie. "Just stretch a little bit more and yer there!"

Toby let out a squeak. "Oh no! There's somethin' behind yer, Usha!"

A flicker of torchlight and a gruff command sounded through the dusk and, fearing another spear-thrust, she spun around to see. Her mouth dropped in shock.

"Arlo!" she cried. "No! Arlo!"

The boy was standing on the cliff top within a circle of flaming torches, his head shaved, and dressed in wolfskins like the others. Next to him stood the white-haired old man bearing a curved jar, and in front of them strode Goren, his face now distorted with an expression of hideous joy.

"So, dead-flesh! Are you prepared to bear penance for the crimes of your fathers? From your death will come a new member of the tribe of Goren, as he abandons his last links to the City of the Dead. And do not fear that no one will know your end. Your stripped skeletons will be left for the next patrol to discover, and show how the Wolf-men treat their mortal enemies."

Arlo raised a flaming torch above his head. The light danced on his features, hard and set. It was as if he didn't see Usha, didn't recognize her. . .

"Stop!" Usha screamed. "Arlo, what are you doing?"

The boy took a step forward, holding the torch in both hands. Around him the wailing grew to a horrible climax and the drummers beat their drums in a frenzy. The air pulsed, grew thick with the fumes of the tarry torches and the thump of heels on turf. Then, with one sharp gesture, Goren cut the commotion, and total silence reigned. He turned to Arlo, who stood gazing sightlessly at the helpless Citizens in front of him.

"Child," he said gruffly, pulling the wolf's-head cloak around the boy's shoulders. "Do you renounce the Dead City and all its inhabitants?"

"Please. . ." whispered Usha, more to herself than anybody. "No, Arlo . . . please. . ."

Goren put out a hand. "Child. Give me your answer. Do you renounce these walking corpses so that you can be reborn again as a true Natural?"

Usha fell to her knees next to Talia, trying vainly to

brush off the beetles that swarmed around her. Already the ground was black and seething and in another moment the wounded gladiator would be totally covered. Ozzie and Toby were shouting and trying to kick against their bonds as the bugs teemed up their legs. "Yer filthy Nat," Ozzie was bellowing. "Yer traitor! Thought you'd bring us out here ter die, eh?"

But Arlo stepped forward, holding his flaming torch in front of him like a sword. "I renounce those who wished me harm," he said softly, turning to Goren, "but as for those who have helped me, I won't forget them."

Goren swung round. "What? What did you just say, boy?"

But as the warlord's attention was distracted, the old white-haired man leapt forward and cracked the jar against the back of Goren's head with all his strength. Shards of clay flew into the air and drenched Goren and the surrounding Naturals with honey. Stunned, Goren fell to his knees. At the same moment, Arlo ducked away and raced down the winding path with the old man behind him, sweeping the blazing torch in front of him.

"Quick! Usha! Run!"

Usha leapt up in sudden hope. As Arlo ran towards them, keeping the torch low to the earth, the crawling mass of bugs scrambled away from the heat of the fire, just as the main column of the advancing swarm entered the clearing. Gritting his teeth, Arlo threw the torch into their midst. With a hideous rattling noise the infuriated bugs swerved away and up the bank where Arlo had just come from, towards the confused tribe of Naturals, drenched in honey. Instantly all was confusion and chaos as the tribe broke ranks and scattered, leaving their dazed leader where he knelt.

Pulling a curved knife out from his robe, Arlo reached up to hack Ozzie and Toby free while he tried to stamp the remaining bugs underfoot with a horrid crunching sound. As they nipped at his ankles painfully, he jumped and swore.

Then Onofre was beside them, gently examining the spear that had impaled Talia to the tree. Quickly, and with practised care, he removed the shaft and pressed a pad over it to staunch the wound. "Listen, girl. Can you hold this tight to stop the blood flow?

"Don't call me girl!" Talia ground out, struggling to her knees and grasping the pad tight. Onofre supported her over to the side of the trees where the swamp met the water, calling over his shoulder. "Children! Quick! Follow me!"

Arlo caught hold of Usha, knocked the last crawling insects off her clothes, and the next moment they were sprinting after Ozzie and Toby towards the estuary. Onofre was already pulling out a wide broad canoe and helping Talia into it. With a last effort they reached the shore and clambered in and Onofre handed round thick short paddles for everyone who could to row. As they pushed off into the river and struggled to find the current, Usha grasped Arlo's shoulder and pointed upwards. "Look!"

Arlo followed her outstretched finger and his eyes widened. The cliff face had become an infested mass of wriggling black insects that swarmed up and on to Goren, biting and tearing. As the pain of their attack broke into Goren's stunned consciousness, he stumbled to his feet, beating at the writhing black wave of bugs that covered him, and staggered to the cliff side, screaming. The next second he had either tripped or flung himself over the edge, perhaps to seek relief from his crazed torment in the cooling sea, and with a roar of agony he plunged into the seething waves with a resounding splash.

Moments later, his bobbing pale head surfaced, its features contorted into a mask of fury, and the fugitives could dimly hear him screaming over the hubbub.

"The boats! Make for the oceans! Catch them! Catch them!"

Fearing the Wolf-men were hot on their heels, everyone set about the oars with all their remaining strength. As they rowed, black clouds chased over the dying sun and a cold wind began to blow. The estuary river widened out into the shallow sea over which they had drifted so calmly the night before, but tonight it seemed to boil and swell. Stinging salt spray filled their eyes and mouths, and their oars were almost useless against the force of the waves. The small boat, overloaded as it was, lurched perilously close to capsizing.

Onofre screwed up his face against the approaching weather. "There is a storm coming," he shouted anxiously. "Keep low in the boat, and hold on. We are drifting into the Citizen-patrolled waters now. If we can get back to the swampland, we will have a chance. The Wolf-men will not venture out after us on a night like this."

As dark night fell around them, it became impossible to tell sky from sea. Scudding clouds obscured the moon, and although sometimes there appeared a smudge on the horizon that seemed to be land, and they rowed eagerly towards it, they could never come within reaching distance. Minutes turned into hours. The lurch and sway of the boat and the pain of his bites were beginning to make Arlo feel queasy and he gripped the side of the boat furiously. Somewhere back in the swamplands was Rem, lost and lonely. Bitterness and guilt stung him to the heart. Shutting his eyes, he began to count silently, but it was impossible to concentrate as the scream of the wind and the surge of the sea filled his mind and thoughts.

But somehow, it must have worked, because in the midst of his sickness, he suddenly became aware that some time had passed. The wind had dropped slightly and the boat was floating in a brief lull. The waves no longer plunged and crashed about them. Opening his eyes he could just make out the shadow of Onofre standing cautiously up in the middle of the boat.

"Onofre!" he whispered. "What is it?"

"Listen," hissed back the old man. "Something is out there. Listen!"

Arlo pricked up his ears and concentrated. A clashing of metal and the noise of screaming drifted through the night.

"Who is it?" murmured Arlo anxiously. "Is it the Wolf-men coming after us?"

"No, it is before us, from the shipping lane," muttered Onofre.

Suddenly there was a great whoosh and the whole sky was momentarily lit up by an enormous yellow flare that reminded Arlo of the fireworks at the Circus. Crouched in the bottom of the boat, the fugitives stared up at the silhouette of an enormous boat towering above them that seemed to have magically appeared out of the blackness. In that brief glimpse they saw ladders and ropes thrown over its side and dark figures swarming aboard before the flare faded and left them blinking in the dark. The searing noise of a great horn ripped through the night, three short blasts, followed by three longer ones, then three short blasts again.

"It is a food-ship from the pharms," called the old man over his shoulder, beginning to row urgently. "They are being attacked by another tribe. The Citizens are sending out a distress call, though they will be lucky to get help on a night like this. We must not get mixed up in their battle!"

But the wind was again picking up, and the large waves caught the small canoe on a crest and pitched it inexorably towards the besieged ship. Pull on the oars as they might, they could make no headway against the mounting gale.

"Pull!" shouted the old man, the words almost torn from his mouth by the wind. "Row! Row!"

But with the next surging wave, their boat was plunged down and into the thick of the fight. Around them broken crates of provisions dislodged from the ship's hold – boxes, loose fruit, unravelling packets of soaked bread and biscuits – bobbed on the heaving sea. A rattle of gunfire ripped through the stormy air, and without warning, a man – whether Citizen or Natural they could not tell – plummeted with a shriek from the deck above and into the seething water before them. He floated face down, unmoving. The children turned away from the sight, sickened. Again a lurid flare blossomed into the darkness and illuminated the food-ship, now listing badly to the side, her deck seething with fighting troops. Another roll of the waves, and their tiny boat was thrown almost against her barnacled side.

Usha threw up her arm to shield her face as a deluge of water smashed into the side of the canoe and swamped it. The thin canvas boat sank like a stone beneath them and the next moment they were floundering in the cold salty water. With one arm still unusable in the sodden cast she felt herself submerging. Above her swung something black and tarry, a rope left dangling from the top deck, and with her good arm she reached up and grabbed it. The next second Arlo was beside her, splashing furiously, before he was thrown violently against the hull and slipped beneath the waves.

"Arlo!" screamed Usha, but the roar of the wind and the fighting tore the words from her lips. She tried to reach out but he was too far away. Her foot kicked uselessly through empty air and salt water as she struggled to reach him. Of Toby there was no sign. Her last memory was of Talia and Ozzie, clinging like drowned rats to a capsized box, being borne away on a great wave before a tremendous shrieking and groaning filled the air. The ship had been forced on to a sandbank and its iron hull grated against the shoals with a loud, metallic creaking. Slowly, like a huge giant being forced to its knees, it keeled over and came to a sudden stop, while the waves lashed furiously about it.

As the boat sank below Arlo, the loop of rope that held the small anchor coiled around his leg, caught on his ankle and dragged him down. Onofre caught his arm at the moment of impact, but a forceful wave tore them apart and sent Arlo tumbling into a deep channel of water in front of the sandbank. Instinctively the chill of the sea made him hold his breath as he kicked in panic at the clinging rope that weighed him down. All around him was a rushing and a roaring. Pressure mounted around his ears and eyes as he sank deeper and deeper and his struggles became more and more useless. The urge to breathe was overwhelming and the pain in his chest almost unbearable. His body seemed frozen, paralysed.

This is it, he thought grimly. *We escape the City of the Dead only to die in the Natural sea.*

Images flashed through his head, of the look in Ignatius's eyes as he said goodbye, of Kristo disguised in the soldier's uniform, of the Abbess as she pressed the book into his hand, of Rem as he snarled defiance at the approaching Naturals, of Usha as she spoke out for him in the darkness of the passageways underneath Genopolis. . .

So bright and warm were the visions that he thought his eyes were open and that for one second time had ceased to exist. At the back of his mind he could hear the Abbess speaking, softly and clearly. *Take whoever you may find on your journey*, she was saying, *for there are others here who are also in need of help. . .*

And with that thought came new life and purpose. He would not lead his new Citizen friends out of slavery only to die in the wilderness a few leagues from his family. Strength flowed back into Arlo's arms and legs and he began to kick out again against the encircling rope. He would not fail at the last test, not when so many people, so many Citizens, had risked their lives to help him. He owed it to them to survive. Wordlessly he tried, as the Abbess had shown him, to disassociate his mind from the pain, and it started to dissolve. At last, with one final wriggle, the anchoring rope slid from his ankle and disappeared into the darkness.

Turning his face upwards, he could see the light from the flares sparkling through the water and, kicking his legs, rose up to meet it.

As the ship keeled over, Usha's fingers finally slipped from the tarred rope and she fell backwards with a cry towards the icy waves. But even as she gritted her teeth and closed her eyes, she never reached the water. Instead, a net of rough cords surrounded her and she felt herself being lifted up and swung through the air before being deposited on something slanting, wet and wooden. Stunned, she moved feebly to see where she was, and realized she had been pulled up on to the deck of the ship.

"We got another one!" came a gleeful shout above her and the next second large hands were fumbling at the net and pulling at her. Usha kicked out in defence and felt her foot connect with someone's knee. There was a cry and a curse and the large figure of a man lunged at her.

"Wait!" cried another voice and, as another explosion lit up the sky, Usha could see two Naturals, their bodies bound in rags and holding long knives instead of swords, staring down on her in disbelief.

"It is just a girl!" exclaimed one of them. "Are the Citizens sending their children to safeguard their food now?"

Usha tried to speak but her tongue refused to work. She could only gesture wordlessly towards the heaving sea around them. Then one of them seized the other's arm and pointed. Out of the waves, Onofre, his white hair drenched with seawater and his cheek pouring with blood, was staggering dizzily along the wreckage-strewn shore.

Arlo lay with his cheek pressed into the rocky shingle of the sandbank. His body felt like a lead weight. Half thrown, half tossed by the waves towards the bank, he had seized on to the rocky outcrop with his last strength and there he lay while the storm gradually subsided. Around him floated snatches of laughter, of shouting, of voices calling, but nothing really meant anything to him any more.

A flickering light dazzled his eyes, and he felt himself being pulled on to stony ground and rolled over. He spluttered and coughed as the lights and faces whirled around him dizzyingly. Amongst them he saw Onofre's face, his white hair plastered flat to his skull, pointing at him urgently and saying a jumble of words that he could hear but not understand. . .

". . . that him the Mark look. . ."

". . . others along all Citizens. . ."

". . . Wolf-men flesh-eaters. . ."

". . . call her, she knows, she will see the Mark. . ."

Hands touched his head, pushed it from side to side, examined the back of his skull. The next second they were picking him up, bearing him away, and the dark roaring sensation finally rolled up and overcame him.

Usha woke and found herself lying on a heap of furs. She thought she must have slept for a long time, but without a timepiece or a sundial to guide her she could only guess at the hour. As she moved, she realized her damp cast had been removed, and her arm had been splinted by wooden stakes bound tightly by woven cords.

She lay in a shallow clearing surrounded by tall grasses. Around them the wind of the storm had finally subsided and a soft grey light was flushing the sky, heralding the arrival of a new day. As she gazed wondering around her, she could see Arlo, also wrapped in a fur, asleep next to her. His head was turned away from her, and, where his hair had been cut down to the scalp, she could see a mark like a three-pronged wheel etched into his skin.

How had they come there? Who had brought them out of the sea? Where were Talia, Toby and Ozzie? As Usha sat up dazedly, the grasses surrounding the clearing were parted and in stepped Onofre, now wrapped in a coarse dark cloak. As he looked at her, his blue eyes crinkled into a smile.

Carefully, as if he were a wild animal, she smiled cautiously back at him.

Behind him there was a movement and other figures, all Naturals, entered the clearing. Amongst them was a woman, swathed in a cloak and leaning heavily on a stick. Usha's first thought was that she seemed small but old, stooped and her hair streaked with grey. Then the woman stepped forward and threw back her hood. Despite herself, Usha could not restrain a sudden gasp of recognition.

At a closer glance she could only be in her early twenties but she had seen more than her fair share of hardship, the weather had taken its toll on her beauty and her features bore the marks of many old injuries. But even that could not mask what Usha was seeing. The same face, the same eyes of Arlo, the Natural boy from Genopolis, looked steadily back at her from underneath the woman's tangled hair.

Woken by Usha's excited shake on his shoulder, Arlo rolled over on to his back and blinked in the early-morning light. Like Usha he came to his senses in an instant and looked wildly about him, wondering where on earth they had come to. Then, as he became conscious of the Naturals standing before him, he sat up hurriedly, before he took in the face of the woman standing next to him.

The woman knelt down next to Arlo and looked at him quietly. From all around them there was a ripple of wonder. Despite the differences of age, dress, boy and woman, it was as if each was looking into a mirror. She was perhaps the same age as Kristo, but her eyes seemed as old and wise as Ignatius.

He could find no words to speak. His heart pounded and his lips were dry.

"Arlo," whispered the old man. "This is Kira, the leader of the Orphan tribe. You bear her Mark."

But the woman too seemed struck dumb. Instead, her blue eyes welled with tears and the next second she had clasped him to her and was embracing him frantically.

"I know who he is," she sobbed, and in the midst of her grief she was also laughing with pure joy. "I know who he is."

Arlo had never been hugged before. No Citizen had ever embraced him, put their arms totally around him in love or compassion. It was a new, almost frightening experience to be so physically close to someone.

Suddenly, inexplicably, he found himself fiercely hugging her back.

Later that day, when the survivors had both slept and rested, Arlo and Kira sat watching the sun go down over the horizon.

They had talked and talked but still there was much to be told and much to be explained. Arlo had related the story of his adventures time after time and on every telling there were new things to add and new questions for Kira to ask. Even the sadness Arlo felt at recounting the fates of Benedict and Ignatius had lessened next to the joy of discovering someone so similar to him and yet so different.

Though deeply troubled by the loss of Talia, Toby and Ozzie, it was secretly the thought of Rem, somewhere out in the wilderness, alone and hungry, wandering in lands that he did not know that wrenched Arlo to the heart. Despite his cousin's assurances that dogs had strange powers that could lead them over many miles and oceans to be reunited with their owners, Arlo could not quite believe it. How could Rem ever find him, knowing nothing of where he had gone?

To distract him, Kira told Arlo her memories of the Rebellion, their escape, and how her tribe had survived since then, landless and wandering from place to place, never resting, never safe. They had resorted to capturing the Citizen food-ships that passed down the shipping lanes while the waters were still high. She had planned this attack as their last before the shallow sea dried up and the imports from the pharms stopped coming for the next few months. During the storm much of the food had been washed away or spoiled and even now many of her Naturals were searching the shoreline for supplies to salvage. Once the food had been collected, they would start the long trek back to their summer-hideout, where the provisions would last them through the harshness of the coming months.

Yet, they were both agreed, the storm had been more of a blessing than a curse. Without the strong currents and winds, the small canoe might never have been blown into the shipping lanes. But more often than speaking, they would gaze at each other sometimes and smile. At these times, Arlo felt an odd sensation, unsure whether to laugh or cry. He felt himself get red with embarrassment when she put her arms around him or pressed her lips to his forehead, but none of the other Naturals seemed to think her actions odd.

But all this time, Usha stood alone on the stony bank as she had for most of the day, looking down the long shore and scanning the flat waters for her Citizen friends. Since the ship had capsized, there had been no sign of them. She had pointed out the direction she had last seen them as they were carried off by the waves, and the Naturals had even ventured off on a search, but one by one returned with nothing save broken crates or waterlogged bundles of bread or fruit.

Despite Arlo's attempts to draw her into the conversation, Usha withdrew to the bank to be alone with her thoughts. Her eyes clouded to a steely darkness as she watched the sun sink beneath the waves in a fiery ball beside the gutted hulk of the food-ship. She had escaped, true, but at the expense of the very people who had helped her. It was all her *fault*. . .

Then a shout from the shoreline roused her and she looked up sharply. People were starting to run down towards the sea and there was a flurry of movement down by the water's edge. Hardly allowing herself to hope, Usha started to slide down the shingle that led to the water, pelted along the shore and forced her way through the crowd of Naturals thronging on the sand. She only had eyes for Ozzie and Talia, dragging an unconscious Toby along between them, their clothes as ripped and bedraggled as if they had been all around the world and back in them.

"Thought yer'd get rid of us that easy, Sis?" muttered Ozzie incoherently as Usha stumbled towards them, her arm outstretched in greeting. "Fat chance, I say. Do these Nats happen ter have a bit of chorley by any chance? I could really do with some right now."

That night under a yellow moon, Naturals, Citizens and one Gemini sat cross-legged around a long flat stone together and shared out some of the perishable provisions lately raided from the food-ship. Kira had called a special banquet in Arlo's honour, having, as she put it, lately returned from the Dead. Only Toby still drowsed in his feverish slumber, ministered to by Onofre and another Natural who tried to soothe his sickness with herbs from the wild lands.

Nobody seemed to mind that the bread was a little damp or salty, or that the dried meat was soggy, and the pockmarked apples seemed the best they had ever eaten. There was even a flagon of (slightly watery) chorley to warm their chests.

"You need to eat well, children," said Kira, smiling at them all kindly. "Tonight we start the return to the summer caves. It is a long and difficult journey, and you cannot do that on an empty stomach."

Yet despite his fatigue, Arlo was tingling with excitement. To be amongst his own people, to live and breathe the same air as they was all he wanted. After all he had been through, a trek through dangerous country at his cousin's side seemed easy. He could not wait to get started and see his new home. If it were not for his guilt and sadness over the loss of Rem he would have been perfectly happy.

But Usha, not for the first time, hesitated at the thought of venturing deeper into the wilderness. The sights, sounds and smells of the Region were still unfamiliar to her and she was wary of Naturals and animals alike. Despite the care shown to the Citizens by the Natural tribe for their part in Arlo's safe return, she still felt different from both Citizens and Naturals in a way that she could not quite describe. Arlo's attention was suddenly all for his new cousin, and since their shared ordeal in the sea, Ozzie and Talia had teamed up together, first re-enacting for the pleasure of the group exactly what had happened when the wave swept them away. Now Talia was relating in great detail the races she had won back in Genopolis, and Ozzie hung on every word, nodding with interest. "That's amazing, Talia. . ." he kept saying. "What happened next?" And Talia, swelling with pride at having so attentive a listener, carried on embroidering her achievements until it seemed that there was not a medal or a wreath in the City that she had not worn.

In the strange world that she occupied between Natural and Citizen, once more Usha felt a strange longing for the place others called home. Arlo had found his, but would she ever find hers? Talia and Ozzie had left theirs long ago and seemed to have no need to return. But where would her home be? Could a Gemini ever really call anything home?

As she glanced up, Kira's eyes were fixed on hers. "Are you ready to come with us, Usha?"

But Usha did not need to reply. As if she already understood, Kira reached over and patted her.

"Do not worry. One day you will find a place to call your own. Where we are going now was not always our dwelling. When I was a child the place of my birth was destroyed and I went in search of another. Sometimes homes need to be built rather than found, and not everyone has one to return to. You are not alone, Usha, you can make your own home with us."

Around them the bags were packed and ready to go. Swathed in cloaks and bent low by parcels of provisions, the Naturals were already preparing to move off. The stretcher holding Toby was held between two Naturals, and as Usha bent over to see him she saw the freckled face suddenly twist and his eyes flicker open.

"Toby! Toby!" she cried, and instantly the others were pressing around him. Toby blinked up sleepily at the faces gazing down at him. "Is it over? Are we back at Nanda's now, Usha?"

"No, Toby," Usha soothed him. "We'll get back

there one day, but before then we're going somewhere a bit more exciting."

Arlo took Usha's hand, and together they followed the twinkling lights of the torches as they walked down into the valley, on the path towards home.

Arlo and Usha's story will continue in
Return to Genopolis.

CHRIS WOODING
STORM THIEF

In the midst of the ocean is the city of Orokos. No one can enter, and no one has ever left. At its heart stands the Fulcrum, source of the probability storms that change whatever they touch, rearranging streets, turning children into statues of glass, remaking the world over and over…

Rail has struggled with the effects of one such storm for years, ever since the Storm Thief stole his breath. Now he and his friend Moa eke out an existence stealing to order. Until a raid leaves them in possession of an unknown artefact. Something that sets them running for their lives…

A stunningly imagined, darkly thrilling
novel from an award-winning storyteller.

Rail

Dark-skinned,
dreadlocked.
Thief, and now runaway…

Moa

Pale as milk,
eyes smudged black.
Rail's trusted friend.

Vago

Winged monster,
creator unknown,
past forgotten…